Chaos Embraced

Book Two: Chaos Reigns Saga

Carol Hightshoe

WolfSinger Publications  Security, Colorado

For permission requests, please contact WolfSinger Publications at
editor@wolfsingerpubs.com

2nd Edition
Originally Published by Double Dragon Publishing 2010

ISBN 978-1-936099-62-7

Printed and bound in the United States of America

Chapter One

Myrith waited by the door to the basement, her impatience showing as she gripped and released the hilt of her sword. Kyrianna had gone down several minutes ago to face the shrine of Thynitic alone. She had promised to give her friend ten minutes, before going after her, but was worried even that would be enough time for the Lady of Chaos to exert her influence over the girl. She had seen Kyrianna's reactions to Thynitic's symbol several times and each time it appeared they were getting stronger. It had taken both her and Tristan to drag Kyrianna out of the shrine several days ago when she had been mesmerized by the symbol above the altar.

"She's had long enough," Myrith said, reaching for the door. "Tristan, come with me."

"What's wrong?" Kyrianna asked stepping through the door.

"We were coming to get you." Myrith watched her friend closely. Previously, she had picked up a sense of some evil power having touched Kyrianna's soul. Now, that taint was gone.

"Thank you," Kyrianna said. "However, my business is concluded. It is time we left this place."

Myrith nodded and placed a hand on her friend's shoulder. "That it is," she said. Yes, the power she had sensed was gone. Perhaps their initial fears about Thynitic could be forgotten.

"We will need to return to Duvshire so I can pay you what was promised as well as to clear up the matter involving Myrith," Tristan said.

"I suggest nothing be said regarding the ledgers or the nature of what we found here," Kyrianna said. "Don't put the mayor or his son in a position where they may believe they must take action to protect their own interests." She smiled at Tristan. "At least not until you're ready."

"I agree that would be for the best," Tristan said, returning the smile.

"We should get going," Myrith said, turning to the group. "There is no way to know if that assassin is still tracking Tristan or not." Her gaze lingered on Tristan for a moment then shifted to

Kyrianna who had gone pale.

"What's wrong?" Myrith asked.

"I had forgotten about him."

"You said something in the maze about being tired of assassins in this world trying to kill you, no matter what form took," Myrith said.

"What?" Tristan stared at Kyrianna. "Were you attacked also? Why?"

"I was going to see if Tyril had the power to send me home or at least suggest someone I could talk to. I was attacked in the woods. He used a poisoned blade." She glanced at Myrith then dropped her head. "It was Elvioril who fought him off."

"What!" Myrith grabbed Kyrianna's chin and forced her head up. "Elvioril rescued you from an assassin and you didn't interfere when we fought." She jerked her hand away from the girl's face. "If you had said something, that fight might not have happened. I thought he was chasing you with the intent of hurting you. Then when he wouldn't respond to me, only kept charging and yelling his insults and challenges." Myrith took a step back and shook her head. "Kyri, why?"

"He was a midnight elf and a follower of Thynitic, I didn't trust him. You gave him an opportunity to stop and he charged and attacked you; you were defending yourself."

"Why would this assassin attack you?" Tristan stepped between Myrith and Kyrianna.

"From what I learned; true elves on this world have a strong hatred of those with mixed blood—to the point of killing them as well as their families," Kyrianna said.

"You said nothing about this," Tristan said.

"I had other things to worry about at the time," Kyrianna whispered.

Myrith slammed the door to the basement shut then headed for the main doors. "Let's get moving."

~ * ~

"Myrith, do you want to press on or make camp?" Kyrianna paused and looked up at the darkening sky. "It's only a few more hours to town, but it will be full dark soon."

"I would prefer to get back to town as soon as possible," Myrith said. She turned and looked back at the others. "And the rest of you?"

"I agree."

"Press on."

"A real bed."

Myrith shook her head and grinned at the last remark, which had come from Hendandra.

"Unfortunately, while I agree with pressing on," Tristan said, "I believe we should wait until morning to actually enter Duvshire."

"We can camp just outside the town," Myrith said.

"Sorry, Hendandra," Tristan said. "However, if you stay another night in the town, I will pay for the finest room, in whatever passes for an inn at this time, for you for the night."

"Agreed!"

~ * ~

Kyrianna led the group to a small clearing just outside Duvshire and Myrith watched as she carefully checked the tracks in and out of the area before deciding it was suitable for a camp. She remembered the doubts she had about this girl when she first joined their group. While she still did not know very much about Kyrianna's background, she had come to trust the girl during these last few days.

She glanced around at the rest of the group and frowned at the look she saw on Laraf's face as he watched the girl. There was a longing there. A longing she doubted Kyrianna was willing to return.

"We still need to set watches," Myrith said as several people started unrolling their bedrolls. They were tired, she knew; she and Kyrianna had pushed them pretty far this day in order to reach this spot.

"I'll take first," Kyrianna said immediately.

Myrith glanced at Laraf.

"I'll stand watch with Kyrianna," Tristan said before anyone else could say anything.

"Very well," Myrith said. She turned away from Laraf to see Tristan watching him also. "How long do you estimate before dawn, Rangerette?"

Kyrianna glanced up at the sky then inhaled deeply. "About six hours," she said, looking at Tristan who nodded.

Myrith looked at the others and shook her head. "Can you handle three hours on your watch? You can wake me and Laraf when you are done."

Tristan shrugged then nodded as he glanced at Kyrianna. Kyrianna nodded slowly. “I’m sure we can manage.”

Chapter Two

Myrith looked around as they entered the small town of Duvshire. The area where the inn had been was cleared and new construction had already begun.

Tristan pointed to a building near the site. A sign on the wall read, 'Temporary home of the Wailing Banshee.' "I think we could use a good meal and I will need to talk to the merchant holding my funds," he said. "For now, I will pay for the meal."

"Sounds good to me," Hendandra said, heading for the building.

Myrith only shook her head as she and others followed.

"I won!" a voice yelled as the group entered the tavern. Marlene jumped up from the stool she had been sitting on and applauded the group. "Less than two weeks and the majority of the group is still in one piece." She walked over to the table where Mulbanith was sitting and held out her hand. "My winnings—please."

"I disagree. They had outside help," he said.

"That was never stipulated." Marlene punched the older man on the shoulder. "Now, pay up, you grouch."

Mulbanith continued to grumble under his breath as he handed the serving girl a black pouch.

Marlene tucked the pouch into her skirts then came over to the group. "Congratulations on your survival and apparent success," she said as she led them to a large table.

"If you don't mind my asking, how much did you win?" Tristan asked after she had taken their orders.

"Fifty silver," she said, grinning.

"Then congratulations to you as well," Myrith said.

"And my congratulations to you and your friends," another voice said behind her.

Myrith turned to see Mayor Ustedler standing behind her, his son only a few steps away.

"It would seem you have satisfied the provisions of the test. Therefore, the matter involving the death of the elf Elvioril is closed and you are cleared. It would appear you do indeed hold the favor of the Battle Maiden." The mayor nodded his head slightly to Myrith then glanced at Tristan, turned and walked away without saying anything to the young man.

"Lord Mayor," Kyrianna called.

"Yes." He turned to look at her.

Myrith raised an eyebrow as she watched Kyrianna. *What is she up to? She was the one to advise against telling the mayor anything about what we found at the estate.*

Kyrianna bowed deeply. "Lord Mayor, I was wondering if the guards had found any trace of the elf Legewyd while we were gone."

Myrith continued to stare at Kyrianna. *Legewyd? What are you doing, Rangerette?*

"Legewyd?" The mayor glanced at Myrith for a moment. "Ah, yes," he said turning his attention back to Kyrianna. "The elf, whom it is believed was responsible for the fire, which destroyed the Wailing Banshee. I am sorry to say no trace of him has been found."

Kyrianna bowed again. "Thank you for the information, Lord Mayor."

The mayor nodded then left the tavern.

"Well?" Myrith asked as Kyrianna returned to the table. "What was that about?"

"Legewyd is our assassin. I wanted to know if he was still out there," Kyrianna said. "

"I thought we were already assuming he was still out there and still a threat," Myrith said.

"We also learned the mayor didn't make any effort to even have Legewyd apprehended," Falden said. "His body language was stressed when Kyrianna asked the question. He was concerned we may have learned something he didn't want us learn." Falden looked at Kyrianna. "However, your own manner appeared to put him at ease. When he answered the question, it is my opinion he was only thinking of the previous accusation."

"That was the idea," Kyrianna said with a smile. "Thank you for your observations."

"I doubt this is an appropriate location for this conversation," Jerietlan said, looking around.

The others followed his gaze around the room. While no one in the tavern appeared to be listening to them, there were a couple of guardsmen in the room for dinner.

"Where do you go from here?" Tristan asked as Marlene came back with their food and drinks.

"Those from this land will most likely be returning to their homes, while Kyrianna and I need to find a way back to our own worlds," Myrith said.

"You could stay here," Laraf said, glancing at Kyrianna.

Kyrianna glanced down at her wrists and the marks placed there by Frayrith and Dwycia then shook her head. "No, I need to return to Rhysia and Nydith. My family is there."

Myrith nodded. "I too need to return. There is business I should be attending to in my own land." Her hand tightened around the hilt of her sword.

"I understand," Tristan said.

Myrith closed her eyes and refused to react when she saw Tristan's gaze dart to Kyrianna and back to his plate. *So, he has an interest in Kyrianna as well.*

They continued their meal in silence. As they were finishing, Tristan again broke the silence.

"Those of you from Shokar, where are you from?"

"All over," Hendandra said. "I have a home in Raspa; I believe Falden is from Gormanghast; Jerietlan is from Irrmar and Nirev would be from Domar. Laraf indicated he lives in this area now, but he is not from here originally. Somewhere to the south, but not one of the larger cities."

"That is more information than I believe anyone has shared," Myrith said.

Hendandra grinned. "I have an ear for picking up subtle inflections in speech. I knew where each of you were from within a day of meeting you, except for Kyri and Myrith of course."

Falden and Jerietlan both started laughing. "I should have known," the mage said.

"Since so many are from Shokar, I have a request to make," Tristan said. "Would you consider escorting me back to Raspa? Keep in mind there are mages in Raspa who might be able to send Kyrianna and Myrith home as well. I would be willing to help you engage their services. Those from Shokar could also find a member of the Wayfinder's Guild to transport them to their homes as well."

Myrith looked around at the members of the group and saw the nods of agreement. "Agreed," she said.

Hendandra looked at Tristan. "You promised me the finest room in whatever passes for an inn in this place for the night," she said with a pout.

"That I did. Raspa will only be two days' journey from here; do you prefer to re-equip yourselves and rest or start today?"

"Personally, I'm not comfortable with staying in this town another day," Kyrianna said. "But I am not adamant we should leave now. I'll abide by the group's decision."

Myrith glanced over at the guardsmen still in the room and saw they were watching their group. "I agree with Kyri. However, I would prefer to leave as soon as we are ready."

"Damn," Hendandra muttered. "It's going to be a while longer before I get that comfortable bed."

"I'll talk to Mulbanith and see if he will open the store for us at this time." Laraf left the table to talk to the merchant.

A short time later, Laraf returned to the table. "He will open the store in ten minutes," he said as he took his seat.

"Good. That gives us time to finish," Myrith said. She opened her money pouch and tossed a gold coin onto the table as the others left silver coins. She smiled at Tristan who had offered to pay for the meal. He still had their reward to pay and she knew it would take a great deal of influence on his part to convince a mage to open a portal to two different worlds. They shouldn't be taking advantage of his generous nature. She shook her head as he started to drop his own coin on the table and pulled a second coin from her own pouch and dropped it by his plate. "This one is on me," she said.

Tristan nodded then smiled.

Myrith glanced at the coins on the table and smiled again. *Probably a bit much for the meal and tip*, she thought. *However, it will help make up for those who don't tip at all.* She remembered all too well her days working at the Silver Dragon. Being a server in an inn could be exceptionally hard work and they had to put up with abuse from the patrons with only a friendly smile as they continued to bring their drinks and food. While she had seen nothing to make her think Marlene was being forced to perform other services, as she had been, she knew they could spare the coin and the girl would welcome it.

~ * ~

"Good morning," Mulbanith said as they entered the store. "Lord Duvall, I believe we should take care of our business while your friends look around." He bowed his head slightly.

"You have the draft I gave you to hold," Tristan said. "I will need you to draw up six for one thousand gold each and the remainder can go into a separate draft." He glanced around at the others and Myrith followed his gaze to where Kyrianna was examining several bows.

"Perhaps you should run a credit for each of us and then take care of anything that might be left over," Myrith said.

"It would save on the accounting," Mulbanith said. "Now, as to my fee." He pulled out a sheet of paper and passed it to Tristan.

Tristan shook his head. "That was never agreed on. I will however, reimburse you what you lost on your bet, plus an additional ten gold."

Mulbanith frowned then nodded. "Agreed." He turned his attention to Myrith. "For you?"

Myrith glanced around again, then shook her head. She had the armor Tristan had given her as well as the sword Hendandra had recovered in the temple. Her other gear was in reasonable shape, and it would not be cheap to hire someone to send her home. "At this time, I do not require anything."

"Very well." Mulbanith handed her a yellow slip of paper.

Myrith looked at the paper then glanced at Tristan.

"It is a draft for the funds. It will serve just as well as actual coin with the Wayfinder's Guild in Raspa."

"And it is this Wayfinder's Guild Kyrianna and I must speak to in order to hire someone to send us back to our homes?"

"It is."

Myrith looked again at the paper in her hands then nodded. "Very well," she said. "At least this will be easier to carry than the full amount of the gold."

"If you will excuse me." Mulbanith nodded his head to Tristan and Myrith then went to talk to Kyrianna.

Myrith watched as Kyrianna and Mulbanith spoke for several minutes. The girl nodded then shouldered the bow she had been looking at and passed the merchant the two knives she had picked up in the estate.

Mulbanith pointed to a battered quiver and Kyrianna shook her head. The merchant wrote on one of the yellow papers, handed it to Kyrianna then bowed slightly and moved to talk to Hendandra.

Before leaving, Myrith looked around the store to see Kyrianna still studying a battered quiver with interest. "Rangerette?"

"He calls it a quiver of Dwycia and says it will hold one hundred arrows. Only problem is the cost. While I would like to have it, I will not have any gold left to pay a mage to get me home."

"I doubt that will be a problem," Myrith said with a quick glance at Tristan.

Myrith fought to keep the smile off her face at the slight blush she saw on Kyrianna's face before the girl shook her head.

"Escorting him to Raspa hardly warrants the amount of gold a mage would ask for to perform that high level of magic," Kyrianna said.

She knows how he feels and she has feelings also, but is denying them. This will be an interesting two days, Myrith thought. "Get the quiver. I think you'll be surprised when we get to Raspa." She clasped Kyrianna's shoulder for a second then stepped out of the shop to where the others waited.

It was only a few minutes later when Kyrianna followed her out, the battered quiver on her back along with the bow she had purchased.

"Lord Duvall, which road do we take?" Myrith asked.

Tristan nodded to the left and they headed in that direction.

Chapter Three

There was no other traffic on the road as they left Duvshire and headed toward Raspa. The day was still clear with the sun not yet at its zenith in the sky.

"Rangerette, why don't you watch the back," Myrith said. "We can let Hendandra do some scouting for a while."

Kyrianna looked at her and raised an eyebrow. Myrith stepped closer. "Until we are well away from Duvshire, I want to make sure the mayor hasn't sent anyone else after us. I need you to watch our backs for a while," she said softly. "I'm sure you noticed he didn't mention Sarasnar not being with us. And, after the cleric made such a fuss about going with us to verify the truth of our success or not, I would have expected something to be said about his absence."

Kyrianna nodded her understanding then readied her bow as she scanned the area and waited for the rest of the group to move ahead.

They traveled for almost two hours without anything happening and Myrith called a halt for a short rest. She watched as Kyrianna dropped further back and took up a position just off the road, while Laraf did the same on the other side.

A sudden gust of wind surged across the area from the general direction of the estate. A cacophony of sound blended with a chaotic mass of color that surrounded them. Myrith drew her sword and pushed Tristan behind her and away from the chaos. She glanced back to see Kyrianna and Laraf both running toward the group then everything vanished.

~ * ~

Myrith found herself floating in a gray void filled with mist, obscuring her vision. "Grab each other's hands!" she yelled as she grabbed onto someone she thought was Hendandra.

"Anyone still floating?" she called after a few minutes.

There were no answers. "Hendandra, I think I have one of your hands—do you have anyone else's?" She squeezed the hand she was holding and felt a return squeeze.

"Yes. I have hold of you and I believe Jerietlan," she responded.

"Jerietlan?"

"Hendandra and I believe Falden," he said.

"Jerietlan and Nirev," Falden said.

Myrith waited for a few seconds. "Nirev?"

"Only the mage," the dwarf replied.

"Kyrianna!" Myrith yelled the name into the thickening gray mist.

"Tristan! Laraf!"

There were no replies.

"Myrith, either they weren't caught or they are lost somewhere else," Falden said. "We need to find a way out of this. We can't stay here. I'm sensing power behind this. This environment could become much worse at any moment. We have to leave this place, and quickly."

"But how?"

"Call Riker. He is of the spirit world and might be able to sense something in this fog," Falden said.

Myrith frowned. She didn't like the idea of calling the spirit horse forth in this place. She looked around at the thickening mist. The only way she knew the others were there was the slight tug on her left hand where she held Hendandra's. There seemed no other way out of this place and if Falden was correct, they could all be in serious danger soon. She sighed and focused her mind on the spirit horse. "Riker, come to me," she called.

The horse appeared next to her, his ghostly eyes wide as he looked at her. She carefully sheathed her sword and grasped the reins. "Can you find a way out of this fog?"

The horse bobbed his head once and began "swimming" away from the area. Myrith slid her hand to the saddle and let the horse pull her and the others through the fog.

After what felt like an eternity, the horse brought them to a shimmering doorway on a rocky outcropping. "My thanks," Myrith said, patting the horse's neck.

The horse nodded his head then vanished.

"I have no clue where this portal leads, do we risk it?" Myrith looked at the others.

"I don't think we have a choice but to do so," Falden said. "A storm appears to be headed this way."

Myrith turned to see the fog and mist beginning to turn black and swirl violently as it approached their location. "Hang on to each other; I don't want to risk anyone else getting separated," she said, taking Hendandra's hand again and stepping through the portal.

Once again, she found her senses being assaulted by swirling colors and various noises. The intense colors burned her eyes and she bit her tongue to stop the scream that threatened to escape her throat. As she continued to fight the chaos surrounding her, she felt Hendandra's hand being torn from her grasp then blackness surrounded her.

~ * ~

When the blackness lifted, she found herself standing on a large field where a battle had been waged. Before her was a woman dressed in full plate armor. She immediately knelt before the vision of Mykaylene.

"My Lady," Myrith said softly.

"Myrith, circumstances have thrown you into a difficult situation forcing you to accept a new deity, one whom you truly do not know much about. Because of this, I understand your hesitancy to call on me for aid and your lack of proclaiming my name or your faith.

"However, you will be entering a realm outside the normal planes of existence. Only if your faith is strong will I be able to aid you."

The woman and the field faded and Myrith found herself on the floor of a cavern, a cold breeze flowing from the only apparent exit. She looked around and saw those who had been in the mist with her had made it at least this far. There was something going on here she didn't like. Mykaylene had visited her in a vision, and warned her that her faith would have to be strong for the goddess to aid her in this place. She had never been one for spending long hours in study, but she did know the gods didn't communicate very often with their followers, at least on her world they seldom did. When they did speak, it was usually because something was going to happen which could have serious consequences.

Jerietlan had warned them of that same possibility when Hendandra and Laraf mentioned receiving dreams which called them to choose a deity to follow. Kyrianna had been warned by one of her patrons someone was coming. As the unnamed party had been referred to as a she, the warning couldn't have meant Mikyl Duvall. So was something still after them? Had she and this group been deliberately separated from Kyrianna, Tristan and Laraf to make them easier targets?

She looked at the others and wondered briefly if they had also had visions in the chaos. She was worried about where Kyrianna and the others had ended up. *Were they still on Shokar? Or, had the portal taken them somewhere else?*

Myrith knew Kyrianna suspected some connection between the two of them and Thynitic because of the manner in which they had been brought together. If the *she* Kyrianna had been warned about was Thynitic—why had they been separated in this way? Surely a goddess would be able to call them away from the others if she desired. She had seen her friend's reactions to the symbols of Thynitic—in the place where they had met and then in the small shrine in the basement of the Duvall Estate. That there was something between Thynitic and Kyrianna seemed obvious then. But the girl had gone down alone to face the shrine and returned, apparently untouched. If Thynitic wanted her, she should have been able to exert her influence over Kyrianna at that time. This had to be something else.

"Everyone ready?" Myrith finally asked. She couldn't dwell on the question of what had happened to Kyrianna and the others. She had to be prepared for whatever was going on here, make sure the ones with her stayed safe and they found a way back to Shokar.

"Not really, but do we have a choice?" Hendandra brushed the dirt and rocks from her leathers.

"No."

"I will need a few more minutes," Falden said softly.

Myrith turned to where the mage was sitting on the floor with his cloak spread out in front of him. His hawk was sitting on his shoulder watching the cloak.

"Any ideas on what happened to the others?" Hendandra whispered as Falden began chanting.

"No. I hope the portal somehow missed them and they are still on Shokar. What we need to do now is figure out where we are and find a way back," Myrith said.

A spot on the cloak glowed for a moment then faded. Falden's hawk jumped from his shoulder onto the cloak and vanished into the fabric.

"What did you do?" Myrith asked as Falden stood and draped

the cloak over his shoulders.

"Until I know where we are and if I want to risk him traveling with us, he is safe," Falden said.

Myrith drew her sword and headed for the only corridor out of the area they were in.

~ * ~

"Chaos take it! What happened?" Kyrianna looked at Tristan and Laraf as the swirling colors vanished leaving only the three of them on the road.

"I would guess it was a portal of some kind." Tristan stood up and dusted himself off.

Kyrianna walked to where Myrith had been standing when she had pushed Tristan out of the portal and knelt down to look at the ground. Only the woman's tracks were there. There was no evidence of struggle.

"The swirling colors and the noise," she said softly. "Chaos." Kyrianna paused and caught her breath for a moment.

"Kyri?" Laraf placed a hand on her shoulder. "What is it?"

"The shrine in the basement of the estate was dedicated to Thynitic, the Lady of Chaos. The swirling colors are her symbol." Her breath caught again. "I could feel her trying to draw me to her in the shrine. Was this some kind of trap on her part? Myrith was taken from her home by a similar portal, as were Falden and Hendandra. Is Thynitic playing some sort of game with us?"

"It will take a powerful cleric to help you get those answers, Kyrianna," Tristan said, offering her his hand.

Kyrianna nodded as she took the offered hand and stood up. "Then the sooner we get to Raspa, the sooner I can try and find my friends. Laraf, you stay close to Tristan; I'll take a scout position several yards ahead. Let's get moving." She held her sword at the ready as she moved down the road.

Chapter Four

Myrith paused at the end of the tunnel as a strong gust of cold air hit her. The wind was bitter, but she suspected it would not be damaging for several days. Still, they had nowhere else to go but forward and pray they found a way out of this place quickly.

Myrith waited for the others before she stepped into the chamber before her. Ice covered the walls and floor and the cold seemed deeper than she had originally suspected. Her lungs felt like they were burning as she breathed the cold air. There were two corridors out of the chamber and she sighed as she glanced from one to the other. Her breath hung like a cloud in front of her as she tried to decide which way to go.

"One way is as good as the other at this point, Myrith. We just need to keep moving before we turn into ice statues," Hendandra said, moving past her. "I'll take the scout position." She moved to the left-hand corridor and carefully checked the passage, listening for any sounds.

"Can't hear anything on this side." She moved to the other corridor. "Nothing here either. Pick a direction."

"Right." Myrith gestured to the first corridor as Hendandra moved ahead of her. She frowned again as she realized the corridor was only wide enough for one person. She wasn't worried about Hendandra being able to get out of the way. The girl was short, not much taller than a child and she was very agile. Hendandra could dive under her as she moved to engage any enemies they met. However, Myrith was concerned she would be the only one in a position to do any fighting that needed to be done and would have to fall before the others could assist her. It was not a pleasant thought.

Hendandra was also the only one with a bow if she was remembering correctly. She was pretty sure neither the cleric nor the mage were carrying ranged weapons, although Falden could cast spells from his position. Her own crossbow had been dropped and forgotten at the Duvall Estate. Nirev would just have to make sure he watched the back so nothing could sneak up on them.

As they moved through the ice-covered corridors, a loud roar from in front of them caught Myrith's attention. The roar was repeated and shards of ice showered down on them from the ceiling as the sound reverberated in the narrow space.

"Hendandra, as carefully as you can, move up and see if you can tell what is ahead of us," Myrith whispered.

Hendandra went pale then nodded and moved away from the group.

It was several minutes before she returned. "Some kind of giant. He is in a room just ahead of us. There also appears to be a person bound in a corner of the room."

"Could you tell anything about this person?" Myrith caught her breath. "Could it be one of the others?"

"I could see nothing familiar." Hendandra paused. "However, I was on the opposite side of the room and the giant was partially blocking my view. It might or might not be one of them, I don't know for sure."

"Did I hear there be a giant up ahead?" Nirev's voice came from the back of the group.

"You did. Now, be quiet and keep a watch for anything coming from your direction," Myrith said.

"Listen, Lady Knight," Nirev said, forcing his way past the cleric and mage. "If there be giants to be fought, then I be wanting a piece of 'em." He slapped his hand against the haft of his maul. "Do ye understand?"

Myrith looked down at the dwarf. "You would let your personal desires put the rest of this group at risk?" she said slowly. "There are only two of us who are trained in the use of a sword. You and I. Yet, you left the mage and cleric guarding our rear in case something should attack us there. I am not impressed."

"Bah, Mulog isn't impressed with ye or yer shiny armor either, Lady Knight. We creep through these halls when we should be calling challenges to the one who trapped us here. Let 'em face our blades so we can force them to release us. This skulking about be ridiculous."

Nirev started to push past her and Myrith placed a hand on his shoulder, holding him in place. "And how does Mulog look on those who forswear their oaths? You swore to follow me as the leader of this group when you joined us in Shokar, sent, you said, by your Lord of Storms. I am certain we will face many challenges and fights in finding our way out of this place. Are you ready to break your oath for the sake of one fight?"

"I gave ye my oath and I will honor it, Lady Knight." Nirev inclined his head slightly, but did not move to the back of the group.

Myrith bit her lower lip as she turned back to Hendandra. This was something she had expected long before now. Women were not warriors where she grew up, it just wasn't accepted. They could train with the lighter blades of the rogue or assassin, but to be a warrior was unheard of. Even in the temple they had first met in, she had expected the others to balk at her leadership, but then that group had had three women and three men in it. The mage did not seem to be the type to want to lead, keeping to himself unless his power was needed and Bukon had stayed in the background as well. Etewyn, well he was Etewyn and really wasn't smart enough to try and lead the group. Now it was only her and Hendandra with three men, one of whom was a trained fighter and a follower of a God who preferred his servants to charge into battle with a challenge on their lips and their weapons swinging.

One problem at a time, she thought. *And first is the giant and whoever he is holding.*

"Hendandra, how big is the room?" Myrith asked, glancing at Falden.

"Only about thirty feet across and twenty feet deep. All of the other corridors are the same size as this," she said.

"Then how did a giant get into this place?" Nirev looked at Hendandra then up at Myrith.

"Good question. Perhaps he is not here of his own choosing and is a prisoner like us."

"Unlikely ye'll get the chance to ask 'em." Nirev slapped his hand against the haft of his weapon. The slap echoed in the passage, like the breaking of a dry piece of wood and Myrith dropped her hand over the dwarf's.

"No more noise," she said.

The dwarf only glared at her. "Listen, if that be a giant in that room, do ye really think it can get to us here? It be too big to fit through this passage as yerself just pointed out. Now, are we going to stand here yammering, or be we finding out if that be one of our friends the creature be holding?"

"Hendandra, what kind of giant was it?"

"Do I look like an expert in giants? It was big and had very pale skin and blue hair. Does that help?"

"Ah," Nirev said, smiling. "Frost giant. Appropriate considering the climate." He paused and smiled. "Another good thing, they not be very smart."

"We will try talking to him first," Myrith said. "If that doesn't work…"

"And it won't," Nirev interrupted.

"If that doesn't work, you'll get your chance." Myrith shook her head. "Hendandra, stay with Jerietlan and Falden. Watch the back; we don't need anything sneaking up on us."

Hendandra nodded and silently slipped past the dwarf and joined the others.

"Do ye speak giant, Lady Knight?" Nirev asked as they approached the chamber.

"No, but I assume you do."

"Ye assume correctly."

Myrith stepped back so the dwarf stood directly in front of her as they approached the chamber where the creature was. It was facing away from them and seemed unaware of their presence.

Nirev looked up at Myrith and she nodded once. The dwarf took a step into the room, his maul held in a defensive position as he moved in and to the side so the mage and cleric could cast any spells they needed to.

Nirev said something in a loud guttural manner Myrith hoped was a semi-polite greeting in the giant tongue. The giant slowly turned toward them, his manner did not seem angry or concerned. Then he stopped and his gaze locked on the dwarf. The giant moved quickly for a creature of his size as he reached for the large axe standing against the wall. Myrith darted forward, kicked the weapon away from the giant's grasping hand, and slashed upward with her sword as Nirev came from behind, his maul swinging at the giant's legs.

Myrith lunged forward, her blade slashing across the lower part of the giant's abdomen. She darted back avoiding the blood flowing from the wound. Several streaks of light flashed past her to strike the giant and she risked a quick glance to see Falden had his hands raised.

The giant roared and brought his huge fists together and slammed them down toward Myrith. She was forced to retreat and found herself sliding on the blood-covered ice. She fought to hold her weapon in a defensive position, even as she felt her balance failing.

"Oh, no ye don't!" Myrith heard Nirev yell followed by the solid thump of the dwarf's maul hitting the giant's leg.

The giant roared again and tried to turn. This time he was the one struggling on the slick ice and another blow from Nirev's maul caused his leg to buckle and he fell to the ground.

Before the giant could get up, Hendandra darted in and stabbed him in the side of his neck with her rapier, opening an artery. She danced back in time to avoid the blood. As she moved back, Nirev raised his maul then brought it down onto the back of the giant's neck.

Myrith stood slowly, her back braced against the wall to help maintain her balance. Once she was sure of her footing, she walked around to face the dwarf. "An impressive display, Nirev. Thank you."

Nirev only nodded as he checked the giant's body for anything useful.

"Myrith," Hendandra called from where the unknown person lay. "He's not anyone we know," she said softly.

"Still, we have an obligation to assist if we can. Someone get a fire going, he's half-frozen. Jerietlan, give me a hand here." Myrith rolled the body over and gently slapped the elderly man's face a couple of times.

He frowned as his brown eyes opened and he looked at her. "Who are you?"

"I am called Myrith," she said.

"Here." Hendandra held a couple of blankets. "They're a bit smelly, but they should help warm him up."

The old man looked from Hendandra to Myrith and back, his brow creased with confusion. "How did you get here?"

"We were trapped in some sort of portal that brought us here," Myrith said.

"I am called Argrala, and I was trapped here by a sorceress who is using this place to draw power from the four elemental planes so she can control them. This is not my normal form; this is the one she has trapped me in for trying to interfere in her plans. There are four layers to this place in keeping with the elemental planes. Throughout these layers she has trapped creatures that make their homes in environments related to the appropriate plane. This being the plane of air—she has both air and cold creatures. Very few of whom came of their own accord."

"Is there a way to stop this sorceress?"

"We must get to her before she can consolidate her power. I have the items needed to perform the rituals to dismiss the elementals guarding the gates between each layer. However, those gates are well hidden and even after we find our way through them we still have to locate the keys to her stronghold and her chamber. I doubt this frail body, which she has trapped me in, has the strength to accomplish the task."

"Then let us aid you," Myrith held out her hand to the old man. "Unless we can find another way out of this realm, I suspect we will have to face this sorceress in order to get back to our homes."

"You are correct. It is only through her you will be allowed to leave this place. I pray to the Lady I am not too much of a burden for you. I have no true magic to speak of and my skills with the blade were hardly adequate before she sapped my strength and youth."

Myrith smiled at the man. "Do not worry about that." She looked at the others. "We have not been traveling for long, and this battle was not that hard. Do we want to rest here, now that a fire is going or do you want to continue on?"

"Continue on. The sooner we are out of this infernal cold the better," Jerietlan said as he began rubbing his arms. "Every time we stop, it seems to get worse."

"I agree," Hendandra said.

Falden nodded.

"If you are ready to move on, Argrala, we can go."

The elderly man nodded as he rolled the blankets together, used a length of rope to tie the ends together and draped the roll over his shoulder. "We may need these later," he said as he stood and waited for the others.

Myrith only nodded.

~ * ~

Kyrianna paused and inhaled deeply of the late afternoon air. Her mother had taught her how the scents of the earth changed during the day. Always at their brightest and most distinct just after the sun rose, the warming of the earth during the day would stir the air and blend them together, smoothing and diluting them until the cooling of the night would cause them to settle and separate. She glanced up at the sky and frowned; the scents she was picking up were cool and starting to separate into their individual selves, the way they did when they camped last night. At this time of the day, she would have expected them to have blended into a single, harmonious melody that spoke of the warm earth and the life that surrounded her.

She held her hand up and signaled to Tristan and Laraf to wait as she began scanning the area, both of her swords now in her hands. Something wasn't right, the air was turning colder and she felt something beginning to prick at her skin. She moved quickly to get out of the cold, but found herself surrounded by a swirling fog of ice and snow that moved with her. "Laraf, get Tristan out of here!" she yelled over the noise of the storm.

She watched as Laraf grabbed Tristan's arm and pulled him away from the storm. She again tried to move out of the ice and snow that surrounded her, but again it moved with her. "Chaos! What is going on here?"

The cold was growing deeper and she saw ice forming around her blades and beginning to move up her hands and arms. "Fray-rith!" she called out, but she didn't expect an answer.

~ * ~

Myrith paused as she looked at bodies of the winter wolves that had attacked them. For three days—at least she thought it had been three days as they had camped and slept three times—they had been wandering in this frozen maze of ice and they seemed no closer to finding their way out of the area than they were when they arrived. She glanced at Argrala and frowned slightly. Other than the initial information he had given them when they found him, he had said very little to her or her companions. At least he was keeping up and staying out of the way.

"Myrith, look at these," Hendandra called from where she had been checking a pile of bones and rags in the corner of the wolves' den. Hendandra held up a pair of silver bracelets, each one with a silver ring attached to a chain. On each of the bracelets was etched a unicorn and wolf. More sparkles among the torn cloth revealed matching earrings and a necklace.

"Too bad Kyrianna's not here, she would have loved those," Myrith said.

"I know." Hendandra gathered the jewelry as well as a few scattered gems into her bag. "I think I'll hold them for her—for when we get back."

"She's probably already home by now," Myrith said.

"You think so? I doubt it. She's probably trying to find someone to locate us and send her here."

"You have another companion in this place?" Argrala said from behind Myrith.

"Actually, there were three others traveling with us when we were brought here. We do not know what happened to them."

The old man nodded then turned away muttering under his breath.

"We'll camp here." Myrith said. "Nirev, see if any of the pelts are salvageable as blankets."

Myrith continued to watch Argrala; there was something bothering her about him. While she couldn't sense any evil in his aura, Falden had sensed something on the old man when he was looking for magical items. She tried telling herself it was because this sorceress, they were trying to get to, had changed his form and appearance, but she knew there was more to it than he was telling them. He seemed to be constantly watching and listening to the group and to her in particular. She was used to being watched; if her flaming red hair wasn't enough to hold most men's attention, then her looks usually were. But Argrala wasn't looking at her in the same way the patrons of the Silver Dragon had looked at her. There was interest, but it was more as if he were evaluating or judging her.

She looked around at the others. Falden had started a fire and Nirev had skinned several of the wolves and added the pelts to the growing piles of blankets. He was now cutting up one of the carcasses and laying the meat across the fire. For a moment, she was reminded of Etewyn and his unusual dietary choices. *At least it can't be as bad as whatever type of reptile he was cooking that night in the temple was*, she thought. She shook her head slightly. The thought was inappropriate to the warrior's memory.

Hendandra was sitting as close to the fire as she could without risking her clothing catching on fire. The smaller woman had already appropriated two of the wolf pelts and was huddled under them shaking. Myrith was worried about what would happen if they had to rely on Hendandra's skill to disarm any traps they found. She herself was also feeling the effects of the cold; she had almost dropped her sword twice during the fight with the wolves as her fingers started going numb. The only ones who seemed unaffected were Nirev and

Argrala.

"Let's get some rest and start out again in a few hours. Falden, can you ward the area?"

Falden didn't respond, he only raised his hands and began chanting. "Done. It will last for six hours." He reached out and touched Myrith's shoulder. "You will be alerted if anything attempts to enter."

Myrith only nodded as she settled against one of the walls, her sword across her lap. Sleep claimed her quickly.

~ * ~

Myrith could hear one or two of the others already stirring as she sought the waking world. Before she was fully awake, she heard a voice whispering in her mind. "Mykaylene," she whispered.

:*You have a friend trapped here*, the voice said softly. :*A very dangerous opponent is holding her and her time is short. She is near.* The presence faded from her mind.

"Kyri!" Myrith threw the blanket someone had draped over her to the side as she stood quickly. "We need to get moving," she said, grabbing her armor.

"What's going on?" Hendandra looked at her from under the wolf pelts she had claimed.

"Kyri's here and she's in trouble," Myrith said, looking at the others as they started scrambling to get their things together.

Hendandra grabbed her arm. "How do you know?"

"Mykaylene spoke to me as I was waking. She told me I have a friend trapped here and her time is short. The only person she could have been talking about is Kyri."

Nirev began helping her with the straps and buckles of her armor. "And did the Battle Maiden tell ye which way to go, Lady Knight?" He glanced at the two corridors leading out of the area they were in.

Myrith stopped and closed her eyes for a moment. "No she didn't, but I will trust her to guide my steps." Once the last of her armor was secured, she grabbed her pack and headed into one of the corridors, leaving the others to catch up.

She paused when she came to a corridor that crossed the one she was in. Listening carefully, Myrith could hear the sound of something large moving to her right. She moved back from the crossroad. "There appears to be something to the right, be ready," she said softly.

The corridor opened into a small alcove that allowed the group to see a large chamber beyond. Resting in the chamber was a large creature with multiple heads on long slender necks. The reptilian creature was purplish in color and frost was coming out of its mouths as it breathed.

"Any sign of her?" Myrith glanced down at Hendandra who was scanning the room from where she knelt just inside the doorway.

Hendandra nodded and pointed to the far corner of the room where a shimmering wall of ice stood. Myrith studied the person on the floor behind the ice. She recognized the long golden-brown hair that lay in a tangled mass covering the person's features. The leather armor could have belonged to many people, but the pendant with the carved unicorn on it was visible on the girl's chest. Myrith looked at the layout of the chamber.

"Falden, can your magic attack the creature without putting her at risk?"

Falden looked past her to where the creature was resting and nodded. He moved his hands through several patterns as he chanted softly. A few seconds later a small bead of fire flew from his hands to explode near the many-headed creature.

As the heat and flames subsided, Myrith started to dash forward only to have Jerietlan place a hand on her arm as he called on Mykaylene's power. A tower of flame flowed from above them to engulf the creature as it swirled around it.

When the firestorm faded, the creature raised six of its nine heads and roared. The other three heads were charred and the necks rested limply on the ground. Myrith raised her sword and charged into the weaving, twisting heads. Her sword flashed as she slashed and parried the snapping teeth. Next to her stood Nirev, his maul swinging as one of the heads hit the ground. From behind them a streak of flame shot out and hit the bleeding stump of the severed neck.

"Chaos," Myrith said as one of the heads darted down and she felt the teeth grab and tear at her left shoulder. She dropped her shield and swung her sword as hard as she could in an arc toward the retreating head. The sword sliced deeply into the underside of the neck, and blood poured over her. Another streak of fire hit the injured area charring it and Myrith jumped back to avoid the falling neck.

"Back to the doorway!" Jerietlan yelled. "I can call another firestorm down on it."

"No! Save your power for any other creatures we may face this day." Myrith darted forward, her blade leading as she plunged it deep into the creature's body. She glanced up to see Hendandra standing behind the beast, her rapier also buried in its body.

"So what was this thing called?" Hendandra asked, looking at Falden.

"A hydra. In this case, one that was adapted to cold climates. We are lucky we were able to take it out so quickly; each of those heads is able to exude a cloud of frost, much like a white dragon's breath weapon," he said.

"Yeah, lucky. I'm sure Kyri would find it interesting you used her favorite curse." Hendandra pulled her rapier out of the hydra's body and walked around to look at Myrith's shoulder. "Nasty bite there, you better let Jerietlan look at it," she said.

Myrith shook her head and sheathed her sword. She then pressed her right hand against the injury, the power of Mykaylene flowing through her to heal the wound. "What are you talking about? Kyri's favorite curse?"

"I heard you yell chaos," Hendandra said.

"I didn't—"

"Myrith, over here! You were right—it's Kyrianna!" Jerietlan called.

Myrith turned and moved quickly to the side of her friend.

"Rangerette. Kyri!" Myrith slapped her friend's face gently. There was a slight moan and a brief fluttering of the girl's eyelids. "Mykaylene," Myrith whispered as she placed her hands over the girl's heart. After another minute, Kyrianna's eyes opened and she sat up shivering.

"Tristan!" Kyrianna's eyes fluttered as she grabbed for her sword.

Myrith jerked the sword away as Kyrianna pulled it from the sheath. "Kyrianna!" She slapped the girl again as Hendandra quickly pulled her other sword away.

"Myrith?" Kyrianna's eyes moved slowly as she glanced around. "Jerietlan? Where are we? What's going on?"

"Easy, Kyri." Hendandra draped a blanket around the girl's shoulders. "We're really not sure either."

Myrith turned and looked at the others. "Get a fire going. I don't care how."

"I've got it," Falden said, making several gestures with his hands and a fire appeared next to the still-shaking Kyrianna.

"Tristan?" Kyrianna's gaze darted around the room as she tried to stand up.

Myrith grabbed Kyrianna's shoulders. "He's not here. What happened?"

"Who is that?" Kyrianna said through chattering teeth. She glanced past Myrith and Jerietlan who were rubbing her arms and legs to get her warmed up.

Myrith glanced over her shoulder for a moment. "He says his name is Argrala. He claims to be here to stop a sorceress from taking control of the elemental planes." She paused and looked Kyrianna closely. "How did you get here?"

"It was a couple of hours after you were pulled into the portal. I was several yards ahead of Laraf and Tristan, when I was caught in an ice storm. It must have been of magical creation as it moved with me and I was unable to get out of it. I told Laraf to get Tristan out of the area and I saw them moving away. Ice tendrils wrapped themselves around me and I lost consciousness until you woke me."

"Kyri, that was approximately three days ago." Myrith stared at her friend; searching the younger woman's dark green eyes for any traces for deception. There was only confusion.

"Three days." Kyrianna's face went pale again.

Jerietlan placed a hand under Kyrianna's arm. "If you're feeling better, we should get moving. You'll warm quicker once you get your circulation flowing," he said.

Myrith stood and offered her hand as well.

"I would recommend the lady wear this for a while." Argrala held out a small red ring. "It will generate warmth around her so she is able to function better."

Falden took the ring and held it for a few minutes. "He is correct." He held it out to Kyrianna.

Myrith glanced at Argrala. The old man was now shivering and holding a blanket around his shoulders. "My thanks. It will be returned before too long." She handed the ring to Kyrianna who slipped it on a shaking hand.

"Thank you," the girl whispered as she picked up her swords and held them in her right hand. She clasped Myrith's with her left and slowly stood. She sheathed the weapons and looked around at the group. "Thank you for finding me."

"Thank Mykaylene. It was She who told me you were here."

Kyrianna bowed her head respectfully. "My thanks to your goddess as well."

~ * ~

"Dragons," Hendandra said softly as she approached the group. "Not sure how many, but they appeared to be fairly young whites." She trembled as she spoke.

"Dragons be evil incarnate," Nirev said. "And depending on their age they can assume other forms. We dare not pass them by."

Myrith glanced at Jerietlan and Falden and saw their nods of agreement.

"Myrith, should we be going out of our way to attack everything in this place?" Kyrianna asked.

Myrith stared at her friend. "We need to explore every area until we find a way out. We were brought here against our will, with no knowledge of this place. These dragons could be guarding the exit."

Kyrianna shook her head then turned to the old man standing in the back of the group. "Argrala, you claim you came here to fight this sorceress. Do you know anything about the layout of this area?"

Argrala shook his head. "No, my Lady, I do not know where the portal is. I only know it will be guarded by elementals, and there are no other ways off the layers other than through the portal to the next."

"Then it is doubtful these dragons are guarding the portal," Kyrianna said.

"If it were not for what ye said about dragons back at the estate, I would say the cold had warped yer thinking," Nirev said. "These be dragons. They be evil and must be destroyed."

"Why?" Kyrianna shook her head.

"Are ye daft, elf? They be dragons. That be enough."

"Dragons are only seen in dark times, Kyrianna," Falden said. "They are harbingers of evil and chaos. They are feared by all."

"That they are considered harbingers does not make them evil themselves."

"Bah." Nirev stepped up to Kyrianna, his maul raised slightly. "When dragons be about, only evil follows. They be not omens of evil—they be the ones who bring it."

"And I will not let evil go unchallenged," Myrith said. "Nor will

I let any part of this place go unchecked until we find the way out." She turned and headed down the corridor. She didn't glance back. However, she released the breath she was holding when she heard the others following her.

"Myrith, wait," Falden whispered.

She glanced at the mage to see him gesturing and chanting softly. Two streams of fire flowed from his hands and into the room. A roar echoed through the area and Myrith reached for the wall as the corridor shook and ice fell around them.

"Who are you that you dare to attack those who have done nothing to you?"

Myrith spun toward the unidentified speaker, her sword leading. He brought his own weapon up and blocked her blade as a blast of cold air hit her.

"Identify yourself!" She watched the young man closely as he took a half-step back. He was dressed in worn gray leathers with a chain mail vest. In his hands he held a double-bladed sword in a defensive position as he looked at her.

Myrith raised an eyebrow as she studied the young man. He had pale blond hair and ice-blue eyes—very similar to the faded coloring of the dragon on the sign at the Silver Dragon where she had grown up. As she examined his aura, she could detect no traces of darkness in his soul, but there was a feeling he had been touched by some power—not unlike what she had sensed from Kyrianna when she had met the girl. Although the darkness she had sensed on her friend was not present on this person.

She risked a quick glance back at the others. Kyrianna was on the ground and Jerietlan was sitting next to her. Falden stood with his hands raised and Nirev was standing behind the mage. There was no sign of Hendandra or Argrala.

"I am Andrinor," the young man said. His gaze moved around the rest of the group then back to her. "I come from a village in the Dragon Flame Mountains; sent here by Ghainaess to defend Her children."

"I do not know the one you have named, but I am aware these creatures follow the path of darkness," Myrith said.

"Their path does not matter," Andrinor said. "They are children of the Great Mother, Ghainaess. You attacked without provocation and that puts you in the wrong."

"And what of my friend who was hurt?" Myrith felt her grip on the sword tighten. She glanced back toward Kyrianna. The girl was sitting up, but shivering violently as Jerietlan draped a blanket over her shoulders.

"That is the price you will pay for this attack. I suggest you and your friends leave now." He shifted his weapon in his hands.

"They are evil; I cannot just pass them by." Myrith took a step back and stared at the young man. She didn't understand why he or Kyrianna couldn't see the need to destroy evil. She had been called by Geladas to fight evil and even though she now followed another she still took that charge seriously. It made no sense to her how those who did not follow the dark paths could stand by and let evil continue.

"Myrith."

She turned and saw Kyrianna getting up, Jerietlan supporting her. The girl was still pale and shivering. It hadn't been that long since they found her trapped behind a wall of ice; now she had been hit by that icy cold blast. If she had still been wearing the ring Argrala had loaned her, she might not have been as badly hurt by the dragon's breath. But the old man had not been able to bear the cold for long and as soon as her involuntary shivering had stopped, Kyrianna had given the enchanted item back to him.

"He says he comes from the Dragon Flames and he has named Ghainaess," Kyrianna said. "She is the Great Mother of dragons and is generally counted among the deities of light."

"You know of the Great Mother?" Andrinor said.

Myrith turned back to the young man who was staring at Kyrianna, his weapon held slightly lower as he took a step toward her.

"I am from Nydith and have some knowledge of all the gods of our land," Kyrianna said, holding out a shaking hand.

Andrinor started to take her hand, but hesitated and Myrith took a slow breath as she saw the young man's eyes go to where the tips of Kyrianna's ears showed through her hair. "You are an elf," he said.

Not again, Myrith thought.

"So, now you judge me on my heritage," Kyrianna whispered. "Something similar to what you have accused Myrith of doing."

Myrith relaxed as Andrinor nodded his head. "You are correct," he said. "I should not judge you based on the history of others. You have done nothing to me or against Ghainaess' children. However, I do have reason to judge those who would attack without provocation." He turned to glare at Falden.

Myrith moved to stand between Andrinor and Falden, her sword again raised in a defensive position. "Perhaps it would be best if we parted company at this time. I will not attack the dragons whom you defend. However, I will fight in defense of myself or others," she said.

"As is proper," Andrinor said, nodding his head slightly. "May the Great Mother spread Her wings over you as you travel."

Myrith motioned the others to leave the area and waited a few moments before she turned and followed them. She glanced back to see Andrinor turn toward the dragon's lair.

"So yer going to let him intimidate ye, are ye?" Nirev said, looking up at Myrith.

"He did not intimidate me. It was not worth arguing with him," Myrith said. "However, it might be a good idea if one of us went back and checked on him."

"Why?" Argrala asked. "He is of no concern to us. We must find the sorceress."

"And if the dragons are guarding the way to your portal from this area to the next, they might allow him to pass through. One of us, who can move quietly, could go back and watch to see if he leaves the area through their lair." She looked down at Hendandra.

"No. I'm not going anywhere near those things," Hendandra said, taking a stumbling step back.

"I'll go," Kyrianna said, readying her bow.

Myrith nodded. "Be careful."

"And how long do we wait?" Nirev asked.

"Until Kyrianna returns," Myrith said. "I trust her judgment in this matter."

Nirev only shook his head. "Trusting an elf's judgment," he whispered.

Myrith fought the smile she felt forming. For whatever reason, Nirev seemed to enjoy harassing Kyrianna about being an elf. However, she honestly didn't think it was because of any hatred he had for elves or for Kyri.

"Hendandra, will you move toward the lair enough to see Kyri and let us know if there is a problem?" Myrith glared at the smaller woman until she finally nodded.

Hendandra tossed her pack at Myrith as she moved away from the group following the corridor back to the dragons.

"I think there's a problem," Hendandra called as a blast of cold air rushed through the corridor.

Myrith tossed Hendandra's pack toward her as she ran toward the lair.

"This does not concern you," she heard Andrinor say as she saw Kyrianna take a step back from the entrance.

There was a roar, followed by a deep voice that had to be one of the dragons. "You claim to serve Ghainaess, yet you sought to trick us into lowering our guard so these could attack us."

"No!" Myrith saw Andrinor look up at the dragon then glance back toward her and Kyrianna. "I would not betray Her children!"

"No!" Kyrianna yelled as the male dragon's claws raked across Andrinor's back and the young man fell to the floor.

Myrith charged toward the dragon as it reached down, grabbed Andrinor's arm in his mouth and threw him across the room. There was a solid thud as the young man hit the far wall. Her sword plunged into the dragon's chest as she felt heat and heard the roar of flames behind her. A loud crash followed, but she didn't dare take her gaze from the dragon.

"Leave them alone." Andrinor's voice was weak but insistent.

Myrith jerked her blade out of the dragon and took several steps back as fire began flowing from the ceiling to engulf the creature.

The dragon roared again and ice shards fell around him, only to turn to vapor as the fire continued. Only after the dragon fell did the flames begin to fade, leaving a scorched husk where the white dragon had stood.

Myrith took a deep breath and glanced around; the others were safe though Kyrianna looked almost as bad as when they had found her. Jerietlan was tending to the girl, so she wasn't worried. "No," she whispered when she caught sight of a pale shimmering. The female had laid three eggs, now there would be no one to care for the hatchlings when they emerged. She couldn't leave them here to hatch alone, only to starve or fall victim to a predator. There was only one thing to do. She raised her sword and took several steps toward the nest.

"No!" Andrinor stepped between her and the eggs.

Myrith glanced at where Andrinor's weapon lay against the far wall then back at him. His eyes had narrowed slightly and he stood there trembling. She was reminded of a coiled snake waiting to strike.

She didn't step back, though she lowered her blade a few inches.

"What will happen to them when they hatch, with no parents to care for them?"

"Ghainaess will care for them or not as *She* determines. It is not for you to decide. They are *Her* children and I will not let you touch them."

Myrith nodded her head once. It was obvious she would have to kill the young man before he would let her touch the eggs unchallenged. She sheathed her sword and took a step back. "Very well, if that's what you want."

Andrinor didn't reply, only continued to stare at her until she turned to leave the lair.

Myrith motioned the others several feet down the corridor, then paused and glanced back at the dragon lair. She could hear Andrinor's voice, but they were too far away for her to understand his words.

"How are you feeling?" Myrith turned to Kyrianna.

"I'll be fine," Kyrianna said.

"We must move on," Argrala said, stepping between Myrith and Kyrianna. "I have no doubts Torliana is able to spy on us while we are in these elemental layers. We cannot give her time to prepare."

"Torliana?" Myrith looked at Argrala.

"That is the name of the sorceress who is doing this," he said.

"Is there anything else you can tell us about her?" Myrith asked.

"She is an elf," Argrala said. "That is all I can tell you."

"Can you describe her?" Kyrianna's asked.

"She is a little taller than you," he said, turning toward Kyrianna. "She has midnight dark hair and black eyes. There are silver flecks in her eyes, almost like stars floating in the night sky."

"A midnight elf?" Myrith asked as she watched Kyrianna's eyes go wide.

Kyrianna only nodded.

"Do you know the name?"

"No," Kyrianna whispered. "But I thought I felt something when he said it." She looked up at Myrith and shook her head. "It's gone now."

"Kyri?" Myrith placed a hand on the girl's shoulder. "Have you heard Thynitic whispering again?"

"I thought I heard something when I was caught by the storm, but I don't know if it was her."

"What happened in the shrine?" Myrith tightened her grip on

the girl's shoulder.

"I renounced her. I dropped the pendant on what was left of the altar and said she had no claim on me."

"Then what?"

"I left. Nothing else happened."

Myrith reached down and lifted a slender silver chain from around Kyrianna's throat. She jerked the chain, breaking it.

"Myrith?" Kyrianna's hand reached for the chain.

"If you left it, then how is it you are wearing it?" Myrith held the oval pendant up, the colors swirling and shimmering across its surface.

"I don't understand." Kyrianna's voice was only a harsh whisper. "I dropped it." She took a half-step back.

"Kyri?" Myrith dropped the pendant and grabbed for the girl, but found herself only grasping air as her friend turned and ran down the icy corridor.

"Myrith?" Hendandra picked up the pendant.

"After we find her," Myrith said.

She didn't wait for the others as she followed Kyrianna. Fortunately, this corridor didn't branch off and she found the girl huddled on the ground at the entrance to the dragon's lair. Andrinor knelt next to her, one arm around her shoulders.

"First you attack those who have done nothing to you, now it appears you attack those you would name as friend," Andrinor said as he looked up at Myrith.

"I did not attack her. Something upset her and she ran off. I thank you for your concern."

"Myrith, what's going on?" Hendandra asked.

Myrith looked at Hendandra then back at Kyrianna. "It is not my place." She knelt down next to the girl. "Kyri?"

Kyrianna looked up at Myrith, her dark green eyes wide. "What does she want with me?"

"I doubt it is anything we would understand." Myrith pulled Kyrianna to her feet.

Kyrianna nodded then stood and offered her hand to Myrith. "Perhaps you're correct. I have no desire to serve her and she has no claim on me."

Myrith gripped Kyrianna's arm. "Of course I'm right." She paused and locked her gaze with her friend's eyes. "Even if she thinks she has a claim on you, I will not allow her to have you."

"Thank you."

"Will someone please tell me what is going on!" Hendandra stepped between Kyrianna and Myrith. She held the pendant up and waited.

Myrith glanced at the colors emblazoned on the oval-shaped disk then at Kyrianna. The girl was staring at the pendant, but didn't appear to be enthralled by it. "It belongs to your lands," Myrith said.

"Yes, it does." Kyrianna took the pendant from Hendandra and dropped it into her pack. "As for your question." She took a deep breath. "I believe Thynitic was trying to call me to her service when we were in the temple. I have renounced her and that should be the end of it."

"No," Myrith said. "Not should. It *is* the end of it." She looked around at the others. "We need to be moving."

"Ghainaess has directed me to travel with you. She wishes me to seek the one who created this place and brought Her children here." Andrinor knelt before Myrith, his weapon on the ground in front of him.

Myrith glanced at Kyrianna who nodded. "Very well. However, I will have your pledge you will not challenge my authority and will follow my orders while you are a part of this group."

He raised his right fist to his heart. "You have my pledge. My sword will be raised only in defense of you and your friends, never against you. I only ask that you understand I serve one higher than you; I will not attack any of Her children without cause. If you provoke them, you must face them without me."

Myrith looked down at the young man. Her first instinct was to send him away. She didn't like him adding conditions to his pledge to follow her. However, she heard a voice in her mind whispering. :*His Goddess considers him one of Her children. Would you ask him to fight a sibling with whom he had no quarrel, only because you had a quarrel with them?*

:*No, my Lady, I would not. But to refuse to fight something that is evil, is that not evil in and of itself?*

:*Would that life were truly that simple. A mother does not see her children as good or evil. She sees them only as her children. Ghainaess requires he see Her children in the same way.*

:*I do not fully understand, my Lady, but I accept Your words and his sword.*

:*A willing heart is the beginning of understanding.* The presence faded from her mind.

"I understand this is a requirement of the goddess you serve. I would not come between you and her. You have shown me the depth of your loyalty to her and her children. May I prove worthy of the same." Myrith held out her hand.

Andrinor took her hand, stood up and bowed his head. "It will be as the Great Mother has directed."

Myrith returned the bow with a nod of her head, then drew her sword and headed down the corridor.

~ * ~

Sounds of growling filled the corridor and Myrith called a halt as Hendandra moved forward to see what was ahead of them.

"More of those damn wolves," Hendandra said as she returned.

"I'll go," Kyrianna said softly.

"Right, and get yourself killed trying to befriend one again, like you almost did last time; I don't think so. You'll stay in the back of the group this time as a guard for Falden and Jerietlan," Myrith said.

Kyrianna grinned and nodded. "Very well." She readied her bow and moved to the back.

Myrith shook her head and moved forward with Nirev and Andrinor behind her. The three of them waded into a carpet of white fur as a large pack of wolves came at them. From behind them, a spark of red shot past to explode into one of Falden's fireballs at the far back of the chamber. They had to move quickly to avoid the edge of the explosion, but the wolves weren't so lucky. Howls of pain filled the room, echoing off the walls as the flames faded.

As they dodged the teeth and claws of the closest members of the pack, Myrith heard a scream come from near the back of the group. It was followed by another, more familiar scream that ended abruptly. She lashed out with her sword trying to take out the remaining wolves quickly. That last scream had been Kyrianna's. The last time she had heard her friend cry out like that had been when the worg had almost killed her at the Duvall Estate. The only thing that had saved her friend then had been Tristan, putting himself into direct danger to administer a healing potion.

She lunged forward, her blade stabbing the last of the wolves. She jerked the weapon free as she turned and hurried to the back of the group.

A corridor led off to the side and she saw Jerietlan kneeling next to Kyrianna. Behind him stood Falden and the bodies of three human-appearing women.

"Hags," was all Falden said.

Nirev came up and looked down at Kyrianna. "Can ye do anything?"

"It is not a physical injury; it was some sort of magic the hags cast as one. Something seems to be pulling her spirit from her body. I can do nothing to prevent it, she has to fight this battle herself," Jerietlan said.

Myrith nodded then reached down and picked Kyrianna's lifeless body up. "Kyrianna, fight it," she whispered. She paused for a moment. "Mykaylene, please help her return to us."

"We'll rest here," Myrith said following Hendandra into another, smaller room.

"No other exits from this room," Hendandra said.

"Good, only one way in." Myrith motioned for Jerietlan and Falden to set up a bed for Kyrianna. With care she placed the girl in the blankets.

~ * ~

Mykaylene, we need to find a way out of here, Myrith thought as she watched the crackling fire after the others had fallen asleep. *I do not want to bury any of my companions in this place.* Falden warded the area and Hendandra hung several of the wolf pelts over the door trapping the heat in the small room. Myrith hadn't realized how much feeling they had lost to the cold until her hands and feet began tingling then almost burning as they warmed back up. Jerietlan had mentioned something about a spell that might help them handle the cold better and he was still in meditation hoping to be able to cast it in the morning.

She glanced over at Kyrianna who was now tossing in her sleep and hoped that was a sign the girl would be back with them soon. She also wondered what nightmares might be haunting her friend as she felt her own eyelids dropping.

~ * ~

Myrith's eyes snapped open at a low growl and whine. She looked around to see a large black and silver tipped wolf nosing at Kyrianna.

"Kyri!" Myrith jumped up drawing her sword.

The wolf looked at her and took a defensive position in front of Kyrianna.

"Myrith?" Kyrianna's voice said as she looked out from under the blankets.

"Don't make any sudden moves." She never took her eyes off the wolf.

Kyrianna sat up slowly then smiled. "Shadow?" She grabbed the wolf and hugged him tightly.

The wolf barked playfully as Kyrianna let go of him then grabbed the blanket in his teeth and pulled it away from her.

"I take it you two know each other," Myrith said, sheathing her sword.

Kyrianna nodded. "Frayrith sent him to me when She first accepted my pledge to serve Her. When the portal grabbed me and brought me to the temple, he was left behind. It would appear she has seen fit to send him to me again. His name is Shadow Seeker."

Myrith knelt down so the wolf could get her scent and held her hand out to him. She was surprised when the large creature suddenly pounced on her and licked her face, before bouncing back over to Kyrianna.

"He's a little playful," Kyrianna said as the wolf pounced on her.

"Great, another mouth to feed," Nirev said as he crawled out of his blankets.

"Well, at least now she won't be trying to make friends with any more winter wolves," Hendandra said as Shadow Seeker came over and licked her face.

The wolf greeted each member of the group with a lick, except the dwarf, whom he quickly sniffed and trotted away from.

"He has dog breath and wet dog smell and he doesn't care for me," Nirev said with a snort. "No accounting for taste."

Myrith shook her head as Kyrianna and Hendandra laughed. "Okay, let's get moving. I want out of this frozen hell."

The two girls stopped laughing and quickly gathered their gear and joined the rest; the wolf staying close to Kyrianna's side.

"Wait," Jerietlan called. He closed his eyes and chanted softly. When he opened his eyes, his hands were glowing with a soft blue radiance. "This will help to shield you against the effects of the cold. He touched Myrith on the shoulder and she felt herself warm slightly.

Andrinor stepped back from the cleric. "I do not require this shield."

Jerietlan nodded and went around to the others. Myrith raised an eyebrow when the cleric paused and looked down at Shadow Seeker.

"While his coat will protect him against a normal winter chill, this is an elemental cold," Jerietlan said.

Kyrianna nodded and the cleric reached down to touch the wolf on the head.

"You'll thank him later," Kyrianna said, looking down at the wolf.

~ * ~

Myrith wasn't sure how many days they had been wandering in the ice-covered passages, but it was definitely too many. "I've had it!" She slammed her fist into the nearest wall as her voice echoed though the corridor.

"Myrith, I hate to say this…" Hendandra looked up from the parchment she and Kyrianna were looking at.

"What!"

Hendandra took a step back and Kyrianna placed a hand on her shoulder as she looked up at Myrith.

"We appear to be back where we started," Kyrianna said, handing the scribbled map to Myrith. "Neither of us can see where we missed any passages either."

"So there is magic or something blocking the passage out of here. Great! We can retrace all of our steps and have Falden searching for traces of magic every step of the way. Or maybe we'll get lucky and stumble into the passage."

"Hendandra and I have been studying the map and we think we have the areas where there might be an additional passage narrowed down to these four," Kyrianna said, pointing to several marks on the map. "One of those areas is this wall here."

Myrith looked at Falden who only shook his head. "I am not sensing any magic on this wall."

"Fine let's move to the next area." Myrith crumbled the map in her hand.

"That does not mean the passage is not here," Falden said quickly. "A powerful enough mage can mask the presence of magic after they cast a spell. Or it might not be masked by magic at all."

"Fine! Riker, come to me!"

The ghostly warhorse appeared and stared at her.

"As you are of the spirit world, can you move through this wall and verify whether there is another passage on the other side or not?"

The horse looked at her, his eyes appearing to grow wider at the request she was making. After a few minutes, the horse bobbed his head and moved past her toward the wall, catching her foot with one of his hooves as he passed her.

"You did that on purpose," Myrith muttered.

"Yes, he did, but you deserved it," Kyrianna said. "Riker was the mount of an apparently highly respected knight, before he was slain by the son of that same man. Being treated like a secret passage detector won't go over very well with his feelings."

Myrith stared at Kyrianna then nodded. "You're right. I'll apologize before I dismiss him."

"Good idea."

The horse paused as he passed through one section of the wall then stepped back and looked at her. Myrith stepped over and pushed against the section of wall only to see her hand vanish into it. She stepped through then back. "Another corridor," she said, looking at the others.

Myrith took a deep breath then looked at the horse. "I'm sorry," she said bowing her head slightly. "And, thank you."

The horse glanced down at her foot and brushed his head against her cheek before he vanished.

Myrith smiled as she stepped through the wall again and the others followed her. The long hallway ended in a small room with a small air elemental watching them.

Argrala stepped in front of her. "This I can deal with; if you will allow me." He pulled a small censer out of his robes and took several steps forward. He raised and lowered the chain holding the censer and let it swing slowly in front of him. Smoke began to flow from the burner as he spoke softly in a strange language. When he finished, the small elemental vanished, only to be replaced by a larger one. Five more times, Argrala raised and lowered the censer and spoke softly and each time one elemental vanished to be replaced by a larger one until the last one vanished and a doorway framed in fire appeared on the back wall.

Myrith waited as the others stepped through the doorway. She frowned when she saw Hendandra pick up something from the floor as she passed through.

Myrith stepped through the portal, then turned to see it vanish leaving only a glowing red wall.

Chapter Five

Myrith cringed at the heat; it felt like someone had wrapped a hot, wet shroud around her when she stepped through the doorway. Rivulets of water began to flow under her armor and she shifted as her skin began to itch. She glanced around at the others and saw the heat glistening on their faces as they tried shifting their armor around. Her hair, normally bright red, had darkened with her sweat and lay plastered against her neck. She pushed the lank, wet hair back from where it had draped itself over her shoulder. Hendandra was trying to tie her long blonde hair up on top of her head and Kyrianna had pulled hers back into a loose ponytail.

She watched as Andrinor poured some water into his hand and offered it to Kyrianna's wolf. Despite his obvious discomfort, Shadow Seeker looked up at the girl for permission before lapping the water up. The wolf's panting eased only a little, and his head and tail still drooped. If still seemed odd to her that Kyrianna's patron had expended power to send the wolf here. If she had the power to reach into this place, why hadn't she pulled Kyrianna, and the rest of them, out?

:*The wolf was sent as more than a companion,* she heard Mykaylene whisper. :*He is a guardian and a watcher. There are things that have been set in motion that must be finished.*

Myrith frowned slightly, wondering what the goddess had meant; but her presence was gone. She looked around at the chamber they were in and shook her head. "Let's get moving," she said. "We still don't know what's going on here." She headed down the corridor and the others followed her.

As she walked through the passageways, Myrith wasn't sure which was worse—the cold of the last area or the heat of this one. Every surface radiated the heat, reflecting and amplifying its intensity. For a moment, she debated calling Riker and asking him to explore the area in his own way to find the passage out quickly. However, she dismissed the idea. She had insulted the ghost horse the last time she had made such a request and if he went off on his own, she had no way to protect him if he were to encounter something that was able to harm him.

~ * ~

The days passed much as they had in the previous area. The creatures they encountered here all seemed to have a connection to fire, just as the previous ones had to cold or air. With the oppressive heat, Myrith was calling for rest stops earlier in the day than she had in the cold and she doubted they were resting as long as they had been before.

Jerietlan was casting a spell to create water for them several times a day and used a variant of the spell he had used to protect them from the cold as they rested to allow their bodies to cool and relax just a little before they began their search again.

"Another group of fire giants," Hendandra said, coming back from checking another room.

Falden raised a slender crystal wand and moved to where he could see into the chamber. Myrith and Nirev stood to the side as he muttered something and pointed the wand into the chamber. A blast of ice and snow erupted from the tip of the wand.

When the severe cold and hail from the spell subsided, Nirev rushed into the room, yelling a dwarven battle cry and swinging his maul. Myrith and the others followed him.

Three of the black-skinned giants turned to face the charging dwarf. Falden raised his hands and launched several bolts of arcane energy at the one furthest back, rocking it.

Nirev brought his maul into an overhead swing that hit the knee of the first giant causing it to roar in pain and drop its sword. Myrith charged up and dropped her shield. Taking a two-handed grip on her sword she struck the back of the giant's other knee, cutting through the leather and cloth of his armor and clothing. The giant's knee buckled and she struggled to pull the blade free from where it had become pinned. Nirev struck his side again and the giant fell backward yanking Myrith's blade from her grasp.

"Sorry about that, Lady Knight!" Nirev yelled. "Ye have another blade, do ye not?"

Myrith didn't bother to answer as she pulled the sword pin from her surcoat and it grew into a full bastard sword.

"Nice trick that," Nirev said.

Andrinor moved to the second of the giants, his double-bladed weapon held in both hands as he parried the giant's powerful blows. He didn't even flinch as Kyrianna's arrows flew past his head to land in the giant's chest.

Hendandra dodged between the giants to get behind the one Andrinor was facing and darted in quickly, her rapier stabbing the back of his knee, the highest place she could reach on the creature. The blow was solid though and the giant roared. As he tried to turn to see who had attacked him, Andrinor brought his weapon into a single powerful swing that connected with the giant's hip.

Andrinor had to jerk hard to pull the blade free of the leather and cloth that tried to bind it and was sprayed by the rush of blood from the wound.

Falden continued his arcane attack on the third giant and was rewarded as the creature fell against the back wall and slid to the floor. He cast a final arcane bolt at the last standing giant as one of Kyrianna's arrows pierced its eye. As the giant fell back, Hendandra tumbled away from him and over by Andrinor.

"Nice shot," Myrith said, looking at the arrow in the giant's eye.

"Doubtful ye can do it again," Nirev said with a snort.

"You're probably correct. Care to find out?" Kyrianna let her hand reach toward the quiver on her back. She grinned as the dwarf shook his head.

"The next time we run into something to fight we can find out," Nirev said.

"That we will." Kyrianna looked at Myrith and smiled.

"Hey, guys, look at this," Hendandra called from a corner of the room. She stood in front of a large steel chest covered with gold inlaid symbols.

"Well, now, this be interesting," Nirev said, looking at the chest. "These be the symbols of the various races of giants."

Hendandra looked at the dwarf and motioned him back with her hands. "I need a little room to work here," she said, pulling out her lock picks. She knelt down in front of the chest and began studying the lock. She slipped first one then a second pick into the lock and carefully twisted them as she listened to the clicks of the tumblers. After several seconds, the lock opened and Hendandra pushed the lid back. Inside was a large sword, covered with the same runes as the chest.

Nirev reached past Hendandra to pick up the sword and carefully removed it from its sheath to study the weapon. "Nice work, this," he said.

"What's this?" Hendandra reached into the chest and pulled out a piece of parchment. She glanced at the note and handed it to Myrith.

Myrith glanced at the note and frowned. "Unfortunately, I can't read this. Nirev?" She held the note out to the dwarf.

Nirev placed the tip of the sword on the ground then took the note in his free hand. "Greetings Droeig," he said after a moment of studying the note. "As I promised, here is the ancient sword of the giant king. With this blade, you will be able to unite and lead all the races of giant and giantkin. Again my thanks for your aid in this endeavor—Torliana." He finished reading the note, handed it back to Myrith and lifted the sword to look at the rune-covered blade.

"Torliana? That was the same name you gave us, wasn't it, Argrala," Falden said.

"Yes." The old man glanced at Kyrianna for a second. "She is a mage of considerable power and also a cleric of a dark goddess, one whose power she seeks to steal for her own."

"You told us she was seeking to gain control of the four elemental planes," Myrith said.

"As a daughter of chaos, she has numerous plots and schemes going."

"Daughter of chaos?"

Myrith turned to stare at Kyrianna. The girl's voice had been a harsh whisper and she had gone pale and her right hand tightly gripped Shadow Seeker's fur. The wolf leaned against her as if supporting her.

"Do you know the name of this goddess she serves?"

"I do not know her actual name, only that she is called the Lady of Chaos," Argrala said.

"Thynitic," Kyrianna whispered. Her eyes were wide and white ringed with fear.

"Something's coming down the other passage," Hendandra said, standing and drawing her rapier.

Nirev started down the passage holding the sword he had taken from the chest, Myrith and Andrinor followed him.

Another fire giant stood in the hallway and Nirev froze with the sword held ready to strike it. The giant leaned forward; his own sword ready to hit Nirev, but was frozen in place and unable to move as he glared at the dwarf.

Myrith and Andrinor both swung at the giant breaking it out

of its trance as it turned to attack them. She was surprised at the power Andrinor had as the two of them worked together against the giant. The young man grinned and raised his blade in salute to her as the giant fell to the ground. She nodded then turned back to where Nirev still stood unmoving.

Jerietlan approached and placed his hands on Nirev's shoulders and chanted softly. The sword dropped from the dwarf's hands and he snapped out of the trance. "What happened?"

"It would appear the sword of the giant king not only protects the wielder from attacks by giants, it also prevents him from attacking them," Jerietlan said.

"You and the giant looked like a pair of statues glaring at each other," Andrinor said. He laughed as he slapped the dwarf on the shoulder.

Nirev only glared at Andrinor as he sheathed the sword and attached it to his pack.

"You're going to keep that, after what happened?" Myrith said, looking at the dwarf.

"Of course. I am. While it may not be my first choice for fighting giants, it still be a valuable item and a well made piece of steel." Nirev picked up his maul and headed off down the corridor. "Are ye all going to stand around talking or are we going to find our way out of this place?"

Myrith only shook her head as she and the others followed Nirev.

~ * ~

"This is getting ridiculous!" Kyrianna yelled as they paused in one of the small chambers while Jerietlan called on Mykaylene for the power to fill their waterskins and other containers. "We still have no clue where to go or what is going on." She slumped against the wall and let her body slide to the floor. "Chaos take it, we don't even know how long we've been here." She wrapped her arms around Shadow Seeker who nosed gently at her face and whined.

"We'll camp here," Myrith said, shaking her head. "Hopefully we can start again with cooler attitudes after we get some rest."

Kyrianna looked up at and nodded her head. "I apologize for my outburst," she said.

"Get some rest, Kyri. I'll wake you for the last watch," Myrith said. "Nirev, you take the first watch, Andrinor, the second, I'll take the third and Kyri gets the fourth. Two hours each."

His water creation spells completed, Jerietlan began casting the spell that would help protect them from the heat. He paused as he got to Kyrianna and Shadow Seeker. "Kyri, I only have enough spell power left to shield one of you." He started to touch her shoulder.

She pulled away from his hand. "Give the spell to Shadow; except for Andrinor, he's in worse shape than any of us here."

"As you wish." Jerietlan reached down and touched the wolf's head, the glow on his hand fading.

Kyrianna smiled as the wolf's breathing eased. "Thank you."

Jerietlan only nodded as he walked away.

"Was that wise?" Myrith said, walking over. "I know you have a responsibility to protect him, particularly when he can't take care of himself. However, you do him and the rest of us more good if you are rested and ready for the day. He can stay out of battle easier than you can."

"And I can cope with the discomfort better than he can, as I am better able to understand what's going on. I'll be fine."

"Okay, get some sleep, then." Myrith moved to her bedroll and stripped off her armor, leaving only the tunic and pants she wore under them on. She glanced around at the rest of the party as she did every night and as usual, no one was paying attention to her. Once again, she chided herself for letting her experiences in her former life cloud the way she expected people to react. But, no matter how many times she tried to tell herself to stop worrying, she couldn't. Some things became too ingrained and impossible to let go of.

She saw Kyrianna remove her leather armor and carefully dry the material with a cloth from her pack. Her light tunic and hose clung to her skin as tightly as Myrith's own did, yet the girl didn't seem concerned about the males in the party as she dropped onto her bedroll, the wolf licking her face a few times before he lay down several inches away from her.

She grinned as Kyrianna reached out and moved the wolf's head so it didn't point at her. "Ugh, hot dog breath," the girl said softly as she turned to face away from her four-footed companion.

~ * ~

Myrith woke to Andrinor's hand on her shoulder. "Your turn," he said.

As she put her chain shirt on, Andrinor stiffened then turned toward one of the passages. "What's wrong?" she asked.

"Thought I heard something," he said, taking a step toward the corridor.

Myrith nodded toward Kyrianna and Nirev as she grabbed her sword. Andrinor moved to wake the other two then stepped quickly into the corridor.

Kyrianna grabbed her bow and quiver, not bothering to put on her armor as she took a position behind the others, Shadow Seeker next to her, an arrow nocked and ready. Myrith tapped her on the shoulder as she moved past and stood next to Nirev and Andrinor.

Three large black canines with glowing red eyes approached from the corridor. All were growling and radiating heat. Myrith stared at them, they seemed to be similar to the hellhounds they had faced before on this layer, but these were each the size of a heavy warhorse. She glanced at the two on her right. While this corridor was large enough for the three of them to stand together, only two of the creatures could attack at a time.

"Watch it, Kyrianna; that was close!" Myrith yelled as an arrow flew past her to strike one of the creatures. "And do us a favor; go after the one in the back. I think the three of us can handle these two." She held her sword ready waiting for the large canines to get close.

"Very well," Kyrianna said as another volley of arrows flew past Myrith.

The war hounds, as Myrith thought of the creatures in front her, had tough hides and she frowned when her sword only glanced off the one in front of her. Andrinor had switched to using only one of his blades and putting more power into the swings. Blood sprouted from the hound as the weapon sliced into the side of its neck.

She wasn't able to see Nirev, but could hear the hound he was fighting yelp several times. Then a loud cry of pain from the dwarf as the creature lunged forward.

"No!," Andrinor yelled, his blade disengaging from the creature they were fighting as he shoved Nirev aside and stepped between him and the second one.

"Nirev!" She heard Kyrianna yell the dwarf's name as arrows continued to fly toward the hound in the back of the group.

Myrith jumped as a large grey streak flew past her to hit the war hound. "Kyri, control your companion," Myrith said turning toward Kyrianna.

Myrith stopped when she saw Argrala standing behind Kyrianna, a tendril of multi-colored mist flowing around the two of them as Kyrianna released another arrow. She followed the flight of the arrow as it flew past her to bury itself in the creature's eye just as Shadow Seeker jumped back from its claws. "Shadow," she whispered then turned back to face Kyrianna. She heard the wolf growl softly, but the mist and Argrala were gone.

Myrith shook her head, she needed to speak to Kyrianna but there was still one of the creatures left to deal with. She stepped back as the creature lunged for her then brought her blade up and thrust it into its mouth with all her strength. She saw Andrinor bring his blade down on the creature's neck as she jerked her sword back. The war hound fell to the ground with the others.

"There," she said directing Jerietlan to Nirev as he came into the area. The cleric was already chanting as he ran. He placed his hands on Nirev's chest calling on Mykaylene's power to heal the fallen warrior.

"Kyri, will you take the watch, while we try to get some more rest?"

"Yes."

"Good, wake me in two hours. We will continue our search of this place in four."

~ * ~

"Kyri?" Myrith sat up as the group began stirring the next morning. "You didn't wake me to take a watch."

"I was fine and you needed the rest," Kyrianna said.

"You still having bad dreams?" Myrith asked.

"Not ones I can remember," Kyrianna said kneeling down next to Shadow Seeker and offering him some water. "I just wake with the feeling something was haunting me as I slept. It's like there was something watching me, judging me. Wanting to control me in some way, but I can never remember the dreams."

Myrith took a deep breath and nodded. *If she can't remember them, then that might explain why she hasn't talked to me.* She was worried Thynitic was still targeting her friend.

"You don't think...," Myrith let her voice fade.

"I don't know." Kyrianna's voice was barely louder than a whisper and Myrith saw her shudder. Shadow Seeker put a paw on her arm and focused his eyes on Kyrianna and Myrith saw her relax slightly.

Myrith glanced at Argrala and saw he was watching Kyrianna with a slight smile on his face.

"Kyri…." She stopped as she felt a sudden chill wrap itself around her.

"Yes." Kyrianna looked up. The fear was gone from the girl's face.

"Let's get moving," Myrith finally said, turning away.

~ * ~

"Enough of this game, whoever you are!" Myrith threw a handful of coins she had picked up at the nearest wall. "I have had enough!"

Only silence greeted her.

"Feel better?" Hendandra asked, picking the coins up and dropping them into one of her sacks.

"No. I just want out of this place. That last pack of hellhounds we encountered almost did you and Falden in."

"But they didn't." Hendandra visibly shuddered as she glanced at the mage for a second.

"Thank Mykaylene for that," Myrith said. "Next time we might not be so lucky."

"Do we have any choice in this though?" Kyrianna looked at her then glanced at Hendandra.

"I guess we don't. Let's get some rest. You can take first watch, Kyri; I'll take the second and Andrinor can take the third."

"Three hours for me and Andrinor. You get only two, taking the middle."

"Since you insist, agreed."

As she lay down on the blankets, Myrith glanced toward the girl who was walking slowly around the chamber. Kyrianna stopped at one of the corridors and seemed to be staring into the reddish light that filled this place. She took a step forward, slowly drew her long sword and glanced toward Myrith. "Something moving this way. Not very large and moving cautiously."

Kyrianna paused for a moment. "The step is heavy. Whatever it is, it is on two legs."

"Hold your blades, warriors," a deep voice said from the shadows of the passageway.

Myrith noticed Kyrianna's hand tighten on her blade even as

she moved it into a low defensive posture. There had been a definite reptilian hiss to the speech patterns of the one approaching. "More salamanders?" She kept her voice low hoping only Kyrianna would hear her.

"I don't think so. I don't detect the odor of sulfur like I did with the salamanders we've fought here. This has a more metallic taste to it. I would suspect dragon, but it's not large enough."

Myrith frowned as a tall shape moved toward them; a reddish-gold glow surrounded it. "Mykaylene's Blessing on you," she called. The creature paused for a moment then stepped close enough for her to see his features. He was almost a foot taller than she was and his skin was covered in gold scales. A large sword was strapped to his back and his hands appeared to be closer to claws than fingers. His face while vaguely human held a pair of slanted eyes the color of molten gold. From his temples, a pair of long, smooth horns swept back, trapping a mane of long dusty blond hair.

"I greet you in the name of Ghainaess," he said, bowing deeply.

"Though I am unfamiliar with your kind, considering the nature of the one you have named, you are welcome in our camp," Myrith said, returning the bow with a polite nod.

"Even in my world, my nature is considered unusual; even more so than that of your companion." He nodded to Kyrianna.

"That you name the Great Mother tells me you are from the same lands I am," Kyrianna said slowly. "If I had to guess, I would say one of your parents was a gold dragon."

"You are correct. My father was a gold dragon. However, most pairings of dragons and humans do not result in such obvious links to the draconic heritage. It is my understanding there is a human village in the Dragon Flame Mountains where dragons have mated with humans many times in the past, and none of those births have resulted in any such as I."

"May we have your name?" Myrith asked, extending her hand.

"Vyroris."

The half-dragon took her hand gently and she could feel heat in the golden scales.

"I am called Myrith and my friend is Kyrianna."

"May the Great Mother spread Her wings over you and your group."

"How did you come to be here?" Kyrianna asked as they returned to the camp.

"I sought one of power to send me here. It was a difficult task as this is a closed plane created by an evil sorceress for the purpose of channeling and controlling the power of the four elemental planes. It was made even more difficult as there are almost none in Rhysia who are able to channel arcane magics. I finally sought the favor of one of the Divine in order to get here." He paused and his gaze moved to the area behind Myrith and Kyrianna. "I am currently searching for another who came here for the same purpose. He is called Argrala."

Both Myrith and Kyrianna glanced toward the elderly man sleeping near Jerietlan.

"That is Argrala?"

Myrith looked at the half-dragon. "That is the name he gave us."

Vyroris walked over to the man, knelt down and placed a hand on his shoulder. "Argrala?"

The older man blinked then sat up and stared at the half-dragon. "Vyroris." He reached up and clasped the hand on his shoulder. "It is good to see you. Took you longer than we anticipated."

"It did. There are no mages on Rhysia with the power to create a portal to this place. I had to travel to the elven lands south of the Sea of Dreams to find one who could send me here and even then, I had to seek the aid of one of the Divine. Now, tell me what that witch did to you."

The old man smiled for a moment then nodded. "Her power caught me as I was attempting to enter the plane and even though I was able to force my way through it, the chaos she commands changed me into this."

"Then we will have to force her to return your true form to you." The half-dragon glanced around at the sleeping group. "These are the heroes you foresaw coming here?"

"Excuse me," Myrith said, looking from Vyroris to Argrala. "The heroes you foresaw coming here?"

"Yes. In my attempts to understand what Torliana is trying to do here, I saw a group coming to this place to challenge her. However, the outcome of that challenge remains shrouded in chaos. There are at least two who appear to have gained the attention of the power Torliana serves." His gaze darted from Kyrianna to Myrith then around the room before returning.

"And you didn't think to tell us this when we found you?" Myrith said, frowning.

"And I was to trust you completely upon first meeting you? I have traveled too far to accept things at face value; something I would caution you against doing as well." His gaze darted to Kyrianna for a moment then back to Myrith.

"Myrith, you're going to take the middle watch," Kyrianna said. "You should get some rest. I will wake you in three hours." She turned to the half-dragon and Argrala. "If you two wish to continue your discussion, please do so in quieter tones as the others still need rest. We can continue the introductions in the morning, or what passes for morning in this place."

"The half-elf is correct," Vyroris said.

Myrith saw Kyrianna's head drop slightly at the way Vyroris said half-elf. She thought for a moment about telling her friend more about her own background and that she, like Kyrianna, was also half-elven and from a place where elves were even more hated than Kyrianna's home. She turned her head and decided it really wouldn't do any good to tell her at this time.

Myrith glanced over at where Andrinor was snoring. He had slept through the half-dragon's arrival, it would be interesting when they met in the morning.

~ * ~

Despite the looks Vyroris received from the others when Myrith introduced him the next morning, they didn't seem too upset to have him join the group. Considering the attitude many of them had for dragons, she was surprised. Andrinor had been the biggest surprise, only bowing slightly to the half-dragon, before returning to readying his gear.

As they were getting ready to move on, she saw Vyroris move to the back of the group, to stand with Argrala. The half-dragon was watching the old man closely, but she had no way of judging his emotions.

"Myrith, I think we should head south today," Hendandra said as she picked up her pack.

"It's as good a direction as any, but why? And honestly, can you tell me which direction is south?" Myrith glanced at Kyrianna who only shrugged.

"Leikor is guiding me in that direction," she said, glancing at one of the passages. "And he said we should travel south today."

"Leikor?" Myrith looked at the smaller woman.

"He is the god of rogues and tricksters on Shokar," Jerietlan said with a frown. "He is not one to be trusted."

"Look, your goddess led you to Kyrianna. I'm sure there is a reason Leikor wants me to go in this direction." Hendandra shouldered her pack and started for the passageway.

"Hold!" Myrith reached out to grab Hendandra's shoulder, only to have her dodge and dart away.

"Chaos!" Kyrianna dashed after Hendandra, the wolf right on her heels followed by the half-dragon. "Hendandra, wait!"

Myrith looked at the others. "Jerietlan, you and Falden stay with Argrala and follow us." She turned and ran after the others as fast as her heavy armor would allow.

The sounds of yelling and ringing metal soon reached Myrith's ears as she forced herself to move faster. *What has that little thief gotten us into now?* She tightened her grip on her sword.

She ran around one corner into a chamber to see a fire giant moving away from her and toward another passage. She didn't slow her speed as she charged the creature and swung her blade at his legs. The giant howled with pain as he tried to turn to see what had struck him. She dodged to the side as Falden entered the chamber and pulled a wand from his robes.

The giant was surrounded by a swirling storm of ice and snow. She didn't have time for the magic to subside as she could still hear shouts and ringing metal in the distance. She darted into the storm and swung her sword again. Falden put the wand in his belt and began casting his bolts of energy at the giant. Just as the magic of the storm subsided the giant began to fall and Myrith barely made it out of his way as he hit the ground. Not waiting for the mage to reach her, she began running toward the now fading sounds of battle.

She rounded another corner to see two fire giants on the ground along with Kyrianna's wolf. The girl was bandaging Shadow Seeker's wounds and Vyroris was standing near another corridor apparently on guard for other possible attacks. "Where's Hendandra?" Myrith demanded as she stopped.

"We lost her, for the moment," Kyrianna said. "As soon as I tend to Shadow's injuries, I will have him track her."

Myrith took several deep breaths then nodded. As she waited

for Kyrianna to finish with the wolf, she called on her own healing gifts and placed her hand on her own chest. Jerietlan and the others came up as the magic faded and she felt herself slightly revived from the fight and run.

Jerietlan looked at her, raised an eyebrow slightly then dropped to his knees beside the wolf and called on his own healing power. Shadow Seeker whined softly as the sword cut along his ribs closed and the bleeding stopped. He reached up and licked the cleric in the face before getting up and sniffing the air and ground.

The wolf paused several times as he checked the floor of the passageway and moved to the doorway where the half-dragon stood. Barking once and glancing at Kyrianna the wolf trotted off following what Myrith hoped was Hendandra's trail.

The group moved a bit more cautiously through the twists and turns of the passages the wolf was following. Nobody wanted to run into anymore fire giants, or anything else, unprepared. Kyrianna was the one in the lead as she had the better chance of tracking the wolf, and when three short barks sounded, took off at a sprint.

Myrith followed her and stopped short when she found Kyrianna kneeling next to Hendandra who was lying on the floor near an open doorway.

"She's unconscious," Kyrianna said. "However, I can find no sign of injury."

"The others will be here shortly. Jerietlan can check her." Myrith moved to the open doorway and took up a guard position.

When the last person entered the area, Hendandra stirred and her eyes opened. "What's going on?" She glanced from Kyrianna to Myrith then to the others. "How did I get here? In fact where is here?"

"What's the last thing you remember?" Jerietlan asked.

"Getting up this morning and being introduced to Vyroris. Why? What's going on?"

"You don't remember telling me Leikor was directing you to travel south this day?" Myrith looked down at Hendandra.

"No. Why would I do that? Yes, I occasionally swear by Leikor and will offer him a thank you when I have a run of good luck, but I am not a devoted follower of the Trickster. I only do the little I do because he is seen as the patron of rogues."

Hendandra stood up and brushed the dust off her clothes. "Now, will someone tell me what happened?"

Myrith looked around and saw the others looking at her, waiting for her to explain.

"After we woke this morning, you told me you thought we should go south today. When I questioned why, you said Leikor was guiding you in that direction, just as Mykaylene had guided me when we found Kyri." Myrith paused for a moment. "Then Jerietlan commented on the nature of Leikor and said he was not one to be trusted. Before a decision could be made regarding today's travel you took off and we followed you. This is where we found you, unconscious until a few moments ago."

Hendandra only stared at her. "Why don't I remember that?"

"It is possible Leikor was able to possess you for a short time," Jerietlan said. "It is he who could have been in control since you woke this morning, until we found you just now."

"Great. Just what I need, a god I really don't care about trying to control me." She walked to the doorway. "I guess we should at least see what he thought was so important for me to find." She stepped into the chamber and Myrith followed her.

Other than a plain wooden chest against the far wall, there was nothing else in the room. Myrith reached down and grabbed Hendandra's shoulder as she approached the chest. "Do you really think this is a good idea?"

"Only one way to find out," Hendandra said. "Don't worry, I'll be careful."

Hendandra approached the chest and knelt in front of it. Her nimble fingers moving slowly over the surface as she studied it. After several minutes, she nodded and turned her attention to the lock. It was almost five minutes before she sat back and removed her picks from the pouch she kept on her belt.

Myrith found herself holding her breath as Hendandra worked the lock.

"Got it," Hendandra said as she lifted the lid of the chest. There was a flash of light and the lid closed immediately. A deck of cards rested on the lid. Myrith glanced around, and saw everyone in the group was holding a card in their hands, with the exception of Argrala who stood just outside the room watching them.

"What is this?" Vyroris said, turning the card in his hand over to look at it. There was a brief flash of light and where the gold half-dragon had been standing was now a small white rabbit.

"No one else look at their cards," Myrith said, moving toward the chest. She stopped as laughter filled the room.

"It is not that easy, Warrior of the Battle Maiden. Once you touch the card, you are bound to its effects. The only thing you have any chance in is the way you turn the card over. If it is upright when you turn it, the effect may be positive; if it is upside down the effect may be negative. Either way you will at least take your chances with one of the cards in my deck. The little one will take her chances with two." The voice dissolved into laughter again.

"Leikor," Jerietlan said.

"Ah, the priest remembers his lessons in the other gods of Shokar."

"Why?" Hendandra asked softly.

"You ask why? Think on this, little thief. What did you do that caused you to be sent away from your home by the priestess of a goddess you thought to steal something from? That one and I are allies in many ways and you upset her with your theft. Therefore, you have the card you received as the chest was opened and after all of your friends have received their *gifts*, you will spread the deck out and draw one last card. No matter which card you draw, if it is upright, you will reverse any negative effects your friends have received; however, if it is upside down you will remove any benefits they have received and make permanent the negative effects of the cards they hold." Laughter filled the room growing louder with each passing moment. Then it stopped altogether. "One last thing—unless the effects are immediately obvious, no one here will be able to tell anyone else about what they received." The presence vanished.

Myrith looked at the others and slowly turned her card over as they did the same. It looked like the type of card fortune tellers used with a brightly colored design on it. She frowned as she looked at the card. It appeared to be the death card. *How can this be positive? Well, at least no one has dropped dead. Maybe it is positive in that it doesn't have a negative effect.*

"Hey, where did my gem pouch go?" Falden said suddenly.

Myrith's hand went to the small money pouch she carried only to find it gone. There were looks of puzzlement on the faces of the others as well as they checked for their money.

"It would appear someone's card caused us to lose our money," Myrith said. "At least we don't appear to need any here. And I'm sure we will continue to find other items of value."

Hendandra looked around at everyone. "Is that everyone?"

There were several nods of assent.

"Then let's go." She started to stand up and found herself instead turning back to the chest, her hand fanning the cards out. "Guess he's not going to let me leave without drawing that last card." Her hand moved slowly over the cards. With care, she drew one out of the middle and slid it toward herself. She stared at the card for several heartbeats before finally lifting one side and flipping the card over. It was upright. She spun around as the white rabbit changed back into the half-dragon.

"Let's get out of this place," Hendandra said, standing up.

Myrith stared at the half-dragon. Instead of the nose he had had prior to his transformation, there was now a pink twitching rabbit nose. "Uh, Vyroris." She touched her own nose and pointed toward his face.

The half-dragon touched his nose and his eyes widened. He looked around at the others. Kyrianna was fighting not to giggle as she pulled a small mirror out of her pack and handed it to him.

"Oh, dear," was all Vyroris said as he handed the mirror back.

"Leikor is credited with having a very unusual sense of humor. Guess he thought he should demonstrate it," Jerietlan said.

"It also ensures we have a visible reminder of what happened," Falden said.

"I'm sorry," Hendandra said.

"Just what was he referring to?" Myrith placed a hand on Hendandra's shoulder before she could move away.

Hendandra glanced at Falden who only shrugged. "I'm not sure." She stared at the floor.

"Hendandra." Myrith took a step toward the smaller woman.

"It may be because Falden, Bukon, Etewyn and I stole back some artifacts of Rhyra from a temple of Ballan."

"Continue," Myrith said.

"I used the excuse that I needed to make an offering to Leikor to visit Ballan's temple since they are allied deities and Leikor's temple was closed for the Masquerade Rites."

"So you made it seem as if one of Leikor's faithful was involved in a plot to steal from one of the darkest and most evil goddesses in the Shokarian pantheon," Jerietlan said. "No wonder he was upset. Ballan probably told him to discipline you or she would take it out of his hide."

"What's done is done, if this is the worst that came of Leikor's interference…" Falden let the sentence trail off.

"You are correct," Vyroris said. "We should probably continue on. We passed several passages coming here that we should check for the exit."

Myrith paused and looked over at Andrinor who, like Nirev and Argrala had not entered the small room. The young man's hands were clenched tightly and he was glaring at Hendandra.

"It is not her doing," Myrith said softly.

Andrinor jerked his head around to stare at her. "It was the one she follows."

"True, but it was not her." She placed her hand on Andrinor's shoulder. "If you are given the opportunity to speak to Leikor about his treatment of Vyroris, I will have your back."

Andrinor nodded. "We have to get out of this place first."

"True." Myrith glanced back at Hendandra then sheathed her sword and started back the way they had traveled. "Let's go."

The first passage they came to was a long narrow corridor, ending in a dead end. "Kyri, you and Hendandra check it out. We'll follow you," Myrith said.

Kyrianna nodded and motioned for Hendandra to follow her down the passage. Myrith watched as they approached the far wall. Kyrianna stepped back after a moment of examining the wall and let Hendandra search it carefully. The thief drew one of her daggers, and placed it against the wall and pushed. The weapon went through as if there was nothing there.

"Once again, I believe I am the best to go through the wall first," Argrala said softly.

Myrith nodded and motioned the old man through; then the others as she waited to follow.

In the small chamber on the other side of the illusionary wall was a small creature made of living flame. Its body danced and swirled in the patterns of a fire and two bright yellow eyes looked out at them. Argrala removed a brazier from his robes along with several pieces of wood, a small silver dagger and a small block of incense. He placed the wood in the brazier then chanted a few words as the wood caught fire. He continued chanting as he picked up the incense and the dagger and began shaving the block, the flakes falling into the brazier.

As the smoke from the fire began to grow, the small fire creature vanished and was replaced by a larger version. Again a total of six creatures appeared in the room and were dismissed by the old man. As the last creature vanished, a pool of brackish water appeared in the center of the room.

"It would appear the portal to the next layer is through the pool," Argrala said as he collected his equipment.

Myrith nodded as she watched Hendandra carefully checking the room. In the far corner the small woman reached for something on the floor, but her movements were too swift for Myrith to be sure what, if anything she picked up.

Myrith shook her head; she would have to talk to Hendandra about this at some point. For now, though, they had to figure out what to do here. "You or me this time?" She glanced at Kyrianna then the pool.

Kyrianna laughed and pulled a coin out of her pouch. "How about we let chance decide?"

Before Kyrianna could toss the coin into the air, Falden dove into the pool.

Myrith looked at her friend and they both dove after the mage.

Chapter Six

Instead of having to swim to a portal, Myrith found herself standing in what appeared to have once been a hedge maze; one that had been turned into a marsh. "This is just wonderful." She frowned at the sucking sound made by the ground as she lifted first one foot then the other out of the grasp of the muck. She glanced at Kyrianna to see her scowling at the mud, but the girl didn't seem to be as hampered by it. The mage was over to the side and while he was moving in mud over his ankles, he definitely did not appear to be affected by the environment at all.

The wolf appeared next, landing next to Kyrianna and splashing her with the brackish water. Shadow Seeker looked around and whined softly as he shook himself, spraying more water and mud on his friend.

Myrith waited as the rest of the group appeared. "At least we don't have to deal with the heat anymore," she said as Vyroris appeared last with Argrala.

"True, but I doubt any of us really want to wade through a marsh for as long as we were in that other area either," Kyrianna said, looking around. "We are going to have to find places when we rest where both our equipment and we can dry out properly or we won't make it out of here due to sickness."

"I seriously doubt any of us are going to be able to sneak up on anything," Hendandra said.

Myrith glanced at the smaller woman and realized that while the mud was only up to her ankles; Hendandra's stature had her standing in water and muck up to mid-calf. Movement would be slowed considerably if they tried to move with any stealth at all. She glanced over at Kyrianna. The girl had been a member of the Thieves Guild and also had wilderness training. "Rangerette, I have a feeling you can move through this better than the rest of us. I want you to take the scout position and one of us can keep an eye on Hendandra to make sure she doesn't fall into any sinkholes and get swallowed up by this place."

"What's that?" Hendandra looked up at Myrith and frowned.

"What? Sinkholes? Those are..."

"No, that buzzing noise. Kyri, do you hear it?" Hendandra drew her rapier as she looked around.

"I do. Possibly a large swarm of insects or..." Kyrianna paused as several large insects flew over the hedge and began to fly toward them. "Stirge! Don't let them bite you!" She drew both of her swords and moved to stand back to back with Hendandra as the others began to pair up also.

The swarm circled a few times, before they finally darted in, attacking with their long needlelike beaks. The stirge were quick as they wove around their blades, attempting to stab each of them.

"Chaos!" Myrith heard Kyrianna yell and she risked a quick glance at the girl to see one of the insects on the back of her neck.

"Hold still," Hendandra said as she raised her rapier and skewered the stirge on it.

"Thanks." Kyrianna hit one diving at Hendandra cutting it in half and splattering them both with blood.

Myrith found herself swinging at two of the insects and smiled as her sword cut through them both quickly.

There were a few more yells from others as the remaining bloodsuckers managed to find targets before they were finally cut apart.

"Who was actually stabbed by one of the creatures?" Jerietlan asked as he opened a pouch on his belt.

Myrith frowned as everyone, except herself and Hendandra indicated they had been hit by the insects.

Jerietlan shook his head. "I do not have the proper herbs with me. The weakness from the blood loss will pass when we rest. If anyone feels themselves getting worse—please tell me."

"Let's get moving," Myrith said. "The sooner we can get out of here, the better off we'll be."

"Myrith," Hendandra said. "If I can get you to carry some of my stuff, I may be able to move through this easier, and should still be able to scout for the group."

"What do you want me to carry?"

Hendandra handed her the three magical sacks she had been using to carry the majority of the coins and gems they had found so far. "Falden told me I shouldn't put these into my backpack as they each create some type of dimensional space to allow them to hold as much as they do. Apparently, if one is put into the other, it can cause both to be destroyed."

Myrith smiled as she took the sacks. That Hendandra would actually give up carrying this wealth in order to work as a member of the group surprised her. She had expected the thief to try and make off with as much of the gold as she could when they finally got out of this place. Maybe there was hope for her after all.

Hendandra nodded her thanks then moved to the only passage out of the area. Myrith was impressed as the small woman moved silently through the water and muck.

A short distance down the path, Hendandra paused then turned and returned. "Black dragon," she said softly. "It appeared to be asleep."

"That's a stroke of luck," Vyroris said, drawing his great sword off his back. "Perhaps we can get by him, without the need to fight."

Myrith drew her sword and glanced at Kyrianna and Nirev, who both stood ready. She nodded and the four of them moved slowly through the passage. As she expected Andrinor stood back and waited—not moving to attack the sleeping dragon.

An explosion roared in the passage as the three of them approached the dragon's lair. Myrith looked back to see Falden floating in the air above the hedges. The mage smiled and waved to her. She turned back to see Vyroris charging in to face the dragon and Kyrianna releasing a volley of arrows.

She and Nirev charged up to stand beside the half-dragon and Myrith found herself dodging the black dragon's teeth as its head snapped forward. Another volley of arrows flew past her head and the dragon roared. Myrith found herself backpedaling as a wave of heat hit her. She risked a quick glance upward and saw Falden still floating in the air. The mage's hands were again moving in a complex pattern and Myrith continued backing away from the dragon as another ball of fire hit just behind it. A final blow from Vyroris and the dragon hit the ground, splashing all of them with the foul marsh water.

"Myrith," Hendandra called from the far corner of the lair. "Look at these."

One large chest and another smaller one sat in the corner. Hendandra carefully checked both of them, then opened the lid on the larger one. The gleam of sentryl greeted Myrith's eyes and she reached in to lift out a finely woven chain mail shirt, which she handed to Hendandra. "Here, you didn't replace your armor in

Duvshire and you should have better protection since you are the scout."

"But I need to be able to move as quickly and quietly as possible."

"There is magic woven into that," Falden said. "And considering the material, it should weigh about the same as what you are already wearing."

Hendandra glanced up at Myrith and nodded. "Thank you."

Myrith bowed her head slightly then turned back to the chest. Also in the chest was what appeared to be a full suit of armor crafted from the scales of various dragons.

"Leave that." She heard Vyroris say as she lifted the patchwork armor out of the chest.

"If no one else wants it, I'll take it," Jerietlan said.

"No!" Vyroris stepped between Myrith and Jerietlan. "This armor is a travesty and must be destroyed. The dragons this came from were not honored by those who took these scales for their own gain."

"What does it matter if it gives me better protection than that which I currently wear?"

"The difference is these were noble creatures—children of Ghainaess. I will not allow them to be dishonored," Andrinor said stepping forward.

Vyroris, placed a hand on the young man's arm. "Would you care to see me wearing armor forged from leather made of human skin?" He asked Jerietlan.

Myrith handed the armor to Vyroris. "You may dispose of this as you see fit."

"I meant no offense. Dragons are viewed very differently on Shokar," Jerietlan said. "You have given me something new to think on."

"Then there is no offense taken." Vyroris bowed his head slightly. "We will return in a few minutes." He turned and left carrying the dragon scale armor. Andrinor followed him.

Myrith watched as Vyroris and Andrinor left, then glanced at Hendandra. The thief nodded then moved to follow the pair.

"Rangerette, I believe this will interest you." Myrith lifted another chain mail shirt out of the chest. The links were even more finely woven than the one she had given to Hendandra. The armor was longer than what she wore during her watch, but it wasn't a full suit either. It was split, the sides tapering down to just about mid-calf. Unlike most chain mail, the right arm was not covered and the left only went to just above the elbow. "Looks like whoever designed this had an archer in mind."

Kyrianna took the armor and slid a hand over the glistening metal links. "It is of elven make. Archers are more common than swordsmen among elves," she said.

"Then I guess it is yours," Myrith said.

Kyrianna only nodded as she began stripping off the leathers she was wearing and changing into the chain mail.

"I believe these will be better off in Kyri's hands as well," Falden said, lifting a quiver and arrows out of the smaller chest. "Interesting," he said, looking at the arrows. "There is a strong enchantment on them. Each arrow is enchanted to become ten separate arrows when fired, each one doing considerable damage to the target they hit. The bow also has an enchantment on it that will encase the arrow in ice when it is released." He handed the quiver to Kyrianna who quickly attached it to her belt and withdrew one of the arrows to inspect it.

"A word of caution," Falden said. "Those arrows can be just as deadly to the one using them as their target. If you slip on the release, the arrow may explode killing you."

"Be careful," Myrith said.

"Good advice." Kyrianna slid the arrow back into the quiver and closed the travel cover over it.

"With the way she shoots, I doubt it will matter," Andrinor said stepping back into the area.

Myrith glanced back at Vyroris who had returned and now stood with Argrala watching them. "May I have a word with you?" she asked, motioning the half-dragon out of the area.

"Is there a problem?" Vyroris asked.

"You invoked the name of Ghainaess, who is the Great Mother of dragons when you joined us, yet you attacked this beast without hesitation. Then there was your reaction to the dragon scale armor. It seems a contradiction."

"While I honor the Great Mother, she is not the one I ultimately serve," Vyroris said. "I am a knight of Sontryantyloth—He Who Watches."

Myrith's hand went to her sword as she took a step back. "I do not care for deceptions, Vyroris. Explain yourself."

"There was no deception. All I did was greet you in her name. I never claimed to serve her. If you failed to ask the question, that is something I am not responsible for. However, rest assured, the one I serve has sent me here for the reasons I have explained. Argrala came to us looking for assistance in preventing Torliana from gaining control of the elemental planes. As he has also said, we believe she seeks to steal the power of the goddess she serves. This is something He Who Watches does not wish to see happen; as it will disrupt the Balance of Order and Chaos. Because of this he sent me to assist you. It was Sontryantyloth who directed me to greet you in Ghainaess' name, as he said you would recognize it and accept me by it."

"I still do not understand. If you serve a god of the dragons, how do you fight them without hesitation?"

"He Who Watches does favor the draconic races as they are the firstborn of the elder races, but he considers all to be his children and he does not favor one over the other in matters such as this. The Balance is what is most important. In this place the Balance has been greatly tilted toward evil and chaos. In order to restore that Balance, we must face Torliana. To do that, we must survive to reach her. I will fight anything that stands between me and that which I am required by him to do. I follow you in this place for as long as our paths run together."

"Very well." Myrith moved her hand away from her sword and nodded before returning to the others.

"Standing around isn't getting us any closer to getting out of here," Myrith said, looking around at the others. "Let's get moving."

Hendandra grinned as she headed for the next passage. She moved ahead of the others and into a small open area. After a few minutes, she returned with a small blue creature with skin that glistened with water droplets following her. "This is…"

"Skylar," the creature said as he stepped past Hendandra. "My name is Skylar. What is your name?" It looked at Myrith then turned to the others, repeating the question each time. Myrith frowned when the creature paused, then turned away from Argrala without asking his name.

"Hendandra?" Myrith glared at the smaller woman.

"I found him in the next open area. He seemed friendly enough and wanted to follow me."

The small blue creature glanced from Hendandra to Myrith.

"Can I go with you, please, please, please? I don't like this place. I don't even know how I got here. Hendandra is my friend. I want to stay with my friend." He moved closer to the girl.

Myrith looked around at the others then shrugged. "I guess you can travel with us," she said after a few minutes.

"Thank you. Thank you. Thank you. Now, I can stay with my friend, Hendandra. Thank you."

"You're welcome. Now, can you please be quiet?" Myrith glared at Skylar.

"Quiet? I can be quiet. Yes, I can be quiet." Skylar covered his mouth with his hand and backed behind Hendandra.

"I'll keep him out of trouble," Hendandra said.

"Very well." Myrith turned to Kyrianna. "We need to find a place where we can camp."

"I know a dry place," Skylar said then stopped as he again covered his mouth with his hand.

"If you know a place, then tell us," Myrith said.

Skylar shook his head, still holding his hand over his mouth.

"You did tell him to be quiet," Falden said.

"This is ridiculous." Myrith knelt down in front of the creature and held out her hand. "Skylar, if you have information we need or can use, please tell us."

Skylar took a step out from behind Hendandra and lowered his hand slightly then grinned. "I will show you." He started to leave the area.

"Wait," Hendandra said. "We need to move cautiously. There are things here that want to hurt us."

Skylar looked around at them then at the dragon that lay on the ground. "Okay. I stay with you," he said softly as he again moved toward the exit. "It is not far."

They followed Skylar and Hendandra through the wet passages to a small area elevated about a foot higher than the rest of the maze. It was dry inside the hedges and Myrith watched Kyrianna as she moved carefully around the area checking the ground.

After about five minutes, she turned to Myrith and nodded. "Should remain dry through the night, at least. I can find no areas where water is seeping up."

"We can camp here then." Myrith glanced up at the sky above the maze. She had no way to read the grayness. Despite a pale glow, there was no sun or moon visible in the sky. Nor was there any evidence of approaching twilight in any direction. Everything was gray in color with the same pale glow casting shadows.

"Reminds me of the sky above the Mushroom Forest," Kyrianna said.

Myrith jerked her head back up at the area where Kyrianna was staring then let out a slow breath. She had expected to see one of the flashes of swirling colors that appeared several times in that other sky. There was nothing here, only gray. She turned her attention back to the group without remarking on the absence.

"Where did you learn to be a squire?" Myrith asked after Kyrianna assisted her in removing her armor.

"My father, uncle and brother all served with the city guard. I was allowed to train with them for a while," Kyrianna said as she wiggled out of her own armor.

Kyrianna removed a comb, brush and several cloths from her pack and called Shadow Seeker over. She got the wolf to lie down then lifted one of his paws and began combing the fur between the pads, removing the balled-up mud. Myrith laughed when he nipped at Kyrianna's hands and she slapped him lightly on the nose.

Vyroris and Argrala had moved to one of the corners and were sitting quietly as the half-dragon cleaned and checked his blade. Hendandra was sitting with Skylar; the two of them talking quietly as he was showing Hendandra how to play the violin she had taken from the Duvall Estate.

As usual, the mage was sitting a bit separate, but closer to Kyrianna than anyone else, studying one of his many scrolls and books.

"Watches tonight: myself, Vyroris, Kyrianna, then Andrinor," Myrith said. She held up her hand to stop Nirev's protest. "You'll get your turn tomorrow," she said.

~ * ~

Myrith stood up and dusted off her pants as she completed her morning prayers then reached for her armor. The rest of the group was also starting to stir. Andrinor nodded to Kyrianna as she finished putting on her armor after completing her prayers and meditations. The girl moved to watch the passageway as Andrinor moved off and knelt down also.

"Myrith!" Kyrianna called.

She looked up to see the girl had drawn both of her swords and was standing ready as an older human male approached. The man was wearing plate mail, but carried no obvious weaponry. She concentrated for a moment, and found nothing in the aura surrounding him.

"I greet you in the name of Mykaylene," Myrith said. "I am called Myrith Lake."

"I am Ashe," he said as he looked around at the others, a deep scowl on his face.

"How may we be of assistance to you?" Myrith continued to study the man. What she could see of his skin was heavily scarred and leathery.

"I doubt you can be of assistance. I am here to find the one who created this place and kill her. I will be continuing on my way after I have a moment's rest."

"We also seek this mage. Might it not be better if we travel together?" Jerietlan stepped forward.

"Torliana is a mage now? At one time she was a monk training in a temple of Hellavar; the temple where I was the Keeper of the Flame, before she and her foul goddess destroyed it and all who were there."

"And which of the Fire Lord's temples would this have been?" Jerietlan asked.

"I can no longer recall the name. It has been taken from me, just as my own name has been. Torliana came to the temple, shortly before I arrived. She was an elf training to be a Flame Dancer of Hellavar. Trying to shed the chaos inherent in her nature to follow his Order. For four years, I watched her walk the path of Order, fighting her own nature and becoming one of highest ranked of the Kindling. Then at the end of those four years, she called forth a storm of chaos that swept through the temple destroying the Order. She turned all those there against each other. In the end, I, the Mistress of the Flames, as well as the three seniors of the order faced a host of chaos demons.

"When Torliana came to me, the bodies of my brothers and sisters in the flame lay at my feet. She laughed as she opened a portal to the lower planes and called forth the chaos demons to drag me to their mistress. I was tortured for almost twenty years by the vile servants of her evil goddess.

"I have tracked her since I was freed from that place and I will see she pays for the destruction of the temple and the deaths she caused that night." He looked around again at the group; his gaze stopping for several minutes as he first seemed to study Myrith then Kyrianna. "Maybe you can be useful. Since you also seek the one responsible, perhaps it does make sense we should travel together."

"Very well," Myrith said. "Kyrianna, you and Shadow can continue with your guard position while the rest of us get ready."

"What about me? I can stand a guard position. Me and Hendandra," Skylar said suddenly. "Can we take the guard position? Kyrianna stood watch last night, let her rest some more before we leave."

"Mykaylene, give me strength," Myrith muttered.

"Do you wish it gone?" Ashe looked from her to Skylar.

"I wish I had never agreed to let it travel with us," she said.

"Very well." A ball of flame appeared in the palm of his right hand and he walked over to look down at the small creature. "I suggest you leave."

Skylar stared at Ashe then glanced at Myrith. "Good luck," he said as he hurried out of the area.

"That wasn't fair," Hendandra said, looking at Myrith.

"Never said it was. As soon as everyone is ready, we need to get moving."

Myrith watched as Hendandra moved to check the next series of passages relaying information to her and the others. They came across very little as they traveled.

"Myrith," Hendandra called back softly. "I'm not sure what we have here. They seem to be nothing more than floating lights."

"I'll take a look," Kyrianna said, moving past her.

After a few minutes, Kyrianna motioned Myrith forward. "They're wisps—they glow in a manner similar to fireflies. However they also generate lightning which they can use to attack other creatures."

"They're also emitting an aura of evil," Myrith said as she drew her sword.

"Lady Lake, I do not recommend engaging these creatures," Ashe said. "There are other ways through this area."

"I do not pass evil by," Myrith said. "Let's go."

Kyrianna shrugged as she drew her swords and stepped forward.

The wisps floated into the passage and Myrith frowned as all but three floated high over the group and past her. The first three hovered around Kyrianna, but only one was within the reach of her blade. She heard shouts coming from the back and realized the others had floated down to attack the rest of the group.

Myrith concentrated on the wisp just behind her friend trying to draw its attacks. Kyrianna screamed as three bolts of lightning jumped from the three wisps to hit her at the same time.

Myrith frowned as her blade only glanced off the glowing ball of light that floated just behind Kyrianna. She saw Kyrianna hit the one in front of her; her blades also appeared to glance off the wisp and the three of them again sent bolts of lightning into her. This time, the girl fell. Myrith cringed at the howl from the wolf that echoed in the narrow passage. She dropped her shield, grabbed her blade in a two-handed hold and put all of her strength into a blow that only gave the creature pause. Someone touched her shoulder and she glanced to the side to see Ashe moving past her to sit next to Kyrianna, a scroll in his hand. He reached out and touched the wolf as well, barely avoiding a snap of sharp teeth.

Myrith ignored Ashe for the moment and turned back to the wisps in front of her. She stopped her swing in time to avoid Shadow Seeker who had pounced on one, and was ripping into it with his teeth and claws. The odor of burnt dog hair stung her nose as the wolf padded back to sit beside his fallen friend.

"I will not harm her any more than she has already been hurt," Ashe said to the wolf as it began growling.

Myrith finally finished off the two remaining wisps and turned to see others had fallen and Jerietlan healing numerous wounds. She turned back to Kyrianna and knelt next to her friend, watching as Ashe read from a scroll in his hands.

The cleric read slowly, pronouncing each word clearly. As he finished speaking, the scroll glowed for a moment then vanished in a burst of flame. Ashe reached down and grasped one of Kyrianna's hands tightly. "Kyrianna, hear me. Return to your friends," he said softly.

Myrith released the breath she had been holding as she watched her friend's eyelids flutter slightly. "Kyri," she whispered.

Kyrianna's eyes opened and she stared at Ashe for several heartbeats. Myrith frowned as the girl's eyes grew wide and she pulled away from him

"Thank you," Kyrianna said weakly as Ashe helped her to stand up. She turned and moved quickly away from him.

"You okay?" Myrith reached out and laid a hand on Kyrianna's shoulder.

Kyrianna's eyes darted to Ashe then she backed away a couple of steps and closed her eyes.

"What's going on?" Myrith stepped in front of Kyrianna and glared at her.

"Nothing." Kyrianna swallowed and looked down. "Don't worry about it."

Myrith glanced over at Ashe and saw him watching the two of them, but he didn't say anything.

"If there is anything that might put this group in danger, I can't ignore it. What is going on?" Myrith frowned as the others stared at her and Kyrianna.

Myrith lowered her voice. "You promised to tell me what was going on. Don't break that promise, Rangerette."

Tears filled Kyrianna's eyes and she caught her breath. "This has nothing to do with Thynitic or her calling to me," she said, taking a step back. "Myrith, please trust me. This is not anything that will put the others at risk." Kyrianna still refused to look at her.

"I cannot be expected to lead this group if people will not tell me what is going on. Someone else can deal with those who want to keep secrets." She reached out and lifted Kyrianna's chin. "You think you know what's best for the others and what will and will not affect them—you take charge."

"My oath is to Myrith," Andrinor said suddenly.

"I stand with Andrinor," Vyroris said.

"Are you suggesting I lead this group after you have just said you don't trust me?" Kyrianna stared at Myrith. "You would follow me after that? I doubt it."

"Yes," Argrala said. "If she truly follows the path of Order and not that of Chaos. If she says she will follow you, she will. Even as you lead her into the heart of Chaos."

Myrith jerked her head up and started to turn toward the old man.

"Even though she relies on her own power too much and not the group as a whole, Lady Lake is the only one who can lead this group," Ashe said, stepping over to stand next to Kyrianna.

Myrith stared at Ashe for a moment. "What do you mean by that? There is only one person I can rely on—myself."

"So you do not trust any of your companions to use their abilities or judgment, when your own can be so easily deceived," Ashe said.

"I want to know why you are here." Myrith stepped away from Kyrianna to stand in front of Ashe. "And why my friend reacted in fear when she saw you."

"I have already told you. I am here to destroy Torliana for what she did to me and the others of my temple. I spent twenty years in the abyss as a toy for the amusement of her foul goddess. I was tortured over and over. My body was killed, but my soul was trapped by her magics. She brought me back time and time again so she could continue to torment me. I owe her much for what she has done." Ashe paused for a moment. "Understand this, Lady Lake; I do not care anything about you or your group. All you are is a means to an end. All I care about is getting to Torliana and making her pay for her crimes. I vow to follow you as the one who leads this group as long as our goals remain the same.

"As for your friend's reaction…"

Myrith frowned as she now sensed a change in Ashe's aura; there was now a strong sense of evil radiating from him. Her hand dropped to her sword, but she did not draw it. She glanced at Kyrianna and saw the pain in her eyes as she nodded slightly. This was what her friend had sensed when Ashe had touched her soul and drawn her back. *Why hadn't she said anything?* Myrith paused as she thought about the question and she realized the answer. If Kyrianna had said something about sensing the evil in Ashe's soul, it would have prompted a confrontation between the two. Something that could have had the same result as the current argument was having on the group. Ashe was a strong cleric and his power might be needed to help them. Kyrianna had realized this but had also thought she wouldn't be unable to accept him because of the evil taint on his soul. She took a deep breath as she realized her friend was correct.

"Everyone, please leave this area." Myrith glanced around at the group. "I must seek Mykaylene's guidance," she said.

As the others filed out, Myrith drew her sword, stuck it into the ground and knelt in front of it. She glanced up briefly to see Kyrianna watching her from the passage. "I am sorry you don't think you can trust me, even after everything else we've been through together," she said then turned to leave.

Myrith didn't reply as Kyrianna walked away. She listened to the girl's footsteps as she splashed through the marshy passage. She was sorry she could no longer trust Kyrianna as well.

Once everyone was gone, Myrith turned her thoughts to the goddess who had called her: Mykaylene, the Battle Maiden. She had always thought those who were called as holy warriors as being called to destroy evil—no matter what form it came in. Now she was being asked to accept a man who radiated evil in his aura as a member of her group. A man who had said he didn't care about the members of this group, but had spent his power to bring Kyrianna back from the realms of the dead. A man who had said he would follow her as the only one who could lead this group as long as their purposes ran together, as they did now. Her instincts were telling her he was a man whose word they could trust once he gave it. Still, to work closely with him was something she didn't think she would be able to do.

"Mykaylene, I ask for your guidance," she whispered.

:*The one who is now called Ashe was not always as he is now*, she heard the goddess' voice in her head. :*His soul has been tainted by the hatred that has grown in him for many years. See what brought this to be.* The voice faded and Myrith found herself looking down on a large temple. While the structure was impressive from its size, it was not a grandiose cathedral. The style was simple, utilitarian and very ordered. Even in its simplicity, there was something that spoke of power and majesty.

She seemed to fly through the stone walls into the heart of the building. In the hallways, bodies littered the floors. She floated above the carnage and up a stairwell to a small office. In the office stood the man she knew as Ashe facing an elven woman with long black hair and eyes as black as a moonless night. On the ground were four bodies. Two appeared to be monks from their robes, one was a cleric and the third was a knight. As she watched the soundless scene, a portal opened behind Ashe and several clawed hands reached through to drag him from the office. Blackness filled her eyes for a moment then cleared as she saw Ashe, his naked body held upright in a frame made of obsidian as the elven woman slowly peeled the skin from his chest. She would pause periodically and cast minor healing spells to slow the flow of blood, and keep the pain levels just below the threshold of him being rendered unconscious.

"By all the gods," Myrith said as she tried to turn away from the scene.

:*For almost two decades, he survived this and other tortures. Now, see what he once was and can be again*, the goddess' voice said.

The scene faded and Myrith found herself watching as Ashe entered a chamber in the temple where three adults and a young boy of about seven years waited. This time she could see and hear what was going on.

One of the two women in the room stood next to the boy. "The boy's parents died on the road between here and Irrmar, Keeper. I am his aunt and I offer him a place to stay," she said.

The other woman looked at the first then turned to Ashe and bowed her head respectfully before speaking. "Keeper, she has no husband; she only wants a slave for her fields. We offer him a real home without harshness," she said, smiling at the boy.

Ashe looked down at the boy. "It would appear you are blessed with two possible homes, young man," he said gently. Myrith was surprised at his voice. It was smooth and resonated with power. The voice he spoke with now, while it still resonated with the same power, was harsh and rough.

The first woman spoke again. "Ask him who he wishes to stay with, Keeper."

Ashe looked up at her. "Why? So he can be forced to choose between two homes? If that really mattered, why did you come to me?"

The woman scowled as she took a half-step back.

Ashe seemed to study the woman and the couple standing before him. "It is the custom for the closest relatives to care for those who are orphaned and that is how it shall be." He slammed his staff against the floor like a gavel. "However, since these people have voiced a concern, I shall come to your house one year from this day. I shall judge your treatment of the boy and if I find it harsh, so shall I be."

The woman's face grew pale as Ashe watched her. "There is no fear for the just," he said. "Do you wish to say something, my Lady?"

"I release the boy to your judgment, Keeper."

"Very well, the boy shall stay with these people who also offer him a home." He turned to the couple as the woman held her hand out to the boy. "However, I tell you the same. I will bear witness to your treatment of the boy."

"We welcome that day, Keeper," the man said as he placed his hand on the boy's shoulder and bowed his head.

The scene faded and Myrith found herself kneeling in a hall, a woman in shining plate mail armor standing before her. The woman took a step toward her, and Myrith bowed her head. "My Lady," she said.

"Myrith, there is still a part of the one you know as Ashe which can be brought back from the darkness he has fallen into. Shokar will need his strength and power in the coming years. I charge you with setting an example and guiding him back from the darkness." The woman paused. "Your companions will all need your strength in the coming days, but most especially Kyrianna. She will face a tremendous trial and if she falters, she could be lost to the darkness and chaos forever."

The goddess reached out and lifted Myrith's chin. "Be strong; set an example of the power of light. Bring him back from darkness and find a way to save her from it."

The vision faded and Myrith found herself still kneeling in the muck. She stood slowly, letting her muscles recover from the prolonged time in the water and the chill that had invaded her body. She pulled the sword from where she had put it into the ground and wiped the blade clean.

Though she had no clear answers, she now had a path to follow and two souls her goddess had charged her with protecting and saving.

Myrith looked up as Kyrianna entered the area with the others. "We were getting worried," she said.

"Has Mykaylene answered your questions?" Jerietlan looked at her, his head tilted to the side.

"She has." She looked at Ashe. "Do I have your word you will follow me as the one who leads this group?"

"You do." Ashe bowed his head slightly as he answered her.

"Very well." She glanced at Kyrianna who looked quickly away. "Let's get moving."

"Myrith, we left several areas behind us we should clear before moving on," Jerietlan said. "I can take Andrinor, Falden and Hendandra to check the areas to the south—or what we think is south—then meet back with you and the others, while you check the areas to the east."

Myrith nodded. "Don't take too long. I want us to meet back here in an hour."

"Agreed."

Myrith watched as the others headed off. She turned and

looked at those still with her. Kyrianna continued to refuse to meet her eyes and she found herself wondering at the goddess' words regarding her friend. *What trial is she going to face?* They had seen nothing here to suggest anything was targeting any of them specifically. As for losing her to the darkness, that made even less sense. At no time since she had met Kyrianna in that first temple, had she seen the girl even come close to doing anything which could be considered evil. Though, withholding the information regarding Elvioril as she had might be considered by some as approaching that line.

Was Mykaylene warning her Thynitic was going to begin calling Kyrianna again? That couldn't be. The girl had renounced the Lady of Chaos, and apparently had not received any indication the goddess was still interested in her. At least Kyrianna had not told her of any. Although—the pendant Kyrianna claimed she left in the shrine had been around her neck when they found her.

She was sorry she had hurt Kyrianna's feelings by not taking her word earlier, but she had known she couldn't take that chance. Kyrianna's actions had betrayed fear when she saw Ashe sitting next to her after calling her back from the realms of the dead, instead of the surprise and gratitude Myrith would have expected to see.

Once again, Kyrianna had chosen to withhold information. Was there other information she was withholding? How could she protect Kyrianna as Mykaylene had charged if the girl was unwilling to trust her? How could she continue to trust Kyrianna after this? Thynitic was the Lady of Chaos and Myrith had no doubts she was also a mistress of lies and deceit.

"Let's go check out those missed areas," Myrith said. "I don't want to end up backtracking to find the exit from this area, like we did in the first one." She motioned to Kyrianna to take the scout position and followed the girl into the passage.

They encountered nothing in the two open areas they found then returned back to the area where they were to meet with the others. An explosion echoed in the maze and Myrith looked at Kyrianna as she spoke one word. "Fireball."

Kyrianna ran out of the area, following the passage the others had taken. "Kyrianna, wait," Myrith called as she started after her.

~ * ~

"What happened?" Myrith looked around the area the others were in and frowned. Andrinor was on the ground covered by

Jerietlan's cloak and a black dragon lay dead near him.

Hendandra looked up from the chest she had just opened. "Andrinor changed into a silver dragon and defeated the black over there." She pointed to the dead dragon.

Myrith looked back at the unconscious man and the dragon. "He became a silver dragon?"

"He has been called by Ghainaess to be one of her initiates," Vyroris said. "She has given him the power of the silver."

Myrith frowned as Ashe walked over to the still unconscious Andrinor and placed a hand on his forehead. "What are you doing?"

"Waking him. We cannot afford delays. She will be watching us and learning everything she can to prepare her defenses."

Andrinor stirred and opened his eyes. He sat up slowly, keeping the blanket over him. "Do you mind?" He glanced at the pile of armor then at the others.

Myrith nodded then motioned Kyrianna and Hendandra out of the area as she followed them.

Andrinor dressed quicker than she would have thought possible in the chain mail he found in the dragon's lair. Like the leather he had been wearing previously, this was sleeveless, the portion covering his upper body more closely resembling a long vest than actual armor.

Hendandra took the lead as she led them back to the area they had started from. Myrith glanced down the northern passage. "We'll go this way," she said after a moment.

They wandered for several hours, fighting battles against various water creatures until they finally came to another room elevated above the muck and relatively dry.

"Chaos," Kyrianna muttered as a familiar blue creature turned to look at the group. "Myrith, that's…"

"Skylar," Hendandra said, walking up to him.

"My friend, Hendandra." Skylar wrapped his arms around the girl and smiled.

After a moment his eyes met Myrith's and he stepped back from Hendandra. "Is the one with the fire still with you?"

"He is," Myrith said, nodding once.

"Oh." Skylar paused for several minutes. "No matter, you are welcome to stay here while you rest."

"We thank you for the offer," Myrith said. "We want to finish checking this part of the maze and perhaps we will return to this spot when we are done."

"Oh, as you wish."

"Make note of this location on your map, Kyrianna, and let's move on."

They continued to the north and found a large open area. The water became deeper as they waded into the area. In the far corner, a pile of rust-colored serpentine scales lay coiled. The head was vaguely dragon shaped, and the eyes were closed. Myrith motioned for the group to back out of the area carefully.

"Andrinor, Vyroris, do either of you recognize the species?" Myrith spoke quietly.

"No," they said together.

"There was a second passage into the dragon's lair," Hendandra said. "Perhaps we should split into two groups so as to have two different attack angles on it."

Myrith looked at Hendandra and nodded. "Good idea. Andrinor, you take Hendandra, Ashe, Kyrianna and Falden to the other passage. Ranged and magical attacks are preferable while it is asleep." She glanced at the others.

"Agreed," Kyrianna and Hendandra said as they readied their bows.

Myrith stood just outside the lair in the first passage, watching for the others. Andrinor finally stepped into the lair leaving room for Hendandra and Kyrianna to flank him, their bows up and nocked. She glanced at Jerietlan and nodded as he cast his spell. A pillar of fire flowed down from the sky and surrounded the dragon for a brief moment. As it faded, a small streak of fire flew from behind Andrinor to erupt into an exploding ball, followed by a volley of arrows from Kyrianna and Hendandra.

Myrith drew her sword and dashed forward with Nirev and Vyroris. The dragon's head snapped at the dwarf and he twisted out of its way as Myrith's sword landed on its long neck. Vyroris' great sword followed her own strike cutting deeper into the flesh of the dragon. Andrinor darted forward and drove his blade into the top of the dragon's head as it turned to grab her, pinning it to the ground.

Myrith and Vyroris dodged the thrashing body of the dragon as the young man held tightly to his weapon keeping the head trapped against the ground.

"It is an Abyssal Dragon," Ashe said as the dragon's death throes finally stopped. "A creature normally only found living in the great river that flows through the layers."

Andrinor jerked the blade of his weapon free and walked around studying the dragon.

"Why?" Myrith asked.

"She said this was an abomination, created by the demons of the Abyss," Andrinor said as he looked down at the serpentine body.

Myrith nodded then moved to check an adjacent area. She motioned Falden and Kyrianna over. "Another one," she said.

This dragon, while asleep, appeared to be sleeping fitfully and stirred slightly. Myrith watched as Kyrianna reached for the quiver of enchanted arrows on her belt and drew one out.

"Frayrith and Dwycia guide my shot," Myrith heard the girl whisper as she nocked the arrow.

Kyrianna took a couple of careful breaths then held it for a heartbeat as she released the arrow. As soon as it was clear of the bow, the arrow became ten. All ten struck the dragon and the creature roared with pain, then dropped to the ground—dead.

"Nice shot," Myrith said. "Make sure you save one of those for Torliana."

"Of course." Kyrianna turned and walked away.

~ * ~

"No!"

Myrith's eyes opened and she grabbed her blade as Kyrianna's scream echoed. She looked over to see the girl sitting up, her eyes wide with fear as she held her dagger in her hand.

"What happened?" Myrith knelt next to Kyrianna, taking the dagger from her hand. The girl only stared at her.

"Kyrianna?" Myrith gripped the girl's hand tightly.

"A bad dream. A voice in my head." Kyrianna stopped, her breathing labored, coming in short gasps. "I can't remember anything specific, now." She continued to stare at Myrith. "Only that the voice said, 'Just as your mother served me, so you shall also.' Who is she? What did she mean?"

"It was only a dream, Kyri. It means nothing. You already serve Frayrith, the Lady of the Forests. Didn't your mother also serve her?"

"She did."

"It was probably only this place twisting your dreams. I doubt there is anything to worry about. Complete your morning prayers and you will feel better." Myrith stood then reached down and placed a hand on Kyrianna's shoulder, squeezing gently. She frowned slightly as she turned and saw Ashe staring at them, studying Kyrianna closely.

:*Is this the beginning of what you warned me about, Mykaylene?* Myrith sent the silent thought, but didn't expect a reply.

"I promise to be good, if you will let me travel with you," Skylar said as they were preparing to leave.

Myrith looked at the creature and nodded. "Very well, you may journey with us."

"Thank you." Skylar bowed then skipped over to Hendandra.

"Why do you keep watching me?"

Myrith spun around at the anger in Kyrianna's voice. She was staring at Ashe, her hands on her swords.

"Kyri," Myrith said softly as she moved to stand next to the girl.

Ashe looked at Myrith and shook his head. "I have warned you she is watching us. Her dreams this past night have confirmed not only is Torliana watching us, but her goddess is as well. Torliana has been in and out of Thynitic's favor many times over the decades. After she destroyed my temple, the Lady of Chaos sent her to another world to learn in one of her temples. That world was yours. And that temple was the one your mother also served in for a time, where she held the Lady's highest favor, before she turned on and renounced the goddess."

"No! My mother is a follower of Frayrith, the Lady of the Forests." Kyrianna shook her head and took several steps back from the cleric.

Ashe only looked at her and shook his head slowly. "That she may be now, but there was a time when she served the Lady of Chaos."

"No," Kyrianna whispered as she turned away.

Myrith could see Kyrianna's body trembling and her knuckles turn white as she gripped the hilts of her swords. She took a step closer to the girl. "Just as your mother served me, so you shall also," she heard the girl saying softly.

Kyrianna spun around, tears in her eyes. "It was Thynitic in my mind, Myrith. It was Thynitic."

"You don't know that. I have only known you for a handful of moon turnings, but I have seen you follow your Lady of the Forests faithfully. So much so, she sent your companion to you from your world. If she felt you would abandon her to follow this Thynitic, I doubt she would have done that."

Myrith reached down and scratched the wolf's ears as he whined and nosed at Kyrianna's hand.

"I hope you're right, Myrith. I hope you're right."

"Considering how you obviously feel about the members of this group, why did you bother expending the power needed to bring her back?" Falden asked as he looked at Ashe.

"Her presence will be needed when I finally confront Torliana," Ashe said, looking at the mage for only a moment before turning his attention back to Kyrianna.

"Needed how?" Myrith asked.

"That I do not know. I only know she is needed."

"Let's get moving," Myrith said. She saw the panic-stricken look on Kyrianna's face as her eyes went wide, but she didn't know what to say to the girl.

~ * ~

"Myrith!" She spun around as Hendandra yelled.

A brilliant light surrounded Andrinor as he dropped his sword, removed his armor and jumped into the air.

"Andrinor!" Myrith watched as the silver dragon he had become circled above them. The dragon roared and exhaled a cloud of ice.

"A spell designed to destroy the intelligence of the victim and turn them more beastlike, as well as increasing their strength," Falden said, looking at the damaged rune stone on the ground.

"Can you help him?" Myrith looked at Falden and Jerietlan.

They both shook their heads. "Not unless we can get him back down here. This is a strong spell and the longer a person is under its effects, the harder it is to remove," Jerietlan said.

Myrith glanced at Ashe, who nodded.

"Will he recognize us, or will we have to fight him in this form to try and help him?"

"Unknown," Falden said.

"Hendandra, grab his equipment and let's follow him." Myrith motioned Kyrianna to take the lead as Hendandra and Skylar slipped to the back.

"Then we need to find a way to get him back down," Myrith

said. "I don't want to attack him and have to fight him in his dragon form, but if that is the only way…"

"Let's take a look around for a few minutes," Argrala said. "Perhaps we can find something." He glanced up at Andrinor and shook his head.

"Let's hope he retains enough intelligence to recognize his allies if we must go into battle again," Myrith said.

"Bah, he be in dragon form and thinking like one. His intelligence be never that high to begin with, since he follows one of the dragon deities. We will be having to fight him," Nirev said.

Myrith watched as Vyroris stopped and turned to face Nirev. The half-dragon's face was impassive as he looked down at the dwarf.

Nirev paused for several seconds as he looked up at the sky. "Let's pray we don't have to kill him," he whispered.

Vyroris tilted his head slightly, then nodded as he turned away from Nirev without saying anything about the insult the dwarf had offered to dragons.

Myrith paused and looked around at the large open area they had entered. There were several places where the others could hide while she faced Andrinor. She nodded slowly and prayed he still had enough intelligence to recognize her.

"Kyrianna, Falden," she called. "I want you two over here with me. The rest of you, find somewhere out of sight."

"Out of sight of a dragon?" Jerietlan stared at her.

"Do the best you can. With luck, his attention will be focused on me."

"Shadow, stay with Hendandra," Kyrianna said.

Myrith waited until the others were away from her then turned to Falden and Kyrianna.

"Falden, can you fire a couple of bolts of energy past him? I want it to look like an attack, but I don't want you to hurt him."

Falden nodded.

"You have the trickier part, Rangerette," Myrith said. "I want you to hit him."

"What?" Kyrianna took a step back. "And have him turn me into an ice statue? Not a good idea."

"He has used his breath weapon once," Vyroris called. "He should not be able to do so again this quickly."

"Aim for the tail, so you don't injure him," Myrith said.

"*Should* not be able to." Kyrianna drew an arrow and sighted carefully. "So there is a chance he can. Wonderful." She took a deep breath. "Falden, get his attention."

Falden nodded and raised his hands. Two streaks of light flew past Andrinor's head and the dragon turned toward them.

"Frayrith, guide my aim," Kyrianna whispered as she released the arrow. Andrinor roared as the arrow impeded itself in his hind leg. "Chaos!" Kyrianna took a step back.

Myrith raised her blade and stepped forward waiting. Andrinor exhaled, but there was no ice; only a deep chill that surrounded her. "Andrinor," she said as the dragon landed in front of her. "You gave me your pledge your sword would be raised only in defense of me and my friends, never against me. Is this how you honor that pledge?"

The dragon paused, his head lowered as he watched her.

"Jerietlan, you have him on the ground, dispel the magic," she said.

Jerietlan made several gestures with his hands then slapped Andrinor's tail. The dragon shook his head slightly then changed back to his human form and grabbed the cloak Vyroris held out to him.

"Kyrianna?" Andrinor reached down and jerked the arrow from his leg.

"We needed a way to get you back on the ground so the magic could be dispelled," Myrith said, stepping between Andrinor and Kyrianna. "I told her to hit you—carefully."

"You were affected by a spell which temporarily destroyed your intelligence making you more animalistic," Ashe said.

"In yer case, that not be a major concern," Nirev said.

"Nor would it have made any noticeable difference in you," Andrinor said.

"If Torliana is watching us, it is possible she set that trap specifically to force Andrinor's transformation," Argrala said.

"For what purpose?"

"As this spell reduced his intelligence, in addition to causing a release of his dragon form, it is possible she was hoping this would cause him to attack us," Ashe said.

"She didn't plan on the strength of the oath he gave Myrith when he joined us," Kyrianna said.

"It would appear you are correct." Ashe glanced at Andrinor

for a moment before turning toward Myrith. "And that is one of her weaknesses. She often underestimates her opponents."

"Let's get some rest," Myrith said. "We still have to find a way out of this area and to the next one."

"Four elemental planes then her stronghold," Falden said. "We have encountered air, fire, now water—that leaves earth."

"Hey, didn't the jars in that temple also represent the four elemental planes?" Hendandra asked.

"Yes, they did," Falden said.

"Temple?" Ashe looked at Hendandra and Falden.

Myrith watched Kyrianna walk away from the others as Hendandra started telling Ashe about the temple they had all met in, including the way each of them had been brought there. Ashe turned to look at Kyrianna when Hendandra mentioned the various symbols that seemed to be tied to Thynitic in that temple.

He continued to watch Kyrianna as Hendandra told him about the Duvall Estate. Ashe never took his attention off Kyrianna.

"Was she calling to you there as well?" Ashe asked when Hendandra finished.

"What?" Hendandra looked up at Ashe.

"Kyrianna?" Ashe took a step toward her.

Myrith moved to stand between the two of them.

"I would ask you the same question, Lady Lake," Ashe said. "Has she been calling to you?"

"What reason would Thynitic have for calling me? She is a goddess of Kyrianna's world, not mine."

"Yet she is the one who brought you to that first temple, and probably the one who brought you here."

"We have no way of knowing that." Myrith frowned as she thought about the similarities between the portal that had opened in the Temple of Geladas and the portal on the road from Duvshire.

"Kyrianna?" Ashe called. He stepped to the side, but did not attempt to move past Myrith.

"Yes." Kyrianna's voice was a harsh whisper as she turned to face the cleric.

"I have heard her voice calling me since before I was exiled from my home. And now you tell me there was a time when my mother served her." She closed her eyes. "I doubt I can keep fighting her."

"Yes you can," Myrith said. "I will not let her have you."

"That you have been able to resist her call for this long shows you can continue to fight her," Ashe said. "Perhaps that is why you will be needed when I face Torliana."

"If you hadn't called me back, I wouldn't have to keep fighting her," Kyrianna whispered before turning away again.

Myrith let her go. She knew she would have to keep an eye on her friend. She had heard that same tone of defeat in the voice of one of the girls at the Silver Dragon years ago. The girl didn't have the courage to kill herself outright, but had instead willed herself to die, not wanting to live anymore as what she was. There had been nothing she or the others could do and day by day, they had had to watch as Lilith grew weaker and weaker until after about a week, she was finally gone.

~ * ~

A small fountain of water floated at the end of the corridor. "Argrala?" Myrith called as the water shifted and a pair of eyes appeared.

The old man shuffled past her and removed a small chime from his pocket. He began chanting then struck the chime with a silver rod as the elemental vanished to be replaced by another, larger one. Five more rings of the chime and five more elementals then a stone archway appeared in the hedge behind where the elementals had been floating.

Myrith again waited as the others stepped through the portal. Just like the other two times, Hendandra picked something up from the ground before stepping through.

Chapter Seven

A long stone corridor greeted Myrith as she stepped through the doorway.

"All but one of the doors is locked," Hendandra said as she and Skylar came up. "I count ten total. Both ends of the corridor are solid walls. Neither I nor Kyri heard anything moving in the unlocked room."

"Then that's where we start." Myrith walked to the first door in the corridor. "Anything?" she asked as Kyrianna glanced at her.

"Nothing that I can hear."

Myrith nodded as she drew her sword. Kyrianna slid her fingers into the thin slot on the stone slab that made up the door and pulled it open slowly. The door swung easily and silently, not even scraping on the stone of the floor as it opened.

Myrith stepped into the room. "Nothing here, except some writing on the back wall," she said.

The door opened the rest of the way and the others entered the room.

Myrith walked to the back of the room and looked at the writing. The script reminded her of the runes on the statues of the temple. "Kyrianna, can you read this?" She remembered the girl had recognized the writing in the temple as being an ancient form of the language from one of the three races of elves on her world. She had been able to read only a few of the runes at that time. Perhaps she could do better here.

Kyrianna stared at the writing for several minutes, not saying anything. The only sound Myrith heard was a sudden intake of breath as Kyrianna trembled violently. "Kyri?"

"It reads: 'To reach the other side, the Goddess you must invoke. As you pass through these rooms, her name you will learn. In the last room on this side; with reverence one descended from the daughter who defied, must call on the Lady or passage will be denied.'" Kyrianna's voice was only a harsh whisper as she spoke.

"Your mother's title was 'The Daughter of Chaos,'" Ashe said from behind them. "And, she defied the Lady of Chaos by renouncing her."

"That means what?" Myrith said, turning to face the cleric.

"That means, Lady Lake, she will have to call on Thynitic when we reach the end of this passage if we are to continue any further," Ashe said.

Myrith looked at Kyrianna and frowned at the paleness of her face. "We'll rest here," she said, turning away from the writing. "Watches will be myself, Andrinor, Vyroris and..." She paused for a long breath as she glanced back at Kyrianna still staring at the writing. "And Nirev," she finally said.

Behind her she heard Kyrianna spin around, but she ignored the girl. Kyrianna had her own fight to concentrate on and she couldn't trust the girl not to lose focus on the group because of it. Mykaylene had charged her with watching out for the girl and giving her strength for her trial. She only knew one way to do that—force her to stand on her own and accept that this was something she had to do. That was how she had managed to survive those long years at the Silver Dragon. It was something she had to do and she had learned to accept it. She had also learned during that time she would never be able to rely on anyone other than herself.

~ * ~

Myrith looked again at the writing in the small alcove. Kyrianna sat with her back in the corner of the area still sleeping. The wolf lay near the opening, his dark brown eyes watching the movement of the others closely.

"We need to get moving," Myrith said, looking at the wolf.

Shadow Seeker raised his head and looked at her for a moment, then stood and padded softly back to Kyrianna. He nosed at her cheek then sat down and pawed at her wrist whining.

"Okay, okay. I'm awake." Kyrianna slapped lightly at the wolf as she opened her eyes.

"When you're ready, we should get moving," Myrith said.

Kyrianna gathered her gear, belted on her swords then turned to face Myrith. "I'm ready now," she said.

"You're neglecting your morning prayers and meditations." Myrith stared at her friend.

"That's my business! Not yours!" Kyrianna moved to the door.

Myrith shook her head. *This isn't good.* From what Mykaylene had said, Kyrianna's soul could be in jeopardy during this journey and now she was deliberately choosing to ignore her goddesses. Still, forcing the girl to perform the rituals of her morning prayers wouldn't help her any and could cause other problems. She had seen with Lilith that pushing someone to do something only caused them to give up even quicker.

She looked up as Hendandra and Andrinor came back into the room. "Anything?"

"The door is still locked, and I can find no way to open it. Perhaps there is a trigger in this room," Hendandra said.

"By the way, Myrith," Andrinor said, "it would appear there are several dragons in the next room. It was difficult to understand them and the only thing I'm sure I understood correctly was that they were hungry."

"Then I suggest we end their hunger," Nirev said, lifting his maul and starting for the door. He was stopped by Andrinor standing in his path, his sword held in a defensive posture in front of him.

We don't need this, Myrith thought as Vyroris stepped between the young warrior and the dwarf.

"Myrith, there's something back here," Hendandra called from the alcove. She pointed to a small button near the floor on the back wall.

"Give the rest of us a chance to get into position outside the other room then push the button and let's hope it only opens that one door," Myrith said.

"Shadow can push the button with his nose," Kyrianna said. "That way no one has to stay behind."

The wolf trotted over to the button and sat waiting. "I can let him know when we're ready."

Myrith looked from Kyrianna to the wolf and back. "I don't want any more noise being made than has to be."

"Shadow Seeker and I are bonded. I can communicate mind-to-mind with him."

"Interesting. I have never heard of this type of bond before. Except for the bond between a mage and their familiar," Falden said. His hand rested for a moment on his cloak and Myrith wondered briefly how Talon was doing confined to the pocket Falden had created for him.

"It was a gift from Frayrith and Dwycia when they brought him here," Kyrianna said. She frowned as she glanced toward the wolf before heading out the door.

Myrith walked out into the corridor to see a silver dragon sitting at the next doorway. Hendandra was putting Andrinor's equipment into her backpack and Nirev was standing next to the dragon.

"You're blocking the door," Myrith said, kicking the dragon's tail.

There was a faint click and Andrinor roared as he hit the door with his right foreleg and released a cone of freezing air into the room. He moved forward just enough for Myrith and Nirev to slip past him then stood up. Myrith laughed when she saw Hendandra and Kyrianna kneeling on either side of the dragon's tail, their bows readied.

There were five juvenile blue dragons in the room and she motioned for everyone to hold their attacks as she listened to Andrinor speaking to them in the hissing draconic language.

"Children of the Great Mother, I am one of Her chosen warriors. Allow my companions and I access to your lair and we will leave you in peace. Do not interfere with us or I will be forced to deal with you."

She cringed as the five dragons only laughed. There was another roar and she jumped as lightning danced across Andrinor's scales.

The dragon warrior's head darted forward and he grabbed one of the younger dragons by the neck and dragged it within range of his powerful claws.

Myrith dodged as one of the dragons came at her. A volley of arrows came from under Andrinor to strike the dragon he had grabbed. On her other side, she heard a yell from the dwarf, followed by the thud of something large hitting the floor. Gripping her sword tightly Myrith moved further away from Andrinor, then turned back to engage the dragon snapping at her. This one was still covered in frost from Andrinor's breath attack and its reactions were slowed as she scored several hits before it opened its mouth and released a bolt of lightning at her.

She fought to maintain her hold on her sword as the lightning caused her muscles to contract and twitch. As soon as she felt herself more in control of her body, she stepped in and jabbed her sword into the dragon's chest. Two arrows flew past her to strike the dragon just above her sword and the dragon began convulsing. She yanked her sword free and stepped back as the dragon fell.

She turned to see one of the blue dragons on the ground in front of Andrinor. Kyrianna and Jerietlan seemed to be handling the last of the dragons themselves. She stood and watched Kyrianna for a moment, her two blades dancing in a mesmerizing pattern the blue dragon was trying to follow as Jerietlan's spear found its heart.

Kyrianna's blades made two quick cuts across the neck of the dragon and blood flowed over her as the dragon raised its head and roared once before it fell to the ground.

Andrinor hissed softly as Jerietlan placed his hand on his chest. Myrith watched as the burns on his scales healed.

"Dragons always have something worth guarding," Myrith heard Hendandra say. She turned and watched as the girl carefully worked the lock on a chest in the corner of the room. Hendandra pulled out three wooden bucklers and a pair of gauntlets that appeared to have been made from blue dragon scales.

Hendandra glanced at Falden. "Well?"

The mage sighed then chanted softly as he studied the items laid out on the floor. "The bucklers and the gauntlets all have protective magics woven into them," he said.

"Vyroris?" Hendandra picked up the gauntlets and glanced at the half-dragon.

"I have no need of extra protections." He placed a hand on the gauntlets and closed his eyes for a moment. "The proper rituals honoring the dragons these scales came from were observed, I have no objections to anyone using these."

Hendandra looked up at the doorway, where Andrinor had been. "Guess Andrinor went to check the next door," she said as she slipped the gauntlets into her pack. "I'll just hold onto these for him." She picked up one of the bucklers. "Interesting, wood—not metal. Falden, this is something you may be able to use." She slid one of the bucklers to the mage.

He picked up the buckler and attached it to his left arm then moved his hands and arms through several sweeping movements. "Thank you, Hendandra," he said.

"Kyri, you should take one as well. You can't use a shield when you're using both swords or your bow."

"True. My thanks."

"That makes another item touched by magic you have accepted," Falden said.

Kyrianna only nodded as she slipped the buckler on her arm.

"Kyrianna, take a look at this," Myrith called as she stepped into the alcove.

Four runes were engraved into four tiles on the back wall.

"The runes represent the letters R, S, T, and C," Kyrianna said.

"As you pass through these rooms, her name you will learn," Ashe said from behind them.

"We already know her name," Myrith said, reaching for the tile with the "T" engraved on it.

"Wait, I want to see something first," Kyrianna said as she pressed the tile with the "R" on it. "Shadow, make sure Andrinor is waiting by the next door, please."

Kyrianna waited as Shadow Seeker trotted out of the room. After a moment she reached over and pushed the door release button.

"Shadow says it didn't open," she said.

"Have your pet wait here while we get ready at the next door," Myrith said, pushing the "T" then turning and leaving the room.

Myrith glared at the dragon then stepped in front of him as she waited for the click of the door. Andrinor lowered his head and exhaled lightly, blowing a small cloud of cold air over her.

"Stop playing around," Myrith said. "And make sure you leave room for me at the doors from now on."

"Of course," Andrinor said, lowering his head next to hers. "However, may I suggest you give me a chance to use my breath weapon as the doors open, before you charge in."

Myrith only nodded as the door clicked and she kicked it open.

~ * ~

Myrith was amazed at the group's luck as the last of the gargoyles shattered under Nirev's maul. They had fought their way through eight different rooms facing giants, dragons, gargoyles and other creatures. Surprisingly no one had received any critical wounds and the clerics had managed to keep everyone in fighting condition. Now, however, most of their magic was spent and they were tired. The next room would be the last one on this side and she knew it would be a difficult fight. Then there was Kyrianna to consider. If they were interpreting the message in the first room correctly, she would have to call on Thynitic to get them through to the next area. She didn't need to try and invoke the Lady of Chaos' power while she was worn out from fighting all day. She needed time to rest—

they all needed time to rest before moving on.

~ * ~

"Laraf!"

Myrith sat up as Nirev's voice echoed in the stone chamber.

"What's going on?" She grabbed her sword as she threw her blankets to the side.

"This blasted thief just appeared out of nowhere," Nirev said.

Myrith looked around and saw the others were stirring and gathering around the young man who had accompanied them through the Duvall Estate. *How many weeks or even months ago has that been?* She had lost track of time in this place.

"How did you get here?" Myrith looked at Laraf and frowned slightly.

Laraf smiled as he sat down on the floor. "Shortly after you guys vanished, Kyri was engulfed by an ice storm and taken as well. I stayed with Tristan getting him back to Raspa and helping him to consolidate his position on the council. The ledgers and other information we found at the estate provided proof several members of the Raspan Council were involved in some dark dealings."

"So his position has been secured?" Hendandra asked.

"While not as prominent as it was doing his grandfather's time, House Duvall once again holds a place of power in Raspa. And as an additional bonus for what we did, he has named us as allied members of House Duvall." He pulled several rolled parchments from his pack and handed them to Hendandra.

She opened one of the rolls, read it, smiled and stuck it into her own pack. "A very handy document for ones such as us," she said, grinning at Laraf.

"You still haven't answered my question," Myrith said, interrupting. "How did you get here?"

"I consulted with various clerics and mages. They were unable to locate you, as you were in a place surrounded by strong chaotic magics. It took some time, but I finally found a cleric who was willing to tell me where I could locate Ferdinand." He glanced at Nirev. "You remember him; the big guy with the even bigger hammer."

"I remember him," the dwarf said.

"Unfortunately, no member of the Wayfinder's Guild would transport me to Ferdinand's location—they all said the same thing: it was forbidden by the Circle of Mages, the Church of Mykaylene and the King of Irrmar.

"It took quite a bit of persuasion on Tristan's part, but we finally got one of them to agree to transport me to the small town of Windermere. There, with a letter of introduction from Tristan, I was able to meet with Lady Carolina and eventually the mage Zanif. He transported me to Ferdinand's cave in the Dragonspire Mountains."

Laraf paused for a moment and glanced around at the faces around him. "Where's Kyri? Ferdinand's scrying indicated she was with you."

Myrith's head snapped up and she glanced toward the alcove where Kyrianna had rolled out her bedroll that night. The girl was tossing in her sleep as Skylar sat next to her, his hand resting on her shoulder. Shadow Seeker was asleep and seemed oblivious to his friend's discomfort.

"Deceiver!" Argrala took a step toward Skylar, his body swelled and he grew taller.

Myrith took a step forward as he changed into the same demon they had faced in the temple. The one they thought they had killed. The one who had mentioned two of the daughters working together. *Daughters of Chaos*, Kyrianna had said when they were trying to figure out what he had meant. This was also the same demon who had opened the portal Bukon had vanished through. *Two Daughters of Chaos?* Myrith shuddered though she didn't know why.

"Argrala?" Vyroris had his sword in his hand as he stepped forward.

"Nothing has changed. I am here to stop Torliana just as I told you. She seeks to steal the Lady's power as her own. If that happens and Thynitic loses her place as the Lady of Chaos—Chaos will be unleashed across all existence. That must not happen."

Myrith stared at the large demon that now stood where Argrala had been.

"Yes, Myrith, I am the same one you fought in that other place of chaos." The demon smiled. "Perhaps you should think of this in light of the saying—the enemy of my enemy—"

"Is still not my friend." Myrith raised her sword. "At this moment all I care about is Kyrianna and both of you are a threat to her."

"Hold your blade, Knight of Mykaylene, or Kyrianna will die here," Skylar said.

"Not by your hand." Argrala raised his hands and a portal

opened behind Skylar. Clawed hands reached through and gripped the smaller creature pulling him through the portal. "Tell your mistress the Lady will not allow her to continue corrupting her Chaos."

Skylar only laughed. "The *Lady* is already lost." The portal snapped shut.

"Thynitic has a new offer for you. Leave *this* Daughter of Chaos behind and she will allow you to return to your homes with gifts for each of you. If you continue on this path, you will all fall to Chaos' power." Argrala waved his hand and a portal opened in the doorway behind them. A shifting scene showed several different locations and Myrith frowned when the main room of the Silver Dragon appeared.

"For you, Knight of Mykaylene, you will be able to free your people from the rule of the tyrant Lavial. He is one of Hers and the Lady is willing to remove him from your world and allow you to take his place or install those whom you believe can lead properly. She has no interest in extending Her influence as other concerns are more important at this time. She will leave your world alone and allow those who belong there to return."

Myrith spat on the ground. "I will deal with Lavial without indebting myself to another. I have seen there is no true freedom unless it is properly earned. Nor would I be worthy of such a precious gift if I left another in torment and slavery. Tell your mistress she will not be able to claim my friend so easily."

"I see the Deceiver's work has been done. Very well." Argrala only smiled and turned to Hendandra. "For you, little one, your violin has been enchanted so you can access the abilities of even the most powerful bards. May you find the life you desire."

Hendandra looked around at the others, reached down and picked up her pack, then grinned as several sacks appeared next to her. She grabbed the sacks and stepped through the portal.

"For you, Sorcerer, a ring that will give you the powers of an archmage." Argrala tossed a silver-colored ring to Falden. "The Lady knows how you and your kind have been treated by the council. Now you will have the power to challenge them and force them to acknowledge you and your kind as proper mages."

Falden caught the ring and placed it on his finger. Chanting softly, he stepped through the portal.

"For you, thief, a ring of power. By utilizing the enhanced abilities this ring will give you, you will be able to become the master of the Thieves Guild in Raspa if you choose. Your current alliance with House Duvall combined with the power of the Thieves Guild could make you and your friend Tristan Duvall the most powerful men in the city. You would be able to ensure those who mistreated you in the past are properly punished and others of their kind are unable to hurt anyone else again." He tossed a second ring into the air.

As it arched toward Laraf, he drew his rapier and sliced the ring into two pieces.

"Interesting response. I will take that as a refusal." Argrala laughed as he turned his attention to Jerietlan. "For you, Priest, you will be given a position of honor in Mykaylene's church in Irrmar. You will be revered as one of her most favored followers."

The cleric only nodded as he stepped through the portal.

"Now, we come to two who would harness the power of dragons. For you, barbarian, you will be granted the ability to become a true dragon anytime you desire. You will not be limited as you have been."

"For me to accept a gift like that from anyone other than Ghainaess herself would be blasphemy. I honor only Her."

"You are stronger than I would have suspected for one so recently come into his power." Argrala turned toward the half-dragon. "For you, the one caught between two worlds, you may choose which world you prefer to walk in. You may become a true dragon and soar the endless skies with your brethren or you may choose to have the appearance of a true human but you will retain the immunities and abilities you now have."

Vyroris' appearance changed to that of a tall, muscular human with golden eyes. He looked down at himself and smiled as he stepped through the portal.

Argrala turned to the dwarf. "That leaves only you and the fire cleric."

"Don't even bother; there is nothing you can offer me that be convincing me to leave my friends. I have given my word to follow the lady knight and I be not foresworn."

"Very well, you can be doomed along with her and the others." Argrala paused and tilted his head down to look at Ashe. "For you, Cleric of Hellavar, one who has been feeding his own need for revenge for so long, he can no longer remember who he once was. My Lady offers to restore everything you have had taken from you. Even that which no one else can return—your name."

"I want nothing more than her head on a platter," Ashe said. "She can never return the years or the lives which were taken."

"Then you will receive Torliana's head."

"I will take it myself."

"Very well. Remember there is always more to every story than is known. You blame Thynitic and Torliana for what happened—but there is another who is the one most responsible." He turned toward the portal then paused and turned back to Myrith. "Be aware Thynitic wants Torliana stopped in what she is doing. For now, your paths run together."

The shifting scene in the portal froze for a moment on a room carved from obsidian. Two thrones sat on a dais and on one of the thrones was an elven woman with midnight-black hair.

The demon jumped through the portal and knelt before the woman, who looked up and smiled before the portal misted over.

"No!"

Myrith spun around at the shout from Kyrianna. The girl was still tossing in her sleep.

"My guess would be a nightmare, probably a spell to create one cast by Torliana or possibly even Thynitic herself," Ashe said as he knelt next to Kyrianna.

"Can you bring her out of it?" Laraf knelt next to Ashe and took one of Kyrianna's hands.

"I can try. I don't know if my power will be sufficient." Ashe began chanting softly as he placed his hand on Kyrianna's forehead.

"She's not showing you the complete story," Ashe said softly.

He sat back and sighed. "I have placed a block in her mind; it's up to her now."

"What was she seeing?" Myrith looked at Ashe then down at her friend.

"She was trapped in a repeating nightmare; one that showed her mother destroying an elven community when she served Thynitic."

"Nowhere in all the worlds or planes is there no pain, torment or chaos," Kyrianna said softly in her sleep. "All we can do is accept those strikes which cannot be avoided and give back chaos and pain to those who offend. Kindness should be the only companion to pain and will increase the intensity of suffering and the chaos surrounding us. Do not ignore the sudden whim of compassion; let it always come, but only seldom as to give those who suffer a sense of hope. Hope is consort to chaos and torment is their offspring. Unending torment destroys pain and this in turn destroys the chaos that nurtures us. Act alluring to trap those who would never seek the Lady on their own. Confuse those who think they know the ways of the world around them. Bring pain and torment not only to those who enjoy it, or to those who deserve it, but also to the innocent and those who do not anticipate it. The lash, fire and cold are the three physical pains that never fail the devout. Love, jealousy and hatred are the three pains that should follow in the footsteps of her devout. Spread Thynitic's theology whenever pain is meted out and chaos swirls. Wherever pain is, there is Thynitic. Wherever chaos is, there is Thynitic. Embrace the pain and chaos. Embrace Thynitic."

"No!" Kyrianna sat up suddenly, her eyes wide as she looked up at the others.

"Kyri?" Laraf looked at the girl, his face pale as his body shook. Myrith wasn't sure if it was from anger or fear.

"It was the litany of Thynitic she was reciting," Ashe said.

"What?" Kyrianna's voice was a harsh whisper as she stared at the cleric. "What did you say?"

"You were reciting Thynitic's litany just now in your sleep," Ashe said.

"Kyri, are you okay?" Myrith stood behind Ashe.

Kyrianna only shook her head and slid further back into the corner of the alcove. "Leave me alone! I'm not going any further! I will not invoke Thynitic! I will not let her use me!" She dropped her head into her hands, her sobs echoing in the room.

"Kyri," Laraf placed a hand on her shoulder, "I know what it's like to be trapped by circumstances not of your making. You can't give up. If you do, she still wins."

Myrith stepped between Laraf and Ashe, reached down and grabbed Kyrianna's hands and pulled them away from the girl's face. "Grow up! You have a responsibility and a duty to perform. Perform it."

Kyrianna jerked her hands away from Myrith then clenched her fists as she looked at the unicorn and wolf marks on her wrists. Tears still streaming down her face, she unclenched her fists and dug the nails of her left hand into her right wrist, scratching at the mark.

"Kyrianna, stop it!" Myrith grabbed her hands again and stared at the blood now flowing from her friend's wrist.

Ashe placed a hand over Kyrianna's wrist healing the cut. "Do you need proof you are more than just a tool? Proof your goddesses are with you?" He held out a small unicorn figure.

Myrith released Kyrianna's hands and she reached out slowly to take the figure.

"This is made from the horn of a unicorn," Kyrianna said.

"Do you know where I got it?" Ashe looked at her.

"I hope not from one you killed."

Ashe took a deep breath. "I got it from your mother. It was carved from the horn of the unicorn filly killed that day."

Kyrianna only stared at the cleric.

"Call her," Ashe said, placing his hand over hers.

Myrith frowned as Kyrianna seemed to focus on the carved figure for a moment. *How can she call someone for whom she had no name?*

"The man's name was Cewyr; there is a connection between them both. If you call his name, the unicorn will come to you," Ashe said. "She was meant for you."

Myrith pulled Laraf to his feet then guided him away from Kyrianna and Ashe. She shook her head as she glanced at her companions who had remained behind.

Nirev was standing on one side of the door with Andrinor on the other. Both were fully armored and standing with readied weapons. Laraf was focused only on Kyrianna so he couldn't be relied on if something attacked them. Ashe was involved in whatever it was he was doing for Kyrianna, and was also not prepared in case of a threat. And Kyrianna...*I will not willingly let her have you*, Myrith thought. *Though I feel I am failing and I don't know how to keep you from falling into the darkness.*

Myrith jumped as Ashe was suddenly flung across the room and a unicorn now stood next to Kyrianna. The scarred priest laughed as he got up from the floor and looked at the unicorn.

Myrith only stared at the mare, she was not the pure white normally associated with unicorns. Her coat was silver-gray in color; her mane and tail were gray darkening almost to black at the tips. The tail was thick and flowed to the floor while her mane, just as thick, flowed over her neck to her knees. Her horn, while still golden in color, appeared to be bloodstained. There was something familiar about the unicorn, but she couldn't quite grasp the memory.

The unicorn neighed softly, stepped forward and laid her horn gently on Kyrianna's neck. The girl reached up and put a hand on the mare's cheek as she stared into the clear amethyst eyes.

"She can only be called forth for about one hour a day," Ashe said from where he stood near the far wall.

Kyrianna nodded. "Return to your home," she said softly.

After the unicorn vanished, the figurine of the unicorn remained on the floor. Kyrianna picked it up and slipped it into one of her belt pouches as she looked around. "Where are the others?"

"They are weaklings, we don't need them," Ashe said.

Myrith glared at Ashe for a moment. "We found Skylar sitting next to you, a hand on your shoulder and you in apparent discomfort of some sort. He then offered us a chance to go home along with *gifts* from Thynitic, if we would leave you here. The others accepted the gifts and left."

"You should have left also," Kyrianna said softly as she slid further back into the alcove, pulling her knees up to her chest.

Myrith moved closer to the girl. "Knock it off," she said. "You have a job to do and you need to do it. You know we can't go back, so the only way we have to get out of this place is to go forward and face this Torliana. And besides, what kind of friend would I be if I abandoned you here. We will face her together."

Kyrianna raised her head and looked at Myrith then nodded slowly.

"We still need rest before we move on," Ashe said. "The arrival of your other companion interrupted our sleep and with the loss of the mage and the other *cleric*, I will need to be at my full strength." He paused for a moment. "I can still cast magics that will allow one of those here to maintain the watch and be rested for tomorrow."

"I will take the watch," Andrinor said immediately. He glanced at Myrith who nodded her agreement.

Ashe chanted softly then reached out and touched Andrinor's arm.

"Ashe," Myrith said softly. "What do you think Argrala meant when he said there was another responsible?"

"I do not know." He glanced at Kyrianna then moved back to his bedroll. "It doesn't matter at this time."

~ * ~

"What did you hear?" Myrith asked as Andrinor came back into the room.

"Sounded like two dragons arguing. It seems one of them was sent to retrieve something from the room and the other was refusing to give it up," he said.

"We should wait until they settle their argument," Kyrianna said. "That way we only have to face one and not two dragons."

"True, but if Torliana wants something brought to her that one of them is guarding, do we want her to have it?" Myrith looked around.

Something large hit the wall between the two rooms and they turned as it shook and pieces of rock fell to the floor. "I would definitely suggest waiting," Andrinor said. "It would be a bad idea to get involved in a fight between two dragons. And from the sound of that—one of them is fairly large."

"Get your things together; we'll wait at the door until we are sure the battle is over. I want to get in there before the winner has a chance to heal or leave with whatever it came for." Myrith drew her sword and headed for the door.

"Shadow." Kyrianna pointed to the button. "Wait here. Push this when I tell you."

The wolf padded over and sat by the small button, his tail thumping against the floor a couple of times.

Myrith stood at the door and glanced back at Andrinor. "You should consider putting on your scales," she said as several roars echoed in the corridor from the room. Several more crashes came from the closed room before the sounds died down. "Okay," Myrith said.

The door clicked a few seconds later and Myrith pushed it open as Andrinor exhaled above her. The large blue dragon in the room seemed unaffected by Andrinor's attack and Myrith charged forward. Several arrows flew past her and struck the dragon in the neck. The head darted down at her and she found herself backpedaling trying to avoid the snapping teeth. She swung her sword up and sliced at the dragon's neck. Blood flowed from the wound and the dragon paused and stepped back from her.

"Hold!" Andrinor said moving next to her.

Myrith held her sword in a defensive position as the dragon lowered it's head then raised his gaze to Andrinor.

"You are an Initiate of the Great Mother," the dragon said.

"I am. And She requires that we confront the one who created this place and trapped Her children here. Will you allow us to continue in our task or must we fight you. You are already injured and we have magic and strength of arms."

"I will leave you be. If you allow me to rest and recover without fear of your companions."

Andrinor dropped his head and nodded. "You have my word. You may rest and recover in peace. The room we just left is clear of enemies. As we will be here for a while, perhaps you would feel more secure there."

The blue dragon nodded, then slowly left the area.

"Can we trust him?" Myrith sheathed her sword and glanced at Andrinor.

"Yes." Andrinor slowly changed back and glanced around for his clothing.

Myrith turned away from the young warrior and looked at the back wall. Kyrianna had slipped past her and was now standing in front of the wall staring at the runes carved there. She walked over to stand behind Kyrianna.

"It says: 'Blood of my lost daughter, speak my name and title with reverence and you may proceed. Fail to honor me as you speak and pain and chaos will be the rewards you receive,'" Ashe said.

Myrith placed a hand on her friend's shoulder and felt her shudder. She squeezed Kyrianna's shoulder gently then turned back to the others.

"She's not going to be able to do this," Laraf said. "You can't force her to call on Thynitic!"

"She has to at least try. None of the rest of us can do this; we have no other way through this place and we can't go back," Myrith said.

"And what if she fails?" Laraf stepped between Myrith and Kyrianna, his hand on his rapier.

Myrith glanced at the partially drawn blade, but ignored the obvious threat as she looked past the young man to Kyrianna who had turned to watch them, tears on her face. "I'm more concerned about what may happen if she succeeds," she whispered.

Kyrianna put a hand on Laraf's, forcing the blade back into the sheath then nodded and turned back to the wall.

"One other thing. We really should find a way to get the others back. We may need their help," Andrinor said.

"They were weak. They cannot be counted on," Ashe said, staring at a large chest in the corner of the room. He reached down slowly and passed his hand over the symbol carved in the top then paused before reaching for the lid.

"That they may have been," Myrith said, walking over to stand next to Ashe. "However, I doubt they were sent home or received any of the gifts they were promised," Myrith said. "And, if that is true, I will not abandon them to Thynitic or Torliana's whims, even if they deserted us."

"I do not have the power to bring them back to this location, Lady Lake." Ashe opened the chest.

Myrith looked down and saw a large shield and a black rod. She frowned slightly as Ashe reached into the chest and removed the shield placing it on his arm and balancing the weight carefully. He smiled as he picked up the rod then slid it into a loop on his belt.

Ashe turned to her. "These were once mine and I reclaim them. The Lady's chaotic nature has betrayed her. She should have had them stored within her own citadel in the abyss instead of here." He paused for a moment. "Give me time to prepare and I will summon an efreeti and see if his powers are sufficient to find and return your companions."

"There is no need for that," Laraf said. "I can contact a cleric of Mykaylene who will be able to accomplish the task." He smiled as he pulled out a small globe and held it in his left hand as he drew his rapier and used it to pierce the globe. In front of him, the head of a large man appeared.

"Ferdinand," Kyrianna said as she stepped up beside Myrith.

"Yes?" Ferdinand's voice echoed in the room.

"Several of our friends were enticed away from this place by a servant of the goddess Thynitic. We fear they may have been tricked and are now trapped somewhere," Myrith said.

"Can you bring them back?" Laraf looked up at the cleric.

Ferdinand seemed to concentrate for a moment. "Describe them."

"Hendandra is a short woman with long blonde hair. She has trained as a rogue," Myrith said. "Jerietlan is a cleric of Mykaylene. He is a half-elf. Falden is a human mage. Vyroris is a half-dragon; I believe one of his parents was a gold."

"He is not from Shokar," Ferdinand said.

"No," Kyrianna said. "He is from my world. It is called Rhysia."

The cleric seemed to study her for a moment. "Rhysia," he said. "Is that all?"

"Yes," Myrith said.

"Very well." The image vanished.

A few minutes later, Ferdinand appeared along with Jerietlan, Falden and Vyroris. The cleric vanished again.

"Where were you?" Myrith asked, looking at the three of them.

"Lost on the plane of limbo," Jerietlan said softly. The cleric turned away. "Thank you for sending him."

"Are you okay?" Andrinor laid a hand on Vyroris' shoulder.

"I will be." The half-dragon looked at him. "Your faith in the Great Mother was stronger than my faith in He Who Watches. I sought to hide who I am. I doubt either of them will forgive me."

"She is the Great Mother. She will always forgive her children; they only need ask," Andrinor said.

"Thank you," Vyroris said, offering Andrinor a slight bow.

Ferdinand reappeared carrying Hendandra.

"Put me down!" Hendandra slapped the cleric on the arm several times before he dropped her.

"What in the names of all the gods is going on here?" Hendandra glared at Myrith. "I assume this was *your* doing. I was home, enjoying a nice meal when this person appeared in the middle of my table. Breaking the table, I might add. He barely gave me enough time to gather my gear before dragging me back here. Threatening me in the process."

"Then you are the only one who wasn't lied to," Myrith said. "The others were trapped on the plane of limbo. All we did was ask Ferdinand to retrieve our comrades. I had no way of knowing the demon had actually spoken truthfully to you. You could have been in the same situation as the others. Would you have preferred that?"

"What I would have preferred was being given a choice in the matter. Not having this brute show up and tell me I could willingly accompany him back to this place or he could raise me here. That is what I would have preferred."

"There was no need to threaten anyone," Myrith turned toward Ferdinand.

"You said bring them back. You did not say only if they wanted to return." Ferdinand walked to the back wall and seemed to study the runes for several seconds. "Who is to speak the name?" he finally asked, looking around.

"She," Nirev said, pointing to Kyrianna.

Myrith heard Kyrianna's sharp intake of breath as she glared at the dwarf.

Ferdinand looked down at Kyrianna and said something Myrith did not understand.

"I will not!" Kyrianna took a step back from the cleric, her eyes wide.

Myrith turned as a soft popping sound came from the area of the door. She turned to see an older man, with a long gray beard wearing sky-blue robes step out of a portal. She recognized him as the mage, Zanif, they had found in the holding cells of the Duvall Estate.

"We haven't heard from you in a long time, Bustal," Zanif said as he approached Ferdinand. His hands moved quickly in a complicated pattern and the cleric seemed dazed for a moment then shook his head.

"Too much. Too much chaos. Get me out of here," Ferdinand said. His voice trembled as he spoke.

Zanif reached out and placed a hand over one of the cleric's and they vanished.

Myrith watched as Kyrianna looked around then slowly approached the back wall and stared at the runes for a moment. The ranger turned back and looked at Myrith, her eyes wide with fear. "Myrith," she whispered.

Myrith moved closer to her friend so she would not have to speak very loudly. "I'm here."

"Don't let her claim me," Kyrianna whispered.

Myrith stared at her friend then nodded her understanding as she drew a dagger from her belt. She held the blade in front of her away from the view of the others.

"All I ask is that you be quick," Kyrianna said as she turned back to face the wall.

Kyrianna took a deep breath. "I call upon Thynitic, the Lady of Chaos." Her voice was barely louder than a whisper.

Nothing happened.

"With reverence, it said. That probably also requires you to speak so all can hear you, Kyri," Myrith said.

Kyrianna nodded then dropped her head and stared at the floor for a moment. When she finally raised her head and spoke the phrase again, Myrith heard and felt a surge of power in the girl's voice. Before them the wall dissolved into a swirling portal of color and light. Kyrianna immediately stepped into the chaos. Myrith felt her hand tighten on the dagger as she followed.

Myrith focused her senses on Kyrianna trying to study the girl's aura. She carefully sheathed the dagger she was holding when she did not sense any evil in the person she hoped was still her friend. Once again, they were in a long hallway with a series of doors. And, like the previous one, only the first was unlocked.

~ * ~

"Looks like we're dealing with these again," Hendandra said, pointing to the small button on the back wall.

Myrith looked at the body of the drake in the middle of the room then up at Andrinor. He had not joined in the fight against the dragon. It had not attacked them initially, only refused them entry into the room and had requested they leave.

When it had turned its back, Nirev had charged in with his maul and attacked. Andrinor had stood back and watched as the dragon had not done anything that could be seen as an attack on the dwarf.

She turned back to the wall. There was nothing inscribed on it and she breathed a small sigh of relief no one else would have to call on Thynitic or any of her other possible incarnations to get them through this passage. For now they could concentrate on getting through the various rooms in this hallway and hopefully finding this Torliana soon and then locating a way home.

Myrith moved to the door. She had no doubts Thynitic and Torliana were watching them. They couldn't give them time to prepare. Despite everything which had happened, it was still early. She paused and turned back to look at the others when she realized no one was following her. Most were moving listlessly around the room, almost as if they were lost. Jerietlan had moved to one of the corners and appeared to be meditating as he knelt there. The small silver shield of Mykaylene was in his hands and his eyes were closed.

None of them had been seriously hurt and she didn't understand what he was doing. Her gaze moved to Vyroris who seemed to be avoiding Andrinor. Despite the young man's assurances that their goddess would forgive the half-dragon his weakness, he still appeared to be judging Vyroris harshly. Falden also seemed to be avoiding the others. Hendandra had slumped down against the wall next to the door and looked up at her.

"What gave you the right to have me kidnapped from my home by that madman?"

Myrith sighed as she looked down at the smaller woman. "The fact you have given me responsibility for this group. The fact you have chosen to follow me in this place. That is what gave me the right."

"It wasn't fair."

"And if I hadn't done anything, would it have been fair to Jerietlan, Falden or Vyroris to be left in limbo? I must plan for the worst so all of us have the best chance of surviving," Myrith said. She smiled as she leaned closer to Hendandra and whispered, "And is it fair to the others that you seem to have returned with all the items you left with, except the gold and gems you took?"

"I made sure they were secure. Everyone will be able to claim their share if we get back," Hendandra said.

"And since none of them know where you secured it, what if something happens to you?"

"Then I guess nothing had better happen to me." Hendandra stood up, her hands on her hips as she looked up at Myrith. "If you will excuse me." She moved to the corner and sat back down.

Myrith's gaze swept the room again. Kyrianna was now sitting in the corner of the small alcove, the wolf nosing at her hands. She shook her head as she saw the girl scratching at the mark on her right wrist. He friend's soul was in danger of falling into darkness and she was showing every sign of renouncing her faith in the goddess she said had marked her as one of her chosen.

Faith! Her gaze darted back to Jerietlan, who was still kneeling in prayer. He was seeking forgiveness for his actions, she realized. His acceptance of Skylar's offer would have been a serious insult to the Battle Maiden. He had not only assumed a goddess whose philosophy was opposed to Mykaylene's could elevate his rank within the church of his chosen deity, he had also quit the field; abandoning his comrades. She knew he had a great deal of soul searching to do.

She shook her head as she moved to the center of the room. Despite the early hour, she could not push them any further today. They were all soul weary and would need the rest. She found a crack in the stone floor and grounded her sword into it, point down as she knelt next to it. She would spend her time in vigil seeking guidance from Mykaylene. Behind her she heard the wolf whine and she turned to see Kyrianna approaching Ashe.

"You are one who walks the path of order?" Kyrianna spoke slowly.

"Of that I am sure. Though my soul has known only darkness for too many years, I can truly say I have not strayed from the letter of Lord Hellavar's teachings," Ashe said.

Myrith frowned slightly as the girl knelt down in front of the cleric. She knew Kyrianna feared Ashe, so why would she approach him?

"Can you cast a spell to protect me from her chaos while we rest?"

"Protection from chaos." Ashe blinked several times as he looked at Kyrianna. "Do you fear her nature," he looked up for a moment, "or your own?"

Kyrianna paused for a moment then nodded before answering. "Hers and mine," she finally said. "I am half-elven and I can feel the chaotic part of my nature being called to by her. It is a call I do not wish to answer. I have seen the images she has sent me and I can sense the truth which lies in them. I don't want to risk losing myself as my mother did. Can you help me?"

Ashe nodded. "I will grant your request, for to not do so would violate everything I have come here to do."

Myrith continued to watch the two of them, as Ashe seemed to concentrate for some time before speaking again. He removed several items from various pouches and laid them out carefully.

"I do not envy you. My path was set decades before and was certain and unfailing. I led my temple and its path was the shining one Hellavar set for it. It was a place all could use. Our rules were set and unbiased. Our priests were sought as mediators by the local farmers and the highest lords," Ashe said.

"She came to the temple, just before I did, seeking guidance and purpose. However, in the end, all she sought was the destruction of all I had made and then my unmaking. That is why I was sent to the Abyss. However, my faith was strong; it did not breaking. The demons sought to peel away my flesh and mind one layer at a time. Every moment I was there, I prayed to Lord Hellavar to deliver me from my torment. He did not. Instead of renouncing my faith, I retreated inward, into His scriptures and blocked out all else. Throughout those many years, I reaffirmed my faith, but the constant assault left me with little more than my faith and my final purpose."

Ashe paused and looked straight into Kyrianna's eyes. "You see, we both are lost; you cannot see the road before you and I cannot see the path back from where I am now."

Ashe reached down and picked up a couple of the items in front of him, then began chanting softly. He finished the spell and touched Kyrianna's chest. "This spell will remove any immediate effects and influences she may have placed on you through her nightmare spell. However, it cannot remove any doubts you may have from what you have seen."

Kyrianna nodded as he began casting the next spell.

"This spell will allow me to monitor your physical and mental states. I believe it will alert me to your distress if she mentally attacks you again. It will last throughout the night and into part of tomorrow."

He began casting another spell. "The specific spell you requested will not last as long as either of us would like. A more powerful version is required. However, I will do what I can and the spell will last for approximately three hours. If I sense her presence, there is another spell I can cast that can aid you," he said.

Kyrianna smiled softly then reached out and touched Ashe's scarred hand. "I thank you for your assistance. However, I do have one other question. Are you only thinking of Torliana and her magics or will these spells help me to fight the Lady of Chaos herself?" She paused as she pulled her hand back and wrapped her arms around herself.

"She is calling me to her. Calling to the chaos that is a part of my own nature. I am worried that when I sleep, I will lose even more of myself to her." Kyrianna shuddered.

Myrith fought with the urge to go and sit next to the girl, offering her support. This was something Kyrianna had to do on her own. She had to defeat this darkness calling to her by herself or the battle would never be over. Myrith knew from her own bitter experiences if you let others fight the battles, even if they won, you still lost because you would end up relying on them. When that happened, they would turn on you and you wouldn't be able to defend yourself against them.

"Even now, I can hear her whispering. I don't want to lose myself to her," Kyrianna said.

"Excuse an old man for not realizing the simpleness of your original intent. This last spell will remove your body's need for sleep today. I am mortal, not divine; my magic can help, but not totally protect you from her power. Unfortunately, it is your battle to wage and the prize is your very soul."

Kyrianna closed her eyes for a moment then dropped her head slightly. "I thank you for your assistance. I hope we are both able to find the way back to our proper paths when this is over." She opened her eyes and looked at the marks on her wrists for a moment before she stood and returned to the alcove.

Myrith frowned at Ashe's whispered comment as Kyrianna sat down and began slowly stroking the wolf's ears. "Will your wounds grow as deep?" She glanced at him to see the cleric looking at his own scarred hands and arms.

Ashe raised his head and shook his head. Myrith followed his gaze to where Jerietlan still knelt. After a few minutes Ashe stood and walked slowly to Jerietlan's side. He looked up at her and she saw disappointment in his eyes before he knelt next to Jerietlan, pulled a bracelet out of one of his belt pouches and handed it to the other cleric.

"You must pray over this; asking for Mykaylene's guidance and forgiveness. I will assist you in casting the magics to create a band of faithfulness," Myrith heard Ashe say. "If we are lucky, she will accept this as partial penance for your lack of faith."

Myrith watched the two of them with some interest. Perhaps there was something salvageable in Ashe as Mykaylene had indicated. He had told them he didn't care about any of them, and yet he had used his power to bring Kyrianna back from the realms of the dead. True, the cleric seemed to think Kyrianna was the key to his being able to get to Torliana. But, now, he was helping a cleric of a different church to atone for his lack of faith. Yes, there was something salvageable in Ashe's soul; she hoped they would be able to reach it before they finally confronted this Torliana.

She even understood why he was disappointed in her as she turned away and began her own meditations. As a servant of Mykaylene, he expected her to be the one assisting Jerietlan. However, she knew she didn't have the religious training at this point to guide the cleric in seeking forgiveness, but Ashe would. And his reaching out to help another as he was doing was another step away from the path of darkness he was following.

~ * ~

Myrith looked up as the others began stirring that morning. She was still troubled by what Kyrianna had been required to do the day before in calling on Thynitic. She had seen no changes in the girl's aura and had been relieved she had not been required to honor her promise. Still, though the taint of evil was not there, there was a definite change in her friend.

Mykaylene had come to her during her vigil, warning her Kyrianna had to open a part of herself to the Lady of Chaos in order to channel the power needed to open the portal. She had also cautioned the chaos infecting this place was affecting each of them. The goddess had told her the chaos must be properly contained for now, so the spark of order could be restored. She warned if Kyrianna fell to the chaos or if Torliana succeeded in claiming the Lady of Chaos' power then they risked chaos being unleashed across all the realms of existence.

Mykaylene had then done something that had frightened Myrith, the Battle Maiden had told her there were others who had a stake in what would be happening in this place, but not all of them truly understood the consequences of failure. She then allowed Myrith to see the visions and dreams the others were receiving that night.

Visions from one's gods were private things to be shared only by choice—that Mykaylene thought it important for Myrith to know what others were being told was a burden she didn't know how to carry.

~ * ~

Myrith found herself in a place of empty blackness filled with the sound of laugher. She covered her ears to stop the laughter, but it only seemed to be drilling itself right into her skull. "Stop it! I was promised you would stop!" She heard a voice not her own shout into the darkness. Even though the voice came from her throat, it was Hendandra's. A wisp of blonde hair caught her eye and she realized she was sharing Hendandra's vision. Myrith forced herself to relax as she watched from behind the thief's eyes.

The cackling stopped and left an eerie quiet. She turned her head quickly one way then another but saw nothing in the darkness. Then suddenly, the blackness became the Duvall Estate's main hall, piano and all. Her ears heard the soft strands of a violin. Hendandra turned to regard the musician whom she recognized as Nyssa Duvall. The woman's bow stokes and fingers were practiced and even as they felt their way through the song.

In front of Nyssa sat two empty chairs, both half-turned toward the figure of the deceased noblewoman. A female voice spoke from the chair on the left. "I am sorry. I thought the laughter would make you feel at home. Is this more to your liking?"

"I never want to hear his infernal laughter again," Hendandra said, placing her hands on her hips as she stared at the chairs. "Why do my dreams persist? Is this some cruel joke by the grand trickster? Is this some maddening dream by Thynitic or is this some punishment by the fire cleric for some perceived allegiance that doesn't exist?"

"No, child," a strong male voice answered from the right chair. The voice was smooth and melodious as if every word were part of a larger song. "The master of tricks has indeed left you. Remember, child, it was he you chose, not us. His nature is almost pure chaos itself. He cares not what heartache his lies and misdeeds do to others, only that they bring amusement. By some strange twist of fate, she has interceded with him on your behalf and he has left you."

The female spoke again. "He leaves you to the chaos Thynitic commands. I hardly consider that a blessing, my dear."

The conversation turned away from Hendandra's presence. "You speak of chaos, Rhyra, like you condemn it. Your own nature is hardly different."

Rhyra? Hendandra's mind repeated the name. *The Mistress of Illusion, and sworn enemy of Ballan. The one whose artifacts we retrieved, and whose ring I thought I had thrown away.*

"I refuse to follow laws laid down by others, if that makes me an anarchist—so be it," Rhyra said. "Life is a beautiful masquerade that should be relished and reveled in. You accuse me of being her or him. Show me where I have either spent my life or my divinity in such a manner I have placed others at risk or left them ill for enjoying my presence.

"Tell me, Vesir, are you really better than I with your *holy* stance? You hold your own truths to be self-evident and those of others to be *evil.* How many people have died trying to live up to your measure and how many others died because they refused to try?"

"All were given choices. Conflict is not my goal. I am the embodiment of compromise, negotiation and persuasion. Every intelligent being is imbued with the power of choice. Some choose to live with others in peace without forcing their views on them. Some instead wish to impose their will and rule without the reason that leads to coexistence. The elves, dwarves, dragons, goblins and most of all, humans constantly battle themselves and each other on this path. I am only a guide: A guide who wishes nothing more than for all to walk their own path of life without bringing ill to one another."

Hendandra fought the giggle that threatened to escape when she heard the snoring from Rhyra's invisible presence in the left chair.

"You're incorrigible," Vesir said.

"And you are a bore. God of Persuasion, my foot. Better name for you is God of Long-windedness."

"Your mouth is like your actions, brash and ill-thought out."

"You are questioning my judgment." Rhyra cackled with laughter. "He who would negotiate with demons and devils to save a few misdirected souls, questions my judgment."

Hendandra saw the chair tip back as a beautiful raven-haired woman tumbled onto the floor. Her laughter never stopped as she pointed to the other chair.

"Your actions have made you many powerful enemies, Rhyra," Vesir said.

"Not my actions, but those of others." Rhyra stood up and smoothed the folds of her pale green gown. "I did nothing to hurt your Lord Thedrin. He was taken with the then mortal Astaeda. I simply pretended to be her as he sought to ascend her to his side. I can't help it if he is so easily tricked by a mere mortal's illusion and more so, can't see to forgive such a trick during the centuries that have passed where I have not interfered with his *grand* designs.

"You should thank me, Vesir. It has made him more cautious in his dealings with others. Imagine if I did not teach him the lesson, but some other more malevolent individual sought to masquerade at another time. Besides, I diminished only Ballan's faith and he still ascended his true love to his side a mere week later."

"You are quite mad," Vesir said. "That trick of yours cut deeply into Thedrin's pride. Just be thankful his son has not his father's anger in his heart or you would find yourself quite the deceased immortal. I also find it amazing Ballan has not cut that tongue from your head herself by this time."

Rhyra twirled her body and mist swirled around her like a dancing dress. Her image had not yet vanished, when Hendandra heard the goddess' voice next to her right ear. She turned quickly back and forth to see Rhyra no longer standing beside her but in front of her still twirling. "She can't harm what she can't find," Rhyra said before laughing a light laugh. "She is an ill-mannered sot, that one. She wants power for its own sake. Not to use for any purpose other than to prove what greater depravity she can create."

She finally stopped and turned to face Hendandra. "Did you know she created the first lycanthrope from the she-cat that nurtured Kaleden and Dynissa's foster daughter Shyada? It was Shyada and Dwycia who slew that poor creature. If anyone knows how to make enemies, it is that witch. In one fell action she gained not one enemy but four."

Vesir appeared before Hendandra. He was a handsome half-elf dressed in fine robes with a beaming smile. "If you seek to pledge yourself to this one you should know she is like the mist; never there when the sun or the need arises. She avoids conflict at all turns and never swears allegiance to anyone." He turned toward Rhyra. "Even Resare, Lord of Death, who saved you on that dreadful first night of immortality, cannot count on you to be by his side when it is his time of need."

Rhyra turned away. "Your words cut deep." An image formed in the mists before her.

The goddess was running in the darkest of night over broken ground, her breath short and her footing not sure as she slipped many times. "I was cast down by Ballan's power that day," she said softly. Shadowy visages of half-animal and half-human chased her across the landscape. Each creature a different mix of lineage—wolf, tiger, rat, bear and many others.

She stepped back to Hendandra's side as the rogue watched the images of the past. "You wonder why I don't fight them. Each is a progenitor of their *race*. Massively powerful creatures able to challenge even demon lords, plus the Goddess of Magic had nullified my magic; my only true calling."

Hendandra watched as the goddess tumbled down a dark hill with the nimble creatures behind. Her head slammed hard against a rock, her face twisted in concentration as she attempted a spell. Her face showed defeat as her hands dropped to her sides. The monsters continued to approach, but stopped with a sudden look of confusion. They looked from one side to the other and the look of concern was evident, even in their misshapen faces. The image pulled back as if viewed by a hawk from many miles away. It was not a rock to the goddess' back but a mausoleum and the gravestones and monuments stretched for leagues in every direction. "The great graveyard of Fellsmore," Rhyra said as the image returned to her.

The image of the goddess smiled as she spoke. "Afraid? You should be. This is *his* ground. Your mistress may be powerful, but he is all around you here."

The werewolf leapt at the goddess only to be held to the ground. Clawed bony hands erupted from the ground to grasp all of the creatures' feet and hold them fast. However, the were-things made short work of the annoyances as a woman's cackle could be heard on the wind. As the creatures ripped the last bony hand from the ground, the dirt erupted into a hundred decaying bodies that encircled the interlopers.

Rhyra smiled at their arrival, but her elation was short-lived as rotten flesh also yielded to long claws and sharp teeth. The wind carried the woman's cackle with greater fury as it echoed in the stillness of the graveyard.

The very darkness now swirled around the trespassers and formed animated humanoid shapes. The black things attacked and some of their strikes seem to bite deep, but their opponents still managed to disperse the darklings at a surprising pace. Soon, only the beasts stood before the prone Rhyra. The massive forms stepped aside to reveal a female figure standing on a hill. The figure was that of a beautiful elven woman with long black hair, her face showed no hint of the naiveté of youth or the wrinkles of old age; instead, she had a mature beauty and confidence born of experience. "Is that the best you can do, my old adversary? You grow weak with time," she said.

A rumbling voice, muffled by the dirt of the grave spoke from a swirling blackness that formed above the mausoleum. "I do not care to show my power. Unlike you, I reserve my strength for those who truly deserve it. This one has earned her place among us this day. When Leikor stole his soul back from my realm, I did not pursue him to drag him back. She snatched her own divinity much as the Trickster did. You and I exist only because of our natures, you because the mortals invoke the arcane and I because every mortal eventually passes to or through my realm."

The swirling blackness shaped itself into a large cloaked humanoid with pale white glowing eyes.

"I will not have her usurp my power over any form of magic," Ballan said, raising her hands. "I will end this here and now. Your lifeless husks and apparitions do not threaten my creations. Stop them if you can."

"I am the keeper of all of those who have died. I am even the master of those who have passed and been raised again to the living. We have had these battles before. You will lose."

"Then let's end this argument and bring your worst."

"So be it," Resare said. The Lord of Death waved his hand and five human figures appeared before Rhyra. "If you can defeat them, you can have the illusionist."

Ballan seemed to study the five figures and her eyes slowly grew wide. Three of the figures were encased in shining heavy armor: one a woman with a spear and shield; another, a man with a long sword and a missing right hand, the third held a curved khopesh and shield. The other two were an elven woman dressed in robes and wielding a morning star and the other a tattooed, scale mail wearing male with a great spear in one hand and a shield in the other.

"All those who have died then risen may still serve me as they were when they passed into my realm. *All*, even those who have now attained godhood. Feel honored, Ballan, for today you see what greatness Thedrin, Sost, Mykaylene, Coressa and Nalath can achieve if they fight together as one."

"No!" the goddess screamed as Thedrin led the god-mortals against her creatures. The resistance of the beasts appeared inconsequential as the warriors—supported by the spell power of Coressa—carved through their opponents in minutes.

As the last one fell, Resare spoke once more. "Be gone, Ballan. This confrontation is over."

She scowled at Rhyra and faded from view.

Rhyra rose from the ground and stared up at the Lord of Death. "Do not expect my thanks. I knew if I came here, followed by her foul magic, you would not allow her to have her prize. Though the appearance of the five was unexpected, the result was not. Your enemy is mine as well and nothing more."

The shrouded figure did not move or speak.

The first hint of sunlight touched Rhyra. "With the dawn, my power returns. Fare well, Resare. I trust I will never pass into your realm, but I expect eternity will bring us together at least once more." She disappeared and the image faded.

Vesir spoke again. "See, Hendandra. Even when saved from certain destruction, she offered no thanks or compensation."

"And you require almost full devotion to your ideals of negotiation and peaceful solutions first," Rhyra said.

Vesir turned to Hendandra. "You are at a crossroads, my dear. You have no ties to any god and none truly claim you, as such, your soul can be lost here. If you die, The Lady of Chaos can claim you, as this is her realm and no other god can intercede on your behalf. Be forewarned, little one, as such you will not pass to another place and can only be raised with *her* consent. We have come to provide paths—nothing more."

Vesir gestured toward Rhyra. "She is the Lady of Mists and Illusion. She is patron to many thieves and all enchanters and illusionists. She cares not for law and chooses no side in the war between good and evil." He paused and nodded politely to the goddess.

"I am the Master of Diplomacy, Oratory and Persuasion," he said after a moment. "My guidance is sought by all who wish to find a middle ground and avoid conflict and I am also revered by many musicians and bards. We both will accept you for who you are."

Hendandra smiled as her gaze caught the goddess opening and closing her hands in time with his words.

Vesir stopped and whirled around to see the goddess' hands stroke back her hair. He scowled as if he knew she had been mocking him.

Rhyra paid him no heed. "Choose, Hendandra," she said.

Hendandra glanced from one to the other. She found it hard to believe two gods would be vying for her worship. She was a simple thief and not a person who had any type of influence over others. Still, maybe there was a way to get something out of this arrangement. "What benefits do I get for accepting either of you as my patron?"

Vesir nodded then smiled at Hendandra. "You have chosen late in life to learn the skills of the bard; a path that requires much training and practice to use to its potential. Your talents lie more in other areas. As the Patron of Persuasion, I grant you the following items."

A gold headband and ring appeared in Hendandra's hands. "The circlet will enhance your persuasiveness and the ring will enhance your ability to convince others you are telling them the truth. I do not ask anything for these gifts other than that you continue to consider my offer to be your patron."

"That is all you can offer, Vesir?" Rhyra said. "You ask for nothing—then I dare you to leave her alone until after she makes a choice. I doubt you can do it.

"I am the Mistress of Illusion and my gifts can enhance both your bardic and rogue skills. Therefore, I grant you the following." She reached out and touched Hendandra's armor, which glowed for a moment.

"Your armor has been given a powerful enchantment. You will move silently, become invisible and assume any disguise at will. In addition, the magical protections have been increased."

She smiled as Hendandra's violin appeared in her hands and a soft glow surrounded it. "Even if you decide to no longer pursue the path of the bard, your instrument will be gifted with all the powers of a master. These will only remain as long as you walk your path and continue to practice every day." She held the instrument out to Hendandra.

There was a pause then Rhyra looked at Vesir and smirked. "Since Vesir has already stated no payment, I am forced to do the same. I also promise to leave you alone, *for now.* Just remember whose gifts bring the most value to you as you continue here."

The vision faded and Myrith found herself back in the room. She glanced at Hendandra who was still sleeping. The girl had been given powerful gifts by two gods who were trying to convince her to follow one of them. Both had promised to let her make her own choice with no price attached to the gifts they had given. She wondered which one Hendandra would choose.

Why had Mykaylene allowed her to see Hendandra's vision? There had been nothing there that meant anything to her. She shook her head for a moment then felt herself being pulled again.

~ * ~

Myrith again found herself in a place of empty blackness. Her feet touched a surface that felt solid yet it appeared she was standing on an eternal void. She gripped the rapier at her side as a set of pale white glowing orbs approached. *Rapier?* She looked down at her side and saw Laraf's blade hanging there. *Another vision*, she thought as she again let her mind step back and watch what was happening.

The orbs floated through the emptiness and widened to form eyes. The blackness seemed to consolidate around the eyes. The rest of the plane became a dark gray as the darkness around the eyes formed itself into an ebon-cloaked humanoid figure. Laraf relaxed as he realized the weapon would not be needed, nor would it have provided any protection if it had been. "Resare," he whispered as the figure glided toward him.

As soon as he spoke the name, the blackness became a translucent, armor-clad man. The shield he carried on his obviously broken arm was emblazoned with Mykaylene's symbol. Laraf recognized the apparition as Rhinehart Duvall, Tristan's grandfather.

"Brother cleric and sister warrior have lost their way," the apparition said as he stepped through Laraf.

No surprise there, Laraf thought. *That only confirms my feelings about Myrith's actions yesterday.*

What? Myrith found herself thinking as she tried to sense Laraf's thoughts. There, floating on the surface of Laraf's thoughts was an image of Myrith standing behind Kyrianna as she called on Thynitic.

~ * ~

How dare she? Laraf thought. *She is supposed to be a holy warrior dedicated to good and she gets mad at me for trying to stop her from forcing Kyri to call on an evil goddess.* He had seen Myrith draw the dagger as she stood at Kyrianna's back yesterday. *Not only is she forcing Kyrianna to open herself up to a dark power, allowing that power to try and claim her, she is willing to sacrifice Kyri in the process.*

When he had met the group in Duvshire, he had been attracted to Kyrianna from the start. He wasn't sure why, he had never really found himself attracted to anyone before. She was a beautiful woman, with her golden-brown hair, dark green eyes and elven features. He had pledged himself to protecting her when she had almost died under the claws of that worg at the Duvall Estate and it bothered him that it had taken so long to rejoin the group.

During the time he had stayed with Tristan Duvall, he had come to realize the young nobleman also cared about Kyrianna and he had decided he wasn't going to try and pursue her. Tristan could offer her more than he ever could and as an escaped slave, he would be constantly looking over his shoulder. That was no kind of life to try and share with another. However, all the feelings he had for Kyrianna had come rushing back when he had seen Myrith holding that dagger, ready to use it. There was no way he was going to let her sacrifice Kyrianna; even if it cost him his own life, it wasn't going to happen.

~ * ~

That explains a lot, Myrith thought as she focused back on the image before Laraf.

Laraf turned to where Rhinehart should have now been and instead found himself face-to-face with Nyssa, Rhinehart's wife. Her gown was covered in blood from where her own son, Mikyl, had plunged a dagger into her abdomen. "The little one does not have the heart for this fight." The ghost scattered into a million motes of light.

From behind him another voice spoke. "The half-dragon desperately seeks the power of the dragon." He spun around to see Lord Terissian's bloody corpse melt into his wife's form.

"And the dragon warrior depends too much on that power." Lady Terissian faded into oblivion.

A voice that seemed as old as time spoke next. "The sorcerer wields power but without discipline or direction." He looked down to see Alesandra, Tristan's great-grandmother seated below him as if he stood on a glass pane with her on the floor below. She disappeared.

A familiar gruff voice called from his right. "The dwarf is kept from his potential by the actions of others."

Another familiar, emotionless voice called from behind and he turned slowly. "The fire priest is kept from his greatest power by his own blind hatred." The scarred lips of Ashe mouthed the words, as his body became a rolling tapestry shifting form several times. Some with his body shown broken in one place and then another. Others with his belly torn open or his limbs ripped from his torso. Another showed half his head bitten away as if by some large creature. Laraf closed his eyes as his stomach lurched. Even though it was not really there, it wanted to spew forth its contents.

A sultry voice spoke from just below his nose and Laraf's eyes snapped open to see the striking beauty of Larissa Duvall. Her face exquisite, but her legs broken and her side bloodied by a knife wound. "You have all come to face her trial." She extended her hand to her side as if to hold someone else's hand then dissolved into smoke, only to reform as Wilhelm Terissian with his hand in position to hold hers even though it was now gone. "How much are you willing to lose for your friends?"

Laraf swallowed hard.

Wilhelm stared at Laraf as he mirrored his stance. "Chaos' power swirls around you with every step you take. The path you tread can lead to nowhere but sorrow. However, if your group does not travel the path then many more will take this road to ruin. She is a primordial goddess created by the chaos that formed the universe, but twisted by the pain the races heap upon themselves and others. Her power is also her weakness and it can be easily corrupted by the ever changing chaos she is a part or.

"A single thread is weak by itself, but once fashioned and entwined within a rope, their individual weaknesses are changed to the strength of the whole. Beware the unraveling, Laraf, for it is the beginning of the end."

Laraf only licked his lips as he nodded once.

The young Terissian moved to depart, and Laraf reached out a hand to stop him. "Question. The others were obviously the visages of their death. Why was Ashe so shown?"

He turned, but as an Ashe in his late thirties with a wound in his chest. "I show the visages of those for each time they have visited me. Brular has visited more times than most in recent history."

"Brular? Why? How did this come to be?"

"He was a high priest of a remote temple of Hellavar. His temple was not a shining beacon of light, nor did the base aspects of man corrupt it. His temple provided simple rules all abided by and adhered to. Torliana went to the temple to learn the ways of order. But she became a pawn of Chaos. Chaos used Torliana to destroy the temple like a cancer from within. Her last desecration against the God of Fire was to send his High Priest to the Abyss where demons tortured him daily. She knew the priest would not break in mere days or even weeks so she gave the demons a talisman that bound his soul to his body. The demons used the power of the talisman to pull Brular's soul back from me, even though neither he nor Hellavar willed it. He suffered many years and with each death, he lost part of himself. He has little left but his faith, and even that has been tainted by his hatred."

"Can we trust him?"

"Can you afford not to?"

"You said he is kept from his greatest power. What is that power, if I may ask?"

"The ability to unlock the greatest power of faith within others."

Laraf blinked in confusion, and found himself staring at Kyrianna. "Help me!"

He stretched out his hand to console her only to see her melt into the form of little Melissa Duvall. "The voices will not stop," the little girl said as tears streamed down her face.

Myrith's eyes snapped open and she thought she could still hear the sound of Melissa weeping. She saw Ashe's head snap up to look at Kyrianna for a moment before he shook his head, sighed and returned to his rest. She heard Laraf moving and saw him sitting up, his rapier across his lap as he watched Kyrianna.

I will not let the darkness claim you, Myrith heard Laraf's thoughts echo for a moment in her mind.

~ * ~

As she looked around, she saw the dazed looks on the faces of those she knew had been visited as well as a couple of the others. To her surprise no one said a word about what they had been told or seen. She hated when people kept secrets. She had seen nothing in the visions which had given her any useful information, other than she now understood Laraf was obsessed with Kyrianna. In his desire to protect the girl, Myrith had no doubts the young man wouldn't care if he put himself or the others at risk. Still, it was possible someone might see something she was missing if they discussed what they had seen. However, just as she did not like to discuss the things Mykaylene shared with her, she would not force them to talk about their visions. She knew she had to get them refocused on the task of finding Torliana and getting out of this place. They had to begin working together or they would most likely all perish here. None of them, with the exception of Ashe, was truly here of their own accord. She and her original companions had been snatched from Shokar and brought here. Andrinor claimed to have been sent here by his goddess to seek out the one who was corrupting her children. Vyroris had claimed to be working with Argrala in seeking out Torliana. Yet, Argrala had turned out to be a demon spying on them for Thynitic. Did that mean the half-dragon was also not to be trusted? Other than his weakness in accepting Skylar's lies, she had seen nothing to make her believe he was other than what he claimed to be. Perhaps he had also been fooled by Argrala. Hendandra was still angry over being brought back here by Ferdinand, and Ashe was consumed by his need for vengeance—that made both of them a liability. Laraf had sought a way to join them, and perhaps it had originally been to find and help all of them; now his feelings for Kyrianna were clouding his judgment. Then there was Kyrianna. She knew the girl would trade herself if it meant the rest of them would be allowed to return to their homes. The way she kept scratching at her wrists also bothered Myrith. It was almost as if Kyrianna was ready to give up. That was something she wouldn't allow her friend to do. She just didn't know how to prevent it.

None of them were going to like what she had to say to them this morning, but she had never been one to hold her tongue in the past and she wasn't going to do so here. Getting out of this place alive was more important than risking hurt feelings.

She slowly stood and looked around the room as the others began getting ready for the day. "Good morning," she said, gaining their attention. "I trust you have all rested well. There are things I must say to you and I beg your indulgence."

The rest of the group stopped and looked at her, except for Kyrianna who was sitting in the alcove with her eyes downcast. Myrith swallowed before continuing; she didn't like doing this anymore than they were going to like hearing it.

"As we have seen, this place is filled with chaos. The evil witch who controls this plane and the ilk that inhabit it have sought to control us and to my regret, she has in many ways succeeded. I tell you now; I will not allow her to control me. You have told me several times I lead this group, and therefore you are choosing to be led. With the chaos that already infests this place, we can no longer allow ourselves to be divided on even the tiniest issue. You wish me to lead; then I shall lead. I will brook no more questioning of my authority while we are in this place. I will not risk adding to the chaos that threatens to divide and destroy each of us. With so much chaos affecting all of us, even myself, as it has; we must adhere more closely to the path order if we are to survive." She looked around again, her gaze stopping briefly on Kyrianna, who turned away from the others, before moving to Hendandra.

"To the littlest among us; I know of your kind, and I trust them not. You have withheld information from me and the others. With the intention, I can only assume, of your personal profit. You have sought to keep to yourself that which belongs to and might benefit us as a whole." Myrith paused. She had more she could say, but she realized it could cause more harm than good. Yes, she had no problems risking hurt feelings, but she now realized she should not be the one driving the wedge deeper into the group if she wanted them to take heed of what she was saying.

Myrith turned to look at Laraf and she felt her anger at his questioning of her actions rising again and she took a deep breath to calm herself. "You challenged me yesterday. Do not make that mistake again, for the next time I shall pick up the glove and you will feel my steel. The decisions I make are for the good of the entire group, not just the one, and for the removal of evil."

"Falden, I hold you no ill will. You chose to accept the gifts offered by our enemy. Such is the nature of your kind. But true magic lies in the power of the gods and not in arcane tricks. I hope you now know our enemy is the embodiment of Chaos and is not to be trusted," she said, looking at Falden. She frowned as he only stared at her impassively.

"Though several of you chose to abandon the rest of us, I do not fault you the decision to leave. I do, however, fault you for thinking you could believe the lies of one born from chaos." She walked over, grasped Jerietlan's hand and looked at the bracelet he now wore. "And what penance has Mykaylene demanded of you for your lack of faith? How have you placed the rest of us in jeopardy by your desertion?"

Jerietlan dropped his head. "My spell casting has been restricted to only those spells related to healing," he said.

Myrith shook her head as she released the cleric's hand and turned to Vyroris. "And what of you?"

"That is between me, the Great Mother and He Who Watches," Vyroris said. "Know they both still support this endeavor and therefore I am to continue to follow you. My sword is yours."

"I have stated, I do not hold your choice to attempt to return to your homes against you, only your wisdom in accepting the word of one whose very nature embodies chaos. However, you have also shown by your actions you cannot be relied upon to defend the members of this group or trusted to support us. If you should make the same choice again, I will not expend our energy or resources to find you."

Myrith took a deep breath then moved to the alcove where Kyrianna still sat, ignoring her and the others. She knelt down, placed a hand on her friend's chin, and turned her face so the girl had to look at her. "You are my closest friend, and I tell you this as a friend. It is time for you to grow up. I know you are in pain. I know you feel betrayed. However, your attitude, your desire to remove yourself from the others of this group only serves those who seek to control you. You need to focus your resolve on confronting the one who would torment you and drive you to question not just why this is happening. But," she reached down and put her hand on Kyrianna's wrist, "yourself and your faith." Myrith dropped her voice to barely a whisper. "Rangerette, it was your quiet faith and strength that did more to restore Tristan's faith than anything I did. My ignorance and ego almost lost him completely. What must I do to save you?"

Kyrianna only closed her eyes and while she didn't respond she offered Myrith a small smile. Myrith stood and faced the others, her sword drawn and in her hand. "The time for talk is over. Let our actions this day serve our cause well. And let the witch who controls this cursed place regret the day she chose to deal with us."

~ * ~

Myrith stared at the blank wall in front of her. They had fought their way through the last six rooms, facing creatures with ties to the planes of earth. Her tactic had worked and no one had suffered serious injury as they directed their anger with her harsh words at those they fought.

She glanced around at the others. Most leaned against one of the walls, their weariness evident in hard breathing and pale skin.

"The back wall glows with a magical aura," Falden said from where he stood next to Kyrianna. "There is no discernible pattern to the magic, so I cannot identify what it is. However, I would surmise that is where the exit is."

"Hendandra?"

"Sorry, nothing here," Hendandra said as she searched the area of the back wall. She began moving around the room while waving the others out of her way. "Ah, here it is," she said after several minutes.

Myrith watched Hendandra pick something up off the floor then turn back to the wall as a small compass rose appeared on it with niches at each of the cardinal points. "Anyone have a clue what we are supposed to do now?"

Hendandra reached into her pack and removed three other gems. "I found these on the other elemental layers," she said. She quickly pointed out which of the gems were found on which of the layers. "I just don't know how to place them."

"Haven't we been in this position before?" Kyrianna looked at Myrith. "The temple and the jars. Do you remember the order?"

"You were the one taking notes," Myrith said. "Don't you remember, or have it written down?"

"Sorry, I didn't write down the order of the jars," Kyrianna said softly.

"You were the one who came up with the order," Falden said softly. "Is there a reason you can't remember it now?"

"Other than the fact I don't remember—no."

Myrith was pleased to hear a note of defiance in Kyrianna's voice as she looked at Falden. There was a playful gleam in the girl's eyes softening the glare she directed at him.

Falden snorted then turned toward Hendandra. "The order of the elements in the temple was fire to the east with water opposite and air to the north with earth opposite."

Hendandra placed the gems in the appropriate niches and the compass and gems vanished as a doorway appeared in the wall.

Chapter Eight

"Another blasted corridor of rooms," Myrith said as she stepped through the doorway. "Why doesn't this Torliana just face us instead of playing games?"

"Torliana isn't stupid. She is studying us. She is learning about our abilities and how to fight us. When she is ready, that is when we will face her," Ashe said.

"All of the doors along this corridor are locked," Hendandra said. "However, the end is not blocked and there is another series of doors to the right. The first door appears to be unlocked."

"Did you check it?"

"No. I heard something moving in there," Hendandra said.

"Guess that's where we start," Kyrianna said as she drew her swords and started down the hallway.

Myrith drew her own sword and followed. Kyrianna was waiting for the rest of the group at the first door in the adjoining corridor. "Something reptilian, but I don't think it's draconic," she said softly.

Myrith looked around at the others then nodded and pushed the door opened.

"Basilisks!" Kyrianna brought her left arm up and shielded her eyes with her buckler.

"Don't look at their eyes," Myrith said as she brought her own shield up and stepped into the room.

Myrith frowned as Kyrianna stepped in with her, both of her swords at the ready. The two large basilisks in the room turned toward the group and both moved directly toward Kyrianna.

Myrith stepped to the side, blocking one of the reptiles as Andrinor stepped in next to her. The basilisk they were fighting moved to the side—again toward Kyrianna. She jumped slightly as Hendandra appeared behind the basilisk and attacked the large reptile from behind. The creature turned slightly and she cursed as she saw Andrinor's sword stop its movement. The young man had been turned into a statue by the basilisk's gaze.

"Kyri!" she heard Laraf's shout behind her followed by a loud string of Dwarven curses. Myrith concentrated on the basilisk in front of her; she didn't want to lose any of her other comrades. Hendandra continued to harass the reptile from behind and she took advantage of the creature's distraction to renew her own attacks.

She wasn't sure how much time had passed before the basilisk finally fell. Myrith sheathed her sword and wiped her face as she turned to face the others. Nirev's maul was buried deep in the skull of the second basilisk and Laraf was staring at the statue that had been Kyrianna.

Ashe reached out and touched Kyrianna's hand, his hand glowing with a red aura as he chanted. For several seconds nothing seemed to be happening, then the aura surrounded the stone figure and Kyrianna gasped as she took a breath.

"And Andrinor," Myrith said.

Ashe nodded as he again cast the spell.

"Thank you," Andrinor said.

Ashe didn't answer as he turned away.

"You two ready to move on?" Myrith glanced from Kyrianna to Andrinor.

"Let's get this over with," Kyrianna said. "Shadow." She pointed to the back wall.

The wolf walked to the alcove and sat down facing the wall. Myrith looked at Kyrianna. "Another button?"

"Yes," Kyrianna said.

Myrith nodded as she took a step toward the open door and was stopped by an invisible barrier.

"You have proven to be an interesting group so far," a woman's voice said. "My little elemental realms were never a true challenge to you; only a chance for me to observe you and learn about you. As you may have guessed, you have now entered *my* domain. While you may have handled the earlier creatures as you traveled through the regions of air, fire, water and earth—you will now be facing my pets and my magic.

"I renew the offer of letting you leave this place, however this time the Lady will not interfere and you will be allowed to reach the places you call home. That is—providing you leave now and Kyrianna, daughter of Arielle, remains behind."

"What do you want with her?" Laraf asked.

"The daughter of Arielle? She and I are destined to face each other. Like Brular, I have spent time in the Abyss at the whims of another. In my case, it was at the hands of one who once held the Lady's favor. And, like Brular, I will take retribution for the torments I was made to suffer. However, unlike the cleric, I have risen above blind hatred and will succeed in my plans."

"We are not going to leave our friend here at your or the Lady's request," Myrith said. "If you want her, you will have to go through us to get her."

Laughter echoed in the room. "Think carefully about your decision this time. I control this region and even the Lady will not be able to interfere. I will open the portal and you will be able to leave without any tricks."

There was a long pause before the woman spoke again. "Do not fret, Brular; you and I will face each other again as well, just not yet. Know this, daughter of Arielle, if you leave this place without settling with the Lady, you will be pursued by Chaos for the rest of your life. She will not let you escape as your mother did."

Myrith frowned as a scroll appeared in Kyrianna's hands and she began to unroll it.

"That is something you need to know." Torliana's voice faded.

"Chaos!" Kyrianna yelled as the scroll exploded.

"Kyri! Are you okay?" Laraf asked.

"Yeah, fine. Let's get going."

Before they entered the next room, Ashe touched each of them on the shoulder. "This will protect you from fire," he said.

Myrith stared at several catlike creatures each with two long tentacles growing from their backs. Two of the creatures were twice the size of the others. "What kind of abominations are these?" she heard Kyrianna say.

Falden raised his hands and a bolt of lightning streaked through the air to strike one of the larger cats then arc around the room to hit two of the smaller ones. The mage nodded his head as he stepped to the side to allow Myrith to enter the room.

Myrith frowned as the creatures ignored her attacks and they all moved toward Kyrianna—just as the basilisks had done. The larger cats stayed just out of range of their weapons, their long tentacles reaching over the smaller cats to hit Kyrianna several times.

A fireball exploded in the room engulfing several of the cats. Myrith's blade connected with the back of one of the smaller cat's neck with a loud crunch as it fell to the ground. Another of the cats moved in front of her to claw at Kyrianna, who was standing next to her.

"Kyri!" Laraf's voice echoed in the room as Myrith heard the sound of metal hitting the floor. She risked a glance at Kyrianna who was on her knees as the two larger cats again hit her with their tentacles. She could hear Ashe chanting in the back of the group and a wall appeared in front of the girl, then another behind her. A third wall appeared between Myrith and Kyrianna, and she assumed one also appeared on the other side. Kyrianna was safe from any other attacks; now they could worry about killing the cats.

"Let me out of here," Kyrianna's voice came from behind the walls. "By all the gods, let me out of here!"

"Shut up!" Myrith and Andrinor yelled together as they continued to fight the cats.

"Get me out of here!"

"Kyrianna, shut up!" Andrinor shouted again as another of the smaller cats fell to the ground.

Another fireball exploded in the room, and this time one of the larger cats fell along with the remaining smaller ones. Myrith swung her sword at the remaining cat's neck and smiled as it fell to floor its spine broken by the force of her blade.

"Kyri, move back against the wall—away from my voice," Laraf said. He raised his sword and jabbed it into the stone several times making a series of holes in a large square pattern.

Nirev carefully tapped the bricks, working his way around the area punctured by Laraf's sword. Once he had cracked the stone along the series of holes, he stepped back and swung the maul at the bricks, knocking several of them out of the perforated area.

"Be careful," Kyrianna said from inside the walls.

"Be quiet. We're going to get you out in a few minutes," Myrith said.

Four more swings of Nirev's maul and there was a large opening in the wall. Kyrianna slowly climbed through the hole and leaned against Laraf as he handed her a vial.

"Healing potion," he said.

"Who did that?" Kyrianna looked around at the others.

Laraf and Hendandra both pointed to Ashe who only shrugged. "I could have let them kill you," he said.

"It would appear the creatures in this area are specifically targeting you," Myrith said. "I want you in the back with your bow from now on."

Myrith frowned at the defeated look in Kyrianna's eye, then turned away as Jerietlan came over and checked her injuries.

"Ashe, I would speak to you a moment," Myrith said, walking out of the room.

"Yes, Lady Lake."

"She must be protected." Myrith said after they had moved down the hall a short distance. "I can summon Riker and have him carry her to the ethereal plane with him until we are out of this area, but I doubt she will go willingly."

"You are a Warrior of the Battle Maiden, are you not?"

"I am."

"Yet you would suggest kidnapping one of your companions and banishing her from the field of battle. Do you honestly believe Mykaylene would favor this type of action? And if you did succeed in this action, you realize there are dangers she would then have to face on the ethereal plane. Thynitic is a goddess; she can send her demons to that plane as easily as any other. How will you protect her when you are not there? I will not help you with this. There are other ways to protect her."

Myrith turned and returned to the room, Ashe following her.

"Myrith, I think I may have found something here," Hendandra said, moving toward the wall on the right side of the alcove. "A faint magical aura." Before she reached the area, there was a flash of light, followed by a second a few seconds later.

Myrith took a couple of steps back avoiding the effects of the magic, she hoped. She frowned as several of the group cried out in pain and doubled over for a moment; then the pain seemed to pass as they stood back up and started looking around.

Laraf looked at her, drew his rapier and took several deliberate steps toward her; his weapon held at the ready. Before she moved too far away from the room she saw Andrinor change into his dragon form and turn toward Vyroris, a cone of his freezing breath striking the half-dragon and surrounding him. Vyroris fell to the ground frozen.

"Laraf, what are you doing?" She took several more steps back watching the thief's eyes. The young man's face was drawn and seemed frozen in an expression of hatred as he continued advancing.

"Enough of this," Myrith said. "Riker." She vaulted onto the horse as soon as he appeared and he galloped to the end of the hallway where she sat and watched Laraf. Nirev stepped out of the room and raised his maul as he began charging down the hallway toward her and Riker. She waited until the dwarf was within forty feet then tapped Riker with her heels and the ghost horse galloped past the dwarf and thief to the other end of the hallway.

"I don't know what's causing this behavior, but this is not something you want to pursue. Riker and I can play this game far longer than you can," she said.

A small shape formed out of the shadows as Laraf turned and ran toward her. Myrith shook her head as Hendandra's sword sliced at Laraf's legs and he fell to the ground. Considering the actions of the others, she doubted the woman was doing this to defend her, but instead something had driven her to attack Laraf.

Nirev ignored the two thieves as he continued on toward her.

Myrith watched as Laraf rolled to the side and forced himself to his feet, his rapier held in a defensive position as he fought to maintain his balance. Blood pooled on the ground around his right foot.

Myrith again tapped Riker with her heels and the horse galloped to the far end of the hallway as she avoided Nirev's swing when she passed him. When the horse turned to face back down the hallway she saw Nirev and the other two standing frozen, their weapons on the ground. She nudged Riker and the horse walked up to the dwarf.

"Nirev?"

"Lady Knight. What happened? Something made me want to kill ye."

"I don't know what caused it. But it looks like it's over. We need to check on the others." She slid off the horse and dismissed him. She paused by what was left of the half-dragon's body and whispered a brief prayer for his soul.

"By all the gods," Myrith said as she stepped back into the room.

Both Andrinor and Falden were on the ground writhing in pain. Over by the wall, Kyrianna lay on the floor sobbing. "What have I done?" she whispered over and over. Myrith frowned as she saw the girl digging her nails into her wrists, scratching at the marks on them.

"Laraf, bind her hands, before she does serious injury to herself," Myrith said, looking around the room. She saw no sign of Ashe or Jerietlan.

"Jerietlan," she called.

"Here," the cleric's voice came from the doorway. "Ashe and I teleported out of the room when Kyrianna attacked him."

"Do either of you have any idea what happened?"

"No, Lady Lake, though I would guess this was meant as an example of the power Torliana holds," Ashe said.

"Myrith, she seems to be coming around," Laraf called.

Myrith walked over and knelt down in front of her friend. "Kyrianna, what happened?"

Kyrianna stared at her for a moment, her eyes wide and her breathing coming in short gasps. "Andrinor, dragon but not normal. Something very malevolent and corrupted." She took several breaths. "He and Falden turned to attack me." She paused again her breath getting shorter.

Myrith placed a hand on her shoulder. "Calm down, Kyri. Just tell me what happened."

"I…I…I called on Thynitic's power." Kyrianna closed her eyes and shook her head as she struggled with the rope binding her hands. "She struck them down because I called on her." Tears were flowing freely down her face. "What have I done, Myrith? What have I done?"

Myrith only stared at her friend for a moment. "What! Why would you do that?"

Kyrianna curled into a tight ball and began sobbing again.

Myrith stood and walked away from Kyrianna. She could sense where the evil had touched the girl's soul, but it wasn't truly a part of her yet. "Can you do anything for them?" She looked at the clerics then down at Andrinor and Falden.

"If this was done by Thynitic, it is doubtful either of us will be able to break the enchantment," Ashe said.

"We can't leave them like this," Myrith said as she drew her sword.

She approached her two companions then glanced back at Kyrianna. The girl was watching her, pain evident in her face as tears continued to flow. She had admitted to calling on Thynitic and it had been the goddess who had done this to Andrinor and Falden. She had to know they couldn't leave them in this kind of torment, but how much further damage would it do for her to know she was responsible for their deaths. And as far as Myrith was concerned Kyrianna was the one responsible, her and Thynitic. *Whatever happened, she still should never have called on Thynitic to help her.*

"Wait," Jerietlan said as he grabbed her arm. "The spell has ended."

"Did one of you?" Myrith glanced from Jerietlan to Ashe. Her sword remained at the ready as she looked down at the bodies of Andrinor and Falden; no longer writhing in pain.

"No, we did not do this. Perhaps Thynitic did it. Mercy is considered one of her domains as well," Ashe said. "I can only think of one reason she would have considered showing mercy to them." He glanced toward Kyrianna, who was now lying unconscious on the ground. "She was showing favor to one who asked."

"Let them rest and recover from their ordeal. We all need rest after this," Ashe said. "We can begin again in the morning."

Myrith nodded.

~ * ~

Myrith woke the next morning before any of the others. She frowned at the sight of Laraf sitting next to Kyrianna his hand resting on her shoulder. His protectiveness was getting stronger and it worried her.

She looked around as the others began stirring and Jerietlan moved to check on Andrinor and Falden. Andrinor waved off the cleric's aid, quickly gathered his armor and equipment then headed for the door. She frowned as she examined the young man's aura and saw the darkness that had taken hold there. She started after him as Ashe followed him out the door.

"Andrinor," she called as she exited the room.

The young man stopped and turned. Ashe stepped up to him and placed a hand on his chest and something seemed to explode between them. The cleric took a step forward and slapped his hand against Andrinor's chest again.

"No!" Myrith yelled as Andrinor fell to the ground. "Why?" She drew her sword as Ashe walked back toward her.

"It had to be done. His soul had been corrupted by her power. He could not be left at our backs, not with his abilities," Ashe said. "I bear the responsibility for my actions, not you."

"So, now we have lost two of our companions."

"That is to be expected in a situation such as this," Ashe said.

"Can they be brought back?"

Ashe looked down at what was left of the half-dragon and

shook his head. "I have not the power myself to bring them back. To only resurrect Andrinor will not remove the corruption from his soul and it takes a more powerful spell to bring the half-dragon back. There is a way, but it will cost me much to do it."

Myrith nodded and turned back to room.

"What is the cost?" Kyrianna said from where she stood in the doorway, Laraf behind her.

"Part of my life force," Ashe said.

"Can that cost be shared?"

"Perhaps, but to do so makes it more dangerous to all involved."

Kyrianna turned toward Laraf and held up her hands. He frowned slightly then began untying the ropes. Kyrianna reached for her dagger, never taking her eyes off Ashe.

"You told me you would do what was necessary to bring them back, when we teleported out of the room yesterday," Jerietlan said. "Are you breaking your word?"

Ashe looked at Jerietlan and bowed his head slightly. "I have never lied and I will not break my word. However, this will be very complicated. I will be summoning an efreeti and binding it to my will. Once I begin the summoning no one is to say anything. One misspoken word could get everyone here killed or bound to the efreeti."

"Can you word your binding so the cost is shared by more than you?" Kyrianna asked as she sheathed her dagger.

"It will be tricky, but yes."

"Then I will share that cost with you," she said.

Myrith frowned when Kyrianna turned to look at her. "I will not enter that circle as someone must remain to guard you," she said.

Ashe nodded. "Then I will place a circle of protection about you," he said.

"Nirev, bring Andrinor's body and as much of Vyroris' remains as you can in here and place them near this circle." Ashe moved to the open area of the room and drew another larger circle. The runes were precise and steady.

Ashe began working on another circle, around Kyrianna. After Nirev returned with the body of Andrinor and part of Vyroris' remains, Ashe began working on the circle that surrounded Myrith and the others.

The fire cleric stepped in the circle with Kyrianna, finished the line of runes then turned his attention to the empty circle as he began chanting. Myrith frowned as the language Ashe was using was unknown to her. Her suspicions grew as smoke began to fill the other circle and when it cleared a large demon stood there. The evil radiating from its aura was strong and she had to force herself not to move from the circle she was in.

Ashe continued to speak to the efreeti and soon she saw the half-dragon's body lying on the ground whole. The slight rise and fall of his chest told her he was alive. She watched Andrinor closely as he gasped once and then his breathing also steadied. The cleric had honored his word—even if they had had to force him to do so.

Ashe glanced around at the others then stepped out of the circle and continued speaking to the demon. After he had finished, the efreeti laughed as he looked around at the group and vanished.

"You do not have much time," Ashe said as a glowing light surrounded him. "I have asked for a conduit to be established so you may contact your deities and ask them what you will."

Kyrianna stepped forward. "Why?" She fell to her knees before the portal.

A tall elven woman appeared before the portal, not truly a part of it; her hair and eyes as black as a moonless night. She reached down and lifted Kyrianna to her feet then turned and nodded politely to Ashe. "My thanks for allowing me this opportunity," she said.

The woman turned back to look at Kyrianna. "Daughter of Chaos, you have asked why. That is an interesting question with an even more interesting answer. As you willingly called on the power of Chaos, I will answer your question. You have taken the first step and it suits my purposes to take it with you.

"Your mother and you are descended from a long line that has been devoted to serving Chaos. A line that has produced the most powerful of those whom I have called, that is until your mother left my service. I do not like losing that which belongs to me."

"Thynitic," Myrith said softly.

The goddess looked at her and smiled before turning her attention back to Kyrianna.

"You are the Mistress of Chaos and Lies," Kyrianna whispered. "My mother is of the Taladilith, not the Rynial."

"Even Arielle doesn't know her own lineage," Thynitic said. "Her mother was Rynial and her father was Taladilith. When her husband's people realized she was a Daughter of Chaos, Arielle's mother was forced to leave the Taladilith. Because Arielle's father was Taladilith, the Rynial forced Shyrella to abandon her daughter for her tainted blood. The priestess who made that decision was later dealt with, but by then Arielle had been found and adopted by the ranger Cewyr. As long as she remained in the forests under Frayrith's protection, I could not reclaim her. However, once she left Kilenter, I moved to reclaim my lost daughter.

"Arielle is still lost to me, but now you are here and I will reclaim what belongs to me." Thynitic reached out, lifted Kyrianna's chin and smiled. "You are still confused, but you will find the correct path to me before this is over. You will either do it willingly or I will make your friends suffer for your insolence."

Thynitic reached up and dragged a single nail down Kyrianna's cheek, causing blood to flow into her cupped hand. "Keep this in mind, you and your friends will not be able to defeat Torliana unless you accept the power I can give you and thereby accept your destiny as a Daughter of Chaos." She leaned forward and kissed Kyrianna gently on the forehead.

The goddess smiled again as she glanced toward Ashe. "This one is amusing and I look forward to when he returns to my citadel. I find it interesting he would offer to lose a piece of himself to allow you to contact your deities. However, I cannot allow any of the others to interfere at this time." She waved her hand and Ashe convulsed in pain as the goddess and the portal vanished.

"Looks like we lose another day," Myrith said, looking around. "Ashe needs rest as do Andrinor and Vyroris." She glanced at Kyrianna who had again separated herself from the group by moving to the alcove.

She continued to watch the girl for a while. She wasn't sure what to do regarding what Kyrianna was going through. The girl was quickly losing whatever faith she had had in Frayrith and Dwycia. It was almost as if she had begun to accept what Thynitic was telling her. "She's the Lady of Chaos and Pain, Kyri," Myrith said softly. "She is only saying what she is to hurt and weaken you. Don't let her win."

Kyrianna glanced toward her and smiled weakly.

Chapter Nine

As they prepared to leave the next morning, Ashe walked over and placed a hand on Kyrianna's shoulder then walked away without saying anything to her. He looked at Myrith and nodded. "There are other ways to protect her," he whispered.

"I want you in the back with your bow, Kyrianna." Myrith glanced at Ashe, but didn't question his meaning.

"I need to be in the fight, Myrith, not apart from it." Kyrianna's voice became a harsh whisper. "Please."

"On your head be it. These creatures are targeting you. You put yourself, and the rest of us at serious risk by being in the front."

"I understand." She drew her swords then nodded toward the back wall as Shadow Seeker moved into the alcove.

They fought their way through three rooms before Myrith finally called for a rest. Kyrianna watched as Ashe slowly lowered himself to the floor and began casting his healing spells on himself.

"You cast a shielding spell before we started this morning, didn't you?" She looked down at Ashe.

"You ignore the directives of the person even you have said is the only one who can lead this group. Someone has to protect you from your own foolishness," Ashe said.

"No one asked you to so. How dare you make me responsible for your welfare in that manner!" She clenched her hands tightly at her sides. "If you are hurt due to your own stupidity, then it is on your head and not mine! I will not be controlled. Not by her, not by you, not by anyone!"

Myrith frowned as Kyrianna turned and stalked toward her. She saw the girl shudder at Ashe's next words.

"Pain is an old friend and death holds no release."

Kyrianna paused and stared at Myrith for a moment then turned away.

"I cannot do this anymore." Myrith barely heard the girl's anguished whisper. She grabbed Kyrianna's hand and pulled her into an embrace.

"When I called on her," Kyrianna contunied. "I opened a part of my soul to her and I now have her whispering in my mind trying to draw me to her. She calls to the chaos that is a part of my nature, something you as a knight dedicated to Order or even the Cleric of Hellavar cannot truly understand." Her voice was harsh and Myrith knew she was fighting for control. She pulled away from Kyrianna slightly and guided her to the floor. This was the most Kyrianna had opened up to her or anyone in this place and she didn't want to risk interrupting her.

"I have had dreams and nightmares since before I called on her; dreams I know are true. She has shown me what my mother was, though I have tried to deny it. She has shown me how my mother destroyed an elven community and the man who was once her friend and mentor. She speaks to me constantly, her litany a whisper in the back of my mind engraving itself in my soul. It is only in battle I am able to ignore the whispering and concentrate on something else. My blades allow me peace from her call that my bow does not. To use my bow properly, I must still my mind in a different type of focus than that of melee combat. When I do that, her voice becomes louder." Kyrianna paused for a second then looked up at Myrith.

"I have agreed to follow you. You have proven yourself in the past and I trust you to lead us through this. I only ask that you let me fight my battle the best way I can.

"While I do not want to be responsible for Ashe's safety in this manner, I will submit to his shielding spell if that is what it takes for you to allow me to take my place at your side."

Myrith glanced at Ashe as he stood up and saw the frown on his face as he shook his head.

"I beg you. Do not regulate me to the back of the group, where I will start to worry about you and the others and where I will have to listen to her," Kyrianna continued.

"I have called on her twice—the second time she struck down two members of our group in pain and agony. My fear is growing that she will soon be able to use me in that manner again. Please don't let that happen. Would a friend and a warrior truly deny another friend the chance to defend themselves against their enemies? When a warrior goes into battle, she does not abandon her friends. Nor would they let a friend go into battle alone. Do not reject my skills or my weapons after I have fought alongside yours all this time. Do not turn your back on our friendship. Please help me to fight her."

Myrith looked down at Kyrianna's arms and saw the marks given her by Frayrith and Dwycia had almost faded completely away. She glanced at Ashe as he walked up to stand next to her; his gaze seemed to search Kyrianna's face for several seconds before it dropped to her wrists also. She took a deep breath. For a moment she felt a flash of anger at Kyrianna and she didn't know why. Myrith took another deep breath to calm herself. *Chaos,* she reminded herself. *It has attacked all of us and is making me see attacks from everyone, even Kyri, who is only asking for help.*

:*Very good my sword,* she heard Mykaylene's voice whisper. :*See past your first reaction to the truth of the matter. Your past clouds your perceptions, but it does not control you, any more than Chaos controls Kyrianna.*

"Kyrianna, I understand and I will let you fight where you will. But, please understand that if you fight in the front, you put all at risk. You are being targeted and there are those who will risk their lives to protect you—just as they would any of the others. To put yourself into needless danger puts all at risk." She released Kyrianna's hands and placed a hand on her cheek calling on her healing gifts to heal the scratch Thynitic had made.

"You are not the only one who suffers? Look at Ashe. He wears his pain as one would wear a coat in the rain. Then look at me and see the pain hidden deep within. I come from a race of humans in a world you know nothing of. Long ago, my people fell under the tyranny of a single vile elf. My people have known oppression, torture, atrocities beyond description, and even death at his hand." Her voice dropped almost to a whisper as she looked at Kyrianna. "This tyrant has but one offspring, the bastard child of one of his many rapes of my people. You see before you the likeness of a human. You need only examine my blood to realize the truth. This is the pain I must live with."

"We all have burdens and pain we must bear. You are correct. I am bringing unnecessary risk to the rest. If you and the others want to go back to your homes, I will ask Thynitic to send you back if I stay."

Kyrianna reached into her pouch and removed the unicorn figure. "I would not risk this falling into Thynitic's control. See she is placed into appropriate hands." She slowly drew the short sword and held the hilt out to Myrith. "The same is true of this weapon. It would be best if it was returned to Tristan Duvall."

Myrith looked at the sword and figurine for a moment then shook her head. "Do you think to so easily remove yourself from this burden? I cannot and will not accept your offer. This path is not of our choosing and I shall not tempt the gods by placing myself in a role for which I was not destined. The burden of the unicorn is yours; the burden of this group is mine. So it has been, so it shall remain." She flinched inside at the harshness in her voice. Kyrianna's offer to trade herself scared her and she had lashed out unthinking.

She felt a hand on her shoulder and glanced up to see Ashe standing there. She saw the unspoken admonishment in his eyes as he lowered himself to sit next to her.

Kyrianna dropped her head. "The unicorn was never a burden; however, if I fall to Thynitic, then she will be lost also." She slowly sheathed the short sword then placed the figure back into its pouch.

Myrith shook her head. "That is not what I meant. If you give up those items, then you reduce the reasons you have to keep fighting. The burden of protecting the unicorn is yours and yours alone—just as it your burden to protect Shadow Seeker. They are your responsibility."

Laraf stepped forward and placed a hand on Kyrianna's shoulder. "You know I'd do anything to stop what you're going through. Even die for you if need be."

"Please don't," Kyrianna whispered. "I don't want that—not from you."

Laraf took a step back and nodded before he continued. "Pain doesn't last forever, Kyri. The only things which last forever are the passions that fire your soul."

"There is no passion or fire left in my soul," Kyrianna said softly. "There is only grief and despair. Grief at the pain I have caused and may yet still cause. Despair at the thought of what may still come if Thynitic wins. I believe we can deal with this mage, Torliana. However, it is I who must deal with the Lady of Chaos, apparently alone, and I doubt I am strong enough." She stood and walked away.

"Hold, Kyrianna," Ashe called. "You are correct; we cannot hope to understand your confusion or despair. She has infused you with too many contradictions. You must show us if you hope for us to understand. You must show us for us to help you defeat them both."

Ashe turned to Myrith. "I still possess enough power to link minds as I did when she was attacked by the nightmare spell; however, I can link only two. Myrith, since you have taken responsibility for this group, I believe you should be the one to listen to her."

Ashe turned back to Kyrianna. "I am a man of my word, the same word that bound me to bring the dragon kin back. It is my word I will not harm you or Myrith." He glanced up. "If she is willing, she can see to that for you as well. Do not fear me, I fought Thynitic's mental twisting for almost two decades; she has not found the crack in my mind and I doubt she will. Myrith has a strong mind as well. Let us see what she has tried to do to you."

Kyrianna frowned then drew a deep breath. "If I myself do not understand well enough to put what is happening into words, how can your spells help you to understand?

"I am willing to let you cast your spells, but only if Myrith agrees as well. You have proven your word is true, but I still do not fully trust you. When you first arrived you told my friends you didn't care if any of us survived or not, yet you used your power to bring me back, and you shield me with your spells at risk to yourself. You had to be reminded of your word by Jerietlan or I believe you would have left Andrinor and Vyroris for dead. These actions do not seem to fit together. You obviously have more knowledge of those we face and yet, you tell us nothing of it. I have said I will allow your spell, though I am not sure it will help. I would ask you though; when it is done that you share with us what you know of the one we will face."

Myrith cleared her throat and looked at the cleric. "Unlike Kyri, I do trust you. This may come as a surprise to you. I trust you because my Lady, Mykaylene, assures me there is still goodness in you—a tiny spark, but a spark that I have seen these past days. So yes, Cleric of Hellavar, I will submit to your spell if it is truly Kyrianna's wish. If by doing this it will bring some level of comfort to her, if there is some benefit to be had, I agree. It is not my wish to invade the thoughts of one I hold so dear, but I am willing for her, and for the good of all."

Ashe nodded as he looked into the faces of the two women. "She must pay for her actions. All I have done has been to achieve that goal. You are correct, the dragon kin were brought back only because the cleric forced my hand. If your price is to go into the darkest places within this patchwork of scars, I will take you there through the link as well. But can a weakened mind withstand the horrors there? Words can hardly describe the havoc and misery wrought."

Ashe motioned for Myrith and Kyrianna to move then knelt on the floor and pulled out several pieces of chalk and began drawing a circle of runes on the floor. "A precaution against her influences. Both of you step inside."

Ashe completed the circle and motioned for them to sit. He faced Myrith as he cast the first spell. "I will be channeling her thoughts to yours and back. Ask of her what you will and what she is willing to answer. This will take substantial effort. I will try not to ask any questions as I don't think I can maintain a conversation between us all."

He turned toward Kyrianna and began the second casting. "As to the use of my spells to shield you, I have protected my brothers and sisters in the temple, paladins and monks of Hellavar with such spells. We are stronger together than apart. Let the shields stay."

The spells completed, Ashe spoke once more. "Show us everything, so we may understand."

"Kyri, what is your greatest fear?" Myrith focused her attention on the girl sitting in front of her.

Kyrianna looked at her, her eyes still glistening with her tears, as she spoke slowly. "As I have said, ever since the day I first called on her, I have had her whispering in my mind. Her litany is now inscribed in my soul and if I am not careful, I hear my own voice repeating the words with her.

"She has told me several times you will reject our friendship. That I am only a tool for you to use and you have never truly cared about me as a friend. I don't want to believe her but I cannot stop her whispering in my mind and soul. And when you lash out thinking everything is a challenge to you, it makes it harder to deny what she says." Kyrianna paused and closed her eyes for a few minutes.

Myrith waited, not wanting to interrupt Kyrianna. But, she knew her friend was right, she had taken every disagreement as a direct challenge.

"Even though I have heard her every day since I called on her, this is not the only place I have heard Thynitic's voice calling me."

The trio found themselves standing in a deep forest, shadows filling the area, soon one of them shifted and images began forming in the depths. Myrith frowned as she watched Kyrianna, dressed in the light leathers of a thief, being escorted into a small room. The human guard, who resembled her friend in appearance slightly, nodded toward the small table in the center of the room then took a position in the back corner, where he could watch both her and the door.

Kyrianna walked around the small desk and pulled out the chair facing the door. She looked at the guard, who had positioned himself in the corner to her right. He ignored the look, and she sat down, crossed her arms on the table and put her head down to wait.

A soft voice began whispering in the stillness of the scene. Kyrianna raised her head and looked around. There was still no one else in the room other than her and the guard. She put her head back down and the voice spoke again—stronger.

"Kyrianna, you don't belong in this place," a woman's voice said. The same voice Thynitic had spoken with the day before. "You are too independent to be tied to the rules of the Thieves Guild or the prejudices of Nydith. You know in your heart you will be sent away from here. Keep in mind, when they reject you, you can call on me. I would welcome you as one of my own."

"Who are you?" Kyrianna mouthed the question, but the others could hear her through the link, just as they were hearing Thynitic.

"You will know when it is time." The voice and the presence attached to it faded.

The scene shifted and changed to show Kyrianna kneeling in front of one of the four statues on a darkened bridge. Her hand touched one of the symbols and she inhaled suddenly as a small vortex of color appeared under her hand. "Thynitic," they heard Kyrianna whisper.

Myrith frowned as the scene shifted again to the altar room with the large symbol of Thynitic on the wall. Just as she had noticed at the time, Kyrianna seemed to be distracted by the symbol. Here as they stood together, she also saw the girl close her eyes and take a deep breath as she seemed to sway on her feet.

The scene shifted and changed to show the group in the basement of the Duvall Estate.

"Tristan," Myrith called from another room off to the side. "Could you and Kyrianna step in here?"

The room Myrith was in was small and held an altar carved from what appeared to be obsidian. Several wooden benches sat in front of the altar and a large tapestry hung on the wall behind it. The background of the wall hanging was a deep black that created an illusion of depth in the cloth. Woven into the blackness was a swirling vortex filled with various colors. None of the colors repeated in any pattern and almost blended together at times.

Kyrianna swayed on her feet and leaned back against the wall. "It is a symbol of Thynitic," she said.

"Thynitic?" Tristan said, looking from Kyrianna to Myrith.

"You don't recognize the symbol or the name?" Myrith stared at the young man. "I knew it looked like the symbols we saw elsewhere that we associate with Thynitic, but she is a goddess from another world. I was wondering if this might belong to a deity from this world."

Tristan only shook his head as he looked at the altar and the tapestry. "I know of none of the gods that use this symbol," he said. "Why would there be an altar to a foreign goddess here? The goblins have their own deities; they would have no reason to serve this Thynitic."

"Perhaps she is trying to extend her power beyond Rhysia," Kyrianna whispered. "She is a primordial goddess. One born from the chaos from which the worlds were created. She is very powerful." She blinked several times as she tried to look away from the tapestry, but it held her attention and she took a slow step toward the altar.

"Kyrianna?" Myrith's voice rose. "Kyrianna! Rangerette!"

Kyrianna's breath was short as she continued toward the altar. Myrith became louder, more insistent, but they could hear another voice over hers. A woman's voice whispering something they couldn't quite understand.

"Get her out of here." Myrith's voice seemed to penetrate the haze Kyrianna was in and her steps paused for a second. Tristan grabbed her arm and she jerked away from him to take another step toward the altar. She was almost close enough to touch it and her hand reached toward the smooth black surface.

"Oh, no you don't," Myrith said as she grabbed Kyrianna's other arm. Together she and Tristan pulled the girl from the room.

Kyrianna gasped for breath and shook her head several times to clear it as the whispering voice finally faded. She jumped at the sound of crashing and splintering coming from the small room.

"Are you okay?" Myrith asked when she exited the shrine.

"Yeah." Kyrianna wrapped her arms around herself and walked away from the woman.

She moved to a corner away from the group. She was shaking and her heart was pounding in her throat. As the scene began to fade they could hear Kyrianna's thoughts. *Why was I so strongly affected by Thynitic's symbol? First, back in the planar temple and now here. It makes no sense. Is there something in Mother's past that would make the goddess want to target me?*

The shadows deepened and the trio found themselves standing once again in the forest as Kyrianna spoke again. "You ask what I fear. I fear losing myself to her chaos. I fear losing your friendship and the friendship of the rest of the group. I fear…" Her voice broke and she closed her eyes as fresh tears began falling.

The shadows shifted again and new images appeared.

Kyrianna was sitting alone in one of the alcoves in one of the many rooms they had fought in recently holding the unicorn figure in one hand, the other resting on Shadow Seeker's head.

"Interesting," Thynitic's voice spoke softly. "The chosen of Frayrith and Dwycia asks one who walks the paths of darkness to protect her from the Lady of Chaos. Why did you not call on either of them to protect you?

"Don't bother trying to answer, because I know the reason; you have been abandoned by them—just as your mother was. Only in your case you have been abandoned by both of the goddesses who called you. They sent you here to face me and left you unprepared."

The image wavered for a moment and Ashe's voice could be heard whispering. "Kindling, was this you?" The image again cleared.

Kyrianna glanced down at Shadow Seeker. "They have granted me and Shadow Seeker a bond."

"You are considered wild kin," Thynitic said then laughed. "That is only a minor trick. You have been given no power. All you have been granted is the ability to communicate with that wolf Frayrith gave you to keep an eye on you. And what good has that done you? None that I have seen.

"And the unicorn? The cleric shows off his own tricks and binds you deeper to his purpose. He told you that you and your group are nothing more than tools to be used and destroyed if necessary. You are only a pawn to him. A way of getting to Torliana.

"Remember, you are only a tool in this game, a pawn of those who have more power than you. Call on your nature goddesses, I doubt they will hear you, and if they do, I doubt they will answer. They brought you here to face me and then abandoned you, just as

Frayrith did your mother."

The scene changed again and they watched as a scroll appeared in Kyrianna's hands and she read it.

"Your mother could have prepared and protected you better, Rangerette. Frayrith specially blessed the unicorn horn sword your mother carries. As long as she carries it, Thynitic cannot touch her. She knew what would be happening to you when you were exiled from your home and yet she did nothing. She sent you out to face a powerful goddess she had insulted, unwarned and ill-prepared. Think on that as you continue to fight your destiny. And, remember this, no matter which path you chose—you will face me and the Lady as well."

The scene shifted again, and the three of them watched as Kyrianna followed a woman with long silver hair through a hallway. As they walked past a dusty, coiled whip hanging on the wall, it began to glow. In the center of the coils was a swirling cloud of color: no discernible shapes or patterns, only a chaotic mixture. The woman with the silver hair hesitated as she glanced at the whip. "Not her. Please not her," she whispered.

The scene changed and Kyrianna's voice echoed her thoughts as she stood next to Myrith after the scroll exploded. "She really did know. That explains Father's hand on my shoulder as he left and the stricken look on his face. It no longer held any of the anger he had been directing at me; instead I remember his eyes filled with a deep sorrow as they looked at me. 'I leave it to you,' he said touching the unicorn horn sword my mother carried. The sword, Torliana now tells me, helped to protect my mother from Thynitic's power and could have protected me.

"Why didn't she warn me?"

The shadows deepened again and Kyrianna's voice could be heard in the darkness. "I am sorry about the other day; I do not fully understand what happened. There is much I can never atone for that I have caused to happen."

The shadows shifted and the scene changed to show Andrinor in his dragon form. However there was something wrong; his appearance was twisted somehow, malevolent. His claws seemed longer as did his teeth. His eyes glowed red as he turned his head to look at Kyrianna. He then glanced back at Falden. "Hurt her," he said.

Kyrianna glanced at the swords in her hands and froze as she looked back up at the silver dragon watching her. Thynitic's voice was woven with Kyrianna's, as the words of the Lady's litany echoed in the room.

As the voice faded, Kyrianna dropped her swords and fell to her knees. "Lady of Chaos, if you are so powerful then prove it," she cried out.

A light delicate laughter echoed in the room as both Andrinor and Falden fell to the ground writhing in apparent agony.

"What have I done?" Kyrianna dropped her head into her hands as she fell to the floor. "By the gods, what have I done?" She began sobbing as she curled up on the floor. For a moment darkness seemed to enfold her in its embrace.

"Welcome, Daughter of Chaos," Thynitic whispered.

The scene froze and Kyrianna's voice spoke in the silence. "What happened to Andrinor and Falden is my fault." She turned and looked at Myrith. "Don't blame Ashe for killing Andrinor after his soul was so twisted by her magic. You are prepared to do the same to prevent Thynitic from claiming me. What makes his actions any different than those you may be forced to take?"

The shadows shifted again. Thynitic's voice was again whispering in Kyrianna's mind. "Kindness should be the only companion to pain and will increase the intensity of suffering and the chaos surrounding them. Do not ignore the sudden whim of compassion; let it always come, but only seldom as to give those who suffer a sense of hope. Hope is consort to chaos and torment is their offspring. Unending torment destroys pain and this in turn destroys the chaos that nurtures us." She paused for a moment. "I dispelled the enchantment to show you I can be merciful and generous to those whom I favor, such as you."

Myrith felt her head snap toward Ashe. He had guessed correctly about Thynitic's reason for showing mercy to Andrinor and Falden.

Another voice began speaking, a young girl's and the scene changed to show Kyrianna in the hedge maze of the Duvall Estate, Melissa Duvall standing in front of her. "This is not the path you wish to follow," the girl said as Kyrianna plunged a dagger into her chest.

Only shadows remained as Kyrianna spoke again. "Every day since I invoked Thynitic's name, I have found myself in that blasted hedge maze on the Duvall Estate, watching as I take the place of Melissa's brother when he killed her. Will I end up betraying you as he betrayed his sister and family? I have already caused pain and death to this group, will I cause more?"

The shadows faded and the trio found themselves on a gray expanse. Kyrianna turned as if to walk away then stopped and turned back.

"Can you understand? Even I do not understand. All I know is Torliana is hunting me for some wrong she believes my mother caused her. A goddess who believes I should belong to her is also seducing me." She paused and took a deep breath.

"When I asked my question, it was Dwycia or Frayrith I expected to appear. As I would have listened to either, I did not call on one specifically. Instead Thynitic appeared. Does that mean the other two have abandoned me as she has said they would or do I have a closer tie to her than those who were my patrons?"

She turned to Myrith and slowly drew her sword and held it flat in front of her parallel to the ground. "My blade is yours," she said. "I only ask that you do not take away from me the little control I have in this situation, let me fight against my enemy. Let me remain at your side in this battle."

Myrith shook her head slowly. "My dearest friend, while your visions are cruel and cold, they are also flawed. I never said I believed I would have to kill you, only that I was willing to do so if it meant saving your soul from her grasp. It is my fervent prayer I need never make that choice. I know I seem cold and harsh at times, I am truly sorry, but such is my way. I had never known real friendship until I met you. I was nothing more than a bar wench to be used and discarded by all.

"I have been accused of arrogance and perhaps that is true, for what I say to you now may seem very arrogant indeed. One thing is clear to me from your visions. The greatest fear of the one who would control you is our friendship. Why else work so hard to break it? Why else work so diligently to set us against each other? Even in your visions she mocks our friendship, calling you Rangerette, a name only I have used. Coincidence?"

"A name you have not used but only rarely in these weeks," Kyrianna whispered. She looked up at Myrith. "If our friendship is so important and dangerous to her, why have you stated there is no place for it on the battlefield? Friendships are always important—in every place and every time. To ignore a friendship is to deny it. Yes, a friend will admonish at times when others will not. But they also offer support and comfort. They seek to help each other. They do not only rely on duty and order to guide them." She paused. "I'm sorry. But it has seemed that way with you pushing us as you have, then almost demanding I do certain things. I understand you must think of all of us and not just one, but it seems you were ignoring our friendship."

Myrith shook her head and continued. "And you also ignored our friendship by refusing to tell me what was happening as you promised at one time to do. Then when Ashe resurrected you, you reacted in fear and refused to tell me what was wrong. Your actions caused me to question your intentions and whether I could still trust you as I had."

Kyrianna dropped her head. "Chaos has been affecting all of us since we got to this place."

Ashe looked at the ground for a moment and his voice was only a whisper. "Kindling, what did she say to you?"

"I ask again if it was a coincidence." Myrith reached out and lifted Kyrianna's head. "I think not. As one who has been called to serve her God I am loath to suggest what I now propose. Since you know not what gods have forsaken you, since you know not what paths to take, do not look for solace or guidance there. Instead turn to those here by your side, those who have fought, suffered and even known death in our mutual undertakings.

"I once said I would kill you rather than see you succumb to Thynitic. I said these words because I felt such would be your wish. I ask you now, what would you have me do if she truly wins you over?"

Kyrianna stood there, her sword still held out. She swallowed as she glanced up at Myrith. "I asked you when I finally agreed to call on Thynitic to be quick and that request stands. I do understand why you may have to strike. I do not look forward to that day, but I fear it will come. Thynitic has told us we will not be able to defeat Torliana unless I accept her. I hope that is only another of her lies."

Kyrianna looked down at her sword in her hands then back up at Myrith.

"You say nothing of the oath I have offered you."

Myrith placed a hand on the sword. "I ask not for your sword, but for your friendship. The time will come when our swords shall together vanquish the evil that fills this place and healing may at last begin."

Kyrianna sheathed her sword and finally smiled. "My friendship will always be yours," she said.

"Ashe, I do not require that you show us anything as payment for this," Kyrianna said as she turned toward the cleric. "I only ask that you share what information you have. Will you do so?"

"I will show you what was, what came to pass and my path here."

~ * ~

The grayness filled with swirling images that cleared into a dark jumble of motion. A boy screamed. "Father! Mother!" A fist was seen in the darkness as the boy fell and a woman screamed.

The boy awakened in a cart with several other children, his hands and feet bound. He looked under the driver's seat to see the lights of a city and his head dropped. An armored figure stopped the cart and unsheathed a flaming two-handed sword. A voice spoke in a rumbling, crackling language and the sword was sheathed in blue fire as the scene faded.

The boy was awakened by two voices, yet only the armored warrior appeared to be present. "The church is no place for one so young, Krella," one of the voices said.

"What do you know about it? You are a hunk of metal not flesh and blood. He has no one." The warrior turned toward the boy. "He will do just fine, I will see to him."

The mists swirled and the scene changed. The boy now appeared to be about ten years older and was standing before an older priest who held his hand out offering the boy a flame, which he took. Behind the boy, a female warrior stood smiling.

The mists swirled again. The boy was now a young man walking through great ornate hallways. Whispers followed him as he passed other robed figures.

"The priest who studies spellcraft within the Academy of Gormanghast."

"It is said he is the only priest to petition and succeed at the tests."

"Why?"

"It is said he seeks to master his power and bring the Order of Hellavar everywhere it is not."

The mists swirled again. Sheets of flame danced before the priest as blades pierced the wall without finding their target. However, the priest's morningstar struck without error through the flames.

"That is enough," a voice called. "Drop the spells."

The flames vanished.

A man clad in plate armor addressed the priest. "Excellent. A Tormasian battle mage could have hoped to do no better. Your time here at Tormasus is done. Inform your Keeper I find you worthy."

The mists swirled again. The priest now ventured forth on horseback, the landscape and his companions ever changing as he traveled, with one exception. The female warrior who rescued the boy remained a common image traveling with him.

The mists swirled again. The priest stood on a cliff's edge next to a Halfling clad in hides. Several large lizard-like beasts could be seen in the land below. He and his companion looked out over an ocean where many ships were caught in a storm. A storm battered the ships as huge waves broke their hulls. He turned to the Halfling and smiled. "Live free," he said.

The mists swirled again. The priest stood within an arena with many cheering people. To the side a man in robes wielding a sword had collapsed on the ground. Another man in ornate armor spoke from the ruler's place of honor. "Well fought. We will submit to the arbitration. A man of words and deeds you are. Let us see if your wisdom can heal the Confederation of Rejki."

The mists swirled again. The cleric fought alongside the female warrior again, behind them was another woman, bound by chains.

The woman pressed her advantage forcing her opponent to the ground.

"Mercy," the man said.

Her blade dropped just an inch as she nodded then a dagger was plunged into her side.

"No!" the cleric summoned a torrent of fire to dispatch the woman's attacker, but the blade had done its work. He stared at the blade, the mark of Leikor clearly visible on the hilt.

The mists swirled again. The woman's body had been placed on a table, her sword in her hands. The woman who had been in chains stood next to a taller, older human male clad in the finery of a noble. "We will honor her always," he said. "This I swear to you. She will always be honored by House Vernas."

The mists swirled again. The cleric entered the courtyard of a temple with mountaintops close by. "We honor your arrival, Keeper," a woman in the robes of a monk said, bowing her head to the cleric.

The cleric glanced at the assembled acolytes and priests and his gaze appeared to lock for a moment on a tall elven woman with midnight-black hair and eyes. "An elf who wishes to be a Flame Dancer," the woman said. "Let us hope she can find the inner flame despite her heritage."

The cleric nodded once. "Yes, let us give her hope."

The mists swirled again. The cleric walked down a corridor and called to a figure ahead of him. "Torliana, I would speak to you."

The elven woman with the black hair turned toward him and smiled. "Keeper." She bowed her head respectfully to the cleric, now a couple of years older.

"It has come to my attention that Mistress Rynalia believes you are ready for advancement to the next rank along the path. Do you agree with her assessment of your skills?" The Keeper stood quietly, his deep brown eyes watching her closely.

"I am honored Mistress Rynalia is pleased with my progress and training."

"As you should be. Praise from her is hard-earned but always well deserved."

She looked up for a brief moment then lowered her eyes once again.

"Think carefully on your decision. The next step along the path requires more than skill. It requires a higher level of dedication to the ideals and philosophy of Lord Hellavar. I will never dispute that your skills and knowledge qualify you for the rank of Flame Dancer. However, I am not sure your heart and soul are ready for what is required."

The elf's head snapped up. "I am ready for the trial," she said, her head held high as she looked at the priest.

The cleric nodded once. "Very well. We will prepare for the testing." He gave her another appraising look then turned and headed back to his office.

The mists swirled again. The cleric was in his chambers dressed in his ceremonial robes. He glanced over at a wall littered with rites of judgment issued by several city-states, but at the center was a portrait of a little boy standing beside the female warrior from days past. "How far we have come," he said softly.

He picked up and regarded a parchment with a broken seal on

it. The door opened and he turned to see the female monk who greeted him on his arrival standing there.

"Keeper, the test is almost ready, but there is an issue some of the villagers have asked for your judgment on."

He placed the parchment on his desk and walked past her. "They are in the main chamber, Rynalia?"

"Yes, Keeper."

He moved quickly through the halls, his manner cold and unflinching. He entered a chamber that had a fire pit some ten feet across. "You have come at an inopportune time, please state the problem."

A lady who stood next to a boy of approximately seven years of age spoke. "The boy's parents died on the road between here and Irrmar, Keeper. I am his aunt and I offer him a place to stay."

Another woman, who stood next to her husband, spoke. "She has no husband; she just wants a slave for her fields. We offer him a good home without harshness."

The Keeper turned to the small boy. "It would appear you are blessed with two homes, young man."

The first woman spoke again. "Ask him who he wishes to stay with, Keeper."

The Keeper turned. "Why? So he can be forced to choose between two homes? If that really mattered, why did you come to me?"

The woman stepped back.

The cleric regarded the gathered people. "It is the custom for the closest relatives to care for those orphaned and that is how it shall be." He slammed his staff like a gavel to the floor. "However, since these people have voiced concern for the boy, I shall come to your house one year from this day. I shall judge your treatment of the boy and if I find it harsh, so shall I be."

The woman's face grew pale as the Keeper looked at her. "There is no fear for the just," he said. "Do you wish to say something, my Lady?"

The woman cleared her throat. "I release the boy to your judgment, Keeper."

"Very well. The boy shall stay with these people who also offer him a home. However, I tell you the same. I shall bear witness to your treatment of the boy."

The husband bowed his head. "We will wait for that day, Keeper."

The Keeper turned toward the boy and smiled before he left the chamber followed by the monk.

As they walked through the hallways, Rynalia looked at him. "Keeper, you have been with the church some thirty-five years. Was there ever anything else?"

His steps did not change as he spoke. "There is the Order, nothing more."

Rynalia only shook her head.

The mists swirled again. "Torliana," the Keeper called.

The elf paused as the Keeper placed his hand on her shoulder outside the ritual chamber.

"Keeper."

The Keeper hesitated as he looked at her. "I wanted to wish you success this day," he finally said. He lifted her hand and kissed it gently. "May Hellavar's Flames strengthen and renew your spirit." He reached over and opened the door to the ritual chamber.

Torliana took a deep breath as the heat flowed out of the room and washed over them. The chamber was filled with fire; only a narrow path wove its way through the dancing flames; a path that changed as the flames moved in apparently chaotic patterns.

In addition to the Keeper and Rynalia there were three other robed figures in the room.

"One comes to dance with the flames, to show her dedication to Lord Hellavar; to progress along the sacred path and to divest herself of any chaos that may be a part of her," Rynalia said.

"Let the Dancer step forward," the other three said.

Torliana stepped into the center of the room as the flames died down. "Chaotic forces seek to control the world by destroying Order," she said. "But we know there is no true Chaos. Order binds all things, even those that appear to be in Chaos. There is Order, there is pattern and there is regulation in all things." The flames sprang back up surrounding her.

"Let the Dancer find the pattern in the Chaos, proving Order controls all things and that there is no true Chaos," one of the robed figures said.

"She must not let the Chaos that abides in all living things control her. She must find the Order to the pattern and herself," another of the three said.

"Let the dance begin," the last one said.

Torliana took another deep breath as the flames moved

around her. She appeared to be studying the dancing flames as she allowed her body to move and sway in the same patterns.

"I open myself to the one who purifies with fire," she whispered.

For several heartbeats, she and the flames moved as one. Then she stumbled, missing her step and falling forward into the heart of the fires.

"The Dancer has failed," the Keeper said as the fires vanished. "The testing is concluded." He frowned at Torliana then turned his back on her and left the chamber.

The mists swirled again. "Keeper, I seek your wisdom," Torliana said, approaching the cleric as he stood watching the sunset.

"Whatever I can offer is yours," he said without looking at her.

"I am bothered by something that happened during the testing," she said softly.

"I warned you might not be ready." The coldness was back in his voice.

"I understand that." She cut the statement short. "You have expressed dissatisfaction with my dedication for the past year. If I was such a disappointment to you, why did you assign yourself to be my mentor?" Her anger was evident in her clenched fists. "Perhaps you did not notice, but I did manage to control the flames for a moment."

The Keeper turned to look at her. "And that is my point. You sought to impose your own control; your own idea of Order on the Sacred Flame instead of finding and following the pattern already there. We do not establish the pattern; we only accept and let it control us. Some call it the rule of law. That is the path you must walk if you wish to remain here. Torliana, I do not see you progressing any further along this path, but you are still a Child of the Flame and will always remain so. Good night to you. May the Sacred Flame warm and strengthen you." He turned and walked back into the temple.

"And you," she said to his back.

The mists swirled again and Ashe spoke from the darkness. "The demons came by the dozens and many members of the order and brotherhood succumbed to the Chaos. They turned on each other. The seniors and I were forced to fight a host of chaos demons; one by one they fell, as I was trapped behind a wall of force, unable to call on the power of Hellavar or raise even a simple weapon. Then she came."

The image cleared. The Keeper raised his head as Torliana entered the room. A host of demons lay at his feet, as did four other bodies, including that of Rynalia. "What have you done?" He raised the rod he was holding.

Torliana held out her hand and the rod vanished in a flash of flame, followed by the cleric's shield. "I have only done what you expected me to do, Keeper. I have opened myself to the Chaos of my own nature. And now, it is time for you to know the true power of Chaos." She waved her hand and smiled as a portal opened behind the cleric. Before he could move away, several powerful arms grabbed him and pulled him back through the portal, into the Abyss.

The mists swirled again. The cleric was now chained to a pillar of salt; runes surrounded his feet and the chains that bound him glowed. A powerfully built demon, as tall as a giant, smiled at him. "My Lady has something special for you, Priest." A blood-red amulet dropped from his hand and dangled from his fingers. "An amulet of soul binding. Few have been made but she wanted one just for you. Your torment will be never ending," the demon said, then laughed.

Ashe's voice spoke again. "It was then they began. All the pain, depravity and misery they could possibly inflict on the living they did to me. I was their toy and they could do things to me they could not to others. You see it is a practiced art to torture someone, but not have him or her die and escape to peace. There was no rest for me. Time and again they took me to beyond the pain to death but the amulet would not let me leave for Hellavar's realm of fire. I was trapped in eternal torment. Do you know what it feels like to have your body melted away by acid? To have your face torn off by some creature? To feel your organs devoured by rats while you still breathe? On some occasions they would decapitate me and show me my corpse before my spirit retreated to the amulet.

"Torliana was there at times also. Sometimes to be tortured as a sign of her subservience to Thynitic and other times to take pride in my downfall."

The mists swirled again as the cleric continued speaking. "Time was meaningless to me. I rotted for months and years, but somehow my mind survived."

Torliana appeared in the mists. "Amazing, Keeper, there is still a spark of a man left. Most go mad in days or weeks. Why does Hellavar grant you the strength to keep your mind but allows us to take our pleasures with your body? Why does he love or hate you so much?" The image faded.

"I still don't know the answer to that question," Ashe said softly.

An image appeared of a black vaporous figure. "Resare," Ashe said. "I begged him many times to sunder my existence. He is the master of death. He can destroy souls. Why did he not release me from my torment? I was as much an abomination as any fell undead. Why did the gods let me suffer? Do you know?" The image faded.

The mists continued to swirl for a moment as another image formed of Ashe being carried by a tall winged humanoid. The cleric stretched out his hand to point at an altar where the amulet was lying.

"It was luck a group of celestials had journeyed to her layer to save one of their own. They saw my pitiful condition and took me back to their realm," Ashe said as the image faded.

"It was no favor. It is only a reprieve. When I die they can summon me back to that damned place where they will most likely revel in my anguish once more.

"I toiled for years in the great Celestial library. I researched that vile goddess. The master of the place was not pleased with my obsession."

Another image appeared. A tall slender blue-robed winged humanoid stood above the patchwork of scars that was Ashe. An unheard exchange showed Ashe yelling at the celestial being. As the image faded, Ashe returned to his reading.

The mists swirled and Ashe spoke again. "I was there for twenty years, before I found what I was looking for. I found the place where Thynitic had been first worshipped. I also found that one of her chosen had rejected her. That is correct, Kyri, she can be rejected and that person was your mother."

An image of Ashe and an elven woman appeared. The elf had long silver hair and appeared to be with child as she handed him a small unicorn horn. His face was emotionless as he summoned a portal to another plane and stepped through.

The mists swirled again. "It was my own folly that I tried to come here, to this plane, at that time. Chaos twisted my magic and I was sent to the Astral Plane through a temporal rift. I am unsure of when this was. All I know is I have been chasing her for years."

Another image of Ashe appeared with him walking through a marshy maze of hedges. He stopped for a moment and removed a potion from his backpack and drank the foul-looking liquid. He discarded the vial as the atrophic muscles of his arms regained tone and his hair turned darker. "I have been chasing her now longer than most live and soon I will lose to time, but even that cannot grant me safe haven from that foul amulet."

The mists surrounded them for a moment. "I await your questions."

~ * ~

The mists faded away leaving the trio once again in a gray expanse. Myrith took a deep breath before she finally spoke. "It would seem you and Torliana share history, and training. If such is the case, I ask you, as I have placed my trust in you, will you place yours in me? Since you come from similar backgrounds, and similar training, I ask you a question." She paused then continued. "How could we defeat—you?

"I realize her powers have grown, and she has gained skills outside her training, but I know this also—training and discipline run deep. She will not easily break from the patterns, the conduct instilled in her. Perhaps by gaining insight into the ways of your order, I can gain insight into her defeat."

Ashe looked at Myrith and sighed. "I believe her time with Thynitic would have washed away any ties to her specific training. When she entered the room that day she said it herself. She embraced Chaos and in doing so, she rejected Hellavar. Her religion now is Chaos and she has been in its depths for decades where she was only in the temple for four years. The simple Order of our teachings holds no meaning anymore, but I doubt she has lost the skills learned from the Brotherhood. She is now a powerful sorceress and a cleric. How well she has married those two crafts, I do not know. Her actions at times are erratic and driven by emotion, but she has crafted this place and that takes discipline. The training she received in the temple will mean she can evade lightning bolts and twist out of many fire and other area-related spells. The mage should be made aware not to waste his time with any of those.

"I cannot give you more answers than that on how to fight her specifically. She has been watching, of that I am sure. She cannot defend against every tactic. We must force her to spend her energies on additional defenses that have no real value. We must force her to react to us."

Kyrianna stood there staring at Ashe then blinked slowly. "You visited Kilenter and met my mother only a few days before I was born. I remember she always seemed to have other things on her mind during the day of my birth celebrations. Even though she never neglected the celebration, our guests, or me, there was still something in her eyes, something far away—something she feared when she would look at me. You said you spent years researching the Lady of Chaos. What can you tell me about my mother and Thynitic?"

Mists swirled around them again and revealed Ashe standing in a clearing when they faded.

"Well met on the journey," a woman's voice called out politely.

Ashe's head jerked up as if he was surprised to see her there. He only nodded once toward the elf then turned his attention back to the ground.

"This area is sacred to many in this region. I ask what you are doing here." The elf woman slid from the saddle and stood watching him.

This time Ashe looked at her closely, his eyes finally resting on the unicorn horn sword she carried—still in its scabbard. "I come seeking the one responsible for this."

The elf tightened her grip on her sword and she stared at him. "Why?"

"You are the one." He stepped toward her.

The elf took a step back and drew the sword.

"Stay your weapon, foolish elf. I would not harm you or the child you carry. I seek the one responsible for this—you were only a pawn and not her. She has called another to her service as you were called and I seek to destroy them both. This place called me from my own realm. The power of Chaos is strong here."

"That is because the Lady of Chaos herself appeared in the spot where you are standing after I renounced her. She threatened me and my children; I defend this place to prevent her return."

"Yet, you are marked with the power of another." He pointed to the silver unicorn on the elf's right wrist.

"The Lady of the Forests, Frayrith. She accepted me back as one of her own after I rejected the Lady of Chaos."

"She has bound you," he paused for a moment, "in some way to her service, hasn't she?"

The elf stared at Ashe. "Yes, I and those who follow me are bound to Her service and to destroying the Lady of Chaos if we are called."

"Then we are allies of a sort. For I am dedicated to destroying the one she has chosen as her new agent of Chaos. Perhaps I was brought here so you could aid me."

"Perhaps. However, I cannot offer you my sword at this time. I will not leave my home unless told to do so directly by Frayrith. However, I can give you an item that may aid you." She stepped back and removed a small unicorn horn from her saddlebags. "This is the horn of the unicorn filly killed that day by the Chaos storm. Just as my own sword helps to shield me from the power of the Lady of Chaos, this may also help to shield you. It is the only aid I can offer at this time."

Ashe slowly turned the horn in his hands several times then smiled. "This will be a powerful artifact in the fight against the Lady of Chaos. I thank you for your gift." With a whispered word, the clearing and the woman vanished.

Kyrianna reached into her pouch and removed the unicorn figure Ashe had given her and cradled it in her hand. "You told me the horn did not come from a unicorn you had killed, yet you did not tell me where it came from. This was carved from the horn my mother gave you, was it not?"

"It was," Ashe said. "You also asked about Thynitic."

He paused for several minutes, as if gathering his thoughts. "She is ancient. She predates history. She is the goddess best described as elemental Chaos and what is wrought from interfering with Order. She is not an ascended being. As long as Chaos exists, so does she. She wears the guises of many in all of the pantheons, but she calls Kyri's world home. I don't know why. As she is not ascended, technically she has no one world she originated from, but maybe there is a particular darkness there that makes her thrive. It is only on that world she wears her true identity.

"On Shokar she has infused herself like no other. The pantheon of Shokar is made up of three primal groups: the nature gods led by Kaleden; Thedrin and his court; finally the Bloody Triad led by Lareang. It is false! The books of the library made this known to me. Ballan is a daughter of Thynitic who was ascended as the goddess of dark magic on Shokar. However, she has become an incarnation of the Lady of Chaos, and she has done something truly diabolical. She used her chosen, Coressa." Ashe looked at Myrith closely. "Yes, I said Coressa, the ascended Goddess of Destruction to add another aspect to her worship. In fact there was no ascension; she would not share that power with any. As Coressa ascended, she took her body and summoned her power to place an avatar instead. Her minion, her mirror self is Coressa." He looked up at Myrith. "Know you not what this means? Coressa did not beget Lareang on Shokar, Thynitic did, but do you think she would share her power? No! The bitch created another avatar to lord over her realm of pain and tyranny."

He paused again. "Myrith, Thynitic is not one goddess on Shokar. She is three. The three most hated goddesses are one. Her religions are in fact one. What will become of Shokar if they truly unite as one temple?"

He turned to Kyrianna. "She is the goddess of chaos, retribution, pain and mercy. She will give even her high priestesses great suffering on nothing more than a whim. She will give her greatest enemy free passage simply because of a passing thought. She is madness without structure. Can you imagine serving such a being?" He stopped for a moment. "What would your mind be like? Twisted so your truest friends become your plotting adversaries." Ashe let his voice trail off and seemed lost in thought for several minutes before he continued.

"She seeks power, but it confounds her; for to harness her power, she must first overcome herself and her very nature. That is her true weakness; her very nature."

The mists swirled in front of them showing a castle from within and without. A castle with mutable walls and rooms that seemed to randomly disappear and reappear in different places.

"She makes her home on the sixty-third layer of the Abyss, but she can also be found on Limbo as well. It is this layer where she tortured me. The layer is in a constantly shifting state. Her castle is stable compared to the plane itself, but even in it, the hallways and doors move. The chambers can disappear to various planes and subject her *guests* to unique tortures. It is torment unbounded. It is Chaos unleashed."

Ashe focused his attention on Myrith for a moment. "I am sorry, you follow a goddess of my world and I forget you do not have the religious training a Warrior of Mykaylene would have received in her temples, and do not know of the goddesses I have named. On Shokar, my world, the Bloody Triad and the Court of

Thedrin, of which Mykaylene is a member, are aligned against one another and are generally of equal status, but the temples have different strengths and weaknesses.

"The Temples of Ballan, the Goddess of Magic in all its evil aspects, such as animating and perverting nature or producing lycanthropes, have many mages allied with them. All mages give Ballan at least passing respect, lest some cleric find out and seek to have them killed.

"The Temples of Coressa, Goddess of Destruction, have powerful clerics and armies in their own right. However, they have little direction.

"The Temples of Lareang are smaller, but are growing. And the Goddess of Tyranny and Pain can unite and control her forces effectively. "Under one church, you have tyranny to command, destruction to fill your ranks and dark magic to support them. All under *one* church, not an alliance—*one.* This would mean their combined temples could annihilate the others unless something is done here." Ashe paused and drew a deep breath. "In short, win here or destruction wages on Shokar, for that is where Torliana will strike.

"Kyri, if you give in to her thoughts, and few can fight that madness, do not blame Myrith. It is not a sentence she wishes to pass, but a mercy she wishes to give to your soul and mind."

Kyrianna glanced from Ashe to Myrith and nodded. "I understand. All I ask is if that day does come, that you be quick and see these go to those who are worthy." She held out the unicorn figure and placed her free hand on the silver sword. "As for Shadow Seeker, I hope Frayrith will protect him and call him back to her."

Kyrianna turned back to Ashe. "Myrith has asked about Torliana's possible weaknesses and you have answered that you do not believe the training she received in the temple would have any more bearing with the time that has passed. What else can you show us about her?"

"She tried," he said. "She tried very hard to calm her heritage."

Images appeared of Torliana practicing with the other Kindling.

"She studied hard and her meditations were long but she could not find her own steady centered flame in her soul."

The images changed to show the elf meditating alone in a small room with the sun rising and setting and rising again.

"She was troubled, I know not by what, but she seemed distracted at times. One evening I even found her alone performing an elven festival dance."

An image of Torliana in an almost translucent gown appeared as she glided across the grass and flowers of a small clearing. Her body seemed to react to some imagined music, and also to the crackling of the fire in the center of the clearing. She smiled then stopped in shock.

The Keeper stood before her regarding her. He was looking straight into her eyes.

"It was strange; she seemed at peace at that moment," Ashe said.

The Keeper lowered his eyes and turned away.

"It is alright, Keeper," Torliana said. "I am clothed. The dress is said to be made of moonbeams."

"And little else I may add," he said.

She moved to pick up her robes and the clearing went dark. "There is no need for that," he said. "My spell will provide well enough for the moment."

"I await your judgment, Keeper," Torliana said.

"Judgment? What am I to judge?"

"I have left the temple to participate in a function not sanctioned."

"You did not have Rynalia's permission then?"

"No, Keeper."

"Then she shall judge you, not I. You have offered no affront to Lord Hellavar or myself. You made a fire so you could honor him with being able to watch. There is no sin here."

The Keeper paused for a moment. "Now, I do recall the Kindling of the Brotherhood have whispered Rynalia keeps a brush with a single bristle that is used for cleaning the mediation chambers for just such a disobedience."

The elf laughed for a brief moment but stopped when the Keeper did not join her.

"I do not jest, Kindling. That is what they say." His voice held no humor.

A raindrop fell between them and Torliana looked up. The sky was full of clouds. She frowned as she looked back in the direction of the Keeper's voice.

"Continue your dance, child of flame." He chanted for a moment and waved the clouds away.

"Keeper, does not the Canon of Order forbid interference?" She almost choked on the last words.

"Yes, but interference in moderation does not harm as long as balance is preserved. The rains will come in an hour and when they do, it will be with some force to counter my little intrusion in nature's plan. Has Rynalia taught you to step between the raindrops yet?"

"No, she has not. So you say I should continue and then be on my way back to the temple?"

"Yes, and you shall submit to her punishment. Do I have your word, Kindling?"

"Yes, Keeper."

He turned and began to walk away.

"Do you wish to stay, Keeper?"

He stopped and turned. "I respect your race's ceremonies, even though they stem from a sense of anarchy and disdain of true order. However, I prefer to see the Flame Dancers in their true glory. I would prefer to see one dancer show me her strength and brilliance as she frees herself of her heritage and joins in His divine plan. When you are ready, I will witness your beauty and dedication, Torliana. But for this night, enjoy yourself; I am sure Rynalia will make the price for it quite high."

The scene changed and Torliana sprinted across the temple grounds. She ran through the doors just as the rain began to lick at her heels. The elf gasped for air as the Keeper and Rynalia approached from behind her. With care she removed her pack.

"It would appear this Kindling is not ready for the fire," Rynalia said. "I believe you can dry out in the meditation chambers." She grabbed the backpack and threw it into the courtyard as the rain came in torrents.

Torliana opened her mouth, but slowly shut it as the Keeper looked at her. She nodded silently to the Keeper as she followed Rynalia to the chambers.

As the two monks left, the cleric retrieved the backpack from the muck. He walked toward the monastery's chambers. "How hard it is for some to let go," he said as the image faded.

"Was there anything else?" Ashe asked.

Kyrianna stared at Ashe then frowned and shook her head. "You fool. For one so wise and who had enough knowledge of the world around him he was asked to mediate between nations as you have shown us, you are incredibly stupid." She paused for a moment.

"Kyri!" Myrith grabbed her shoulder.

"Let me go." Kyrianna jerked away from her.

"I do not understand," Ashe said, looking at Kyrianna. "I gave her proper guidance. I treated her properly and even showed her more latitude than most."

Kyrianna took a breath. "Granted this is not my world, however, the movements of the dance you showed us are the same as the dance the twilight elves perform to welcome the coming of spring and the rebirth of life in the forests. It is a dance of fertility and love. For her to ask you to stay and watch was more than an invitation to see her dance. She was offering you a part of herself."

"The elves of Shokar are reclusive and I have not ventured within their woods. I believed she was looking for acceptance and approval."

"Do I have to hit you over the head, Ashe? The woman was in love with you."

Kyrianna waited several minutes before she continued.

"I heard you whisper something while we were watching my visions that came back to me just now. You asked; 'Kindling, what did she say to you?' I would guess she told Torliana you would reject her. She told me my family would do that and I was exiled from my home. She told me Myrith was not truly my friend and would also reject me. We have dismissed that lie between ourselves today and it will not be able to affect me any longer. In this we are stronger. What happened to Torliana that caused her to accept the goddess? Look at what you have already shown us for your answer, Keeper."

The mists again swirled around them and the scene of Torliana and the Keeper on the parapets of the temple watching the sunset repeated itself.

The Keeper turned to look at Torliana. "And that is my point. You sought to impose your own control; your own idea of order on the Sacred Flame instead of finding and following the pattern already there. We do not establish the pattern; we only accept and let it control us. Some call it the rule of law. That is the path you must walk if you are to remain here, Torliana. I do not see you progressing any further along this path, but you are still a Child of the Flame and will always remain so. Good night to you. May the Sacred Flame warm and strengthen you." He turned and walked back into the temple.

The mists faded and Kyrianna only stared at Ashe. "*If you wish to remain here*. That is what you said to her."

The mists swirled again. Torliana stood before the Keeper, amid the carnage in his office. "I have only done what you expected me to do, Keeper. I have opened myself to the chaos of my own nature."

"In her mind you rejected her and she probably expected to be ordered out of the temple for her failure with your statement of, 'If you wish to remain here,'" Kyrianna said.

"Why would she have expected that? The temple rules were quite specific in this. She could not be exiled from the order based on her failure."

"I do not mean to hurt you with my words. But in your hatred, you have missed the fire burning in her soul and the spark in yours as well. If you do not believe the spark was there, why would you rescue her backpack and dress when she had violated the rules of the temple to dance in the moonlight to welcome the spring?"

Kyrianna turned toward Myrith. "I believe we all have much to think on this night. I thank you for listening to me and thereby helping me to see past her lies so we can fight together more effectively. While I prefer to stand next to you in battle, I will stay where you feel I am most effective."

She turned back to Ashe. "Ashe, you risk much with your shielding spell. You have told us the amulet still exists and if you fall your soul will again be trapped in it. Take care in using it, as I do not want to see you lost to her torments again. I have one other question for you, why would Torliana call you Brular? You have told us even your name was stripped from you; could that have been your name before she tried to destroy you?"

Ashe turned away. "I cannot recall if it is or is not. She has addressed me twice by it since I have been here, but is it some ruse. I cannot be sure. Lies within lies within lies with just enough truth to make some believe." He turned back to face her. "I just don't know."

The spell faded and the three of them found themselves back in the room with the others. Myrith took the time to tell the rest about what they saw in the link. Filling them in on the things Thynitic had been whispering in Kyrianna's ear and about Ashe's past and what they learned about Torliana. The only thing she left out was Kyrianna's guess about Torliana being in love with the cleric.

As she finished recounting the images and discussions they

shared while linked mind to mind, Myrith noticed Kyrianna was sitting with the rest of the group and not by herself. *Perhaps this was a good thing after all*, she thought.

"I recall Resare calling you Brular in one of my visions," Laraf said as he stared at Ashe. "Your body kept mutilating before my eyes then returning to its true form. There's more going on here with you than you're letting on, isn't there?"

He continued to study Ashe for a moment. He seemed to be lost in thought as if he was trying to recall some obscure memory. "It-it can't be." His face grew pale and his eyes widened as he stared at Ashe. "You…you'd have to be almost one hundred years old, but that can't be." Laraf paused for a moment as he glanced around at the others, before his gaze finally returned to Ashe. "There's an old story I researched while I was under the tutelage of my mentor, it says a High Cleric of Hellavar—a judge as he was called—tried, convicted and punished a slaver fleet near the isles of Jahli. He saved the entire island of Halflings and sank the fleet. It's said he told their leader two words before the first of the ships started to sink. Live…" Laraf paused, his eyes locked with Ashe's as he waited.

"Free," Ashe said with no emotion.

Ashe seemed to be lost in thought for a moment before he spoke again. "An eternity ago, I traveled the length and breadth of eastern Shokar as a wandering judge sanctioned by many of the city-states; Irrmar, Gormanghast and Tormasus were the most noteworthy, but there were other places where law could never reign. Rejki and Saljora were controlled by greed and avarice.

"One day, my companions and I freed some slaves. They were just small Halfling children who could barely speak. The language they spoke was more grunts and animal noises than a true vocabulary. Krella…" His voice trailed off and he turned away from the group. "She asked me to speak with them. Once it was apparent their minds could not make adequate sentences, she asked me to look into their memories." He turned back and seemed to study Kyrianna and Myrith for a moment.

"The scene was sad. The children had been taken from an island village in the Southern Sea near Jahli. The Halflings, though capable fighters given their savage nature, were no match for the slavers who raided and took their prisoners for sale in Rejki."

Ashe turned to face the entire group. "Slavery is legal in that city and because of the Confederation of Rejki, the owning of slaves purchased there is legal in the signature city-states as well. I would have sent that blight of corruption to the bottom of the sea if Hellavar had granted me the power." He bowed his head. "But things are never that simple."

He was silent for a long while. "From the memories of the children, I was able to discern a general location of the island, so my companions and I set sail. The captain informed us it was referred to as the Isle of Justula and that great beasts; larger than any we had ever seen awaited us. He was quite correct. There are reptiles there as big as dragons." He looked at Andrinor and Vyroris. "Some, even bigger."

He turned toward the tiny rogue. "The Halflings though seemed to have adapted quite well and had placed their villages in places the larger predators could not reach. They had also developed their own totem magic, which manifests from arcane tattoos. Quite unique actually."

He turned away again, but continued to speak. "We returned the children, but were stunned to find these raids were quite regular. My companions visited with one of the chiefs and he informed us slavery among the tribes was common but ritualistic. For the most part, mock battles would be fought between tribes and prisoners both male and female would be taken, but this was more a farce than any real battle and 'prisoners' many times were willing young people who had courted and wished to change tribes. One tribe had the ill-conceived notion of selling some of its willing and adventurous young people to a 'tribe' aboard a ship bound for Rejki. This brought the attention of the real slavers to Justula. The attacks had been persisting for almost a year.

"The tribes had tried to repel the attacks, but they simply did not have the resources. If they abandoned their villages, they would be at the mercy of the 'thunder' lizards of the island. We convinced them to have all of the chiefs gather and sign a treaty that abolished slavery and its practice on the island. They then granted me rights of judgment concerning all established Justulan laws." Ashe laughed lightly as he turned back to the group. "They could not even spell. My name was written as 'Brular Aglis'."

He looked at Laraf. "Thank you. It appears they forgot that little misspelling in the twisting and purging of my memories. It would appear Brular is my first name and Krella Eglis, Paladin of the Order of the Purifying Flame and my adopted mother, provided me with my last. 'Brular Eglis.' It has been a long time since I could remember that name, however I digress." He turned away again.

"We delivered a copy of the treaty and the rite. The slavers were not impressed. I made it clear punishment for any ship engaged in the slave trade that approached within two miles of the isle would be destruction of the ship and the consignment of the crew to the sea. Several powerful water elementals were entrusted with defending against ships if a warning drum sounded. As the ships approached, I turned the sky dark and churned the sea and sky into a raging storm."

He turned to look at Myrith. "My Tormasian tutor on spell tactics once said, 'In battle, those who hold their ground will prevail. Deny them their ground.'"

Ashe looked at the ground again. "The sea prevented their escape and the water elementals shattered their hulls. The hapless crews were forced into the sea. Some came to the island and were eaten by the lizards; the villagers also fed others to the reptiles. Some actually made safe landfall, but only a few.

"I told one of the Halfling chiefs that day to 'live free.'" Ashe paused for a moment then turned to gather his shield. "Enough of the past. Torliana has held back the hand of her judgment long enough. There are more than thirty years of interest for her to pay on her debt and by your words, Laraf, quite a few more that I have missed. Let us go see to her reckoning."

Laraf slowly turned to glance at Kyrianna, then turned back to glare at Ashe. "And you never finished what you started!" His anger evident as his voice echoed in the room. "Because you didn't end what you started...because of you...I went through three years of hell! I could rip your heart out. Give me one reason why I shouldn't! Just one reason!" Laraf didn't move toward Ashe though his body was shaking as he pointed at Ashe. "Some way. Somehow, I will finish it! I'm going to take the head of the snake! No matter who it is!"

Kyrianna placed a hand on the thief's shoulder. "Laraf, even if he had destroyed every person associated with the slave trade in Shokar at that time, someone else would have taken up the job. There will always be those who want to persecute and use others, be careful you don't become just like them."

She glanced toward Ashe. "You did what you had the power and the authority to do at the time. You protected the innocents who asked for your protection. You should be proud of the lives you saved and the justice done that day."

Kyrianna pulled Laraf away from the group to the back alcove for a minute before returning to the group. Myrith watched the two of them even though she couldn't hear the conversation. The girl's fists were clenched tightly and she glared at Laraf just before she walked back to the group without giving him any opportunity to respond to whatever it was she had said.

Ashe looked at Laraf as he walked back. "Think carefully what you ask of me or anyone else for that matter, even yourself, Laraf. What is the price you are willing to pay for justice and vengeance? Your life? Your soul?" He nodded toward Kyrianna. "Would you trade her as well? What of the others? Would you have me pass judgment on the entire city of Rejki?"

Ashe waited for a moment then took a step back. "I could have. I had the power and the skill to use it. The destruction of a city is not a difficult thing." He glanced at Myrith, again with no emotion evident on his face. "A city's strength is its people's sense of security and resolve. The tacticians of Tormasus teach, 'Crush it, grind it and soon the people of the city will be like the dust in your hand. Yours to mold with just a pinch of blood or a flick to be discarded in the wind.'"

He looked straight at Laraf and tapped his rod against the wall. "What is your judgment? What is the sentence, Laraf? And remember that sometimes the act of punishment itself can be a far greater injustice than the original offense. Should I have destroyed the city? Should I have burned every man, woman and child to ashes? Is that what you wish?"

He turned away again. "Is it better to show mercy and sow a few seeds of hope or stomp out injustice and grind the hearts of all into the ground?"

Myrith looked around at the rest of the group. While they were all tired from the battles they had fought that day, Ashe, no Brular, and Kyrianna had been through even additional stress with sharing their memories and thoughts. She had watched them as she had recounted the information after the meld and while Brular had seemed to remain impassive, Kyrianna still had a haunted look in her eyes.

"We all need to get some rest. Andrinor, Nirev, Laraf and Vyroris will take the watches," she said.

Andrinor walked over and pulled Kyrianna into the alcove and whispered something to her then left to take up his watch.

Kyrianna nodded when she finally came over to help Myrith with her armor. "What did he say to you?" she asked.

Kyrianna shook her head. "That is between Andrinor and I; just as there are things that are only between us."

"As long as it wasn't bad." She glanced over to see Andrinor now talking to Brular. The cleric muttered something in the same language he had used to summon the efreeti as the young warrior moved to assume his watch post.

"Seems Brular has made an impression on everyone," Myrith said as Falden approached the cleric.

"So you are the one!" Falden bowed his head slightly. "I stand humbled in your presence. I had heard of the cleric who was allowed into the revered halls of the Academy! Alas, unlike you I have had little opportunity for formal study. What I have learned, I did on my own. Unfortunately, it is all I know. Perhaps in the future I shall have opportunities to learn new and more effective means of wielding my craft. When the time comes, I would welcome any guidance you could give in choosing my new studies and in honing the skills I already possess. Admittance into the Academy is no small accomplishment and I am honored to share the field with you."

Brular reached out and placed a hand on Falden's shoulder. "I am the Keeper of a ruined temple and a ruined life. I humble no one." He paused for a moment as he glanced toward Myrith and Kyrianna, then turned his attention back to Falden. "I will prepare you and your friends the best I can. I must know all of your power. The answer may already be there, you may just not realize the possibilities. If it is not, there is no shame in watching over one's comrades as they fight. The action you hold in reserve may save their lives," he said.

Falden nodded then turned and left the cleric.

Myrith studied Brular for several minutes after she set the last of her armor aside. Mykaylene had charged her with redeeming this man from the darkness he was in. She wondered briefly how far their efforts this day had brought him. There was an obvious difference in his demeanor and his words to Laraf were not those of a man who no longer cared. Perhaps they had put him on the path from the darkness; she only hoped his need to confront Torliana would not push him back toward it.

Hendandra walked over to the cleric and looked up at him, her shoulders set and her face determined. "Ashe, something bothers me about the visions you shared with my comrades. Leikor may be the God of Mischief, and his mischief may indeed cause someone's death, but he is not a God of Death. I find it hard to accept he would be involved in actions to deliberately cause someone's death and find it even harder to accept he would leave evidence such as his symbol on that blade. Isn't it possible other forces were up to no good, including deceiving you and making it look like Leikor was to blame?"

Brular stood there half-turned away from Hendandra as he stared at the wall. "The symbol of Leikor, like so many divine symbols, has its own meaning to many. He is a God of Chaos, Greed, Trickery and by definition, Anarchy. His followers have no code or allegiance even to those of their guilds. The slaver may have been simply a believer of his religion or just a follower of his greedy dictates. The blade is so burned into my memory, not because my mother was struck down by a god's will or a magical blade, which she wasn't, but because her killer used her own belief in mercy against her as he drove the blade home. I find that to be the highest sin."

He turned toward the small woman and stared down at her. "I am not a benevolent judge. I believe people set their own scales. I sentence not as I wish to be judged, but as they would have judged others. I have had slavers put to the sea, and merciful men shown that in kind. There is balance in the world, Hendandra. Where do you wish to set your scales?"

He half-turned then stopped and turned back. "I apologize for my actions and the harsh words I have shown you these past weeks. I prejudged you and that is my crime. You did not earn my ire and even though you worshipped him, you were not a member of his true calling. You never gave me a reason to mistrust you or to insult you." He smiled and offered her his hand. "What is your judgment?"

Hendandra grinned and took the offered hand. "Ashe, I bear you no ill will. I am what I am: a person with simple goals and desires. I have come to admire and respect those in this group, but I do not aspire to such lofty ideals as Myrith. A fine wine, a good pipe, and a comfortable chair are all I desire. Well…maybe a castle, some servants, and a banquet or two would also be nice. Of course, I wouldn't mind being filthy rich either. But until then, my loyalty really does lie with these people."

Brular smiled again, and Myrith was surprised to see the smile reflected in the cleric's eyes. "It is not the trappings of wealth that make a rich life, it is the zeal in which you live it. The Halflings of Justula have little wealth, but their festivals were marvelous nonetheless. You should see one some time, little one. Their revelry is matched only by their stamina."

Hendandra's grin widened as she nodded and took her leave of the cleric. Myrith watched the girl return to her bedroll and frowned slightly. *Her loyalty lies with us?* she thought. *I do not believe her.* When Ferdinand had returned Hendandra to the group, she had given the magical bags back to Myrith to carry. The bags had been empty. According to the thief, since they would most likely have to return to Shokar after they got out of this place, she had seen to the safe storage of the gold and gems. She had no doubts Hendandra would return a portion of what the group had recovered, but since no one knew how much she was carrying or how much had been in the bags, they had no way of knowing how much she was holding back. They would just have to see what happened when this was over.

Chapter Ten

Myrith looked around as the sounds of music awakened her. Hendandra's practice with the violin was not as smooth or harmonious as it had been on previous mornings and she cast a quizzical glance in that direction. Hendandra only shrugged as she stopped playing and packed the violin back into its case.

She frowned when she saw Kyrianna had again retreated to the small alcove during the night. The only difference today, Kyrianna seemed to be more alert to what was going on in the room instead of being lost in her own thoughts.

Brular was sitting with Jerietlan and Nirev talking quietly. Andrinor was sharpening the blades on his sword while Hendandra now sat checking her pack and gear. Falden was studying one of his books and Laraf was sitting with his rapier across his lap watching Kyrianna as she got up. Myrith felt her frown deepen as she looked at Laraf. The young man wasn't hiding his feelings for Kyrianna very well. *There is no place for this on the battlefield*, she thought.

"Morning," Kyrianna said as she approached. "Want some help with your armor?"

"You're not in yours yet," Myrith said.

"I know, but my armor is easier to get into than yours."

As Kyrianna helped her with the plate mail, Myrith again found herself wondering about her friend's background. From what she had seen in the link and based on some of Kyrianna's comments, she believed the girl's brother held rank within the city guard where she lived and her father had influence with the nobles of that city. Yet Kyrianna didn't act like the daughter of a minor noble house in any way. In her experience, those who were used to having power had no problems with trying to exert it over others and refused to give it up unless forced. She had no doubts the girl had been spoiled by her family, but she wasn't arrogant or demanding in her attitudes.

"Let's take the battle to her," Kyrianna said as she handed Myrith her sword belt.

"During the link, the guard who waited with you…" she started.

Kyrianna's head dropped slightly. "My brother Erudus. He was the one who caught me burglarizing the home of one of the council members."

"And he didn't try to protect you?"

"No. His own personal code of honor would never allow him to do that. Perhaps even more so, because he was my brother." Kyrianna looked up at her and smiled. "I'll tell you the whole sordid story another time. For now, we have other things to worry about."

Myrith smiled and nodded. "Glad you're back with us."

Kyrianna glanced at Brular, where he still sat with the other two clerics. "Thank you," she said softly.

"We need to get moving," Myrith said, looking around at the others as Kyrianna put her own armor on. Laraf moved to assist, but she waved him away then turned her back on him. Myrith nodded as she realized her suspicion Kyrianna wasn't interested in the thief appeared to be confirmed. Instead of disappointment, Laraf's face showed only determination as he moved to wait by the door. As she watched him, she remembered the look she had seen on Tristan Duvall's face when he had looked at Kyrianna after they left the estate. For a moment, she wondered if Kyrianna realized the young nobleman also cared for her. She suspected the girl had feelings toward Tristan, from the way she had acted after they left the estate, but wasn't sure. She paused for a moment then remembered how Kyrianna had looked for Tristan when they had found her here—yes, she did have feelings for him.

Myrith had never had anyone who cared about her in that way. She had grown up in a bar and as soon as he had decided she was old enough, the owner had forced her into performing the same work and services as the other women there—even her mother. Senna hadn't even tried to stand up for her daughter; instead, she had taken advantage of the opportunity to make arrangements to leave the Silver Dragon—using Myrith's looks and therefore her potential earnings for Marcus as a way of paying off her debts to him. Marcus had agreed and then added that debt to what he claimed Myrith owed him for the years she had lived there and had not been a working member of the staff. Where her mother's debt had come from she didn't know. He had also found ways to make sure she never earned anything for herself, by adding the cost of damages to her room, or visits by a healer when one of the patrons got upset or just wanted to hurt someone and she became the target. She hadn't fooled herself into thinking he was acting out of concern for her, when he had started to stand up to Jod and his companions that last day. *No, he was only looking out for his own interests and the income he would be losing.*

Myrith shook her head to clear it. *Too many bad memories.* The group needed to be focused; therefore she needed to be as well. She picked up the rest of her gear and looked around at the others. "Everyone ready?"

She nodded as Kyrianna picked up her bow and held it at the ready. *Good,* she thought. *She listened to me.*

Myrith turned her attention to Brular then glanced toward Kyrianna. The fire cleric nodded then stood and moved to stand next to the girl. She saw Kyrianna frown slightly as Brular spoke to her. After a moment, she bowed her head slightly and the cleric touched her right shoulder then her chest.

"I don't like it, but I'll accept his protection spells. You still want me in the back away from the main attacks?" Kyrianna didn't look up at her.

"Yes. Your skill with the bow means you are as dangerous to our enemies from a distance as you are in a melee with your swords."

Kyrianna nodded and stepped back. She looked down at the wolf next to her and he moved to the back of the room to stand next to the door button.

~ * ~

"I think I can hear a couple of people talking, but it's too low to understand," Hendandra whispered as Myrith joined her at the locked door.

Myrith looked around at the rest of the group as they came up to the door. Kyrianna glanced back toward the open door and Myrith heard a slight click from the closed one in front of her. She pushed it open and stepped into the room.

"Thank Ballan," a female voice said from the back of the room. "Someone finally found us."

Myrith tightened her grip on the hilt of her sword as she examined the aura of the woman who stepped out from the shadows. There was a definite taint of evil about this woman and the man who stood behind her. They were both tall with dark hair and dark features—at least what she could see of them. Both were wearing tight-fitting leathers, their hands covered by gloves and their faces obscured by the hoods of their cloaks.

Ballan? Myrith glanced back at where Brular stood watching the pair closely. The fire cleric had caught the name as well. Something was wrong here. Brular had told them last night Ballan was just another incarnation of Thynitic. However, these two had called on her, but appeared to be trapped here just as they were.

She jumped as Shadow Seeker began growling behind her. The large wolf had his head held low in a threatening posture as he took a step past her.

"Kyri, control your companion," she said, moving forward slightly.

"Shadow!" Kyrianna reached down and grabbed the collar the wolf wore. "My apologies," she said. "He is a little high-strung at times and very nervous around strangers."

"There is no need to apologize. It would appear your friend takes protecting you very seriously, that's all. The apparent nature of this place makes all suspect until proven to not be enemies. I take no offense at his protectiveness."

Myrith glanced at Kyrianna who seemed to be watching the two people very closely as she pulled the wolf back a few steps.

"I am Mylia and my partner is Falian. We were brought here by forces unknown several days ago and have been trapped in this room since that time." She held her hand out.

Myrith took the hand and nodded slightly. Behind her, Shadow Seeker continued to growl softly.

"Our supplies are almost gone, so it is fortunate you happened onto our prison," Falian said, moving to stand next to Mylia. "Perhaps you could spend some time telling us how you came to be here as well."

"Yes," Mylia said, smiling. "Sit and tell us about yourselves. Then perhaps after you have rested, we can join together to find a way out of this place."

"We were brought here much like you were, by forces unknown," Myrith said. She did not sit, instead placing her hand on the hilt of her sword as she continued to stand. "We have been traveling through this realm for untold weeks and have learned a powerful mage created this place. We have also gathered information which indicates she is working to control the elemental planes. We have already traveled through areas that seemed to duplicate those planes."

"Please rest yourselves, while Falian and I gather our gear together. We offer you our blades and hope that together, we can find our way out of this place," Mylia said.

"While I thank you for the offer, the taint of evil I sense from you as well as the uneasiness of my friend's companion makes me hesitant to accept."

"That is understandable. Falian and I have performed services as thieves and assassins on many occasions and that is probably what is causing the taint you speak of. However, in a group such as yours, trust between all parties is very important; therefore I will not press the issue. May the gods guide your path." The woman touched her companion's arm and gestured to the pile of equipment in the corner of the room.

Myrith gestured to the door and the others began moving in that direction. Shadow Seeker seemed reluctant to leave and Kyrianna grabbed his collar and a handful of fur as she tried to pull the wolf out of the room.

As she turned, Myrith heard Mylia and Falian rummaging in the pile of equipment.

"I would ask you to make sure the door is left open, please," Mylia said.

"Of course. May your goddess guide you safely out of this place," Myrith said as she turned and headed toward the door.

There was a whisper of air as an arrow flew past Myrith's ear to glance off Brular's armor. Before she could turn, she felt the thud of an arrow striking her armor as well. Kyrianna released her hold on the wolf, but before Shadow Seeker could attack the two humans, at least a dozen dire wolves appeared along the walls and charged the group.

Brular raised his hands and a wall of flame went up on one side of the room, trapping the wolves on that side behind it.

"They're weres," Kyrianna said, drawing her silver sword as Shadow Seeker grabbed one of the dire wolves that hadn't been trapped by Brular's flames and pulled it away from her. "Don't let them bite you."

Myrith drew her own blade and moved to engage Falian as Kyrianna's sword caught Mylia's and Hendandra darted past the woman to get behind Falian, her rapier at the ready.

"Kyri, watch your back!" Myrith heard Laraf yell.

"I told you to remain out of melee combat," Myrith said as she parried Falian's long sword.

"Next time, I'll retreat out of the room once the battle is started." Kyrianna dodged as one of the dire wolves snapped at her and Mylia began changing form.

Myrith watched as both Mylia and Falian changed to something that was a cross between the wolf and human. Their features had become more canine and their gloves were shredded by the long sharp claws they both now had. Mylia wasn't wielding a sword as her partner was, but she was definitely causing problems for Kyrianna with her claws.

There were several yelps from the area behind the wall of flame, but she couldn't take her attention from the creature she was fighting. Falian had sidestepped away from her and had turned on Hendandra. The girl yelled as his teeth bit into her shoulder. Myrith swung her sword, catching the werewolf in the neck; however the blade didn't seem to do the expected damage. Falian jumped away from Hendandra, who managed to stab his leg once before she fell to the ground.

Myrith glanced to her side as Kyrianna dodged the attack of two dire wolves, just as Shadow Seeker charged into one and knocked it away. The two canines began rolling around on the floor snarling and growling.

There was a sudden flash of light to Myrith's right and she heard the crack of thunder that normally accompanied one of Falden's lightning bolts. The yelps from behind the wall of flame told her the attack had been successful.

Hendandra rolled away from Falian then jumped up and darted in with her rapier scoring a hit on the werewolf's side. Myrith took advantage of his distraction and stepped in, putting her weight and power into the blow as her blade slid into his chest.

As the werewolf fell, his features slowly changed back to human.

"Falian!" Mylia lunged at Myrith, her claws extended.

Myrith turned to the side slightly and the werewolf's claws slid off her armor.

"Chaos!" she heard Kyrianna yell as Shadow Seeker yelped in pain.

Several more yelps could be heard behind her, and Myrith also began to detect the acrid odor of burned hair. She could hear the others behind her as well as the snarling of the wolves, but Myrith couldn't risk checking on them as Mylia came at her again.

Hendandra moved quickly into a flanking position behind the female werewolf and Myrith attacked just as the girl darted in. The werewolf howled as both blades found their target. Myrith twisted her blade as she pulled it back out and lunged in again. She barely avoided the creature's claws as her sword sank into its chest and the werewolf fell to the floor.

She turned to see the others finishing the last of the wolves and Kyrianna kneeling on the ground next to Shadow Seeker. Kyrianna's companion had several long gashes along his side. The wolf whined softly as Brular laid his hands on the injuries. Myrith watched as the wolf's flesh knitted itself back together and his eyes seemed to clear.

"Keep him down for a few more minutes. There is still some internal healing to be completed." Brular stood and moved toward Hendandra, then looked back at Kyrianna. "I found no traces of the lycanthrope disease in his system." The fire cleric placed a hand on Hendandra and nodded. "There are no traces of the disease in your system either, little one." He looked around at the rest of the group. "Was anyone else bitten?"

No one else spoke up as they dusted themselves off. Myrith frowned as Laraf offered his hand to Kyrianna to help her up. She took his hand without saying anything. Myrith turned to see Hendandra checking the equipment and bodies of Mylia and Falian. She picked up the two short bows and placed them in her pack, then shook her head as she glanced over the rest of the items.

"Is everyone healed and ready?" Myrith glanced at Brular then Kyrianna. The cleric glanced toward Jerietlan who had been tending to Laraf and Nirev. Jerietlan only nodded.

Shadow Seeker moved slowly to the back of the alcove and waited as the rest of them headed out the door.

The group was silent as they moved to the next door.

"I don't hear that much," Hendandra said. "A low hissing is all. Maybe it's a sleeping dragon." She smiled at Andrinor.

Andrinor looked her and cocked his head to the side.

"Not until the rest of us are in place. You are not blocking another door and preventing the rest of us from getting into the fight. If you keep that up, you will encounter something even your dragon form cannot cope with and we will not be able to help you." Myrith moved to stand between Andrinor and the door and Nirev moved to stand next to her.

"Yer not leaving me out of this battle," the dwarf said.

Andrinor nodded then tightened the grip on his sword. "I'll wait and see what it is we are facing," he said.

"Myrith, perhaps I can improve our chances with one of my fireballs," Falden said.

Myrith looked at the mage then nodded. "You stand to the side, where you can step out of the doorway easily. I'll open the door."

"Actually, my blade generates a globe of silence," Laraf said. "If I open the door, I can do it in total silence as to not risk waking our opponents."

Myrith glanced from Laraf to Hendandra who shrugged. "My armor allows me to move in total silence, however, it doesn't generate a globe that affects other objects," she said.

"Just make sure you leave room for Falden to cast his spell and for the rest of us to get in," Myrith said.

Laraf nodded as he drew his rapier and reached for the small notch in the stone door. Myrith glanced toward Kyrianna who raised her bow as the door began moving.

Falden stepped up quickly and completed the final gesture for his spell then moved to the side of the door as Myrith and Nirev headed for the doorway. She smiled as Laraf showed the good sense to let her and Nirev enter the room first. She hesitated for only a heartbeat as she saw the creatures that waited for them: Chimera and the color of their dragon head—red. The fireball had no other effect than to awaken the three-headed monsters. She stood her ground as the lead chimera roared with its lion's head then released a stream of flame with its dragon's. She knew Falden and possibly Hendandra were standing behind her and she wanted to try and shield them from the flames. She heard Andrinor curse from the back of the group.

An arrow flew past her ear to strike the first chimera then another. Myrith brought her sword up to parry the attack from the dragon's head even as she blocked the goat's with her shield. Just to her side she saw Nirev swing his maul as he stepped past her opponent to engage another of the creatures.

"Moving past you." Hendandra's voice came from beside Myrith though she couldn't see the girl.

Another volley of arrows flew past her ear.

"Hey, be careful," Hendandra said.

"Sorry, Hendandra, next time let me know when you're going invisible," Kyrianna called.

Myrith cursed as the chimera tried to lunge past her, its dragon's head snapping at her neck as the lion's caught her sword arm. She jerked her shield around and bashed it into the side of the head. The creature released her arm, took a step back and roared loudly.

Myrith frowned as Hendandra appeared behind the chimera, her blade partially buried in its back. The chimera roared again and started to turn. Myrith swung quickly, her sword opening a deep gash in the lion's neck. Blood gushed from the neck wound and the chimera hesitated. Myrith saw Hendandra retrieve her weapon then vanish again. She smiled as she swung again, this time burying her own blade deep in the chimera's chest.

With a bleat from the goat's head, the creature fell to the floor. Nirev had dispatched his opponent and was now moving toward another. Myrith frowned. If the dwarf would stay near the door, they could keep the creatures from being able to flank them. If he kept moving forward, it would put him at risk of being surrounded.

She barely dodged another burst of flame as Andrinor charged past her. All hope of keeping the chimera's attacks limited gone, Myrith darted forward to engage the one facing the dragon warrior. Behind her she heard Falden chanting then he clapped his hands together and a storm of ice and snow swirled around the chimeras. She backpedaled as the hailstones beat on her armor and found herself standing next to Kyrianna as she continued to fire her arrows into the storm. At least two of the chimera fell from the cold and both Nirev and Andrinor accounted for two more. That left only four of the creatures.

"Damn it, Kyri, I told you to stay in the back of the group," Myrith said as the remaining chimeras moved toward her friend, ignoring Andrinor and Nirev. Both of the others took swings as the creatures moved past them, but none of the four even slowed.

Kyrianna dropped her bow and started to draw both of her swords as the chimeras approached. The first of the creatures lunged forward, its claws raking her arms and knocking the swords from her grasp. She fell back against the wall as the dragon's head darted in. Myrith lunged forward, only to be knocked to the side as Laraf jumped between Kyrianna and the chimera.

The dragon's head locked on Laraf and Myrith winced at the

sickening crunch she heard.

"Laraf!" Kyrianna screamed as the chimera dropped the body on the ground. She rolled to the side avoiding the lion's head as Myrith plunged her sword into its heart.

Myrith glanced at Kyrianna who was still on the floor. She didn't have time to wonder what injury the creature had done to her friend as another of the beasts tried to get past her to attack the girl. As she raised her sword, several streaks of light flew past her to strike the chimera's chest. It roared as Hendandra appeared behind it and plunged her rapier into its lungs. Myrith smiled as the creature fell to the ground. She glanced around to see Andrinor, Nirev and Vyroris had dispatched the remaining chimeras.

Brular approached Laraf just as his body was surrounded by a thick fog and vanished from the area. The cleric stood there for several seconds, his eyes closed and his head bowed. "He was called by Resare directly," Brular finally said.

"That's better than the alternative," Myrith said. "At least he wasn't taken by Thynitic."

Brular glanced at Kyrianna then stepped closer to Myrith. "I am only guessing that is who claimed him, Lady Lake. Kyri doesn't need to hear that one who fell placing himself in the way of an attack meant for her may have been claimed by that one." His voice was harsh though pitched so only the two of them could hear.

Myrith glanced at Kyrianna who had finally gotten off the ground, recovered and sheathed her swords then picked up her bow. He was right; they didn't need her falling back into the dangerous depression she had been in the past few days. She nodded her understanding and Brular placed a glowing hand on her arm where the chimera had clawed her. She watched as the skin knitted itself closed. *Too bad Kyri's soul can't be knitted back together as easily*, she thought. *Then again, maybe it has been*. Kyrianna's right arm was a patchwork of scars she had gained in their travels. Claws of demons, scrags and now chimeras had left their marks, just as Thynitic was leaving her mark on Kyrianna's soul.

The group fought its way through three more rooms of creatures including a group of things that at first had resembled large stalactites until Kyrianna walked into the room and they all tried to grab her with powerful tentacles.

The fight had been long and they were all worn out, but there was only one room left on this side.

"I think we should go on," Myrith said. "Falden as well as Jerietlan and Brular still have power left. And the rest of us have been healed of our injuries."

"I still have the availability of my dragon form as well," Andrinor said. "Let's get this part of this cursed place done with."

"The sooner we are done with this, the quicker I can get back to my own home and a soft bed in Raspa," Hendandra said. "Which as I may remind you, I was able to make it to once already and was forcibly brought back here by that insane hammer-wielding cleric."

Kyrianna looked at Hendandra and nodded. "I'm sorry you were brought back against your will. However, none of us are really here by our own will. While I would prefer to know you were home and safe, I am glad you're here with us also." She paused for a moment. "Myrith, if we think we're able to handle another fight, we should press on. Let's take the fight to her."

"Agreed," Nirev said.

Shadow Seeker trotted over to stand by the button. "He's voting we go on also," Kyrianna said.

Myrith nodded as she headed of the room and to the last door at the end of the corridor.

Hendandra slipped up beside Myrith and pressed her ear against the door. "Sounds of movement, but nothing else I can identify," the rogue said.

A look of concentration crossed Hendandra's face then she frowned.

"Hendandra?" Myrith looked down at her.

"Something must be interfering with the magic," she said. "Ah there we go," she said as she vanished.

There was a loud click and Myrith stared as the door began to move. This was the first one that had opened with such a noticeable release of the lock. She glanced back at Kyrianna who already had her bow up and aimed at the crack between the door and the wall.

The door moved a bit more and Myrith heard a creak from the bow. There was no apparent reaction from anything in the room. She moved to look through the crack and saw only darkness. Her sword held at the ready, Myrith stepped into the room along with Andrinor and Nirev.

Waiting for them were several dark-skinned creatures with glowing eyes, long arms, wings and long pointed ears. For a brief moment, Myrith was reminded of a bat. The two furthest away from the door began chanting and moving their hands in complex patterns. She moved to the side as Kyrianna stepped up beside her and quickly released two arrows; one for each of the creatures. The was a flash of light around one of the creatures and it howled in pain, however the other only smiled as a lightning bolt streaked from its hands to first strike Kyrianna and then leap to her, Andrinor, Vyroris and finally Nirev.

"Mages!" Myrith yelled as she charged into the midst of the creatures. "Kyri, Falden, concentrate on getting them out of the fight."

A volley of arrows and several streaks of arcane force were the only answers she received. The creatures between her and the two mages clawed and bit as they fought with a frenzy which exceeded even that of Andrinor when he went into one of his battle rages.

"Pyremar's Fires!"

Myrith risked a glance toward Andrinor who was surrounded by the largest variety of the creatures in the room. There was blood flowing from his arms and neck as he continued to swing his double sword. Nirev was standing with his back to the wall facing four of the creatures and swinging his maul while singing something in Dwarven. Vyroris appeared to be attempting to reach Andrinor, his sword swinging furiously as the creatures swarmed toward him.

Myrith dodged the claws of the creature she was facing to run to Andrinor as he fell to the floor. She frowned at the pool of blood surrounding him. She swung her blade with as much force as she could muster at the bat-like creature that had felled the young warrior. Time seemed to slow for a moment and she shook her head to clear it of a sudden disorientation.

There was the sound of wings and chanting behind her then she heard Hendandra scream. "Kyri!"

Myrith turned just in time to see a large black bird-like creature holding Kyrianna and vanishing. "No!" she yelled as she swung again at the thing in front of her. Her sword left a deep gash across its throat and it fell. There was the sound of an explosion against the back wall and Myrith flinched as the heat from one of Falden's fireballs washed over her.

There were several screams from the creatures toward the back of the room—screams which were cut off abruptly. The dwarf swung his maul hard, opening the abdomens of two of the creatures as they fell to the ground.

"What happened?" Myrith demanded as she turned to face Hendandra.

"I don't know," Hendandra said softly. "That…that…that thing just appeared and touched Kyri then they both vanished."

"It was a chronynian," Brular said. "They are denizens of several planes and while they serve Order, they will also work for darkness. They are able to control time for short periods. By using this ability, they can seem to freeze time while they prepare spells or attacks that take immediate effect when time returns to normal. They can also teleport themselves and others."

"Then Torliana has her," Jerietlan said softly.

Myrith looked around at the defeated looks on the faces of the others. "We cannot afford to be distracted. Kyri's abduction changes nothing! However, it should serve to strengthen our resolve." She paused and glared at Brular for a moment who met her gaze with a slight nod as he stepped forward.

"We must rest and prepare," Brular said. "This is the last room in this corridor and a portal to the next should have activated. Do we rest here, in the previous room or on the other side? If the portal does open, that is," He glanced down at Andrinor briefly. "The dragon warrior has been seriously hurt and we need to see to his wounds as well, before we move."

Myrith nodded. "I agree, rest is needed. Make the necessary arrangements including spells to protect the weaker members of this group. Jerietlan, you and Brular attend to Andrinor's injuries."

Brular motioned Jerietlan to join him then handed the other cleric a scroll. Myrith watched as the two clerics turned their attention to the fallen dragon warrior and began casting their spells.

As Andrinor began to stir slightly, Brular looked back up at Myrith. "I can seal this room from planar and teleportation magic so as to make any new assailant leave us alone; unless they want to come through the front door. After that, I have enough power left to enchant my shield for tomorrow and cast a spell on Hendandra, Falden, Jerietlan and Andrinor so I can monitor their health. Alternatively, I can cast a spell to increase one person's resistance to her magics. I would suggest that be placed on Hendandra. However, it is your decision as to the magic being cast.

"In addition, I will also need to pray with Jerietlan and Nirev to help them access spells with which I am familiar, but they are not." The fire cleric gasped aloud and closed his eyes for a moment.

He opened them slowly and looked up at Myrith. "She is in pain, great pain," he said.

Shadow Seeker gave a loud howl then dropped to the floor whining softly. Myrith glanced at Falden. "He is bonded to her," he said. "He is feeling the same pain she is."

Myrith frowned as she looked around at the group. "Get what rest you can. Tomorrow will tax us all, but our delay taxes Kyrianna even more." She turned and walked to the back of the room, where the portal should have appeared, slammed a fist into the wall and stood there for several seconds before turning back around. "May the Gods of Light be with us."

Brular moved to one of the far corners of the room and sat quietly, his hands moving slowly in complicated patterns. Myrith looked at him then turned to Jerietlan. "What is he doing?"

"He is trying to break the pain Kyrianna is in," Jerietlan said.

Brular paused and stared at the floor for several minutes. "The spell is powerful, but I will try," he said softly. "No! Kyrianna, we will both try!" He closed his eyes and began moving his hands again. He paused again, and Myrith saw the creases in his brow as he began the casting once again.

Jerietlan looked at her. "He is trying to bolster Kyrianna's strength and will from within so she can reject the power herself."

Brular looked up as his hands stilled with a slight smile on his face. "It is broken," he said. He froze then clenched his hands tightly. "No!" Tears came to his eyes. "The spell was broken, but only for a moment." He paused and seemed to gather his thoughts. "She will do great evil to Kyrianna, Myrith. I have seen the strong break in hours, some in days but never longer than that."

Myrith looked at him. "You never broke."

Brular looked up at her. "And was that a blessing or a curse, Lady Lake? There is one other thing I wish to do before we rest for the evening." Brular removed a piece of chalk from his robes and began carefully inscribing a symbol of protection on the floor. Before he finished the design, he stepped out of it. With extreme care, he connected the last lines of the symbol.

He stood up and motioned the others to the far wall as he began speaking in the language he had used when he had called the efreeti. This time though, he had created no circles for the group and the casting seemed to be much shorter as a larger efreeti appeared in the circle.

"Hellavar sends his greetings to his cleric and directs I should grant you one request," the efreeti said, bowing slightly.

Myrith glanced at the others and realized the demon was speaking so they could all understand it.

"I wish to summon the avatar of the Goddess Mykaylene," Brular said.

"You wish to summon an avatar?" The efreeti stared at Brular. "I almost wish I could stay to see the consequences of such an act, but I am not so foolish. As our Lord Hellavar has directed me, so it shall be." The efreeti vanished in a cloud of flame and smoke. In his place, a tall, statuesque woman appeared holding a long spear.

Myrith immediately prostrated herself on the floor next to Jerietlan. She frowned as she saw Brular only knelt on his right knee. However, the goddess only nodded as she looked at the fire cleric.

"You are bold; especially for one who is not one of my faithful, Brular Eglis." She stepped forward, picked up the cleric's shield and examined it. "Why have you summoned me, Cleric of Hellavar?"

"Not for myself, Lady of Battles, but for those who do follow you. I would ask you to forgive Jerietlan for his lack of faith that led him to foolishly accept the lies of Thynitic and restore his full magical abilities. I also ask you bestow upon the Warrior Myrith Lake your highest honors and the powers normally reserved for those who follow the straightest and holiest paths. She will need the strength and blessing only you can give her to see this task, which has been set before her, completed."

The goddess smiled. "Hellavar has spoken truly of his highest servant and his dedication to the Order. Even though she has not yet earned the privileges of the holiest of my faithful, I will grant your request as it serves the Order we all seek to preserve in these times. And I lift the restrictions placed on my wayward cleric. Know this, Brular Eglis, I hold you responsible for the methods in which Myrith wields this new power I am granting. If she falls or abuses the power, it will be you who answers to me for her failings. I also expect you to assist Jerietlan in keeping to the proper path."

Brular bowed his head. "I understand and accept these responsibilities."

"That is good." The avatar vanished from the room carrying the cleric's shield with her.

"What did you do?" Myrith stood up and looked at the fire cleric.

"I asked for the highest blessings of the Gods of Light to be given to you. When you pray in the morning, you will find you have access to power normally only reserved for those who walk the holiest paths of the faithful," Brular said. "We go to face a servant of one of the vilest gods of darkness; you will need that power, Myrith. We all will need it."

Myrith only stared at the fire cleric as he prepared his bedroll and lay down. His request had cost him a powerful magic item in his shield as well as the goddess requiring him to be pledge for her use of this new power. She would never understand that kind of selfless behavior, but she now knew it was also expected of her. She took her place in the center of the room for her watch as the others drifted off to sleep. Tomorrow would be dangerous for them all. For a moment she wondered just how dangerous this time was going to be for Kyrianna.

Chapter Eleven

"What?" Kyrianna coughed as she hit a hard, black floor and a pair of manacles immediately attached themselves to her wrists. She started to get up and was struck by several sharp pains, like being hit by a flurry of needles.

"No one told you you could get up, half-elf," a voice surprisingly soft and melodic despite the venom of the words said. "I would stay where you are unless you want the pain to grow worse." A pair of soft, black, leather slippers moved in front of her.

"That's the first one," the voice said. "I thank you for your service at this time."

Another voice or pair of voices, Kyrianna couldn't be sure, spoke from behind where she was on the floor. "We will honor the agreement that was made. Who is the other you wish to have brought here?"

"The Cleric of Hellavar. He has become too much of a nuisance and he has started them working together. I don't care if he is alive or not. Remove him from them and bring whatever is left here."

"The agreement will be honored?"

"It will. You will have the items I promised and I will return you to your home."

There was a pop behind Kyrianna and she risked shifting her position slightly.

"Well, now this is a pleasant sight," the woman said. "The daughter of Arielle on the floor at my feet." The woman lifted a foot, placed it on Kyrianna's neck and pressed her head against the floor. "While not as satisfying as having Arielle in this position would be, it will suffice." The pressure moved away suddenly. "You may get up."

Kyrianna slowly forced herself to a kneeling position as she quickly scanned the room. The walls, floor, rows of columns and even the large dais and throne all seemed to be carved from obsidian. Dark gray runes and symbols were etched into almost every inch of every surface. "Where am I?" She forced herself to stand and look at the woman who now faced away from her. Her long black hair shimmered with dark blue highlights as she finally turned to face Kyrianna.

"You are where I wanted you to be, Kyrianna Dalynne."

Kyrianna looked into the silver-flecked black eyes of the elven woman and felt her chest tighten around her heart. "Torliana," she whispered the name.

"Very good." Torliana raised her hands and clapped them together a few times. The dark red of her robes swirled around her like pooling blood. "I suppose I should reward your cleverness." She passed her hands through a complicated pattern as she smiled at Kyrianna.

Kyrianna gasped as the spell touched her and she crumbled to the floor. Pain, intense pain. Her mind reeled at the power as she tried to fight the agony that enveloped her. Blackness claimed her and the only sounds she could hear were her own weak whimpers. She had not even the strength left to scream.

~ * ~

Kyrianna groaned as the pain faded. She glanced up to see Torliana standing in front of her, a small flame held in the palm of her hand. "So, Keeper, you continue to spend your power to help those not of your faith. Maybe if you had been more concerned with helping those who followed your god, we would not be here now," she said softly. She waved her hand and the flame vanished. "It is only a moment's respite, Kyrianna. Enjoy it while you can."

She smiled as she looked at Kyrianna. "So Brular knows what I am doing to you." Torliana laughed as she looked at Kyrianna still curled up on the floor. "I thank you for that gift," she said. "Two can play at this game, Brular. How much power are you willing to waste on her?" Torliana laughed again as she began to recast the spell.

Kyrianna closed her eyes, not wanting to see the final hand movements, not wanting to know exactly when the pain would strike. She felt the scream tear itself from her throat as the burning, stabbing and tearing sensations once again assaulted her senses and darkness surrounded her.

~ * ~

She had no idea how long she had been trapped when the pain finally lifted. The agony she had been in stopped suddenly and she gasped as warm air caressed her body. Her armor and gear had been removed and she was standing there only in the long tunic and leggings she wore under it. Her hands were pulled over her head. There was something cutting against her wrists, neck and ankles. Her body protested as she forced herself to move, and chains rattled in the silence of the room.

To her left was a large dais with an ornate throne. Directly in front of the dais, a large circle was inscribed on the floor. An elven woman was walking around the circle studying it. She paused and glanced in Kyrianna's direction.

"The Lady has decided some mercy should be shown and has dispelled the magic, I see," the elf said, walking back over to her.

"Witch! What do you want from me?" Kyrianna lunged forward, but was stopped by the manacles and chains. She stared at the elf standing in front of her. Midnight-black hair and eyes that seemed to flash silver.

"Temper, temper." Torliana raised a hand and smiled.

Kyrianna cried out as pain wracked her body.

"As for what I want from you—that was only a sample." She waved her hand again.

Kyrianna gasped as she found herself in the main hall of her parents' home in Nydith. Her father appeared to be kneeling beside her, concern written on his face. "Ari, are you all right? What happened? Arielle?" His voice was breaking as the scene faded.

"That was the rest of the sample. I have linked you and Arielle. She will know everything you are going through and will suffer the same torments. Your mother was responsible for the time I spent as a toy of the chaos demons. Now, it is her turn to suffer. And suffer you both shall." She waved her hand again.

Kyrianna hung limply in the chains as another wave of pain hit her. This one seemed to radiate from the collar and chains she was wearing and was not as intense as the torture spell. *Was that the same spell Thynitic used on Falden and Andrinor?* She knew in her heart it was and felt renewed guilt and anger at her own actions as well as the goddesses who had brought her here unprepared to face this trial.

:*Just as I released you from her torture spell and restored your strength, I can give you the power to escape this torment,* Thynitic whispered in her mind. :*You can turn the tables on Torliana if you wish.*

"No!" Kyrianna screamed into the silence of the room.

Torliana glanced back at her and smiled then turned away.

Kyrianna watched as Torliana went back to the circle she had been studying. *I thought you were from Shokar*, she thought. *Why would one of the Rynial have been on that world? And why would she have studied in the temple of a foreign god? Perhaps you are not the innocent pawn who was deceived by her lies after all.* Kyrianna fought not to scream as another wave of pain struck her.

~ * ~

Kyrianna raised her head and stared at Torliana as the elf placed a glowing hand on her chest. She took one ragged breath then another as the pain eased. "Why?"

Torliana smiled. "You should know the answer to that question by now. You have been whispering her litany for almost an hour." She stepped back. "Kindness should be the only companion to pain and will…" she began.

"And will increase the intensity of suffering and the chaos surrounding us. Do not ignore the sudden whim of compassion; let it always come, but only seldom as to give those who suffer a sense of hope. Hope is consort to chaos and torment is their offspring. Unending torment destroys pain and this in turn destroys the chaos that nurtures us," Kyrianna said, reciting the rest of the passage.

"You are learning. But there are other lessons, besides the memorization of words, you need to receive." Torliana uncoiled the nine-strand whip she carried and stepped back a few more steps. "Do you know the rest of the words?"

Kyrianna refused to answer.

Torliana flicked the whip so the strands rested lightly around Kyrianna's neck. "Listen well, Kyrianna Dalynne, daughter of Arielle, Daughter of Chaos. Act alluring to trap those who would never seek the Lady on their own. Confuse those who think they know the ways of the world around them. Bring pain and torment not only to those who enjoy it, or to those who deserve it, but also to the innocent and those who do not anticipate it. The lash…" Torliana paused and jerked the whip, the nine strands of braided leather cut deeply into Kyrianna's neck. She raised her other hand and a small globe of fire surrounded it. "Fire." She flung the flames at Kyrianna's chest. "And cold are the three physical pains that never fail the devout." She slid a wand out of her belt and pointed it at Kyrianna.

Ice and hail swirled around her as she fought the scream lodged in her throat. This time she gratefully accepted the darkness that began to surround her as much of the pain vanished.

~ * ~

"That's enough rest," Torliana said, slapping her face.

Kyrianna shook her head and glared at the woman. Torliana's hands glowed for a moment and she touched Kyrianna's chest. She fought tears as the exhaustion vanished and she fully awoke. *The witch cast the same spell Ashe did when I didn't want to sleep. No true rest or respite from her.*

:*I can give you that rest,* Thynitic whispered. :*Call on me and I will give you the power you need to escape.*

:*No!* Kyrianna shouted the word in her mind. :*The price is too high!* Her gaze went back to Torliana, who was casting another healing spell.

"Your friends continue to make progress, Kyrianna. I find them most amusing. However, they will never make it here." She raised her hand and a dark bolt of force leapt from it.

Kyrianna screamed as the bolt hit her.

Torliana cast another healing spell then stepped away. She reached into the air, opened a small portal and removed a silver mirror. "Let's watch your friends as they face some more of the Lady's pets, shall we?" she said and the mirror expanded and suspended itself in the air.

Kyrianna tried to relax as Torliana stood next to her, the mirror hanging in the air where they could watch. The group was working together much better today, and Torliana took note of Falden's increasingly powerful magics.

"The coordination of the clerics and the mage, that would be your handiwork, Brular," Torliana muttered as the group stepped into the hallway from the third room they had been forced to enter. "You will be dealt with soon."

Kyrianna felt tears as she watched, unable to help her friends. The large ornate doors she knew opened into this chamber were easily visible from where the group was, but it seemed every time they took a step, a door appeared before them and they had no choice but to pass through it into a room where they were forced to fight creatures of chaos.

She remembered how Torliana had laughed as various members of the party found themselves with unwanted partial shape changes. Vyroris had grown a set of rabbit ears to go with his constantly twitching nose and Falden was gradually being changed into a hawk.

A Fog of Chaos, Torliana had called the spell. A spell placed in the corridor by Thynitic herself. She shook her head as the image focused on Falden with his bird legs and feet and feathers covering his arms.

The group moved through two more rooms and Kyrianna felt her eyes burning as she watched Myrith stagger from several powerful blows from a gray-skinned, frog-faced creature. The woman was seriously hurt as was Nirev.

Torliana only smiled as she dismissed the mirror. "Perhaps we don't need to watch any more. It would appear to be causing you some distress to see your friends hurt." Her tone was condescending as she started to walk away. Without warning, she spun around and raised her right hand—a dark bolt of force leapt from her hand to strike Kyrianna's chest.

:*I can save them if you want me to*, Thynitic's voice whispered in her mind. :*Call on my power and it will be yours to destroy your enemy and help your friends.*

"No," Kyrianna gasped out the word as pain from the spell on the restraints surrounded her.

Torliana ignored her as she moved to the main doors of her chamber. "I will have to see to that sorcerer as well," she muttered as the door opened.

Kyrianna lost sight of Torliana as darkness claimed her once again.

~ * ~

"Did you have a good rest?"

Kyrianna opened her eyes to see Torliana standing before her. The woman was standing there looking at her, a smile on her lips. Kyrianna felt stronger and realized the witch had again healed her.

"I'm glad you are feeling better; I am expecting another guest shortly," Torliana said.

"What are you talking about?"

"You will see."

Torliana moved her hands in a pattern Kyrianna hadn't seen before as she stepped back several paces. A shimmering wall surrounded Kyrianna then a cloud of darkness covered the area.

~ * ~

Brular took a deep breath and rose from the floor. It was starting again. The weight on his wrists reminded him of previous chains. The only thing missing was the laughter of the demons.

He pulled the chains taut as he forced himself to stand straight and face Torliana as she stepped down from the ornate throne she had created for herself.

She smiled as she stepped up to him, just out of reach of his bound hands.

"Only a precaution," she said with a smile, "mighty *Keeper of the Flame.*"

He closed his eyes as she spat out his old title. The temple was gone, her doing. His title stripped from him, along with everything else he had lost that day and in the decades following. He had bathed himself in his anger, hatred and a hunger for vengeance. He had cast off his name, a remnant of a proud man who had been flayed from his body like so much tissue and sinew.

The companions he had told he would trade any and all of their lives on his path for revenge, had, despite a few stumbles along the way, shown him the strength of their devotion to each other. It was a devotion that reminded him so much of the temple. However, it was not that which had brought him back from the edge of wielding the most accursed magics to achieve his goal. Kyrianna had shared her thoughts, that dark, twisted collage of images. For the first time he could see how Thynitic could manipulate the truth and prey on one's fears and uncertainties. He had endured physical torments like no other who still walked. However, through some miracle of Hellavar, his mind had held. Kyrianna's thoughts disturbed him. He had seen glimpses of Torliana within her. Not only as a Kindling, but as Kyrianna had seen, a woman calling out to him. She was a student looking for guidance and a girl looking for acknowledgement of affection. *What horrors did she do to your mind, before you succumbed, Kindling?*

Opening his eyes, he bowed his head slightly studying the runes engraved on the chains and the inscription carved into the floor where he stood. He shook his head. When he spoke, his words were measured. "Does the favored of the Lady actually fear me this much?"

Torliana's laugh seemed forced as she answered him. "Fear

you? No. It is you who should fear me. You—who would have cast me out."

Brular leaned back as she spoke. He shook his head again, but did not reply.

"You who would not yield to anything, but your precious Order," Torliana said. "You should fear me. There is more at stake here than you know. I will have her power soon and then I will dwarf your status, Keeper."

Brular straightened and spoke softly, as if to a child. "You wish to reign over more destruction. You wish to sow more misery. You are not a god; you are a plague. A plague that needs to be cut from the body before it consumes everything." He narrowed his eyes in sudden realization and understanding. "Even itself."

Torliana laughed again. This time it wasn't forced and it echoed in the large chamber. "What? You don't honestly think that pitiful group can actually challenge me? Now that I have taken you from them, they have no one who truly has faith in their god. They walk alone; in particular the daughter of Arielle. It is her lack of faith that dooms this group in ways they cannot image. It will be amusing to send a creature that can match their powers now."

Brular stood quietly but knew her words were not entirely convincing—not even to herself. As they had rekindled his light, he had shown them the untapped sparks of their faith and the power of their patrons. *They are not alone*, he thought. *They have their gods and more importantly, they have each other.*

"Truth be told, you were the only uncertain factor in that group," Torliana said. "I found your summoning of an efreeti and bargaining with your own life force to restore another surprising. However, the gall you had to draw Mykaylene to this place shocked me. That cost you much. That shield should have been a relic for your church and she took it for your insolence in summoning her. What did it buy you? Nothing." She applauded lightly as she walked around him. "Never would I have guessed you would tap such resources."

He kept his face stoic and his thoughts only a whisper in his mind. *A shield for a knight infused with the most holy of magics. A worthy trade if I can stop this abomination she is twisting you to become. You don't even see it, do you?*

She stopped in front of him, standing a bit closer, with her fingers resting on his chest. "That brings me to my next little issue.

As I am sure you have guessed, I have the daughter of Arielle."

Brular stared as the cloud of darkness dissolved in the corner next to Torliana's throne. Kyrianna hung in a set of chains similar to his own. On the floor several feet from her appeared to be all of her gear and equipment. The mage had left her only with the long tunic and leggings she wore under her armor, nothing else. He paused as a slight sparkle of silver, from what appeared to be a pendant hanging around the girl's neck, caught his eye.

Kyrianna raised her head slightly and he saw the grief and guilt that had taken up residence in her soul multiply exponentially as she looked at him. "No, please, no," he heard the whispered plea.

He glanced from Kyrianna to Torliana and back several times. "You have the one you wanted. What do you want from me?"

Torliana glanced at Kyrianna and smiled. "I want the rest of that group dead. You have come a long way, Brular; it would be a shame for you to fail without having your chance at retribution." She spat on the floor, then stepped even closer, her hand moving up to his throat.

After several seconds of resting her nails lightly on his skin, she stepped back and frowned. "What do you know of being wronged? For four years, I worked to do everything I was expected to do, just to be thrown away."

Brular only stared at her. Not answering the accusation or the anger he heard in her voice.

"Despite that, I still offer you your chance at vengeance," she said. "Defeat the knight and her companions." She walked away from him waving her hand in an absentminded gesture. "Kill them and I will grant you a fair chance at revenge."

She spun around quickly as he responded without any hesitation. He had already made his decision years ago. "No enchanted items or in place magics of any sort," he said, his voice harsh as he spoke. "We face each other only with spells and simple non-magical equipment." He cocked his head to one side as he let his words sink into his former student.

"Well, well, well. That did not take long. The group disappoints you," she said.

"They know not how to match their skills and powers to take enemies down quickly. The seniors from Mount Veri would have buried them in the first moments of combat." Brular paused and pulled against the chains forcing himself to take a step forward as he stared into her depthless black eyes. "Let us stop this silly game. What is the price of failure?"

Torliana smirked as her hand pulled a small blood-red amulet from under her tunic. It hung there on a slender silver chain. "You will be sent back to the abyss for the Lady's pleasure."

"So be it!"

"Brular, no!" Kyrianna fought against her chains.

"She has spirit and strength. It is surprising, isn't it?" Torliana waved her hand.

"No!" The cry dragged out as Kyrianna fell forward; her weight supported only by her bound wrists. "Please, no more," she whispered.

Brular stared at Kyrianna, she had been held by Torliana for several days now. That she had any strength left was remarkable. He glanced at the equipment on the ground.

"Give me her equipment to take with me," he said.

"Why?" Torliana glanced at the pile.

"It is of no consequence to you and if I drop it at their feet, it will break their will and crush their souls. Then it will be all the easier to grind their bodies into dust."

She stared at him for several minutes then took a step back. He could see the anger building as her body tensed and her eyes narrowed then with a wave of her hand, he convulsed in pain. The silver flecks in her eyes were like daggers as her open hand struck his face. "Then it is settled, you emotionless bastard."

Brular looked at her and knew Kyrianna's words were true, even now. For just a moment, he saw her for what she was, not what the Lady had made her. "No, Torliana, it is not settled yet," he said. "First, bring me parchment and a pen. Then prepare a gate and bring to us an efreeti noble. He will bear witness to the contract and if you dishonor it, the efreeti will see to your punishment." His voice was once again that of the great judge who had presided over archmages and generals.

Torliana's hand flashed out and slapped hard across his face yet again. "You think that scares me, Cleric?"

Brular only looked at her, not reacting to the assault. "No. What I expect is if you fail to adhere to the letter of the contract, he will grant me three magical requests immediately and the first thing I will request is that we both be transported to the lowest levels of the Nine Hells and the next one will be to trap both of us there." His voice was cold and stern as he stared at Torliana. "The last I hold for your imagination. What would Brular Eglis, Keeper of Mount Veri, summoner of gods dare to do with his last bit of magic?"

Torliana stepped back, her eyes wide as she stared at the cleric.

"Now, I believe we have an understanding," Brular said as he sat back on the floor. "Bring me a pen."

"You will add the following two items, *Lawgiver*," Torliana said. "First, the amulet will go with you to Thynitic. Second, you will only have one hour from the time you encounter them to settle the matter, great Keeper." Torliana walked slowly around him as he began to write. "After that time, I will bring you back here and you will admit to failure and suffer the punishment already agreed to."

Brular glanced up at Kyrianna and nodded his agreement to the conditions. Her eyes were wide as she watched him. He dropped his head back to the parchment in his hand and finished the contract. "It has been written; summon the efreeti to witness and hold the contract," he said.

Torliana looked down and he watched as her eyes scanned the words on the page. "Very well." She looked back up at Kyrianna and smiled. "Your friends will never have a chance."

~ * ~

Kyrianna felt the shackles disappear and she caught herself as she hit the floor. Her eyes widened; the bare floor below her was smooth and gray. Gone was the black stone covered in runes, except for a faintly glowing circle in front of her. The glowing, reddish hue began dissipating before her eyes.

She looked frantically to one side, then the other. *No throne, no enspelling runes, except this one.* However, she could see a symbol painted in the center of the right wall. She looked at the single rune on the ground as the magic faded. She was not a student of magic, but she had seen this several times in the last few days. Carefully ordered inscriptions of power forming a continuous circle. *Brular, what have you done?*

She tried to stand, only to feel her leg muscles scream at her. Her right hand touched the floor to steady herself. *No!* She looked at the layered and scarred flesh of the hand. *What have you done?* Her mind screamed the question as she collapsed to the floor. *You did not free me. You took my place. Why would you dare to bear more pain for me?*

Kyrianna sat there weeping. She had prayed to be released regardless of the cost, with one exception. She was wrong. This price was also too high. "Why did you do this?" She froze as she listened to the resonating power of Brular's voice mixed with the subtle melodic elven rhythm of her own speech patterns. She dropped her head and closed her eyes. "Now you must also bear my torture." The words were only a pathetic whimper as she fought the anger and despair building in her heart.

"Why did you do this?" Her anger exploded as she screamed the question in the empty room.

She wiped her eyes only to feel pain in both her new body's hands and brow. His body was tired and wounded from all those years he spent at the hands of Thynitic and her minions. Every movement was its own little ordeal. *He knew what she would be doing to me from his own experiences, yet he took my place. He even dared to summon the efreeti again so he could take my place. That's the only way. She paused as her chest tightened. Despite everything, I could never have done what he has.*

Her eyes slowly cleared and she saw his weapons and armor as well as her own equipment close by. Placed on top of the pile was an open piece of parchment. She moved carefully, feeling the constant pain he endured as she reached for the parchment.

Kyrianna, Daughter of Arielle,

First, do not despair for your friends. They will not suffer from my magic. They are safe from me.

She held the letter and thanked Hellavar his servant would not take up the mantle of her companions' destruction. The nightmare of the last few hours wondering what Brular would do ended abruptly and completely in her mind. He had written it and it would be so. Even at his darkest, this man was a man of his word.

She continued to read the letter. "No!" The word turned into a scream of denial that echoed in the room like the cry of a tortured animal. While the first lines of the letter had eased her fears for her comrades, the next ones tore a new hole in her heart.

As I wrote the contract, I knew I was accepting an eternity of torture once more.

"Why? By all the gods, why did you do it?" She spoke the words softly, but knew she would probably never know the real answer. She had heard the words spoken by Brular and Torliana in the mage's chambers and knew what he had just damned himself to in order to protect the others.

What two poor lost souls we are. I am sorry but I dare not try to rip your body and soul from your bonds. Torliana may have expected that and prepared magics to intercede.

I have freed your mind and soul and have given them to my sorry aged husk. I am sorry I could not provide better for you but that is an unfortunate limitation of my abilities as of late. The request (I am sure you recognized my efreeti friend's handiwork) was worded so you will remain in this body until eight hours have passed or the door to this room opens. While I have given you my word they will come to no harm at my hands, I still have business with your friends.

I must atone for my own actions. I must give them what power I have left. I must prepare them for the task I must not do myself.

Use this time well, Kyrianna. I prayed for years to have just one minute away from their clutches. I grant you eight hours. The wall holds a symbol of sleep. If you speak the words 'Hellavar's rest', it will activate. Give yourself over to its magic and sleep. Let your strength return.

The Lady will come for you, I cannot stop that. However, I tell you with every ounce of my being she will bring you to ruin. She will tempt you with salvation then have you destroy your closest friends and loved ones. She will twist you against everything you care to have. Remember these words most of all: The power of a god is a fallacy. *She will turn on you regardless of what she says. She is chaos and it knows no promise or treaty.*

Look at Torliana. I can see Thynitic has done the most insidious thing to the Kindling. Thynitic has twisted Torliana so she resembles herself. A poor lost soul desperate to control the chaos even though she knows in her heart she cannot. She seeks to steal Thynitic's power. She doesn't even realize that every time she takes a bit of the goddess' power, she is in turn losing a part of her very soul.

To be her Chosen is to be lost in a sea of misery and lies. See the lies for what they are, child. They hold no power, only despair. How can you save them if you cannot save yourself? How can you?

My hand grows tired and you should rest. I will watch over the Kindling for you; then I will go see Thynitic. Should I spit in the left eye or the right for you?

Brular Eglis, Keeper of the Flame of Mount Veri.

Kyrianna smiled softly as she read the last line again. *I hope you get the chance.*

She carefully folded the parchment and placed it into her pack. He had given her a gift that would cost him more than she could ever repay and she would never forget him for it. As she tucked the paper into an inner pocket, her hand brushed against the small figurine he had given her before—the silver-gray unicorn. She had called it forth only once, when it had been completed. Ashe, as he had called himself at that time, had indicated the unicorn had ties to her mother's past; the figurine had been carved from the horn of the filly killed on that day.

I have seen what Thynitic wanted me to see about that day, she thought. *Perhaps, I should find out if there is another viewpoint.* She placed the figurine on the ground in front of her. "Cewyr," she said softly.

A soft glow surrounded the figurine then the unicorn stood in front of her. The mare tilted her head to the side as the bright amethyst eyes looked at her. The eyes widened a bit as she looked into Kyrianna's, then the golden-red horn dipped in acknowledgement. "Kyrianna?" The unicorn spoke in Taladilith, the voice as delicate as the wisps of hair that covered her fetlocks.

Kyrianna only nodded and the unicorn lowered herself to the ground in front of her. "You are deeply troubled and soul sick, young one. I have only few skills as a cleric so cannot do anything to ease the sorrow you are feeling."

"I understand that. What I would ask of you is to tell me of that day. I have seen what the Lady would have me see. I need to know the truth of what happened that day."

"Young one, I do not think you need to see again what the Lady of Chaos has shown you. I know what happened that day, and I know she did not need to twist any of those events in what she showed you. However, I will show you what she did not." Cewyr gently touched her horn to Kyrianna's forehead.

Kyrianna gasped as she found herself standing once again in the forest of Kilenter. She watched as an elven woman in multicolored robes knelt next to the body of an old man dressed as a ranger. The woman picked up the man's sword; it was the same unicorn horn long sword she remembered her mother carrying.

Grasping the sword, the elven woman stood up, tears streaming down her face. Kyrianna gasped as she realized it was her mother Arielle.

"Thynitic, you bitch!" Arielle held the sword tightly as she screamed the goddess' name. "This is what you wanted all along, wasn't it! There was never any call from you for me to contact the Rynial, was there? All you wanted was to bring me back here and destroy the only place I had ever found happiness."

Only silence greeted Arielle. "I renounce you and all you stand for. I will never return to your service and will do everything I can to destroy you. This I swear by Frayrith, the Lady of the Forests."

Without any warning, a woman appeared before Arielle. She was tall and slender, her coloring and appearance shifting through the three elven races as well as human. "You have been called as my representative in this world. You are a Daughter of Chaos. Do not think to walk away from me so easily. You will never escape from me or the chaos I can bring to you and your children."

"I renounce you! You have no power over me anymore!" Arielle stood defiantly before the goddess, her hands clasped around the unicorn horn sword.

"In this place, as long as you hold that sword, you are correct. However, there will come a time when you will not have the protections of that weapon. Then, my daughter, we will see what happens. Until one of your blood returns to me, you are cursed. You and those who follow you will know only chaos and confusion. Chaos will follow in your steps." With a burst of blinding light, Thynitic vanished.

"Frayrith." Arielle dropped to her knees as a unicorn stepped out of the trees and stood before her. The woman held out the bloodstained horn. "I beg forgiveness for my actions, though I know I am unworthy to even ask for such."

"Regardless of that, you were first my child before Chaos claimed you. I will not abandon you again," Frayrith said. The unicorn stepped forward and gently touched Arielle's wrist with her horn. Kyrianna watched as a silver unicorn appeared on her mother's flesh. "I am sorry, but I cannot undo the curse she has laid on you. You and your line are bound to me and to fight the growing Chaos. Those of your blood will be the tools I and others will use to prevent Chaos from destroying everything when it becomes necessary."

Arielle bowed her head slightly then nodded. "I accept the binding," she said softly.

The unicorn shimmered and an elf appeared before Arielle. She had flowing silver hair, black eyes and golden skin. She wore the simple leathers of a ranger and carried a longbow and short sword. With a gentle hand, she reached out and lifted Arielle's head. "I too must ask forgiveness. I knew what you would be facing and allowed it to happen in order to bring you to this day. Cewyr's blood is not on your hands alone; it is also on mine." The goddess drew her sword and held it out to Arielle. The metal was the color of dried blood.

As Frayrith spoke, the body of the ranger was covered in a golden mist then vanished. "He was one of my chosen. He will be received with honor." She reached out and laid her sword tip across the unicorn blade Arielle held. The elf's clothes changed into the traditional garb of a ranger. "You are also one of my chosen." The goddess changed back into her unicorn form, touched Arielle with her horn then turned and bounded back into the forest.

Kyrianna shook her head as the scene cleared, Cewyr's amethyst eyes still watching her. "There is always hope, Kyrianna. Your mother served Thynitic for five years and was still able to renounce her and leave her service. Keep that hope locked in your heart. Now, I think you should rest. The priest's spell will not last forever, nor should it."

"Return to your home," Kyrianna said softly.

Cewyr touched the parchment with her horn. "Leave him a message that I wish to speak with him," she said. Mist surrounded the unicorn and when it dissipated all that was left was the small figurine.

Kyrianna looked up at the symbol Brular had placed on the wall. "Hellavar's rest," she said. Warmth embraced her as blackness claimed her.

Chapter Twelve

Brular howled as he found himself stretched by arm restraints and his own weight. He let his eyes scan the room without moving his head. Torliana was looking toward him, concern on her face as she studied him. She then turned back to study the mirror in front of her with its black surface.

"Chaos take him!" The scream echoed in the room. "How dare he taunt me like this?" Her hand closed with her fingers drawn inward like a claw as she slammed it into the mirror. Her face was impassive as a large piece of glass embedded itself in the back of her hand. "He summoned an efreeti and sealed the room to all types of scrying." She turned to stare at Brular as she plucked the glass from her hand.

"What is he planning? He penned the contract himself. Why did I trust him with that? Why am I such a fool?" She sat on her throne for several minutes in apparent contemplation.

Brular's gaze moved around the room. A sudden flash of motion from Torliana's hand and the pain he felt in his temporary body's left cheek told him she had thrown the glass and cut his face. His gaze jerked back to her.

His thoughts were guarded and he concentrated on keeping his features impassive as he watched her. *Kindling? Is there more of you left than I thought?*

A small and distinctly young female whisper came to his mind. :*Kyri? Are you alright?*

His eyes grew wide. For the first time in many decades, Brular Eglis was indeed surprised.

:*You're not Kyri*, the small voice said. :*This is her body. What is going on? Who are you? Where is Kyrianna?* The small voice grew more desperate as it spoke.

The frantic voice was an unexpected distraction. His mind was assaulted by her pleading and he saw Torliana watching him with curiosity. He quickly contorted in mock pain as his mind raced inward.

:*Quiet, little one. She is fine. Let me deal with Torliana's concern or it will not go well for either Kyrianna or us.*

Torliana stepped down from her throne toward him.

The small voice spoke again. :*Little one? Brular? Keeper, is that you? How? Why?*

Torliana was almost within arms' reach. Brular's voice was commanding and reassuring, yet harsh. :*Be quiet, lest she probe this mind; then we both will be found. There are spells that will drag us both from in here and Kyrianna immediately back. Is that what you want?*

:*No, I only want to help her.*

:*Then. Be. Quiet!*

The voice began to sob and he closed his eyes as he concentrated to find it, but there was a sharp pain in his side. His eyes snapped open to see Torliana's within inches of his.

"Aren't you comfortable?" Torliana grinned at him.

He didn't even attempt to speak. To speak aloud would risk doom, not only for himself, but also for Kyrianna and the mysterious voice in his mind. However, most important of all, it would cost him the chance to prepare their companions. Instead, he felt the ranger's strength of body and youth; he lazily rolled her head down to the side. As Torliana reached for it, he whipped Kyrianna's head up and was rewarded with the rocking back of Torliana's head. It was hardly a wound at all, but a mark of defiance, a reason for the feigned pain. He punctuated his wordless response to Kyrianna's imprisonment by spitting.

Torliana wiped her face, which then twisted into a cruel smile. "Good, you have fight left. It gives me something to break." Her hands moved in smooth practiced rhythms.

He recognized the spell and called out in his mind. :*Little one, great pain comes.* Just as his warning was finished, so was her spell and he felt the tears come as his ears burned, his back arched and his distinctly female larynx wailed. From another part of his mind he heard an echoing howl—Shadow Seeker was still linked to Kyrianna. That surprised him. He would have expected the wolf to be linked to her soul and not her body by the bond Kyrianna had described.

The pain passed and, he could see Torliana brooding on her throne. She looked down at the crushed mirror and he could see the smallest smile on her face.

How much of you is left, Torliana? How much? Do you still seek adoration, purpose and security? She has none of that. She can give only constant anarchy and conflict.

:*What are you talking about?*

:*Her, little one. The poor lost Kindling.*

:*Poor! She has been torturing Kyri for days.*

:*True, but is it her hand or that of Thynitic?*

:*I don't understand. You speak in riddles.*

:*Shh. Let me watch and learn. Then I will try to make everything clear. First, who are you and how do you come to be here?*

:*I am Melissa Duvall and I have traveled with Kyri for months, ever since they left my family's estate near Duvshire, north of Raspa.*

:*Melissa. That is a nice smooth name befitting your melodious voice.*

:*I would have you know that I am older than Kyri by almost twenty years. I am more wraith than waif.*

He allowed a laugh to enter his thoughts. :*I am still old enough to be your grandfather and you should mind your elders, Missy. His voice turned into a bellowing laugh.*

:*Missy; that was the name my tutor called me. I miss her.* Her voice became faraway. :*I miss all of them.*

:*It seems we have something in common. We are both alone in this world. All those who cared are gone.*

His eyes focused again on Torliana. *Or, are they?*

Torliana glanced back at Kyrianna and smiled again. She then turned away as if the girl was no longer of any concern to her. She glanced around the chamber then reached up and a small portal opened at the tips of her fingers. She reached in and removed a large book. As she sat on the throne and opened the book the portal closed and several tiles on the floor of the chamber began to glow.

:*Keeper, why did you come? I mean, why did you take Kyri's place?*

:*Because it is where I belong,* Brular said.

:*You belong under the whip of this cruel woman?*

:*I am her Keeper and she is lost in that poor tortured mind. I accepted a duty from Hellavar to watch over this Kindling. I have been negligent. I failed so many years ago to see his true meaning. Now we have come to this. Look at her, Melissa; she doesn't truly know what she is doing.*

Torliana was still reading from the book and more tiles began to glow in the room.

:*Keeper, she prepares to destroy Myrith, Hendandra and the others. She seems quite purposeful. She reminds me of you. She completes her craft without a moment's hesitation. Her path seems clear to her.* Melissa paused. :*Are you trying to confuse me? I don't understand what you mean.*

:*I am sorry, Melissa. I will try to explain.* There was a short pause as Brular took a silent but deep breath. :*Her magic, at least part of it, is drawn directly from the goddess Thynitic. The more she uses the goddess' power, the more her soul becomes tied to the Lady of Chaos.*

:*Tied? You mean like a cleric, right?*

:*No. She has passed that now. She is a Chosen; a person who channels her god's very essence on the material plane. Her soul becomes entwined with her god's nature—in this case, chaos. Each time she uses that power its hold becomes a little tighter, until it can never be separated from her. If the Chosen has channeled enough deific power, they join with their god upon death and become a part of that deity. In the case of the powers of light, it is a bliss of knowledge, power or kindness, for my own it would be brilliance, warmth and order. For hers…* his voice trailed off.

Melissa's voice choked. :*Chaos, misery, darkness, torture, pain, mockery. That is horrible. I know this existence, Keeper. It is horrible. I…* Her voice was quiet for a moment. :*Sorry. I existed for some thirty years trapped as you say. I spent thirty years watching the same events when my brother took the lives of almost all my family. It was so cold in the garden's maze. So cold! I wanted to go someplace warm, but my soul was sealed within the hedges. Every night was a torture; I saw my brother and that knife. I felt that blade. I heard my family's screams. I thought it would never end. Then my nephew Tristan came and he held me. I felt his warmth and his sorrow for what had happened. It was not the warmth of his body but his soul, Keeper. It was as if the sky had opened for the briefest moment and the sun shone on me. He carried my body to the chapel, then he and the others left to see to the others. I was alone again. I sank deeper into the depths, Keeper. Do you know what it is like to find what you have been missing for so long for just the briefest moment and then have it taken away? It is the worst type of emptiness.*

Her voice descended into a series of sobs. :*Later, Kyrianna carried my mother's soul to the chapel within her own body. My mother and I were brought back together after being apart for those long years. I knew companionship, even though it was next to the empty shell of the once living.* She paused for several minutes.

:*Mother, thank you for all those years of waiting for me at the door, calling to me.* Her voice sounded like a soft, distance breeze. :*Keeper, Krella was your mother. Did you love her?*

His voice sounded hollow and empty when he replied. :*Until a few days ago, I would have said yes. However, I have come to realize something: I am not sure I have ever truly loved anyone. My life since the age of five has been duty, dedication, order and service. Not love.*

:*I am sorry.*

:*For what? For showing me for the fool I am? I am a judge who has roamed Shokar for decades. Dedicated to nothing but blind ideals, His greatest servant; one so dedicated that his own life, wants and needs were nonexistent. The perfect servant for the God of Order and Flame. Consumed by the very Order—what a sorry statement of my life. You are more alive than I am.*

Her voice was cool and soothing. :*I did not mean this, Keeper. I only wanted to explain why I chose to come with Kyri. I felt her loneliness even among her companions. My mother felt the loneliness of her soul when they touched briefly. I came to be with her as they came to be with me.*

His eyes returned to Torliana on her throne. :*You are absolutely right, little one. Thank you, Melissa.*

:*For what?*

:*For giving me the power to save her.* He let his gaze rest on the mage. He let the darkness melt to see the woman, the one who had asked him to stay that night in a moonlit grove. *I will stay this time, Torliana.*

His thoughts became structured and unyielding. *First, I must give the others all of my power and magic to stop this chaos.*

His inner voice resonated as if in a great cathedral. *Then I will give everything else to save you.* His thoughts became an unspoken oath. *She will not have you. She will never have you. I swear it. And I will kill her myself if I have to.*

He felt Melissa retreat from his thoughts and he concentrated on studying the power Torliana was calling as she continued to cast her preparation and trap spells. He focused his attention on the magics trying to read the lines of power that still glowed in the room as Torliana moved around casting and activating the spells.

The aura from the spells on the steps of the dais were beginning to fade, but he could still tell each of the affected steps were linked together as a trigger for the same spell on the first set and a different enchantment on the second. There was a single safe route off the dais against the back wall. He nodded at the power Torliana was expending in her efforts; she wanted to take no chances on the group reaching her. The spell on the first riser would unleash a storm of fire, ice and lightning that would assault all in the room for several minutes. The second riser contained a simple but powerful spell that would trap a person on each of the steps.

Torliana was now standing in the center of the room as the tiles on the floor glowed briefly then faded. With her position, he was unable to clearly mark where the trigger rune was being placed in each case, but he was certain the magic was a spell they had already faced once in this place of chaos and torment. With his attention on the floor tiles that were being used as the trigger runes, he almost missed the bright flashes from the columns that told him where the spell would actually emanate from when triggered. Unfortunately, he couldn't tell which of the columns had been specifically triggered to release the spell.

As she finished with the floor runes, Torliana moved between the walls that bracketed the doors into the chamber. Her voice was low as she chanted and he couldn't hear the words clearly enough to make out the spells.

Torliana smiled as she walked across the floor and back to where Kyrianna was being held. "Even if by some miracle they manage to live through what Brular has planned for them, they will not survive entering this room. When this is over, I will escort you to the Lady's citadel where I will begin your training as one of her daughters."

Brular continued to glare defiantly at Torliana, not saying anything as she turned and walked back to the throne. *Two souls I must protect from her chaos and madness,* he thought. *First, protect the others so they can save Kyri. Then I have to salvage what has been damaged and rescue what has been almost lost.* He continued to watch Torliana as she sat down and returned the book she had used for her spells to its pocket dimension and removed another, larger book. A book bound in black with a silver-gray unicorn inlaid on the cover with the portal of Chaos displayed as if it were balanced on the tip of the horn.

:*That book*, Melissa's voice was quaking. :*That's the book Mikyl had.*

:*That is the* Book of Chaos, *little one. It is a relic of Thynitic's church on Kyri's world. How can that be the book your brother had?*

:*I don't know. He got it from someone he met in Duvshire. I went with him and the stable master that night. He told me to stay by the carriage, so I never saw the person he got it from, but it is the same book*. The girl's voice paused. :*Keeper, why does Cewyr have the same coloring as the unicorn on the book? I always thought unicorns were pure white.*

Brular looked at the unicorn on the book and frowned. The image indeed had the same coloring as the unicorn mare summoned by the figurine he had created. :*Perhaps, it is Cewyr's way of taunting the Lady of Chaos*, he thought.

Chapter Thirteen

Brular grimaced as he forced himself to sit up. The spell had transferred him back to his body before the group arrived. He could see the lines of power around the door had not been disturbed; indicating the spell weaving he and the efreeti had created was still in place, as was the shielding spell. Torliana was still prevented from scrying on the room. The unicorn figurine was sitting on the floor with a small piece of parchment next to it. *She wishes to speak to you*, was all it said.

He touched the unicorn figure where it sat on the floor. "Cewyr," he said.

The mare appeared and nodded her head. "Keeper," she said. "There is a flaw in both your and Myrith's thinking. I have touched Kyrianna's thoughts and have seen what has transpired these past days. While you and the knight only seek to save her from the darkness, if Myrith is forced to kill Kyrianna—her soul will go to Thynitic. She is bound to the Lady of Chaos much as Torliana is. She has all but renounced Frayrith because she feels betrayed by her patron. If she is killed in this place…"

"Her soul goes to Thynitic," Brular said, interrupting the unicorn.

"Myrith must understand the consequences of her actions if she decides she must honor her promise." Mist swirled around the unicorn and she vanished leaving only the figurine.

Brular closed his eyes and took a deep breath. He would have to make Myrith understand. If he didn't, both of their souls could be lost if Myrith condemned her friend to Thynitic's chaos. He secured the figurine in Kyrianna's pack and took a seat against the wall and waited for the group to arrive.

~ * ~

"You need new armor, Hendandra," Myrith said, looking down at the rogue. "This looks like it's disintegrating. What's going on?"

Hendandra's eyes widened as she glanced up at Myrith.

Myrith frowned as Hendandra looked down at the floor. "I think I may have managed to get Rhyra mad at me."

"We go to confront the representative of a goddess, possibly even the goddess herself and you managed to get a different one mad at you? What did you do?"

"I don't know! She's the one who blessed my armor and violin and now the enchantments are fading. She hasn't said anything to me about why she's doing this."

"We don't have time to seek an answer to the problem at this point." Myrith glanced over the rest of the group. "Does anyone have any armor she can wear?"

"I have the leather Kyrianna was wearing before we found the chain mail," Andrinor said. "She asked me to carry it because of weight."

"But will it fit?" Hendandra looked around at the others. "I'm a bit smaller than the rest of you trees."

"It had magical enchantments on it. Perhaps it will resize itself," Falden said. "That is a minor enchantment and one that is common on many enhanced items."

"Do you think Kyri will mind?" Hendandra held the armor as she looked at Myrith.

"Of course not. All she is going to care about is that you have a chance of surviving this place," Andrinor said.

"Use the armor, if it will fit," Myrith said. "Kyri will not mind." *And if she does, she's no longer the person I call my friend.*

The group waited as Hendandra changed into Kyrianna's old armor, the leather resizing itself to her smaller stature as Falden had suggested it might. The loss of Brular the previous day had shocked them all. After Kyrianna had been taken by the chronoynian, as Brular had named the creature, she hadn't expected anything to target any of them specifically. But the ice devils had gone after Brular as soon as they entered this room. He had suggested Torliana was watching and evaluating them before; perhaps she saw him as the greatest threat to her and had taken steps to have him removed from the group. If that were true, was she going to be picking them off one at a time—sending creatures targeted to a particular person's weaknesses? It wasn't a pleasant thought.

"Okay, I'm ready," Hendandra said, dropping her old armor. A cloud of dust billowed out of the pile as it hit the floor.

"Let's get going," Myrith said, opening the door.

The fog that filled the corridor these past days was still there and it surrounded them as the room vanished. There was a bright flash of light and the fog also vanished.

"Myrith," Falden's voice called.

She turned to look at the mage and smiled. The changes that had been taking place had all been reversed. Falden was once again himself instead of a patchwork cross between a human and a hawk. "Lady of Chaos, indeed," she said.

"Brular said her own nature was her weakness, remember," Vyroris said as he touched the place the rabbit ears had been. "She would give her enemies safe passage while causing her most faithful servants to suffer great torments—all on a whim."

"Well at least this time it appears to be to our benefit," Hendandra said. She smiled as she looked up Vyroris. "The nose is gone also," she said.

"For now." Myrith looked at the double doors at the end of the corridor. They were only a few yards away, but she had no idea how many more rooms they would be forced to enter before they finally reached them. It didn't matter, they would face whatever Torliana decided to throw at them and the sooner they got started the sooner they would find her and hopefully, Kyrianna.

As she took a step, a door appeared in front of her and Myrith nodded. The game had started again.

The door was partially ajar as Hendandra checked it. She stepped back and shook her head. "I find nothing, but I don't like this," she whispered.

"Do we have a choice?" Myrith asked as she reached for the door. The door opened into darkness and Myrith frowned as water splashed around her ankles. She only took a few steps and found herself against a wall as the others came in behind her and the door shut.

A sudden burst of sound echoed in the small area and Myrith heard the clang of steel as Hendandra dropped her blade and grabbed her ears. A howl filled the room as Shadow Seeker voiced his displeasure at the pain from the noise. As the echoes faded, a flash of light went off above her and Myrith fought the spell that wrapped itself around her trying to bind her. "Show yourself!" she yelled as the effects of the spell faded.

There was no answer and Myrith glanced back at the rest of the group. Vyroris, Nirev and Kyrianna's wolf seemed to be frozen in place. “Chaos take it,” she said.

“Myrith, there appears to be an opening at the top of the wall,” Hendandra said. “I think I can make it up.”

“We need to do something. Go.”

The wall burst into flames and Myrith heard Andrinor curse as the heat washed over them. The witch had prepared well. Brular had been right about her watching and evaluating them. They had been led into this trap. Still, she had no intentions of giving up; if they were going to die, she would find a way to take Torliana with her.

“Leikor’s cursed luck,” Hendandra said.

Myrith looked up to see Hendandra had reached the top of the wall. “What is it?”

“A barrier of some sort—dancing blades.” She paused. “There’s a ledge against the back wall and someone sitting on it.” She paused for a moment. “Myrith, it’s Brular!”

“Brular? No, you’re mistaken.”

Hendandra screamed as the area began shaking violently and she fell from the wall. Andrinor dropped his weapon as he attempted to catch the girl. Myrith fell to the floor as a large piece of the ceiling hit her in the shoulder. She heard a strangled yelp from the wolf. She forced herself back to her feet and looked around.

Shadow Seeker was trapped under a large piece of stone and the blood mixing with the water they were standing in told her the wolf was dead. Vyroris also appeared to be dead, crushed by falling debris. Jerietlan was chanting as he laid his hands on Nirev. The dwarf stirred slightly.

“Why would Brular be doing this?” Hendandra said as Andrinor set her down.

“Are you sure it was Brular?” Andrinor backed away from the flames.

“Yes.” Hendandra’s voice was barely a whisper as she looked at the floor.

“We have to get out of this area and quickly,” Myrith said.

“Not again,” Hendandra said as the ground began shaking.

Myrith dodged several chucks of stone as the shaking stopped.

“Mykaylene protect us,” Jerietlan said as they heard chanting from the other side of the wall. “He’s calling a firestorm.”

Myrith raised her blade defiantly and closed her eyes as flames poured from the ceiling.

~ * ~

Myrith opened her eyes to find herself standing in a room similar to the others they had entered in this corridor. Standing in the center of the room was Brular. Next to him was Kyrianna's unicorn and equipment. "I wanted to show you the type of danger you will be facing when you enter her chamber. You must be prepared for the worst she can throw at you," Brular said.

"I do not have much time, before she calls me back to her. She believes I have agreed to destroy you for her, but she cannot scry into this room to see what is really happening."

"What *is* going on?" Myrith stepped forward. "And what was that?"

"Lady Lake; that is what you would have faced if you had not succeeded in restoring me to who I was before I became Ashe. Torliana offered me a deal: if I would destroy you, she would allow me the chance to face her. As Ashe, I would have agreed. As Brular, I have taken advantage of the opportunity to try and prepare you for her. First, I must atone for some of my actions these past days." He looked at Hendandra. "You whom I prejudged based on your profession and minimal ties to a particular god, I give this." He handed her a small coin. "May your fingers prove more nimble and your movements more graceful." A soft light surrounded her.

"Wait," Myrith said. "You said she offered you a deal; that if you destroyed us, she would give a chance at revenge. What is the penalty if you fail?"

Brular looked at her and shook his head. "That is between Torliana and I. It does not concern you at this time."

"You are a part of this group and therefore it does concern us." She paused and waited for him to answer.

"Very well. I will have your word you will not interfere. I made my decision knowing what the consequences of my actions would be."

Myrith hesitated as she looked at Brular then around at the others. Mykaylene had charged her with redeeming Brular from the darkness he was following and his demonstration of what he could have done, but hadn't, showed her she had succeeded. But what would be the cost of that success? She took a deep breath and nodded. "Very well, you have my word."

"If I fail, the penalty is I will be sent back to Thynitic, along with the amulet, which Torliana has in her possession."

"No!"

"You gave your word, Lady Lake." Brular started to turn away.

"However, I did not," Nirev said. "Nor did any of the rest of us."

"You gave your word to follow me," Myrith said. "I lead and by that I also speak for the group." She looked at Brular. "Is there no way to prevent that from happening?"

"No, Lady Lake. I penned the contract myself and it will be honored as written."

Myrith nodded. "I understand."

Brular turned to Andrinor. "You whom I killed, I give this." He handed the dragon warrior a similar token. "Being brought back from the realms of the dead causes a weakening of your body's strength, may it be restored." A light surrounded Andrinor.

"For the rest of you. Jerietlan; this rod will allow your spells to operate at their maximum level—if you channel the power you would use against those who are undead into it when you cast. To Nirev, I pass my weapons." He handed the dwarf his morningstar and a dagger. "I ask that you only hold the dagger until you are able to rescue Kyrianna, then see it is given to her. I have no doubt she will be hounded by Thynitic the rest of her life. The dagger has been imbued with minor protections against chaos that may help to shield her."

He picked up a letter and turned to Falden. "An introduction to the council of mages. While it is doubtful they will accept you into the Academy at this time, this should allow you access to the libraries and magical research of Gormanghast."

Falden took the letter and bowed deeply. "My thanks."

Brular turned to Myrith. "To you, I give my armor."

Myrith glanced down at the armor she was wearing. A gift from the spirit of Rhinehart Duvall. She would not be replacing it at this time, but could not refuse Brular. "It will be given a place of honor."

He turned at Vyroris. "While not responsible for your death, I also have the same token for you as I had for Andrinor." He handed a small coin to the half-dragon.

"Quickly, before she summons me back to her, there are some things you must know. She has placed several spell traps in her chambers." He used a piece of chalk to sketch the layout of the room. "Here on the first step she has cast a storm spell that will rain down fire, lightning, ice and acid into the room. I imagine she has shielding spells in place that will protect her if it is triggered. The next step holds spells that will trap any who stand there. Only here at the back wall is there a safe way up the steps.

"There are traps in these areas of the floor that will trigger spells from these columns. I do not know the exact nature of the spells, but you have seen some of the ones she has favored as traps in other areas. Expect similar magics here. She has also cast spells here between these walls; however, I was unable to discern what they were." He paused and looked at Myrith.

"Kyrianna is being held here. She has surprising strength for one so young, but I doubt she will be able to fight both Torliana and Thynitic much longer. You must get to her quickly and you must keep her alive."

"Even if…" Myrith let her voice trail off.

"Yes!" Cewyr said as she stamped her right forefoot. "Myrith, she has all but renounced Frayrith. If she dies here, her soul goes to Thynitic. Don't let that happen. Please." The mare vanished leaving only the small figurine on the floor.

"She's right, Lady Lake. It is something I did not think of during our previous conversations on this. But it is true."

"How do I stop her from losing herself then?"

"That I cannot answer for you, but you must find a way. *You* are her friend, *you* must find a way." Brular picked up the unicorn figurine and handed it to Myrith. "She entrusted Cewyr and the silver sword to you."

Myrith looked at the silver-gray unicorn and nodded as Shadow Seeker came over and placed his muzzle on her knee.

Brular paused and glanced down at Hendandra. "There is something troubling you; something serious—what is it?"

Hendandra looked away and didn't say anything.

"She believes she may have gotten Rhyra mad at her," Falden said. "The Mistress of Illusion has said nothing to me regarding this matter."

"What happened?" Brular asked.

"I was approached by both Vesir and Rhyra; both offering to be my patrons. They warned if I did not follow a particular god and something happened to me here, Thynitic could trap my soul. Much as you just warned about Kyri. They both offered me gifts to choose one or the other. Vesir gave me a circlet and ring that enhance my communications and ability to persuade others to think as I want. Rhyra gave me the armor and also enchanted the violin. Both said there were no strings attached to the gifts."

"Vesir follows the dictates of Order and because of that, his word, when given, will be honored," Brular said. "Rhyra, on the other hand, is almost as chaotic as Thynitic in her actions. She is the Mistress of Illusion, not only with her magic, but also with her behavior. No matter what she said to you, she is not bound to hold to it." Brular placed a hand on Hendandra's shoulder. "In many respects she is like a petulant child when she does not get her way. Be wary. When this is over, seek the advice of a cleric of Vesir to aid you in finding a way to apologize to Rhyra."

Brular stood and moved away from the group. "This room is sealed against her ability to scry. Use the time you will have to prepare. Remember, she has watched you and knows how you normally fight; you must change your tactics. It is time," he said then vanished.

~ * ~

"Leikor's cursed luck," Hendandra said as she reached for the door. "It's been sealed."

"Myrith," Jerietlan whispered. "He linked our minds together when he handed me the rod. I can see what is going on in the room as he faces Torliana."

"What! Why?"

"He must have felt it important for us to know what happened between them."

"As the door is sealed, preventing us from leaving at this time, I guess we will have to wait," Myrith said.

Chapter Fourteen

The pain was back; she could feel the cold metal cutting her wrists again. Kyrianna forced herself to hang limply, waiting for her strength to return. A fog seemed to fill her mind for a moment and she felt herself being drawn away once more. The fog cleared and she found herself watching her mother as she jumped on Smokemist and galloped out of the courtyard of the Dalynne Estate.

"Arielle!" Brygan called as the silver-gray gelding galloped out of the courtyard. The woman sitting on the horse didn't acknowledge her husband as they passed him.

Arielle didn't slow the horse until she reached a large clearing in Kilenter. She dismounted, her hand on the whip Kyrianna remembered hanging dusty on the wall, untouched for over two decades. Arielle took a deep breath and looked around slowly. "I'm here as you demanded, Thynitic. Where is Kyrianna? Where is my daughter?"

Another elf, dressed in the multicolored robes of a cleric of Thynitic, stepped out of the trees followed by several more. Arielle spun around; a party of Rynial elves surrounded her. "I'm here on the Lady's business," she said, uncoiling the whip she now held ready.

"No, you are here because the Lady wanted you here. After all this time, she will extract her punishment on you." The priestess uncoiled a whip from her side as well.

Behind and around Arielle the other elves began drawing blades, uncoiling whips and readying their bows as they watched.

"Where is my daughter?" Arielle took a slow step toward the priestess.

"Soon to be a guest in the Lady's citadel. The Lady's Chosen, Torliana, is currently entertaining her."

"Torliana?" Arielle stopped as she stated at the priestess. "She offended the Lady and was sent to the Abyss as punishment. She is now the Lady's Chosen?"

The priestess laughed. "Jealous, Arielle? She has the same blood right to claim the title Daughter of Chaos as you have. Yes,

Torliana has offended the Lady on several occasions, but as befits the nature of chaos, is it she who holds the Lady's favor; just as you hold her disfavor."

Arielle shook her head and took a deep breath as the priestess stepped closer, the whip trailing behind her. Arielle dropped the whip she had brought with her and grasped the unicorn pendant around her neck. "Frayrith protect her," she said as the first stroke fell.

"No!" Kyrianna screamed as the vision faded.

"Well that was interesting, wasn't it?" Torliana smiled. "It would seem the Lady had plans for Arielle."

:*Kyri, she is the Mistress of Lies and Pain, a small voice whispered in her mind.* :*Please don't give in to her.*

"What?" Kyrianna's head snapped up as the presence seemed to fade away to be replaced by Thynitic's.

:*It would seem the Keeper still has a few tricks available to him. I hope you enjoyed your rest, daughter. Before this day is over, you will call on me.*

She closed her eyes as the goddess' voice continued whispering the litany in her mind.

Kyrianna tried to connect with the small voice that had spoken briefly, but the goddess' voice was too strong. She opened her eyes to watch Torliana as she moved around the chamber, checking various areas and the circle still inscribed on the floor. Brular's words in his letter echoed in her mind and for a moment, she could hear his voice over the goddess' as if he were whispering in her ear.

"The Lady will come for you, I cannot stop that. However, I tell you with every ounce of my being she will bring you to ruin. She will tempt you with salvation then have you destroy your closest friends and loved ones. She will twist you against everything you care to have. Remember these words most of all: *The power of a god is a fallacy.* She will turn on you regardless of what she says. She is chaos and it knows no promise or treaty.

"Look at Torliana. I can see Thynitic has done the most insidious thing to the Kindling. Thynitic has twisted Torliana so she resembles herself. A poor lost soul desperate to control the chaos even though she knows in her heart she cannot. She seeks to steal Tynitic's power. She doesn't even realize that every time she takes a bit of the goddess' power, she is in turn losing a part of her very soul.

"To be her chosen is to be lost in a sea of misery and lies. See the lies for what they are, child. They hold no power, only despair. How can you save them if you cannot save yourself? How can you?"

:*Kyri*, the small voice spoke again. :*He's right. Hold on to who you are. Don't become like my brother, Mikyl.* The presence faded again.

Mikyl? Kyrianna's mind raced for a moment, chasing the litany from her mind. :*Mikyl Duvall? Melissa?*

She felt a warmth that reminded her of the little girl who had thanked her and blessed her sword when they had rid the Duvall estate of the evil that had grown there. Then a deep cold settled in her mind as the goddess laughed and began whispering again.

"I suppose one last healing would be in order before your friends arrive," Torliana said, placing her hand on Kyrianna's chest. "That is if they arrive. I trust the Keeper will have finished them by now."

"You don't know," Kyrianna said, forcing a smile.

Torliana raised an eyebrow and glared at her. "You know very well he sealed the room against my scrying." She reached up and dragged a ragged nail down Kyrianna's cheek. "I believe this will leave a nice scar. A souvenir, if you do manage to survive." Torliana stepped back and brought the walls of force back up and moved to stand in front of the circle.

"Brular, your time is up," she said, raising her arms.

There was a bright flash of light and the cleric appeared in the circle, the manacles once again wrapping themselves around his wrists. Kyrianna closed her eyes for a moment as she dropped her head and fought the tears.

~ * ~

"Is it finished?"

"My part is completed, Kindling," Brular said. "Now it is up to them."

Brular watched Torliana as she took a step and glared at him. "You lied to me!"

"I did not lie, Torliana," he said, holding his head high and looking directly into her black eyes. "I have never lied. I accept my sentence as written by my own hand."

"Do you truly think they can defeat me?" She walked slowly around him, the edge of her robes dragging across the floor and completing the circle previously inscribed there. "Has the great Keeper taken leave of his senses?"

He only blinked as he continued to study her. "Can they defeat you? Perhaps. I have given them many protections. However, that is not the point." He paused and watched as the silver in her eyes seemed to flash for a second. "The point is," he said slowly. "It is not *my* place to defeat you. It will not be *my* magic that harms you." He glanced toward Kyrianna, still held in her restraints. The girl had raised her head only slightly, but it was enough for him to see the concern and the fear written across her face.

He returned his gaze to Torliana and saw her eyes grow wide as she watched him. It was several heartbeats before she finally spoke. "You are surrendering?"

Brular bowed his head, not in a gesture of submission, but in a subtle sign of agreement. "If you wish to call it that, then yes. I prefer to call it the dissolution of a war that should never have happened. Several days ago, Kyrianna allowed me to see her visions and in turn I shared my memories. It is funny how another can see something one would never consider." He paused as the emotions he had fought to keep buried for so long rushed forward. The walls built by his ordered life and strict impartial adherence to his faith were finally gone. "I was and am a fool, Torliana," he said softly.

Even as he watched her, he doubted the Chosen of the Lady of Chaos truly understood what he was saying to her. Then again, as passion was also one of the Lady's domains, though one that had been very much neglected over the past centuries, perhaps there was a slim chance she would.

As Torliana continued to stare blankly, he realized this was not what she had expected from him. His voice grew more resounding and his words more powerful as if he were back in the Temple of Hellavar, and he prayed in his heart this mistake could be redeemed. "I was responsible for so many, yet I forgot to concern myself with the one. It was Hellavar who dictated I should concern myself with the one piece of Kindling that would not ignite to his glory and I failed to do so." His voice faded to a soft whisper. "I failed to see that Order is not everything. I failed to understand that Order maintained for its own sake eventually collapses under its own weight. I maintained the temple for what? I gave everything freely to Hellavar. I lived for him and no other—not even myself.

"I am an old man and a child, Torliana. Kyri showed me you looked at me with both reverence and longing and now I understand that I didn't have the emotional being to see another's needs outside the scriptures." He paused and looked her directly in the eyes. "I was here with you last night, Torliana."

She took a step back, her eyes brightening. "Impossible."

"No, not impossible, but difficult. It was I inside Kyrianna's body last night as I let her mind and soul rest in my own shattered body." He continued to stare into her flashing eyes. "I saw you preparing. I saw how you grew angry at my sealing the room from your view. But, most of all, I saw you."

He paused and closed his eyes; calling on the power denied him in their first encounter. The manacles fell from his wrists and the circle vanished in a burst of flame. Torliana raised her hands in preparation for a spell, but held them still as she waited.

"We are quite the pair, you and I," he said, stepping closer to her. "I see Order in all things, yet I cannot understand the simple needs of a woman so close." He reached up and placed a scarred hand on her smooth cheek feeling the difference in their skin. He had been physically changed by his time in the Abyss and she had remained untouched. Yet, he knew they had both been changed mentally and emotionally. "You wrap yourself in Chaos and direct its flow, but cannot see its nature when it is so close to you."

He stepped back for a moment. "You said when we last met I would have cast you out. Why?"

Torliana dropped her hands to her sides and lowered her eyes. "I had violated the rules of the temple many times. I had failed to prove myself as one who could follow the patterns of Order. I allowed Chaos to continue to be a part of my soul. Therefore I would have been cast out of the temple."

"Torliana," he said, shaking his head. "Why would I cast you out? My own laws ruled me and none of them gave me that as a punishment. You know the truth of what I say."

"No!" Torliana raised her hands and stepped closer to him. "I forbid it! I have not finished with him yet."

"The contract was penned and sealed, my Lady," a deep, gravelly voice said from behind Brular. "We have no more time."

He turned slightly to see the portal opening and the demons waiting there. Torliana stepped beside him and moved her hands quickly.

Brular nodded as the red lines of the portal disappeared. "A null magic field," he said. "Impressive. However, you cannot maintain it for long."

Perspiration ran down her face and he knew she was fighting the demons pushing against her defense. "The truth then, Keeper," she said through clenched teeth. "You would not have cast me out."

"No. I would not."

Torliana only stared at him then her body seemed to slump for a moment. "She told me you would cast me out," she whispered. "Like a fool, I believed her!" Her hands clenched tightly and he saw a drop of blood fall slowly to the floor.

"Torliana," he said, placing a hand over hers. "It was not you who doomed the temple. You were also one of those damaged by that night as well. I should have felt your sadness, your loneliness and your vulnerability when you came to me. I failed you. I ask your forgiveness, Flame Dancer, before they take me this last time."

He could see the tears in her eyes and the quivering lip as she looked at him. "No!" The shout echoed in the room. "It *is* my fault; I will hold them." She straightened her back and turned to face the portal as it started to crack open again.

"You cannot," he said, softly placing his hand on her cheek. "No more than you can hold back the sun. I release you from any responsibility concerning the temple or myself. I go now to my punishment. Please forgive me for failing you, Child of Fire." His hand slid down her cheek and neck to grasp the blood-red amulet. With a jerk, he broke the chain.

Her voice was only a whisper. "No."

His arm moved quickly and he released the amulet. It flew through the dimensional crack. "The sending of the amulet was penned as well—at your stipulation. I will not have you suffer the demon's wrath for words laid down by my hand."

He placed his right hand against her face again. "As a judge of Dh'Mark, I pardon you."

He watched the silver in her eyes glow as she fought to maintain her concentration. His left hand reached up, moving from her neck to her ear. "As your Keeper, I absolve you."

She inhaled sharply and he could feel her trembling.

His fingers caressed the tip of her ear. "As a man, I forgive you."

He smiled as she sighed softly and he saw her face relax into the same delicate features he remembered from the night she had asked him to stay and watch her dance. Too late, he realized the moment had also broken her concentration and he felt the claws that reached through the portal to encircle and drag him back to their plane.

~ * ~

Kyrianna frowned as Torliana collapsed to the floor; her sobs echoing in the chamber as the portal to the Abyss snapped shut and Brular vanished. She had been right about what she had seen. Torliana had been in love with Brular, but the thought gave her no pleasure. The Lady of Chaos was also the Mistress of Pain and she took pleasure in tormenting others and using their own weaknesses and fears against them. Even as the portal closed, she noticed a swirling of colors across the black throne—the swirling colors that were Thynitic's chosen symbol. The goddess was still watching them.

She watched as Torliana finally composed herself enough to crawl back to the steps to her throne. Kyrianna cursed softly as the chains binding her rattled in the silence of the room and Torliana glanced in her direction.

"You!" Torliana glared at Kyrianna. "Your mother. How did she reject the Lady without being destroyed?"

"What?" Kyrianna lifted her head slightly and stared at Torliana. "You are the Lady's Chosen—ask her!" There might be a slight spark of understanding at what Thynitic had done to Torliana, but, unlike Brular, she had no forgiveness and no desire to help the other woman.

"I want nothing from her. Her lies cost me everything I had and everything I ever wanted!" Torliana forced herself to her feet and moved to the front of the force cage.

"She has lied to me since I came here," Kyrianna said. "She may have tricked me into calling on her power once, but you haven't seen me betray my friends for her—the way you betrayed the man you loved. You wanted to believe her lies."

"You little bitch!" Torliana moved her hands in a complex pattern and Kyrianna fell against the chains as pain wracked her body.

Torliana turned away as Kyrianna cried out from the pain of the spell. She moved to the center of the chamber and held her hands out from her sides. "Lady of Chaos, you have controlled me long enough. I am your pawn no longer."

Kyrianna's head snapped up as Torliana screamed. A multicolored fog surrounded her and Thynitic's voice echoed in the room.

"You still have not learned," the goddess said. "Even after the previous lessons you have been given, you still have not learned. I remove my favor and strip you of the gifts I have given you. Soon the others will be here and you will have to deal with them with just your own power. Even if you fall, you will not be free. You are mine now and always will be. It is time for another lesson."

The fog vanished and Kyrianna smiled softly as Torliana was flung back against her throne and the doors to the chamber opened.

Chapter Fifteen

"Myrith, he forgave her," Jerietlan said. "He forgave her then went with the demons who were called to take him back to Thynitic. I can still see what he is seeing. We should hurry as Torliana appears to be in shock."

"He forgave her? How can that be?" Andrinor stared at Jerietlan. "What he told us she did to his temple and those there? It makes no sense."

"Of course it makes sense. He saw through the lies of Thynitic to see Torliana as she once was," Myrith said. "He blames Thynitic for what happened to Torliana, not Torliana herself. He is no longer lost to the blind hatred he held when we first met him. He has left the path of darkness he was walking, but at what final cost?"

"Myrith, there's something else," Jerietlan said. "Thynitic just told Brular, 'Ah, she knows I watch her. Good, her skills are coming along nicely.' She was talking about Kyrianna."

"Falden, can you cast a spell that will protect us from all magic? I want to make sure we can get to her."

"I can create an anti-magic field that can surround me and the rest of the group if we stay close together."

"Cast it just before we enter her chamber." Myrith drew her sword. "Let's take this battle to her."

"There is a problem with your plan," Falden said. "All of us carry many items of magic. They will lose their enchantments and we will be without their benefits."

"But we will not be vulnerable to her magic. It be a fair compromise," Nirev said.

"Be sure of that before I cast this spell." Falden looked around. "The armor many of you wear is made lighter because of the magic woven into it. Hendandra's pack contains magic that creates an extra-dimensional space, so it can carry much more than normal. Depending on how much she is carrying, it may be destroyed when its magic is nullified. The same is true of the three sacks she is carrying the coins and gems in. Both Myrith and Andrinor wear objects that increase their strength; those will also be nullified."

"Andrinor and I can remain outside of the spell and carry any extra items that need to be carried. The field only needs to be in effect as we pass through the doors and the entryway. Once we are clear of those unknown spells, you can dismiss the spell," Myrith said.

"That will leave you vulnerable to her magic," Jerietlan said. "I do not like this idea."

"It is the best option we have unless you have another to offer," Vyroris said. "There is another concern for both Andrinor and myself. Because of our draconic heritage, we are both vulnerable to certain elements. I would recommend he and I be the ones who carry the extra items. As we will be outside Falden's spell, magic to protect us from those elements can be cast first, without it losing its protections."

Jerietlan nodded. "Brular showed me another spell that will work well in conjunction with that kind of protection," he said. "One that will take the energy from a specific attack and turn it into healing energy for the one targeted."

"Interesting," Falden said. "If you cast that spell on us, I could safely cast a fireball if necessary and have it heal us and harm our enemies."

"Yes, however, I only have enough power to cast two of them. I would suggest protecting Vyroris and Andrinor as Torliana is sure to know of their individual vulnerabilities and will target them."

"I agree," Myrith said. "Jerietlan, you are still linked to Brular?"

"I am." He paused for a moment. "Torliana has attempted to renounce Thynitic and has had the goddess strip her of some of her power."

"Then we need to move—now." Myrith nodded as the door to the room opened.

Andrinor took Hendandra's pack as Vyroris gathered several items from the others. Myrith motioned for the rest of the group to stand close together as Jerietlan cast the protection spells on the two dragon kin. When the cleric was finished, she readied her sword. "Andrinor and Hendandra, I want you two to get to Kyrianna as quickly as possible. Falden, my stepping beyond the protection of your spell and raising my sword will be your cue to dismiss the field. Let's take the fight to her."

~ * ~

Kyrianna looked up to see Myrith and the others enter the chamber. They were still alive. "Thank you, Brular," she whispered.

Torliana looked up from where she lay on the steps. "Hold, knight of Mykaylene. I have no desire to fight you, but I will not remove my defenses at this time. There are several set spells and traps throughout this room. For your safety, stay where you are."

The group took another step forward before Myrith signaled to them to stop.

"Hold," Torliana said again.

"Why should we trust you?" Myrith demanded.

Torliana stood and looked at Myrith, then glanced toward Kyrianna. "I will release your friend if you leave this place immediately. Do you agree?"

"We cannot just leave you here. Will you go with us?" Myrith's hand tightened on the blade she held.

"No. I will go after my Keeper. Are you willing to go with me to save him?"

Kyrianna saw Myrith take a half-step back as the others looked at her. Jerietlan had slipped back into the shadows of one of the columns and was watching the wall behind Torliana.

Torliana raised her hands and turned toward Kyrianna. "As a show of faith, I will release her before you answer."

Kyrianna watched as Torliana moved her hands through the complicated pattern several times. She could see the wall of the force cage shimmer then brighten each time.

"Thynitic," she heard Torliana whisper.

Kyrianna dropped her head. The goddess was blocking Torliana's magic.

"She is trying to dispel the magic around Kyri," Kyrianna heard Falden say.

Torliana screamed and Kyrianna turned her head slightly to see her being dragged through a portal that had appeared behind her.

Across the chamber, where she could see everything, Thynitic opened another portal. The goddess sat on her black throne laughing. Next to that throne stood Brular. She could see the glow surrounding the manacles he was wearing and Kyrianna closed her eyes as the goddess spoke.

"This is amusing," the goddess' voice echoed in the room. "I could destroy all of you easily, but there is someone who needs to watch as you are ground into dust, one at a time."

:*You can save them*, Thynitic said in Kyrianna's mind. :*Are you willing to watch them all die to save yourself? And, if they do all die, you still will not be able to save yourself.*

Kyrianna closed her fists tightly and tried to close her mind to the goddess' taunting. In the back of her mind, she could hear a little girl sobbing.

As she watched, a group of four buzzard-headed demons walked up to the portal and quietly surveyed the group still standing by the doors.

Andrinor and Shadow Seeker sprinted across the room to stand by the force cage. "Kyri, are you alright?" He looked at her closely.

Her voice was harsh as she spoke. "No."

:*Courage, Kyri*, Melissa said. :*Your friends are strong. There is hope.*

:*Thank you, Melissa.*

"Before we get started, I must deprive you of some of the things you have acquired," Thynitic said, raising her hands.

A pile of equipment appeared in front of Thynitic and she smiled as she picked up the bow Kyrianna had been carrying and handed it, along with the magical arrows, to one of the demons standing near her. Kyrianna grimaced as Andrinor stood clutching only air for a moment before readying another sword. Myrith raised her sword as four demons appeared in front of the group by the doors, each one now surrounded by five others. Myrith and the others engaged the large creatures, and Kyrianna found herself screaming silently as each time one of their weapons hit one of the demons, it vanished. They were only illusions designed to distract her friends from the real creatures.

"Vyroris!" Kyrianna screamed as the half-dragon staggered and almost fell to his knees. His great sword cut across the throat of the demon and blood gushed over him as it fell. Three of the demons that had been surrounding it vanished.

Andrinor looked at her, smiled and moved to stand in front of the steps as another group of the demons appeared and surrounded him.

"No!" The denial did not come out in the scream she intended, but instead was only a weak whisper.

:*The dragon warrior is your friend. He will fall under their blades if you do not stop it. All you have to do is call on my power and you can save him.*

"No!" She shook her head, ignoring the sharp pain from the collar.

Andrinor was able to dispatch one of the demons just as another appeared next to him. This one was larger and he doubled over retching. The demons surrounding him took advantage of his state and began their attacks.

Myrith and Vyroris each also killed one of the demons in the back group and Kyrianna smiled at the frown on Thynitic's face. The group was stronger than the goddess had suspected them to be.

Kyrianna gasped as Andrinor yelled, between coughing and retching. "Fireball! Falden, fireball!"

Kyrianna stared at Andrinor, her breath coming in ragged gasps. "What are you doing?" She could barely hear her own voice.

Falden seemed to concentrate a little longer than normal and the fireball exploded under Andrinor's feet. Kyrianna watched as Andrinor laughed and swung his sword again.

Jerietlan also began casting and through the portal Kyrianna saw a ball of flame streak toward Thynitic, and crash into the goddess' throne destroying it. Thynitic stood from the rumble, a streak of blood on her temple and stared at Jerietlan through the portal. Her eyes were wide with surprise then narrowed as she slowly turned her gaze to Brular. "This had to be your doing," she said.

The demons in the room all turned to stare at the portal, their shock written on their faces as they ignored the group they were supposed to be fighting. Andrinor took advantage of the distraction to move away from the ones around him.

:*See, Kyri. He was actually able to hurt the goddess. There is still hope.* Melissa's voice faded away.

:*Enjoyed that did you, daughter? Let us see if you enjoy this.*

Thynitic looked at the tall demon standing near what was left of her throne. "Kill the fire cleric."

No! Kyrianna screamed in her mind as she watched the demon raise his sword and swing at Brular's neck. Just before the blow struck, the cleric looked right at her and smiled. He spit at the goddess striking her left cheek. Kyrianna closed her eyes and dropped her head as much as the collar around her neck would allow, as the blade sliced through Brular's neck.

"Jerietlan!" Hendandra's voice cut through Kyrianna's grief and she looked up to see the cleric on the floor.

Kyrianna was breathing deeply as she looked around at the others. *There is still hope*, she told herself.

:*You think so. Then continue to wait. Even hope will be gone.*

The demon who killed Brular sheathed his sword and readied Kyrianna's bow. "No," she whispered as he drew one of the arrows she had used to kill the Abyssal Dragon. The arrow flew through the portal and expanded into ten large arrows, each one encased in ice.

"Chaos take you!" Kyrianna shouted as the arrows hit Vyroris and he was surrounded by a shimmering cloak of shifting colors.

"I am Chaos," Thynitic said with a laugh as Vyroris fell back against the wall then slid to the floor. "However, I thank you for adding your curse to what hurt your friend. You have proven you are truly on of my daughters."

Kyrianna looked away as Myrith snapped her head up to look at her.

The demons fighting Andrinor all moved to attack him again as the others renewed their attacks against the group in the back. Another demon stepped up to the portal and smiled. It was larger than the last and had six arms, each one wielding a sword. It looked at Kyrianna and grinned as it dropped one of its own blades and picked up a sword from the pile in front of Thynitic.

:*After this, I begin sending my chaos demons in. Your friends have done well to this point. What chance do you think they stand against them? You can save them from that.*

The new demon transported into the room and turned to look at Kyrianna before turning toward Hendandra.

Myrith, forgive me, Kyrianna thought. *I can't let this happen.* She took a deep breath. "Thynitic," she said softly. "I call on your power."

"You will need to do better than that, my daughter."

Kyrianna looked again at Hendandra who had gone ghost white as she held her rapier in a defensive position and watched the six swords of the demon move in a spinning, weaving pattern.

An arrow streaked from the portal to strike Falden, who collapsed on the floor. Another flew toward Andrinor, and Kyrianna watched as he deflected it with his buckler. Unfortunately, the move left him open and he took several steps back as one of the demons slashed his arm and another left a deep gash across his chest.

"I call on the powers of Chaos!" Kyrianna yelled above the sounds of the battle. "Begone from this place!"

The demons in the room vanished and the force cage surrounding her blew apart. She took a step forward as the chains fell away. The power was there and it was coursing through her. She looked back at the portal and saw Thynitic's smile. "Welcome to your heritage, Daughter of Chaos," the goddess said.

Kyrianna took a step back against the wall and closed her eyes. *No!* Her mind protested. *What have I done?* She glanced back up at the portal in front of her and saw Brular's headless body still lying at the foot of the rubble that had once been Thynitic's throne, then the portal vanished.

Andrinor moved to stand next to her. "Kyrianna?"

She ignored him and looked around at the group staring at her. She waved a hand and watched as their injuries were healed.

"I want to talk to Kyrianna," Andrinor insisted.

"I am Kyrianna," she said. "You and the others should leave, before she forces me to do something to hurt you." She waved her hand again and a portal opened in the entrance to the room. Through the portal stood the Duvall Estate. "Please."

"I'm not leaving you," Andrinor said.

"Neither am I." Myrith walked over to stand in front of her, several of the others joining her. "You once questioned whether I was ignoring our friendship," Myrith said. "There may have been other concerns that made it seem so at that time. However, right now, I have no other concern but you and I will not abandon a friend."

Kyrianna smiled as Hendandra and Falden looked at the group then turned and stepped through the portal. A slight thought on her part and Hendandra's pack was on the floor near her. Her equipment was in that pack and she would keep it.

The chamber shook and cracks streaked across the floor and up the walls. "You must leave," Kyrianna said softly.

"So, Rangerette, you would fail where your mother succeeded," Myrith said, looking at her.

The others looked at the woman with surprise at the coldness of her words. But Kyrianna staggered back a bit; Myrith couldn't have known how her words would cut.

Melissa's voice spoke through her sobs. :*Remember the words of the Keeper.*

The Keeper! Kyrianna's mind again saw the headless corpse on the obsidian floor then raced to the scene of her mother kneeling next to the body of the man she had called her mentor and friend. The image in her mind shifted and she again saw her mother surrounded by the Rynial elves, dropping the whip she had once carried. Thynitic had told Arielle she would release Kyrianna if Arielle returned to her. The goddess had lied to her and would lie to Kyrianna. She was the Mistress of Lies and Pain, the Lady of Chaos.

"No," she said harshly. "I will not be your pawn. I do not belong to you."

:*You think it that easy, daughter? It is not*, Thynitic's voice whispered. :*If I had not been willing to let her go, do you think your mother could have been able to leave me as she did? No. I allowed her to return to Frayrith. Torliana tried to renounce me and I refused to let her get away from me. Think on that, Daughter of Chaos. Remember, if you do leave here today, you will not truly be free; it will only be because I allow it.*

Kyrianna felt Melissa's spirit trying to aid her as best the child could against the goddess. Her internal struggle showed in her tightly clenched fists and the sweat that dripped from her brow. It took time, but she finally felt the goddess' presence retreat from her mind and she collapsed on the ground, sobbing. :*This is not over, daughter*, Thynitic's voice whispered.

Andrinor and Myrith both started to kneel beside her as she felt something grab her from behind and start to drag her through another portal. They both dove to grab her as the portal snapped closed.

Chapter Sixteen

Kyrianna found herself falling and blackness claimed her as she hit a rocky plain. When she opened her eyes, her hands and feet were bound together, and a woman, a demoness, was standing over her.

"You still live—good. The Lady has sent me to fetch you." The demoness held a vial with a potion and placed it against Kyrianna's lips. "Drink."

She tied to pull away only to have the demoness hold her head tightly. "You will drink this or I will force it down your throat." The demoness' fingers moved to press against the pressure point on Kyrianna's jaw, forcing her mouth open. The liquid was warm as it flowed down her throat and the demoness held her mouth shut.

"Now, while we have some time, there are questions you will answer for me." The demoness looked at her as she drew a dagger and held it in her hand.

Kyrianna glared at the demoness. "I have nothing to tell you."

"We will see about that." She smiled then reached out and laid a hand on Kyrianna's neck, her nails cutting into the flesh.

Kyrianna felt a wave of dizziness grab her and she closed her eyes for a moment.

"I believe you will be more receptive to my questions now. We will start with the dragon warrior. Who is he and where does his power come from?"

Kyrianna swallowed and shook her head. "No," she whispered.

"You think you can fight me." The demoness laughed. "You may be able to resist for a short time, but you cannot truly fight it. Now, tell me about the dragon warrior."

"Andrinor." Kyrianna gasped as she fought the demoness' control. "His name is Andrinor." Another ragged breath. "No!"

"You are strong. I should have anticipated that considering your bloodline and how you have managed to fight the Lady's control." The demoness brought the knife to Kyrianna's lips. "I have been sent by the Lady to bring you to her. However, I have other plans for you. You and Torliana have weakened her and there are others here who wish to see the Lady of Chaos fall. If you do not start answering my questions, I will turn you over to her. You have heard what she has done to the Cleric of Hellavar—I can assure you what she has planned for you will make his torments seem mild.

"Your friends will probably be foolish enough to come after you—do you want them to be the ones entertaining Thynitic and her guests as you are forced to watch? Or even to be the one torturing them?"

"He is a follower of Ghainaess. She is the Great Mother of Dragons. It is from her he received his draconic power." The words tumbled out of her mouth as she stared at the demoness.

"That corresponds to what I have learned—good. You are telling me the truth. Now, about the knight. Where is she from?"

"I do not know the name of her world."

The demoness slapped her across the face. "I have watched the two of you for some time, you little wretch. You are friends and you are trying to tell me you don't know where she is from?"

"No. Myrith has told me very little about her past."

"Then what has she told you?"

"She is from a world ruled by an elf tyrant who follows a goddess of pain and tyranny. He has banned the worship of the native gods in favor of the goddess he brought from another world."

"What is this elf's name?"

"Lavial."

"Interesting." The demoness sat back for a moment and smiled. "What else?"

Kyrianna took a deep breath and shook her head. "I don't understand. What else do you want?"

"Who is her father?"

"She suspects it to be Lavial."

"Lavial. Very good." The demoness smiled as she looked away from Kyrianna. "Thynitic, I doubt you have realized the truth about Myrith yet. Very good." She paused and cocked her head as if listening to something.

~ * ~

"Jerietlan, find her!" Myrith grabbed the pack with Kyrianna's gear and draped it over her shoulder. The room was still shaking and one of the columns fell behind them.

The cleric looked up from tending Shadow Seeker, who had tried to follow Kyrianna as she had been dragged through the portal. The portal closed as the wolf hit the wall. The impact and some sort of backlash from the portal had almost killed him.

"We're going after her! Now!"

Jerietlan stood and nodded. He stared at the wall where the portal had been and raised his hands.

"Hold, Priest." A woman's voice cut through the rumbling of the room. "Do not expend your energy in this task."

Myrith drew her sword as she spun around to face the speaker. Two women stood there, one human, the other elven in appearance. Both were dressed as rangers and seemed to have an aura of power about them. Power similar to what she had felt from Mykaylene's avatar. She bowed her head and lowered her sword. "Frayrith," she whispered.

"Correct, Myrith. I am Frayrith and this is Dwycia, my sister from Shokar."

Myrith frowned as two more people appeared in the chamber. Hendandra and Falden stood there.

"Leikor's cursed luck, not again," Hendandra said. "I'm getting very tired of making it home and being brought back here."

"It was not my doing this time," Myrith said.

"The daughter is lost in spirit and must be brought back," Dwycia said. "We ask that you bring her back. I will open the portal for you and Frayrith will return you to Shokar once you have retrieved her. You must hurry as the one who holds her plans to give her to the enemies of Thynitic who will use her against the Lady of Chaos. She will be lost to the darkness in this way just as surely as she would if she willingly serves Thynitic at this time. This cannot be allowed to happen."

"I care not for whatever plots the divine think to play against each other," Myrith said. "I only care about my friend. Open the portal and we will go to find her—even if we go to the heart of Thynitic's citadel itself."

"Spoken like a true friend," Frayrith said.

"There is your portal," Dwycia said. "Hurry."

Myrith didn't wait for the others as she stepped through the glowing portal and onto an empty rocky expanse. Several feet in front of her, she saw a woman with wings turn to look at her. The woman leaned down and picked something up from the ground. It was Kyrianna.

"Myrith!" Kyrianna's cry was weak and Myrith closed her eyes for a moment. Brular and Cewyr had warned her about the risks involved if Kyrianna fell in this place before she could restore her faith in Frayrith; her soul would be lost to the Lady of Chaos. Frayrith and Dwycia had said the daughter was lost in spirit—did that mean the risk was still there?

"Release her!" Myrith shouted.

The woman turned and smiled. "Oh, please," she heard the woman say as she dropped Kyrianna.

A weak cry escaped from the girl, and she didn't move. The demoness looked down at Kyrianna and her lips moved, but Myrith was unable to hear what she said to her friend.

"You think you're ready to confront Thynitic?" the demoness said as she turned and laughed at the group. "You're not even ready to face me." Her wings unfurled behind her.

"A demoness of the lower levels," Jerietlan said. "We must be careful."

"I am called Drezmona and I count many of the Princes and Lords of the Abyss as my allies, as well as few of the divine who make their homes on its infinite layers."

Behind Kyrianna and the demoness, a shape rose from the ground and rose and rose. The eight-legged monstrosity stood protectively over Drezmona and Kyrianna as the group stared up at it.

"A gift from one of those who oppose Thynitic." Drezmona looked at Myrith and smiled. "Interesting," she said. "Much like your brother."

"I have no brother," Myrith said.

"Oh," Drezmona paused as she stepped forward. "Just because one does not live on the material plane, does not mean one does not exist." The demoness walked around Myrith then returned to stand next to Kyrianna. "Your father is an elf and elves live for millennia."

"I don't understand. I have no brother."

"Silly girl. I too have *known* your father. However, I was just wondering what it would have been like if you had been born to me and he to your mother." She smiled as she continued to stare at Myrith.

Myrith frowned as she heard Drezmona's voice in her head. :*You think to protect them. Know this; I will have the dragon warrior at some point. Thynitic will be seeking to punish the cleric and the mage herself. You and your friend also have business with the Lady of Chaos. The rest are inconsequential and disposable. However, I believe my son would enjoy entertaining himself with the little thief. Yes, he would enjoy that quite a bit.*

Myrith felt her grip on her sword tighten and she took a slow step toward the demoness. "He will never have the opportunity." She had understood the implications of Drezmona's threat and also knew the depravities she had suffered in her life would be nothing compared to what a demon would do to Hendandra.

Drezmona only smiled then turned her attention to Andrinor. "You have power."

He nodded. "Supposedly."

She smiled. "If our power were to be joined, our child would be like a god among the demons."

Andrinor took a step back, his hands tight on his blade. "That will never happen."

"We will see."

She reached down and grabbed Kyrianna and pulled her up, her dagger now against the girl's neck. "A truce," she said. Over them, the spider faded away.

"You have done well. There are many who were pleased to see the Lady's power disrupted." She pulled the knife away and stepped back into a portal on the ground and vanished.

Andrinor and Vyroris ran to Kyrianna's side and cut the ropes holding her. They helped her to her feet and held her as she stood there unmoving, her head bowed. Magic swirled around them and they found themselves leaving the Abyss.

Frayrith's magic surrounded the group pulling them from the Abyss as she had promised. However, instead of Shokar, they found themselves in a glowing, radiant landscape. Fire surrounded them, dancing in ever-changing patterns.

"This is not Shokar," Hendandra said, looking around.

Andrinor's eyes were wide, as flames seemed to dance around him. "I don't like this. Can we get out of here?"

A deep, resonating voice seemed to bellow from the flames. "You are correct, little one. This is not Shokar. It is my realm: the realm of order and fire. Do not worry, Initiate of the Great Mother, my flames will not harm you unless I will it."

Jerietlan stepped forward, his head bowed slightly. "Hellavar, Lord of Fire. I have one question if I may."

"Speak, Priest of the Battle Maiden," the voice said.

"All of our gods guided us through visions, but you never spoke to him."

"Wrong." There was amusement in the voice. "We spoke in prayer and deed. He was and is the Order. He served with perfect duty until that fateful day; then he was lost. You brought him back to the ordered glory."

"Why did you allow him to remain in the darkness so long?" Jerietlan maintained a respectful tone in his voice as he spoke.

"His fire was strong, but now it burns like the sun. It is needed to shine the way. It guides even as we speak, but it burns too hot to sustain in the darkness much longer. He will be lost to it soon. Will you take up the mantle? Will you seek to restore his flame to Shokar?"

Myrith stepped forward and knelt before the presence. Before she could say anything, she heard the voices of the others behind her.

"He shall see the sun once more," Jerietlan said.

Nirav's voice rang across the plane of fire. "Thunder and lightning shall rain against her castle."

"The power of the dragon knows no fear or boundary," Andrinor and Vyroris said together.

Falden's voice was low and forbidding as he finally spoke. "Gormanghast sees my kind as a pale imitation. Let us see my magic against a truly worthy foe."

There was a long pause before Hendandra swallowed and finally spoke in a voice threatening to break. "For a friend," she said softly.

"We will take the battle to her very throne room, if necessary," Myrith said as she held her sword out. After a few minutes she stood and looked back at the others. The only voice she had not heard was Kyrianna's. The girl was listless as she stood supported by the two dragon kin. Her eyes were open, but there was no fire in them.

Hellavar's voice resonated again. "Jerietlan, you felt his power, his order. I grant you the power to call on him, but for only a few minutes a day. He can give you clarity and guidance in that time. Chaos will not be able to harm you through the link."

"I accept this gift," Jerietlan said. "I hope to prove worthy of it."

"I have kept you here long enough. The one whose power I

interrupted will be growing concerned." The presence seemed to concentrate on Kyrianna for the briefest moment then returned to the group as a whole. "I send you back to Shokar, with this advice. There is much assistance to be acquired in a short time. Be quick."

The fire faded and the group found themselves on the outskirts of a large city. Myrith looked at the beleaguered group who had fought the Lady of Chaos and saw the tired look in their eyes. However, it was the eyes of Kyrianna that concerned her the most. They were sunken, like her soul.

Myrith took a deep breath and turned toward the city of this world that was alien to her. They needed time to rest and prepare in order to face what was to come.

Chapter Seventeen

As she looked at the city, Myrith's thoughts went back to the words of the demoness Drezmona. *You cannot hope to reach the cleric. You could hardly hope to beat me.* Hellavar said there was assistance to be gained, but first they had to care for their own sorrows and pains. Kyrianna had called on Thynitic's power, had given herself to the goddess however briefly. She had no way to understand what effect that had on her friend's fragile spirit. That Thynitic had thanked her for cursing Vyroris before she had done so wouldn't help the girl.

"Where are we?" Myrith asked.

"Irrmar," Falden said.

"Jerietlan, I believe you said a great hall to Mykaylene was in this city," Myrith said.

"Yes. The Coliseum is here."

She looked back at Kyrianna who was barely keeping her feet, even with Andrinor and Vyroris helping her. "Riker."

The horse appeared for a brief moment, but instead of approaching, he turned toward the city and disappeared. Myrith frowned. That was not like the horse. She called several more times, with no result.

She finally turned to Falden. "Can you take us to the temple?"

He looked toward the city. "I dare not use such magic to enter an unknown city. Gormanghast has many protections, and it is well known many of the larger cities also have similar protections. Though I doubt the quality of their magic, it would be easy for them to detect our arrival. I assume we do not want to draw the attention of the local wizards and clerics with our arrival, particularly for Kyrianna's sake."

"It is a long walk and I doubt she can make it." Myrith sighed and wondered again why the spectral horse had refused to answer her summons. "I will carry her." Myrith moved to gather the girl in her arms.

Vyroris moved quicker. His great sword went into its sheath and he lifted Kyrianna into his clawed arms. "She is no burden. Lead on, Myrith."

Myrith led them to the city gates, which had already been closed for the evening. The guards looked them over and frowned. "The gates are closed; you will have to return in the morning," he said.

Hendandra stepped forward and smiled. "We have been summoned by the Temple of Mykaylene and must make an immediate appearance. Surely, you were informed about this," she said.

The guard looked at his companion who only shrugged. "Very well," he said as he opened the walk-through door to the side of the large gate.

"Hold there," the second guard said, stepping in front of the group, his hand on his sword. "There was no mention of that creature." He gestured toward Vyroris. "He may not enter." Both of them readied their weapons and made warding signs against evil.

Both Myrith and Jerietlan stepped between the guards and Vyroris. "He is with us," Myrith said. "I will be bond for his behavior."

The guards glanced at Jerietlan who nodded. "I as well."

The guards glanced at each other again, their concern written across their faces. "He is dragon kin. Dragons are evil creatures and bring evil with them," the first guard said.

"I am a Warrior of Mykaylene," Myrith said. She held her hands away from her weapons, as she heard her companions shifting their own into position. "I swear by the Battle Maiden there is no evil in the dragon kin. He is a part of our group and he is required to accompany us. If you doubt the truth of my words, you also doubt the honor of the Battle Maiden herself."

The two guards drew themselves up straighter and frowned. "Very well, Warrior of Mykaylene, you and this creature may pass. You will go immediately to the Coliseum and both you and the cleric will be held accountable for its actions."

Myrith nodded then motioned the rest of the group through. She watched Andrinor carefully as he passed the guards. Vyroris was much more even-tempered than the young man and she knew the insults the guards had made regarding dragons would not sit well with him. Fortunately, Andrinor only glared at the two as he walked by.

As the group walked through the darkened streets toward the Coliseum, they received hostile looks from the few people they saw and all those they passed made warding signs as they glanced at

Vyroris and looked away.

"Do not worry that you are hampered by carrying Kyri; I will watch your back," Myrith heard Andrinor say in Draconic. She glanced back to see him now walking behind Vyroris, his two-bladed sword at the ready.

Hendandra glanced at her then darted ahead of the group to ask directions from a couple just leaving a nearby tavern. The man and woman laughed lightly and pointed toward the center of town. "All roads lead to the Coliseum," the man said before they walked off still laughing.

The guards at the temple blocked their entrance as they called for several of the ranking clerics.

The clerics stared at Vyroris and Myrith's hopes her comrade would receive fairer treatment here were quickly destroyed.

"You will wait here until the Shield arrives," one of those who met the group at the entrance said. "It is only because of your presence, Warrior, we have not destroyed this creature out of hand. Your favor with the Battle Maiden is the only thing granting you a hearing with Sarasnar."

"Sarasnar?" Myrith glanced at Jerietlan and saw the young man's nod. The name was the same as the cleric they had spent time with on the Duvall Estate; perhaps that would work in their favor. She bowed her head respectfully as the cleric approached the group.

"He shall not enter. Dragons are evil omens here and we will not risk the temple by allowing this creature inside our walls," Sarasnar said after hearing Myrith's request for the group to be allowed into the Coliseum after their struggles against Torliana and Thynitic.

Myrith took a step back and crossed her arms over her chest. "This is ridiculous. He is my companion and I tell you he is not an evil being. My comrades and I have been trapped for a long while in a place controlled by a mage in service to Goddess Thynitic, the Lady of Chaos, and he has fought by my side throughout. The Battle Maiden herself blessed our endeavors. I do not believe she would treat those who answered her call in this manner."

Vyroris took a cautious step forward, still cradling Kyrianna in his arms. "My Lord, I will not argue your beliefs regarding dragons. The Great Mother has many diverse children across the planes of existence. Perhaps here on your world, her children have a more evil nature; however, I am not from this world and I answered the Great

Mother's call as well as the Battle Maiden's to fight Chaos and preserve the Balance. I harbor no evil intent toward you, your temple or your world."

Sarasnar studied Vyroris closely for a moment then looked again at Myrith and shook his head. "I doubt not your sincerity, but this creature will not be allowed to enter this temple. As it claims to be from another world, I will give it the option of returning there. If it will not accept this option, I will summon the guards to have it removed from the city."

"You would dare threaten my companion!" Myrith's blade flashed in the lamplight as she started to draw it.

"Stay your blade. I have given your companion an option that would not normally be given. Do you wish me to follow the normal procedures and have this creature destroyed immediately?"

Vyroris handed the barely conscious Kyrianna to Myrith, who had to release her sword to hold her friend. "I do not mind going home, Myrith. You will not change their beliefs. I only regret I will not be able to travel with you to rescue Brular, but I will go now to prevent any further trouble."

"Listen to your companion, Myrith. The creature speaks wisely," Sarasnar said. "Concentrate on your home," he said, touching Vyroris lightly on the shoulder. "Picture it clearly." A small portal opened before them and Vyroris smiled as he stepped through.

Sarasnar turned his attention to Myrith and Kyrianna, and his frown deepened into a scowl. "You and the others may remain here tonight," Sarasnar said. "She has been touched by the vilest evil; she may not enter."

Myrith looked down at her friend. "Her soul was touched by a being of darkness, yes. But it does not radiate any aura of evil. You fought alongside her at the Duvall Estate. You should know she does not walk with the darkness."

"The evil is still there. She may not enter."

"I have had enough of this," Andrinor said, stepping forward, his sword held in a ready position. "Our friend needs help and you will provide it or I will know the reasons why; then you will be able to explain those reasons to your goddess in person."

"Andrinor." Myrith shifted her hold on Kyrianna and hit his blade, knocking it to the side as she handed Kyrianna to him.

Andrinor dropped his weapon to catch Kyrianna and glared at Myrith.

Myrith pulled the cleric aside and spoke quietly to him. "She needs the most powerful healing magics you can give her." She paused for a moment. How could she explain what had happened without telling Sarasnar Kyrianna had called on the power of Thynitic voluntarily? "She was possessed by Thynitic, and it took much effort on her part, but she was finally able to reclaim her mind and soul from that one's control. Yes, that evil goddess has touched her, but she does not deserve to be condemned for it. In Mykaylene's name, I beg you to help her."

Sarasnar glanced from Myrith to the still angry Andrinor then to Kyrianna whom he held carefully. "That god's name is not known to us here, but I feel Mykaylene does walk strongly with you." He looked at Myrith and nodded. "Very well, follow me."

Sarasnar led them through several twisting corridors to an area that felt deserted and opened a small room with a single bed. "Put her there," he said. He turned and gestured to the two novices who had followed them. "Fetch healing potions and the elixir," he said.

He gripped his holy symbol and spoke several quiet words, as a soft light surrounded Kyrianna.

Shadow Seeker looked up at Sarasnar and whined as his head moved from the priest to his friend and back.

"She has been seriously hurt," he said. "Deep grief and guilt fill her. This type of damage to the soul is not easily healed. I have healed her body. We can provide something to temporarily remove the anguish and hurt in her soul, but it is only temporary. It will dull the pain for many days though, so she can work through what has happened on her own."

The novices returned and the priest took a glowing vial from one of them and handed it to Myrith. "It is called Glayde and it can only be distilled from the emotions of those experiencing pure joy, such as the union of two who know true love, or an artist completing his life's crowning work. It is a rare and precious substance." He motioned to Kyrianna.

"In this state, she will fight anyone who tries to make her drink a potion. Someone she knows and trusts might be better able to get her to take it. I would not see this wasted by having to fight her."

Myrith nodded then sat carefully beside Kyrianna as she held Kyrianna's head. Andrinor moved to the other side of the bed. "Kyri," Myrith said softly. "You need to drink this." Andrinor helped Kyrianna into a sitting position as Myrith held the vial to the girl's lips. "Come on, Rangerette. Drink it."

Kyrianna slowly swallowed the glowing liquid. After a moment, she sat upright, throwing Myrith back. "Brular!" She started to get up and Andrinor grabbed her arm while Myrith grabbed her shoulders. "Myrith, we have to go after him." She locked her eyes with hers. "Now!"

Myrith and Andrinor tightened their grips on Kyrianna, holding her. Myrith found herself looking into green eyes that blazed with anger. They were not the bright clear green she knew her own eyes to be, but the dark shade of a deep forest, one that shrouded its secrets in shadow. She frowned at the silver that sparkled in those green eyes. "We are not ready," Myrith said softly. "Tomorrow, Rangerette. We'll talk tomorrow. Sleep."

She glanced at Sarasnar who handed her a small vial. "We all need rest. Drink this and sleep. We will go after him. I promise you that."

Kyrianna took the vial and nodded, but did not drink it right away.

Myrith stood and motioned the others to leave the room.

"Myrith," Kyrianna called before the woman left the room. "Thank you."

Myrith only nodded as she closed the door. "Andrinor, you take the first watch at her door. Nirev, the second and I will take the third."

The dwarf looked up at her. "You do not trust your church?"

"I don't trust Thynitic," she said as she stormed away.

~ * ~

Myrith dropped her pack on the floor as she entered the small room she had been given. There was only a single bed and a table in the room. No water basin or other items she would have expected. There was also no shrine to Mykaylene.

She slammed the door behind her. "Chaos take it," she whispered, repeating Kyrianna's favored curse. It seemed as if Chaos had indeed embraced them, but they had escaped it for now. She had managed to redeem Brular, as Mykaylene had directed her to do, but he had fallen into Thynitic's hands. She wasn't sure she had saved Kyrianna from the darkness trying to call her friend; only time would be able to supply the answer to that question.

She would be going after Brular. She had seen what Thynitic

had done to the priest before and she would not leave anyone to that torment. The others had said they would also go; even Kyrianna was ready to go after him as soon as the potion Sarasnar had given her had begun to take effect.

Going after Brular would mean going into the Abyss, to Thynitic's very citadel itself. She prayed they would be ready.

About the Author

A native Texan, Carol found her way to her current home in Colorado by way of a five-year detour in The Nederlands - courtesy of her husband Tim and the US Air Force.

An avid reader at a young age, her strong desire to write came from her love of (her husband calls it her obsession with) Star Trek. It was this early love of Star Trek that led her to the Science Fiction and Fantasy genres.

In addition to her writing she has worked as a receptionist/office manager for two veterinary clinics, a deputy sheriff in El Paso County Colorado and for the Professional Bull Riders.

She has been published in various anthologies and magazines including "Creature Fantastic", PanGaia Magazine, "Stories of Strength", Baen's Universe, Tales of the Talisman and Kepler's Dozen. Her books include: *Call of Chaos*, *Chaos Embraced*, *The Road into Chaos*, and *Chaos Challenged.*

Carol has also edited several anthologies for Sky Warrior Books including: "Zombiefied", "These Vampires Don't Sparkle", and "The Dragon's Hoard".

In addition to her own writing, she is the editor and publisher of the online e-zines: The Lorelei Signal and Sorcerous Signals as well as running her own micro-press - WolfSinger Publications.

Answer the Call

Call of Chaos - Book One: The Chaos Reigns Saga

The exiled daughter of a minor noble, Kyrianna Dalynne, finds herself trapped in a temple dedicated to Thynitic, The Lady of Chaos. She and her companions, are charged with finding an ancient artifact before the ones guarding the portals out will allow them to leave. As their search continues, Kyrianna begins to question if there was a specific reason she and the others were brought to this place.

After the guardians claim the artifact has been secured, they offer to open the portals to allow the group to return to their homes. Instead of the familiar forest of Kilenter, Kyrianna finds herself in another world. Her companions from the temple arrive several days after her.

When one of the members is accused of murder, they are tasked with assisting Tristan Duvall, who must face the demons and ghosts of his family's past in order to claim his birthright as a nobleman of the city of Raspa. Kyrianna finds herself attracted to the young man and facing the difficult decision of accepting his invitation to remain with him or return to her own home.

Now Available from WolfSinger Publications

The Road Into Chaos - Book Three: The Chaos Reigns Saga

After escaping from Thynitic's control, Kyrianna and her friends find themselves back on Shokar. All but one—Brular, the priest of Hellavar, who sacrificed his freedom to protect them, is now a prisoner of the Lady of Chaos.

Each member of the group is given a different vision to follow as they seek aid in rescuing Brular in the short time they have before they must journey into the Abyss to challenge Thynitic herself.

As they seek aid from various areas of Shokar, they find their efforts blocked by the temples of Mykaylene and Hellavar. They also learn others are preparing for a coming war against a group they only call the Faithless.

All of them find something unexpected, including Kyrianna—who finds a way to return home as well as an unexpected romantic entanglement.

Kyrianna must make choices—to accept her feelings for Tristan Duvall and risk losing her friend and companion—the unicorn Cewyr. To return home, to a family willing to welcome her back or face the Goddess Thynitic and eventually her own destiny as a Daughter of Chaos.

Coming Soon from WolfSinger Publications

Chaos Challenged – Book Four: The Chaos Reigns Saga

FOR A FRIEND

Those were Hendandra's words when the group was asked to go to the Abyss to rescue Brular from Thynitic.

Now they find themselves facing the horrors of that cursed place, along with nightmares from their own past as they struggle to reach the Lady of Chaos' citadel.

The closer they get to their goal the more dangerous their journey becomes and another deity enters the game—one who says she opposes Thynitic, but whose actions indicate she also wants to stop Kyrianna and her friends from facing the Lady of Chaos.

Even as she tries to fight her destiny as a Daughter of Chaos, Kyrianna finds herself being drawn deeper into Thynitic's plans.

Will she finally be able to separate herself from her destiny when she faces Thynitic or will the Lady of Chaos finally be able to claim her soul?

Coming Soon from WolfSinger Publications

www.ingramcontent.com/pod-product-compliance
Lightning Source LLC
Chambersburg PA
CBHW061611170626
46811CB00001B/389

* 9 7 8 1 9 3 6 0 9 9 6 2 7 *